Cruel

Susan Lewis is the bestselling author of twenty-eight novels. She is also the author of *Just One More Day* and *One Day at a Time*, the moving memoirs of her childhood in Bristol. She lives in Gloucestershire. Her website address is www.susanlewis.com

Acclaim for Susan Lewis

'One of the best around' *Independent on Sunday*

'Spellbinding! . . . you just keep turning the pages, with the atmosphere growing more and more intense as the story leads to its dramatic climax' *Daily Mail*

'Mystery and romance *par excellence*' *Sun*

'Deliciously dramatic and positively oozing with tension, this is another wonderfully absorbing novel from the *Sunday Times* bestseller Susan Lewis . . . Expertly written to brew an atmosphere of foreboding, this story is an irresistible blend of intrigue and passion, and the consequences of secrets and betrayal' *Woman*

'A multi-faceted tear jerker' *heat*

Susan LEWIS

Cruel Venus

arrow books

Published by Arrow Books 2009

6 8 10 9 7

First published in Great Britain in 2000 by
William Heinemann
Random House, 20 Vauxhall Bridge Road,
London SW1V 2SA

www.randomhouse.co.uk

Addresses for companies within The Random House Group Limited can be
found at: www.randomhouse.co.uk/offices.htm

The Random House Group Limited Reg. No. 954009

A CIP catalogue record for this book
is available from the British Library

ISBN 9780099534358

Typeset by SX Composing DTP, Rayleigh, Essex

Penguin Random House is committed to a sustainable future for
our business, our readers and our planet. This book is made from
Forest Stewardship Council® certified paper.

Printed and bound in Great Britain by Clays Ltd, St Ives plc

For Pat

I should like to express a huge thank you to Chiara Lima and the staff of the Palazzo Sasso, in Ravello, Italy. A superb hotel, with exceptional service and a wonderful location. Highly recommended.

I should also like to thank Don Tate, a great friend and lawyer, for expertly guiding me through the trial in the book – any errors that remain are entirely mine.

Love and thanks also go to Fanny Blackburne, Lesley Morgan, Denise Hastie, David Christian and Chris Witty.

ALLYSON

Chapter 1

'Is it true? Are you sleeping with her?'

The sound of him crunching into his toast followed her question. Then he turned a page of the newspaper to pick up the last part of a story in the sports section.

She didn't look up either, simply continued to gaze at the paper as though absorbed. The question hung in the air with the smell of coffee and the warmth of the heating. Her voice hadn't sounded shrill, or panicked, not even accusatory. She wondered how many women knew what it was like to pick up a paper and read, along with the rest of the world, that your husband was having an affair. She imagined every woman knew exactly what she'd do, she'd always known too, until now.

It was Sunday morning. The newspapers were piled up at the end of the kitchen table, and the autumn sunlight pinged off the china. In front of her was one of the more scurrilous tabloids bearing the front-page headline 'Bob's Secret Love'. Not a particularly imaginative headline, but it was a great picture. No surprise there, he was a good-looking man. He always photographed well. Had quite a fan club now, especially here, in the village, where they spent most weekends.

Allyson wasn't a lover of sports; couldn't stand football, hated cricket, detested rugby and put up with tennis. It had never come between them though; he had his job as a freelance commentator on TV sports, she had hers, hosting *Soirée*, a nightly magazine show. Allyson and Bob Jaymes. They'd been together since their early twenties, had fervently supported each other's careers, and now they were a pretty famous couple, though she was possibly more recognizable than he was, not only because of the programme's high profile, but because of the embarrassing regularity with which she was honoured for her work with the underprivileged. They went to all the right parties, were invited to all the first nights, all the benefits, balls, weekend hunts, summer villas and winter ski trips. They entertained here, at their farmhouse, quite regularly, and at least twice a week at their London flat. Their lives could easily be described as blessed, though of course they weren't without their problems, but whoever heard of anyone sailing through eighteen years of marriage without problems? Of course, not having children helped, but testing though they were to any relationship, children were by no means the only cause of marital unrest.

To remain childless was a decision they'd made early on in their relationship, though lately they'd been talking about reversing it and taking the plunge into parenthood that so many of their friends were deliriously enjoying and bitterly regretting. Now she was getting used to the idea Allyson had to confess she wanted it much more than she'd realized, in fact secretly she was already sorry they'd waited this long.

Her dark blue eyes scanned the story again, skimming fast over the words as though speed might render them benign. That Bob was being accused of having an affair with Tessa Dukes wasn't something she could allow herself to take in. If she did, she'd have to accept it could be true, and she wasn't going to do that when it was so patently absurd. No, the Sunday papers generally yielded up material worth pursuing for the show, which was why she read them, and it had to be said that this story definitely didn't make the grade. The problem was, it was there, and false though it had to be, *please God!* it couldn't be ignored.

Putting the paper down she refilled her cup with lukewarm coffee. She loved this farmhouse kitchen with its handcrafted cabinets, rows of copper pots and arrangements of dried herbs. The view, down over the valley to the village, was spectacular today. The seasonal shift in colours spread over the hillside like a busy artist's palette, and the sky was so clear, just one small mass of fluffy white cloud.

'I think you heard my question,' she said, feeling an odd reluctance in her legs as she got up to make more coffee. She'd left the paper so he could see it, so he couldn't miss it.

He glanced over at it, then laughed. 'You're taking that seriously?' he said, his amazement sounding comfortingly genuine.

'Are you telling me I don't need to?' she responded, watching the water stream into the jug.

'Oh, come on, Ally,' he said, reaching for the *Telegraph*, 'you know what the tabloids are like. They'll print anything they think'll make a story. Look what they did to Gascoigne and his missus.'

Allyson turned round. Her shoulder-length blonde hair was in an untidy knot at the top of her head, her blue fleecy pyjamas fell loosely around her small, slender figure. Considering the kind of issue they were facing she could have wished she looked a little more attractive. 'Paul Gascoigne deserved most of the publicity he got,' she reminded him. 'Maybe you'd like to try another example.'

Bob's round grey eyes grew large with surprise. 'Ally, it's the *News of the World*, for God's sake. No-one ever believes the *News of the World*, so why don't we just let this go?'

'So you don't care what they're printing about you? Or about Tessa Dukes, my *nineteen*-year-old-assistant?'

5

'Why the hell would I care what they're printing about her? I barely even know the girl.'

'So how come they've got a shot of you coming out of her flat?'

Bob turned the paper round and frowned as he looked at the front page. 'You know where that is,' he said, finally. 'It's the building Danny Jacobs just moved into. He's one of the producers at the Beeb, in case you'd forgotten. His flat's on the second floor, or maybe it's the third. You can check easily enough.'

'I know who he is,' Allyson responded. Though she snapped, relief was starting to release the tension inside her. How desperately she wanted to believe him. It was pathetic really, but she didn't even want to think about what it would mean if any of this were true. So why not believe it? The tabloids were well known to fabricate scandal in order to increase sales, and she and Bob were nothing if not prime targets. Indeed, all that was really surprising about this was that they had never been targeted before.

He really was handsome, she was thinking, with his large grey eyes, round, rugged face and quirky mouth. He might not be in quite as good shape now as when they'd first met, but who was, twenty years down the line? In Bob's case he'd managed to maintain his sportsman's physique until just a couple of years ago, when the first signs of middle-age spread and too much partying had started to show. But Allyson couldn't imagine any amount of passing years, or addiction to the high life, diminishing the incredible warmth of his character, or the magical intensity of his laughter-lined eyes. Funny, when you'd been married a long time, how you forgot to notice those things. They were just there, like the monthly bills and pile-up of laundry. More diverting of course, but just as constant and rarely much change – except for the times when crises hit, but those times weren't often and when compared to the disasters and catastrophes some couples suffered, Bob's occasional problem with drink and erratic struggles with self-esteem were really very minor and generally swiftly overcome. Less so lately, it was true, for these past few months he'd started getting into self-pity in a pretty big way, and she had to confess that it stretched her patience no end to know that so much of his resentment was directed at her. It was because she came from an established and wealthy family, and had had many of the advantages that weren't available to someone like him. Which was nonsense, of course, because his working-class origins had done nothing to stunt his education, had, if anything, broadened his social skills to a degree many people from her kind of background never got to achieve, and had propelled him into an extremely prominent and highly paid career. It was true his job didn't provide him with the kind of security he craved, but no freelance job ever did, and if he weren't allowing that chip on his shoulder to get so out of hand, as he seemed to be lately, then he might not be putting so many employers' backs up and finding himself overlooked for some of the plummer assignments.

However, it wasn't often that cracks appeared in the famous Bob Jaymes charm, and though he sometimes complained that she made him feel inferior with her fabulous connections, public adulation, and irritatingly saintly image, she was never backward in reminding him that his inferiority was a product of his own addled mind, and if he weren't so prone to feeling hard done by he might get a glimpse of how incredibly fortunate, and talented, he actually was. And while they were at it, this sense of entitlement he seemed to be whipping up into some sort of frenzy lately was starting to become more than a little tiresome, because no-one was *entitled* to anything, and as he could easily be deemed one of life's achievers it might be a good idea for him to recognize that he'd *earned* his privileged place in the world, which

7

was much more admirable than having it handed to him the way she had.

Pushing aside the criticisms and swallowing the irritation she knew she was stirring up as some kind of defence, she thought about what a deeply caring and sensitive man he could be, with enormous dash and charisma, and the kind of allure that was extremely appealing to the opposite sex, especially those who were impressed by fame – and plenty were. However, Allyson had long since overcome her insecurity where other women were concerned, for though Bob could be an outrageous flirt and was quite capable of giving some poor girls the wrong impression, their marriage had never suffered anything even approaching a crisis on that front, which was maybe, perversely, what was making her so nervous now.

Feeling the relief of moments ago start to evaporate she said, 'So why are they saying you're coming out of Tessa's place?'

'How do I know? Where does she live?'

'Peckham.'

'There you are. Danny's place is in Peckham. Could be they're in the same building, or same street. Most of those houses look the same.'

Allyson switched on the percolator and went back to the table. As she sat down she was watching him, once again engrossed in the paper, and apparently not in the least bit bothered by his own personal appearance in the headlines. So why should she be? After all, it did stretch credibility somewhat, him and Tessa Dukes, especially when he was such a dedicated social climber – not something Tessa could give him a leg up with. On the other hand, he was in his mid-forties now and there was never any telling what a man might do when struggling with the encroaching horrors of middle age and mortality. And with all the self-doubt and insecurity he'd been exhibiting lately, along with some sudden outbursts of impatience with her, she was pretty certain he was limbering up for a nasty first few rounds in the arena of midlife unrest. It unnerved her to think of it, for enough of their friends were experiencing it for her to know how damaging, even devastating, it could be. Just thank God she and Bob had such a rock solid relationship, and that she loved him enough to go the course with him, and know that when her time came he would go it with her. She wished she could say that for more of their friends, for it was amazing how many of them, when sucked into the emotional holocaust of midlife crisis, had come out the other end with an overriding hatred of a spouse they'd spent the past ten or fifteen years, if not adoring, then certainly fondly enduring.

But she couldn't see that happening to them. They were too much a part of each other now to be easily torn apart, and she didn't feel anywhere near the kind of exasperation with him that some of her friends felt with their irritating bedmates. In fact, she could go as far as to say that he hardly got on her nerves at all, except maybe when he started whingeing about how infrequently they had sex. That usually happened when they'd somehow spilled into a third consecutive week of non-conjugal bliss, which was increasingly how she saw it, for she had to admit that she'd become just a teensy bit bored, sleeping with the same partner all these years. Not that he didn't do it for her any more, he just didn't do it quite so often, or quite so explosively, as he had during the early years. But a wickedly obscene fantasy entailing lots of tarty behaviour with men in hard hats usually took care of that, and, of course, at the end she was always relieved it was Bob she was with, for she truly didn't harbour any secret desire to engage in real sex with anyone else.

Maybe real sex would be a good idea now, she thought. If nothing else it might dispel some of the horrible anxieties gathering inside her, anxieties she'd very much like to destroy before they had chance to take

9

root. She could start by sliding her feet nonchalantly on to his lap, the way she often did when they read the Sunday papers. Sometimes he'd massage them, which would very occasionally lead on to other things. The problem was, she didn't know if she wanted to go through with it after such a shock. In truth she didn't think she could.

As though sensing some of the turmoil going on in her head, he looked up. For a long moment his eyes locked with hers, then leaning forward he cupped her chin in his hand and kissed her softly on the lips. 'It's not true,' he said gently.

She forced a smile, and waited for a renewed buoyancy in her spirits. After all, what was wrong with believing him? She'd never had any reason to disbelieve him before, so why start now?

He sat back, still looking at her, then lifting her feet onto his lap he began to massage them. After a while he turned back to the paper, though he continued to toy with her toes. She watched his hands and wondered if they were hands that had recently caressed the teenage Tessa? The question lodged with immense weight in her heart, seeming to depress the beat.

Reaching for the *Observer* she laid it on top of the *News of the World* and started to read about the upcoming American Presidential elections. She wondered how many of the candidates had had oral sex with an underling. Then hearing the crunch of Sid Carter's milk float on the gravel outside she wondered if he'd ever had oral sex. Smiling inwardly she went to get her coat, then padded down the hall to the front door.

'Hello Sid,' she called, her breath visible in the crisp morning air, her skin goosing as she pulled her coat tighter around her.

'Hello,' he said gloomily. Sid was always gloomy. Maybe a spot of oral sex would cheer him up. She wasn't volunteering. 'How many pints today?'

10

'Two, same as usual,' she said. 'And three sliced wholemeal loaves. We've got the kids from Hobert Hall coming over this afternoon for the cricket match.'

'Your husband there then, is he?' Sid asked, in his gruff west country burr.

'Of course he is,' Allyson replied. 'Where did you expect him to be?'

It wasn't in Sid to look uncomfortable. 'Well, after what we read in the paper this morning,' he said bluntly, 'Elsie reckoned you'd have kicked the bugger out.'

'Come on Sid,' she chided, 'you know better than to believe what you read in the papers, especially that kind of paper.'

'No smoke without fire, is what I say,' he muttered. 'How many loaves was that?'

'Three. And a dozen eggs.'

She waited as he trundled back to the milk float, and waved out to Mrs Briggs, who was walking past the end of the drive with Klutz, the dog. Actually, it was Bob who had named the dog, as it kept blundering into walls and falling off the kerb. Mrs Briggs had thought the name hilarious and often boasted to her neighbours that it was Bob Jaymes, yes *the* Bob Jaymes, who'd given her beloved pet such a sophisticated name.

They were fortunate in the village they'd chosen for their country home, just outside Bath, as the locals were mostly friendly and seemed rather pleased to have a couple of celebrities in their midst. Not many of their London friends could boast such warmth from their rural neighbours, and the rip-offs they'd endured brought many a dinner party to the brink of outrage or hilarity.

She inhaled deeply and looked around. God, she loved it here.

'Everything all right, dear?' Mrs Briggs called out. 'Anything I can do?'

'Everything's fine, thanks,' Allyson called back. 'Are

you still coming this afternoon to help with the kids?'

'Of course. Still going ahead with it then?'

Allyson hid a momentary irritation. 'I wouldn't want to let them down. Nor would Bob.'

Mrs Briggs only nodded, but Allyson could see she too was surprised to hear that Bob was around.

'Here,' Sid said, thrusting two hand-labelled jars at her. 'Lemon curd. For the kids. Elsie's coming up later with a couple of jam tarts.' His eyes met hers. 'Lucky you'm not bombarded up here,' he grunted. ''Swat usually happens when someone gets theirselves in the paper, innit? Got every Tom Dick and Harry with a camera hanging around after.'

Just what Allyson had been thinking. 'Bye Sid,' she said. 'See you later, if you're coming.'

She waited for him to turn his float round, milk bottles jangling, Radio Four churning out the Sunday morning service. Down the hill the church bells were clanging melodiously into life, nearer to home the birds were engaged in a shrill, happy chorus. She glanced at the surrounding bushes and trees to see if she was being watched. There was no sign of anyone. Hugging her groceries she turned back inside and closed the door.

She could hear Bob moving about upstairs, floorboards creaking as he walked from bedroom to bathroom; the howl and thud of the pipes as he turned on the shower, the hiss and whine of the radio as he searched out a sports station. It was so normal it almost made her shudder, for it made her think of some dreadful sci-fi movie she'd once seen, where the world was going about its day in blissful ignorance of the asteroid that was about to smash it into oblivion. Likening Tessa Dukes to an asteroid was a touch melodramatic, but there was a horrible chance the effects of this 'exclusive' had hardly yet begun, and the results could be as catastrophic to her life as if someone really had blown apart the world.

Except all that had happened was that Bob had been

photographed coming out of Danny Jacobs's building, which could be the same building Tessa lived in. Tessa, of whom she was so exceptionally fond. Tessa, the intriguing young beauty who'd made Allyson's life so much easier since she'd joined the team. Intriguing, because the girl almost never talked about herself except in the most general terms, was clearly nervous of strangers and had a way of looking at a person as though he or she might prove the hidden key to a mystery. From her work with abused and abandoned children Allyson knew the signs when she saw them, though Tessa didn't strike her as a classical, or in any way severely damaged victim, more an extremely bright young girl who might have had to fight an overbearing father for the freedom to shine. If that were the case then she'd certainly succeeded, for her academic qualifications were more than impressive, despite the abrupt departure from London Polytechnic, where she'd just completed the first year of a three-year course in media studies. Allyson had interviewed more than two dozen candidates for the position of her personal assistant, but she'd known immediately Tessa had walked in the door that here was the assistant she wanted. The dark-eyed Tessa with her shaggy black hair and rosy red cheeks not only exuded intelligence and ambition, she also radiated a very clear need to feel she belonged somewhere, which, for someone like Allyson, was the most irresistible quality of all. If the girl had had a difficult start in life, then she deserved the kind of break Allyson could offer, and not once in the four months Tessa had been with her had Allyson experienced a single moment of doubt over her decision. If anything, she was increasingly thrilled by it, for once Tessa had overcome her initial shyness she had blossomed into an exceptionally warm and friendly young girl. All her colleagues liked her and were helping Allyson to groom her for bigger and better things, the way Allyson had with two previous assistants, one of whom was now a reporter on *Soirée*, the other an associate producer at the BBC.

Allyson was trying to remember if Tessa and Bob had ever met, and decided they must have, for Bob was a regular visitor to the *Soirée* office and studio, and Tessa's desk was right outside Allyson's door. However, Allyson was failing to come up with the scenario of when this meeting took place, which, for some reason, wasn't having the comforting effect it should have.

Going back to the kitchen she began putting away her groceries and wondering why the phone hadn't rung. True, her parents would never read the *News of the World*, nor would most of her friends, but someone had to know about the 'exclusive' by now. So why hadn't anyone called? Most particularly, where was Shelley? Shelley Bronson got every Sunday paper. As *Soirée's* editor and senior producer, she was obliged to read them before the Monday meetings when topics for that week's shows were locked in. Plus, and it was a big plus, Shelley Bronson was Allyson's closest friend. So why wasn't Shelley on the phone demanding to know what the hell was going on?

Allyson cleared the table, loaded the dishwasher, then went upstairs. She loved this house. Absolutely adored it. It was at least two hundred years old, creaked and groaned like an arthritic old codger and made her feel as safe as a child in a womb. *She couldn't bear to lose it!* She'd fought so hard to make it beautiful, rising to the contest of wills as the house tried to refuse renovation and she had insisted. It had defied her every step of the way, besting the efforts of a dozen designers and workmen with its determination to remain a ruin. But in the past couple of years it had settled into its defeat as though the victory of style, taste and comfort was all its own. It had even absorbed the extra wing as a parent might an offspring that totally resembled itself.

'Don't you think it's odd there's no press outside?' she remarked to Bob as he stepped out of the shower. She squeezed a line of toothpaste onto her brush and began to clean her teeth. In the mirror she watched him as he towelled himself dry. There wasn't much left of the tan he'd acquired in France that summer, but unless she was mistaken he seemed to have lost some weight. The possible meaning of that thundered to the front of her mind. She shoved it away sharply. She wasn't going to allow this paranoia to take hold, or before she knew it she'd be checking his credit cards and sneaking looks at his diary. Everyone's weight fluctuated from time to time, why should he be any different? And there was nothing new about the fact that he looked closer to thirty-five than forty-five, he'd always looked young for his age. So had she, though she was younger than him, for she'd yet to reach forty. That treat was coming up in the middle of next year. Extraordinary, for she certainly didn't feel forty. It sounded like an age that belonged to older people, and she definitely didn't consider herself an older person.

'What?' she said, spitting out a mouthful of tooth-paste. 'What did you say?'

'I said, thank God there isn't. Any press outside.'

'But don't you think it's odd? You know how they go and stake people out after that kind of story? Even old Sid remarked on it.'

'They probably know by now that the *News of the World* got it wrong,' he said, walking across the spacious, Victorian-style bathroom to get a can of baby talc from the antique brass-framed cabinet that hugged the wall behind the bath.

Loving him for being so unruffled by it all, Allyson dried her mouth and went to put her arms round him. He smiled, giving life to the roguish grin she adored.

'You really did take it seriously, didn't you?' he teased. 'You were worried.'

'No, I wasn't,' she denied. Then, 'OK, perhaps I was, a bit. She's a pretty girl, and the men in the office are all crazy about her.'

Bob grimaced. 'What's the matter with them, looking at her when you're around?'

'She's twenty years younger, and available,' she said, putting her lips very close to his.

He kissed her, then looked into her face, and she wondered if he meant it when he told her she was even more beautiful now than when he'd first met her. She couldn't really be considered a beauty, but she certainly felt more attractive now. However, the confidence that came with success was probably responsible for that.

'If it were anyone but Vic Stafford you were going to see,' she said after he kissed her again, 'I'd insist you be late. But Vic won't stand for it.'

'We can always catch up with this later,' he said, smiling into her eyes. 'After the kids have gone back to Hobert Hall.'

'If we've still got the energy.'

Looking regretfully down at his semi-erect penis, for she actually was in the mood right now, she moved away and slipped out of her pyjamas. She was petite and pale-skinned, and saddened by the way her large breasts were starting to sag. Bob insisted they were fabulous, which she loved him for, but unlike the drop-dead gorgeous Shelley she'd never go topless on the beaches of Cannes. She did go along with all the cleavage and leg shots the publicists insisted on though, and thanked God for smart lighting and airbrushes.

'OK, I'm off,' Bob said, putting his head round the door, some ten minutes later. 'I'll get the bus from Vic, then go over to the station to pick up whoever's coming. What time does the London train get in?'

'Half past twelve. Take them all straight to the pub. I'll meet you there. I'm going to make a start on the sandwiches, then I'll pop over to the Hall to check how many kids are coming.'

It was only when he'd gone that Allyson remembered Tessa was due to arrive on the train. Her heart reacted with a disturbing lurch as she wondered what it would be like for them, having to face each other after that morning's story. She pictured them meeting, awkwardly, trying to laugh off the absurdity of their rumoured affair. *But maybe it wasn't a rumour! Maybe they were desperately in love.*

No! No they weren't.

Shelley would be on the train too, which could account for why she hadn't called. Except Shelley had a mobile phone.

Everyone else on the train would have read the paper, the premier-league footballers Bob had roped into the kids'-celebrity cricket match in the field next to their house, the handful of soap stars and kids'-TV presenters. The children at the Hall, who all had Down's syndrome, were already so excited that Mrs Gore was having trouble keeping them calm. Time to concentrate on them now, and abandon this ludicrous mind-trip to the brink of disaster.

Allyson was on her way out of the door when the telephone finally rang. 'Yes, hello Vic,' she said, when she heard the surly man's voice at the other end.

'What time's he coming?' Vic growled.

'He's already on his way. Should be there by now.'

'I'll wait five more minutes,' and the line went dead.

Allyson hung up, picked up her bag and was about to leave when the phone rang again.

'Darling, I've just been informed of that nonsense in the *News of the World*. I imagine Bob's going to sue.'

'Hello Mother. He hasn't mentioned suing, but it could be an option. How's Daddy?'

'He's right here. I called Uncle Cecil and he gave me the number of a good lawyer. Apparently the man's handled plenty of libel cases and has a good record of winning. You could donate your compensation to one of your charities.'

'Good idea.' Allyson smiled. 'I'm glad to hear you so convinced it isn't true.'

'Preposterous, darling. Bob would never dream of being unfaithful, any more than you would. Trouble is, this sort of thing has a way of putting ideas into people's heads.'

'Well, there's a happy thought.'

'How did Bob take it?'

'He didn't seem very interested. Laughed that I thought it could be true, but on the whole I'm not sure it's really sunk in that the story's there.'

'Any more press lurking around?'

'No. Don't you think that's weird?'

'Mmm. I'll hand you over to Daddy. Sorry we can't make the match, but we'll be sending a handsome donation.'

Her father's voice came uncertainly down the line. 'Hello? Who's that?'

'Hello Daddy. It's me. Allyson.'

'Who?'

'How are you feeling today?'

'Who is this?'

'I should be able to pop over on Tuesday.'

'It's Howard Butler-Blythe speaking. Identify yourself please.'

'Bye, Daddy. Love you.'

She rang off, feeling a sharper edge to the sadness of her father's fading mind than she usually did. She missed him so terribly, and how hard this had to be for her mother.

Having put on the answering machine, she managed to escape the house before being intercepted by any more calls. The fact that there were no lurking photographers or persistent hacks was helping her to breathe more easily, for she'd decided that their absence could only mean that Bob was right, they had already discovered their mistake and were busy devising some kind of page-twenty-five apology.

Bob was sitting in the driver's seat of the bus he'd collected half an hour ago. Now, with time to spare before he was due at the station, he'd pulled into this hidden little picnic glade and parked.

It was starting to warm up outside. There was no wind, and the occasional leaf that fell from the densely clustered trees merely wafted to the ground in its own lightness of being. His eyes were transfixed by Tessa as she came towards the bus, her short, shaggy black hair and deeply flushed cheeks making her seem even younger than she actually was. She wasn't tall; her body was plump and soft, like an overripe melon; her normally timid eyes were glittering now with a light that cut right through him. The smile on her full, sulky lips quivered with a lethal mix of modesty and mischief.

By the time she reached the bus his pulses were thick and throbbing. The door was already open. He watched her come up the steps, knowing that beneath her long dark winter coat she wore nothing more than a pair of black vinyl thigh-high boots. Her eyes were on his as she stopped in front of him and allowed him to open the coat. As he pulled it apart desire cut through him in a long, painful groove. Her breasts were fleshy and round, irresistible and perfectly made for sucking and squeezing. Their nipples were blood-red and hard from the cold. Her tummy bulged from her waist, creating a softly pliant mound above her pubis. Where there should have been a tangle of thick, curling hair there was only the tenderest and most succulent of flesh. He'd shaved her himself the day before, in the bathroom of her tiny flat, which was a few doors away from Danny Jacobs. The flat where he now spent every available

19

minute, either making love to her, talking to her, bathing her, reading to her, or sometimes just watching her.

He lifted his eyes back to her face, and inserted a finger between the lips he had shaved. She was so moist he could feel it, hot on his hand, and wet on her legs. He pulled her closer and took a fat, juicy nipple into his mouth. He sucked hard, twisting his tongue around it and pushing his fingers deeper inside her. Having her come to him like this had brought him close to the brink, if he penetrated her now he would lose it.

Getting up from his seat he stood over her, then lifted her mouth to his. She tasted of peppermint and coffee. Her skin, beneath his fingers, was as soft as a baby's. He pulled it, pushed it, bunched it in his hands and squeezed it, while feeling himself swimming in the vortex of emotions she aroused in him, the agonizing desire to love her, the fear of its intensity, the horror of its consequence.

'Did you see the paper?' he said gruffly.

'Yes,' she answered.

Her black eyes were fringed with long, dense lashes, her pale, cool skin was blotched with patches of red. He looked at her and felt a thousand knots twist around his heart. He knew he should say more, but he couldn't discuss it, he had no idea what he wanted to say. All he knew was the glowing allure of her face, the tender trust in her eyes and the enslaving beauty of her body. His need for her was like a silently raging tide, way beyond any semblance of control, long past any chance of reason. He had to have her. Whatever it meant to his life now, or in the future, he had to have her, possess her, make her his and his alone.

Turning her round, he steered her halfway down the bus then stopped and removed her coat. His hands moved to her breasts as he pulled her back against his chest. Then he whispered in her ear what he wanted her to do. Without hesitation she put a knee on each of the seats either side of her, leaned forward and rested her hands on the seats behind. The fleshy roundness of her bottom was wholly exposed, her black shiny boots made an unsparingly erotic contrast to her colourless skin.

He pushed into her, big and hard and almost ready to explode. She was trapped by the seats, anchored to him by the brutal ramming of his hips. He pushed her head down and penetrated harder. He wanted to slap the rippling flesh of her buttocks, but he was too far into her, too close already to letting it go.

'Harder. Give it to me harder,' she begged, repeating the words he'd told her he wanted to hear. And as he gripped her hips with his hands and pumped her with a ferocity that caused him to grunt with exertion, she gasped, 'Don't stop. Just fuck me! Fuck me.'

She went on. The words she used, and the way she spoke them, drove the power of his orgasm to an excruciating pitch. He wanted never to stop coming. He wanted his cock hard in her like this for as long as she could take it. And he knew she could take it. She could take it like no-one he'd ever known. She wanted it like no-one he'd ever known. And anything he wanted, *anything*, was all right by her, because all she really wanted was whatever made him happy.

Moments after he exploded inside her, he could feel himself hardening again. Knowing it, she got to her feet and led him to the back of the bus. Pushing him down on the seat she sat astride him, taking him into her fast and starting to move with electrifying vigour, her breasts quivering and bouncing, her black eyes watching him closely. He looked back, feeling the slap of her buttocks on his thighs, and making her pant and groan as his fingers slid between her legs. Her small, chubby hands gripped her breasts and he ducked his mouth to the solid dark red buds of her nipples, sucking them tightly and cruelly until their bodies were thrown into the tumultuous sensations of climax, engulfed by the chaotic throb of exhausting release.

In all his life he had never known a woman like this. A woman who was no more than a girl, whom he'd taught to fuck like the most experienced whore, and who was now as consumed by him as he was by her.

'Don't tell me, you've got to go!' She pouted as he gently withdrew.

He looked at his watch. 'I'm due at the station in ten minutes.'

She climbed off his lap and sat beside him, crossing her legs on the seat and entwining her hand in his. 'How did Allyson react to the paper?' she asked.

He looked at her and wondered what she was really thinking, for everyone knew how devoted she was to Allyson, the heroine who had plucked her from some Allyson-imagined hell and was now turning her into a rising star. It hadn't stopped her falling for Allyson's husband though, had it? Nor had it stopped Allyson's husband falling for her. If anything Allyson's husband was out of his mind with lust, maybe even love for the girl, and was fast losing the struggle to keep it in check, for why else would he be here, so close to home, where anyone might discover them, if he wasn't having a problem with control?

'How did she take it?' he repeated. 'I'm not sure. She was prepared to believe it.'

'But you told her it wasn't true.' Her big eyes looked up at his, her kiss-reddened lips were apart and inviting.

Unable to stop himself he kissed them, for a long and deliciously arousing time. 'I sidestepped it,' he said finally.

'But you're going to tell her?'

A stab of guilt penetrated his chest, stopping his breath. He looked away. But unable to keep his eyes from her, he looked at her again. Yes, he'd tell Allyson if he was forced to, he'd tell her everything in all its crazed and obsessive glory, all its inexorable, brainwashing might, if it was the only way he got to keep this girl.

Tessa's eyes went down. His own fell to her breasts and watched them rising and falling in the labouring heaviness of her breath. How could he stop himself touching them? They were so heavy and soft and unbelievably responsive, like Tessa herself, who never stopped him whatever he wanted to do.

'I don't think you should tell her,' she whispered, watching his hands as he caressed her.

He was surprised, and relieved. 'I thought it was what you wanted,' he said.

'What I want is *you*,' she cried earnestly. 'Not to hurt Ally. I really like her. A part of me actually loves her, you know, like a sister or something. She gave me my job. She really trusts me.' She covered her face with her hands. 'God, I hate doing this to her. I hate you for making me.'

'Hey, no-one's making you,' he said gently. 'Remember it was your idea to drive down last night and stay in a hotel. Your idea for us to meet here, before I go to the station.'

'You don't get what I'm saying,' she protested. 'I mean, you make me because I can't resist you. Because there's something in me that has to do whatever you want me to do. I feel like a slave to the need you've created inside me.' Her voice lost its passion. She was suddenly very young and confused. 'It's weird. I've never felt anything like it before.'

Two tears trickled down her cheeks. He caught them with his fingers, and touched them to her breasts.

'You frighten me,' she whispered.

'Sssh,' he soothed.

'Do you love me?' Her lashes were wet, her lips were moist and tempting beyond endurance.

He kissed her softly. His passion for her was right there, burning in his fingertips, on his tongue, in his eyes, in his loins. It dominated his senses, consumed his mind. 'You know I do,' he said.

'But what about Ally? She's your wife! The whole world knows how much you love her.'

'Ally is Ally,' he replied. He didn't want to think about her now, he didn't want her to spoil a single moment of this precious, stolen time.

'What does that mean?'

He tilted her mouth up to his and kissed her. 'Come on, I'll walk you back to your car,' he said.

Her Beetle was parked further down the track. They walked hand in hand, her head leaning against his shoulder, her coat wrapped warmly around her naked body. In the misty bands of sunlight, streaming through the golden, leafy trees, they looked like ghosts passing through a timeless glade of sparkling autumnal beauty.

'What's going to happen?' she said, stopping to look up at him as they reached her car.

'I don't know,' he answered. He leaned forward and kissed her lingeringly.

'I'll drive straight to the house,' she said, 'as though I've come from London. See you there?'

'We're meeting at the pub,' he told her. Then looking anxiously into her eyes he said, 'This afternoon's going to be tough, for us both. Do you think you can handle it?'

'It'll be tough for Ally too, after the papers.'

He glanced away for a moment, looking back along the hazy, glistening track as though he were looking back at his life. Allyson, his wife, the only woman he had truly loved – until now. How could he do this to her? What the hell was he thinking?

He turned back to Tessa, then putting a hand behind her head he pulled her mouth hard against his, defiance and anger pushing aside the savage onslaught of guilt.

Chapter Two

The bell over the pub door clanged as Allyson walked in, a mobile phone pressed to one ear, and a heavy bag weighing down her shoulder. She was wearing tight black jeans, snug little ankle boots and a thick cable-knit sweater that seemed to engulf her. Her sleek blonde hair was swept casually to one side, her neat, attractive features were lightly made up and currently drawn in a frown. 'Can't you just tell her to go to hell?' she grumbled, giving a quick wave to Ron, the landlord, as he ducked into the kitchen to investigate a loud crash.

At the other end of the line Shelley sighed. 'Wouldn't I love to,' she replied. 'But I'll have to go and find out what the old witch wants.'

Allyson knew that their illustrious old cow of a programme controller, Stella Cornbright, was unlikely to be summoning Shelley to her home on a Sunday afternoon for tea. So, whatever it was it had to be serious. She glanced around the pub. It was still early. There were only a couple of locals, over in the corner playing darts, out of earshot. 'Do you think it's got something to do with what was in the paper this morning?' she asked, keeping her voice low as she dumped her bag on a tapestry-covered stool and sat down on a comfy bench seat.

'No,' Shelley answered, her tone indicating that she'd been expecting the question. 'If it were, it would be you she was demanding to see, not me.'

Allyson waited.

Shelley said no more.

'Is that it?' Allyson said tightly. 'You obviously know what I'm talking about, so don't you have something to say?'

'Not right now,' Shelley answered. 'But I don't mind listening to what you've got to say.'

Allyson gave an incredulous laugh. 'You're making it sound as though I have to excuse myself, or something,' she cried.

'I should think that was the last thing you had to do,' Shelley replied. 'What did Bob say?'

'Not much. Except that Dan Jacobs probably lives in the same building as Tessa. If not, the same street.'

'How very convenient.'

Allyson's face darkened as her heart thudded an extra beat. 'I'm not sure I like the sound of that. Don't you believe him?'

'Do you?'

'Why shouldn't I?'

'Only you know the answer to that.'

Allyson was so thrown by the turn the conversation was taking that she decided to drop it, at least for now. 'So, did Stella give you any idea what she wanted to talk about?' she said, turning to look out of the window.

'No.'

'Oh God, looks like Tessa's car just pulled into the car park. She must have driven down.' Then, 'I thought she was getting the train.' Her mind had gone from nought to sixty in less than a second and the conclusion was turning her cold.

'Bet you're looking forward to seeing her,' Shelley remarked dryly.

Allyson couldn't help smiling, for she could easily imagine the droll expression on Shelley's beautiful face. 'Even more than you're looking forward to seeing Stella,' she responded.

26

'Are you going to fire her?'

Allyson laughed. 'Who, Tessa? Not today,' she answered. 'I need to keep a perspective on this, because there's a huge chance the *News of the World* have got it wrong. You know what they're like. Anyway, I'm not sure I've got the power to fire her, have I? So it might be you I'll be coming to for that. Or Stella.'

'Stella,' Shelley answered. 'We can hire, but Stella fires. I'm calling the Monday meeting for twelve tomorrow, by the way. Edmund and Debbie are on the early morning shuttle from Glasgow, they'll need some time to get their acts together before we get under way. We should be a full team tomorrow. A rarity. Are you driving back to London tonight?'

'Not if the meeting's at twelve. I'll stay down an extra night. Oh shit, I wish you were going to be here. This thing has really thrown me. And here comes *Soirée*'s answer to Christina Ricci, looking like she's just been screwed all the way to senselessness and back.'

'Goodness me, that can't be darling, brilliant, got-to-be-rescued little Tessa you're talking about, can it?' Shelley teased. 'And she always looks like that, which accounts for the high visibility of all the male tongues in the office. God, she makes me feel old. I could forgive her for a lot, but definitely not that.'

Tessa was hovering uncertainly, and because Allyson was still laughing at what Shelley had just said it was easy to smile as she waved the girl over. 'Give me a call later and let me know what it's all about,' she said to Shelley.

'I take it you mean Stella,' Shelley responded. 'Sure, if I have time. I'm out for dinner tonight, with David Billington and a couple of his clients.'

'Sounds like fun. Give him my love.'

Allyson put away her phone and forced another smile as she looked at Tessa. God, this was difficult. What was she supposed to say to a girl who was rumoured to be having an affair with her husband? A girl who she happened to be inordinately fond of, and about whom she had always felt very protective? In fact she'd probably grown a little too close to Tessa, and knew that Tessa was very attached to her too, which was why it just wasn't conceivable that Tessa would betray her this way. The poor girl was looking so terrified right now that there was simply no way that menace of a newspaper could be right.

'So how does it feel to be famous?' she said, making an attempt at levity.

Tessa's youthful dark eyes were dimmed by nerves as she put her coat on a chair and sat down. 'Given the choice, I wouldn't have gone for it this way,' she replied, trying to match Allyson's wryness.

Allyson laughed. 'No, I would have preferred you to take another route,' she said, 'but it's done now, so we'll just have to wait for the fuss to die down, then put it all behind us.'

Tessa's eyes were disconcerting in their frank, searching efforts to gauge what Allyson was really thinking, and not enjoying being probed quite so deeply, Allyson reached over for her bag to take out her purse. 'My parents want Bob to sue for libel,' she said, without really knowing why.

Tessa seemed to flinch. 'Can he do that?'

'I'm not sure, I haven't given it much thought. But yes, I guess he can, if it's not true.'

'Oh it's not,' Tessa assured her.

Allyson smiled warmly, and could have hugged her for sounding so convincing. 'What'll you have to drink?' she said.

'Whatever you're having.'

'Ron,' Allyson said, as the thickly bearded landlord re-emerged from the kitchen. 'Come and meet my assistant, Tessa Dukes.'

Ron's small, watery eyes rounded with amazement,

leaving Allyson in no doubt which Sunday tabloid the paper boy tossed over his garden gate. 'Your . . .?' He looked at Tessa and his normally florid complexion deepened to scarlet. 'Tessa,' he said, pronouncing it Tesser. 'Nice to meet you. Heard a lot about you. From Allyson, like. Says how good you are at your job.' He glanced at Allyson, as though seeking assurance that it was all right to say that.

Allyson's expression was friendly.

Ron looked at Tessa again. Tessa was smiling, shyly, the way she always did with strangers, especially men, and Allyson watched the cordiality of Ron's smile start yielding to a bemusing haze of unexpected attraction. The girl certainly had a way with men, there was no doubt about that, and the fact she seemed not to know it was probably what made it so potent. Her appeal was very definitely of the Lolita variety, for there she sat, looking no more than sixteen, skirt barely covering her buttocks, boots tugged up over her knees, and the exposed, cold-mottled flesh of her thighs looking as succulent as cake. And as for the big braless breasts that were amply evident beneath her tight-fitting light blue sweater, and the lips that looked permanently ravished, it was enough to make Allyson want to stuff the girl in a sack and smuggle her swiftly out of sight. Startled, Allyson pulled herself up sharply. She'd never looked at Tessa that way before, but there again Tessa hadn't been coupled in a scandal with Allyson's husband before.

'We'll have two lagers and lime,' Allyson said to Ron. 'I'm reckoning on us being around fourteen for lunch.'

'Roast beef today,' Ron told her, dragging his eyes from Tessa. 'Got some nice fresh runner beans off John Turner up at the farm. Wanda says she's going to doing something fancy with 'em.'

'Roast potatoes?'

''Course. Wouldn't be a Sunday dinner without roasters, would it? Got some nice colly and a bit of cabbage too. And Wanda's doing her home-baked apple crumble and ice cream for pudding. Says Bob called her up and asked special.'

Allyson laughed. 'She spoils him.'

'Well, it's a bit of a favourite with everyone round here,' he said. 'Hope you're going to have some, young lady,' he said to Tessa. 'Can't be doing with all you London types who won't eat a square meal.'

'Oh, I can't pass up on Wanda's legendary crumble,' Tessa responded, peering at him bravely from under her lashes.

Allyson's smile lost some warmth. How did she know the crumble was legendary? Who, except Bob, could have told her? No! No! She'd just said it to be polite.

The pub door opened and a few more locals came in. Allyson wasn't sure she wanted to go on introducing Tessa and watching the reactions, for those who didn't get that particular paper would certainly have been informed by those who did, and Ron would no doubt find a way of letting everyone know that the 'Secret Love' was actually sitting at a table over there with Allyson.

Allyson got up to greet her neighbours and ask after their families, the way she usually did. She knew she was being rude not introducing Tessa, but bless the girl, she seemed to sense the awkwardness so was making herself busy fetching the drinks from the bar. A couple of the newcomers threw astonished looks in her direction, probably drawn to the jostling breasts under the tight blue sweater, for they'd be something of a treat in this wintry outback where the desire to be warm triumphed every time over style.

Then Bob arrived from the station with a busload of celebrities and the small, oak-beamed bar was soon full to overflowing. Allyson watched him as he ordered pints and vodka martinis for their party, then swung behind the counter to mix the martinis himself, while

Ron and his two barmen mastered the pumps. Allyson's first martini slipped down so fast that her head started whirling, but the second seemed to steady her up and got her joining in with the loud and lively chat that was erupting all around her. Wanda and her waitresses bustled in and out of the tables, taking orders and delivering mouth-watering lunches, Wanda's high heels tapping on the flagstones and her newly permed hair frizzing in the heat of the kitchen. There was a roar of laughter as Wanda treated Bob to a cheeky pinch on the bottom, and the old lady almost disintegrated with delight when he put his arms around her and smacked a kiss on her age-puckered lips.

Later, after downing her second martini, or was it her third, Allyson got involved in a rowdy game of darts with two of the footballers and a young couple who'd just taken out a giant mortgage on a draughty little cottage at the end of the street. Bob, she noticed, was engaged in some hot dispute with the farmer, Jack Turner, and Reg Singer who ran the village shop and post office. Tessa was glowing and blushing as she listened to the hilariously tall tales being bandied about by a noisy group of locals and Londoners, where the men involved appeared as keen to make her laugh as they were to ogle the blue sweater. Allyson hiccuped through another urge to go and cover the girl up, but it was soon vanquished, for though her sight was a bit blurry, and her perspective was temporarily askew, she was managing to hang onto the assertion that she was responding irrationally, and that Tessa had every right to show off how lovely she was. But even through the vodka she could sense how alive her doubt still was, and it seemed that not even Bob's apparent lack of interest was managing to uproot it. Nor were the martinis managing to drown it.

It had never been clear if anyone in the village ate Sunday lunch at home, certainly they were all in the pub by one, and no-one ever left much before three. Reverend Beesely and his wife Mary were usually the last to go. Today, though, it seemed that the celebrities would be the last out, and, laughing as Bob slipped an arm round her shoulders, Allyson wondered what kind of event the cricket match was going to turn into.

'I'm just off to pick up the kids,' Bob shouted in her ear. 'We should be back at the house by three thirty.'

'How much have you had to drink?' she shouted back.

'Half of bitter,' he answered, giving her a wink, then catching her as she wobbled. 'How much have you had?'

'I stopped counting after three. By the way, I was trying to remember if you and Tessa have ever met.'

Bob looked across the bar to where Tessa was now talking to a couple of the soap stars. 'You know, I don't think we have,' he said. 'Maybe a brief hello at the office. Which one is she? The one over there with Mandy and Frank?'

Allyson knew the devilish spirit of drink was goading her, but she was too far gone to smother it. 'Come on, I'll introduce you before you go,' she said, grabbing his hand. 'She's a great assistant, did I ever tell you that?'

'Yeah, you told me,' he answered, following on behind.

Looking back over her shoulder she gave him a saucy wink and said, 'What's she like in bed? Is she great there too?'

Bob's insides churned, for the tease had barbs and he knew it. But deciding that the safest bet was to keep it all on the surface, he said, 'Oh, she's the best. Just the best.'

Though Allyson's heart did a sickening dive, she continued to smile, and made herself remember that this was only play, and that a hot denial might well have been far greater cause for worry.

'Tessa!' Allyson cried. 'I want you to meet my husband, Bob.'

Tessa turned round, flushed and sparkling, but her

smile was already fading as unease clouded her eyes and made her mouth tremble.

'This is Bob!' Allyson declared. 'Apparently, you're having an affair with him.'

Bob took Allyson's arm and tried to pull her aside. 'The joke's gone far enough,' he said in her ear. 'You're embarrassing the girl.'

'No I'm not, am I?' she demanded of Tessa. 'How am I embarrassing you?'

Those nearby had stopped to listen. Over in the corner, the kids' presenter and Mrs Briggs were attempting to dance to Abba, while Ron rang the bell for last orders. 'So you live in the same building as Bob's producer,' Allyson affirmed, slurring slightly. 'Did you hear that, everyone? Just because Tessa here lives in the same building as Bob's producer she's supposed to be having an affair with him. Bob, I mean, not the producer. Now tell me, isn't that a joke!'

There was some uneasy laughter as again Bob tried to pull her away.

'No, don't,' she said, shrugging him off. 'I'm just telling everyone that you and Tessa have never really met before today, but you're still supposed to be having an affair. Crazy, isn't it?' she said to Mary Beesely, the vicar's wife. 'I mean, how can you have an affair with someone you don't even know?' She turned to Tessa. 'This,' she declared, putting an arm round her, 'is my wonderful assistant Tessa. I know I've told you all about her, and now here she is, in the flesh. She's fantastic. She wants to become a reporter and I'm helping her get there, because I think she'll make a brilliant reporter. But I'll be sorry to lose her, because she's the best assistant I've ever had. And she's not, I repeat not, having an affair with my husband. Are you?'

Tessa's voice was small as she said, 'No.'

'You see,' Allyson shouted. 'She's not. And just for the record, Bob and I are still every bit as much in love as

33

we've ever been . . . Correction, we're even more in love than ever, and if things work out, we're going to be starting a family. Aren't we, Bob?'

Laughing, Bob pulled her into his arms and held her tight. 'That's enough now,' he whispered. 'You've made your point. I'm going to get the kids.'

'But you didn't even say hello to Tessa!' Allyson objected.

'Hello Tessa,' he said.

'Hello,' she responded. The colour in her cheeks was flooding right down to her neck, making her look so innocent and tender and afraid that it wrenched the anger from Bob's heart and replaced it with a searing desire to protect her.

'Tell you what, Tessa,' Allyson cried. 'Why don't you go with Bob to get the kids? Then you can actually get to know one another.'

Tessa was looking more miserable by the minute. Bob's anger was back. 'Ally, let's leave it now,' he said shortly. 'I'll see you in half an hour, back at the house.'

As he walked away he took Wanda to one side. 'Give her some coffee,' he said. 'She's never been able to handle martinis.'

'Leave her to me,' Wanda said. 'I'll have her sober in no time. What about the lass? She looks a bit lost, standing there like that.'

Bob turned round. Allyson had now moved into the centre of another crowd, leaving Tessa standing alone. Her head was bowed and Bob ached to take her in his arms and soothe away the pain. 'Poor kid,' he murmured. 'What do you think I should do?'

'Oh, go on with you,' Wanda said. 'I'll get her chatting to someone else, don't you worry.'

Bob started to leave, and Wanda turned away to clear glasses from a table. It took her by surprise when Bob suddenly came back. 'You know what, I'm going to take her with me,' he said.

Wanda blinked. 'I thought you was going to leave her to me,' she said, taking a moment to adjust.

He didn't answer and Wanda watched in confusion as he brushed past her to get to Tessa. The young girl's eyes looked big and grateful as he spoke to her, and it was only after they'd gone out of the door that Wanda thought it strange that neither of them had looked at Allyson. You'd have thought one of them would, she later remarked to Mrs Briggs.

From where she was now sitting, in one of the bay windows, Allyson stopped listening to those around her and watched Bob lead Tessa to the bus. Her heart was pounding and her face was turning numb as every instinct in her screamed to make itself heard. *It was true! He was sleeping with the girl. Oh my God! Oh my God! It was true.* But no! No, no, it couldn't be. Push it aside, smother the paranoia and remember who had started the rumour. They always got it wrong, *always*, and maybe her mother was right, Bob should sue.

She was staring hard at the bus, watching it pull away. Her mind's eye showed her visions of them kissing, their hands entwining . . . It was hard to breathe, dread was billowing up inside her like a great suffocating balloon. She had to be wrong, it had to be drink that was frightening her like this, making her get everything out of perspective and think that their lives were going to be wrecked. She needed some coffee, she had to sober up and remind herself calmly that Bob and Tessa both loved her far too much to do this to her, and there was *just no way this was going to wreck their lives*, because there was no 'this' and because she believed wholeheartedly in the strength of their marriage, which could overcome even 'this' if there really was a 'this', which there absolutely was not.

The spacious sitting room of Shelley Bronson's Kensington flat was littered with the Sunday papers.

The remains of a late breakfast were still in evidence, and a stack of hand-labelled video cassettes had broken down into an untidy pile in front of the TV. Otherwise the room was pure elegance and style, with its sensuously lit Icart nudes, stylish Thirties furniture and rugs, and splendid original art deco fireplace. It was all so beautifully reminiscent of old Hollywood that both her home and her magnificent collection of ceramics and glassware had recently been featured in *Interiors* magazine. But not even the tasteful and unusual elegance of her surroundings could compare with Shelley herself, whose hauntingly dark beauty, languorous movements and thoughtful, almond-shaped eyes created a woman who was so exotic and sensuous that she aroused interest and caused intrigue merely by existing. But she was a very private woman, with few friends and a marked distaste for publicity, which in itself gave rise to all manner of speculation, for her dark, velvety eyes radiated the kind of promise that could incite male fantasies beyond normal limits, and often left other women feeling benign and gauche in her presence. Shelley liked it that way, for there was no reason for anyone to know about the dark, disturbing rivers that ran through her psyche, because everyone had them. The trauma of her father's death when she was only twelve, and the catastrophic relationship with her mother that had followed were the major causes of whatever doubts and insecurities she might have now, but they were nobody else's business, and certainly not for public appraisal.

For Shelley, her outward appearance and the image she created was all that mattered. She was forty-two, almost six feet tall and had the most perfectly formed body it was possible for a woman to have. She was also incisively intelligent, with great poise and confidence, and had very little time for fools, of whom there seemed to be lamentably plenty amongst the males of her acquaintance. She had yet to meet a man who could match her, in the bedroom or the boardroom, though she wasn't the kind of woman who went for long without sex, she simply indulged herself with the husbands of others, who would naturally want no scandal or commitment. There was only one exception to the non-commitment deal, though not one that she ever discussed, even with Allyson, her closest friend.

Shelley was thinking about Allyson now, as she took part in a conference call with *Soirée*'s other two producers, Alan Rich and Hayley Brocket, who would surely have seen that morning's exclusive in the *News of the World*. It was probably only a matter of time now before one of them brought the subject up, possibly in the hope of getting the low-down from Shelley, though they had to know how unlikely that was. As they talked Shelley wandered aimlessly about her apartment, the lush satin of her robe slipping down over one shoulder to reveal an exquisitely pert breast, and the flawless olive-dark skin. When finally she sat the robe fell apart exposing the silken firmness of her thighs, and as she unclasped her glorious chestnut hair, letting it tumble loosely around her shoulders, Hayley finally got round to the subject of Allyson.

'So how do we handle the "Secret Love" at the meeting tomorrow?' she asked. Then quite bluntly tacked on, 'Is it true, by the way?'

'What do you think?' Shelley responded, enjoying the sensation of her fingers as they moved through her hair.

There was a moment's silence at the other end before Alan said, 'Have you spoken to Allyson today? How did she take it?'

'Probably the way you're imagining,' Shelley responded. She got to her feet and went into the bedroom to stand in front of the mirror. Untying the robe she let it pool at her feet.

'Isn't Tessa going down there today?' Hayley asked.

'Mmmm.' Shelley was checking her flawless skin for the first signs of a blemish.

'I doubt she'll go now,' Alan said.

'She's already there,' Shelley informed them.

'My, she's got guts,' Hayley remarked.

'Why? If she's innocent?' Shelley said.

That stopped the conversation. Obviously both Hayley and Alan had presumed the story was true.

'OK, the line-up from Monday to Wednesday is looking good,' Shelley said. 'Let's see what comes out of the meeting tomorrow. Are there any Hollywood stars in town, we could probably do with some light relief on Wednesday – that show's looking a bit heavy right now.'

'Allyson wanted it that way,' Hayley reminded her.

'OK. We'll talk tomorrow and I'll fill you all in on what Stella Cornbright has to say.'

'Hey, Shelley, before you go,' Alan said. 'I was with Tim Forster last night. He'd really like to meet you.'

Shelley's immaculate eyebrows rose. 'Tim Forster the night-club owner?' she said. As Alan answered she turned back to the mirror and imagined herself standing in front of Forster like this. It would blow the man's mind.

'That's him,' Alan was saying. 'He couldn't stop talking about you. Wants you and Allyson to join him for dinner after the show on Friday. In other words, he's after some publicity for his club.'

'I don't think that's all he's after,' Shelley responded. 'Tell him I'm a lesbian and Allyson's an electronic invention,' and she rang off.

Glancing at the delicate gold Cartier watch on her wrist she toyed with the idea of calling Allyson to find out how things were going, but the Hobert Hall kids were due to arrive any minute, meaning Allyson would probably be too busy to talk. The notion of calling Bob on his mobile appealed for a moment, but then she dismissed it, and going into her bedroom she took out an exquisite set of black satin underwear and laid it on the bed. She loved beautiful things, especially those that caressed her skin and made her feel so desirable. Her creams and lotions were all from the most expensive perfume houses of France and Italy, and her clothes were either silk or cashmere, leather or suede.

After showering, she dressed slowly, savouring the pleasure of satin, then cashmere, then leather as it covered her lovingly scented body. She wasn't unduly worried about what Stella Cornbright had to say. The show's ratings were down, it was true, and Allyson's popularity had been waning these past few months. However, this scandal would turn that around. The nation would take her right to its heart now, the way it always did when a wife was cheated on by her husband, especially publicly. And the fact Tessa was so young and Allyson was fast approaching forty could, perversely, work even more in Allyson's favour than the cheating itself, for how could a middle-aged woman be expected to compete with a teenage girl?

Shelley sighed, for she knew that this kind of pain was new to Allyson, and she couldn't help wondering how she would handle it. Of course, Shelley would be there for her, and of course, it could all blow over. However, Shelley doubted that, for she knew very well that this obsession had hit the man like a raging tornado, and there was just no knowing how much havoc and devastation it was going to wreak, or indeed how many lives it would leave destroyed in its wake.

She sighed again as she reflected on what fools men were, and Bob Jaymes surely had to take the prize for being the biggest.

The cricket match was a triumph for the kids. Despite their handicaps they threw themselves wildly into the game, and came out so far ahead that the losers deserved nothing less than the bombardment of cream cakes and soggy fruit they got. Thanks to Elsie Carter and Jack Turner there was plenty of both.

Allyson rarely loved Bob more than at times like this, for he got so involved with the children, and had such a great time himself, that it seemed like he never wanted it to end. She had no idea how many of the children recognized him from the TV, but it didn't seem to matter, he was their hero. He was the one who visited them each month with Allyson, who took them on day trips to Weston or Longleat, and he was always interested in what they were doing and what they had to say. He was so good and kind and full of crazy fun that their reward was to make him the prime target when it came time to let fly with the ammunition of cakes and fruit. Allyson and Tessa were right in there with them, letting him have it too. Allyson wasn't sure if she detected some vindictiveness behind Tessa's pitching, which would have been quite out of character for Tessa, so perhaps it was her own missiles that were sailing through the air with such lethal intent.

The footballers and soap stars sacrificed their dignity too, but it wasn't long before they started fighting back and there wasn't a single person on the field who wasn't covered in goo. A couple of photographers, one from the local paper and another from a tabloid, took plenty of shots and Allyson felt a tightening in her chest as she wondered if Bob and Tessa had been captured together. No doubt she'd find out the next day.

She hadn't yet passed comment on how he'd taken Tessa to pick up the kids, mainly because she was at a total loss how to play it. The thought of them together on that bus was making her feel sick inside, but she had to keep reminding herself that those torturously erotic images were a product of her rabid imagination, not of reality, so she must get a grip. Not that she was really in danger of losing it, she just didn't know what to say when she brought the subject up, which presumably she should. Or should she? Oh God, why did all the answers get spirited off the minute a crisis turned up?

Except there was no crisis, there was only her husband, who was making his way towards her with cream all over his face, and looking so wicked and humorous that she had to laugh. As he reached her she began mopping him up with a paper towel, then she shrieked as he suddenly scooped her up and spun her round. The spectators, who'd come to watch the game, were delighted, and after taking their bows Allyson turned to Bob with a huge, friendly smile and said, 'So, did you screw Tessa on the way over to the Hall?'

His face was hidden as he had resumed wiping the cream from his eyes. When it emerged he was grinning. 'Of course,' he said. 'I wasn't going to waste the opportunity, was I?'

Allyson hoped her look of scepticism disguised her misgivings. 'Out of interest,' she said, 'is she going with you when you take them back? Could be another opportunity, though hopefully not in front of the children.'

She was already turning away, but he grabbed her arm and spun her back. Then tilting her chin so that her mouth was very close to his, he said, 'Stop this. You're tormenting yourself.'

She swallowed hard on a sudden rush of anger, and guessing they were being watched she put on a showy act of intimacy as she looked up into his eyes. But the caustic response she was planning got suddenly swept away by a wave of unease. 'Can you stay here tonight?' she asked. 'My meeting's not until twelve tomorrow.'

He was still looking at her, and she could see his anger retreating too, until finally there was only concern in his eyes. 'I'll fix it so I can,' he said, and after giving her a lingering kiss on the mouth he went to start packing the kids into the bus.

'How much do you think we raised?' Tessa said, coming to join Allyson.

Allyson turned round, concealing the jolt in her heart with a vaguely distracted smile. How close had the girl been standing, she wondered. Close enough to hear what she and Bob were saying? Her limpid black eyes showed only a quiet eagerness to share her information, and perhaps a faint hint of surprise that Allyson was failing to reply. Oh God, this was an impossible situation, with so many emotions and loyalties getting her in such a state of confusion. So maybe she should just keep remembering that she adored this girl, who she knew would never do anything to hurt her, perhaps then she would stop this nonsense and start behaving like the calm and rational adult she was. 'Five hundred,' she guessed, looking round at the clutches of spectators.

Tessa's face broke into a delighted smile. 'Better,' she cried. 'Nine hundred and twenty.'

Allyson was genuinely impressed. 'Fantastic,' she said. 'There were obviously more people here than I realized.' How hard it was to care about anything else when your life could be falling apart. But it wasn't. *It wasn't!* 'You'll have to get on to Wendy Peacemaker in the morning,' she said, 'find out how much we've totalled so far. We should be up around fourteen thousand by now, almost enough for a bus. My parents are donating, by the way. You'd better call my mother tomorrow and remind her. Oh, and find out when the guy from Human Rights Watch is flying in from the Balkans. He's on Wednesday's show, but I think he arrives on Tuesday. Sort him out a hotel, and if he's up to it, Bob and I will take him to dinner.' Had it really been necessary to add that?

'Which restaurant?' Tessa asked, as she noted down her instructions.

'Let me see. What about the Pharmacy in Notting Hill? No, let's take him to ... Hey, Kathy, what was that

42

restaurant you were telling me about earlier?' she shouted over to one of the soap stars. 'The one on Fulham Road.'

'It's on Brompton Road,' the actress answered, wandering over, a couple of autograph-hunters in tow. 'I'll call you tomorrow with the number.' She finished signing, then turned back to Allyson. 'This has been a terrific day, Ally,' she said. 'Those kids are something else.'

'Aren't they?' Allyson agreed, smiling. 'Are you going to come into the house for a drink before you leave?'

'Sure. Lead me to it.'

'What about you, Tessa?'

'Um, I'd like to,' Tessa answered, starting to blush, 'but I don't like driving in the dark, so I should probably start making tracks.'

'OK,' Allyson said, and because it was something she normally did, she gave the girl a hug. 'Drive safely now, won't you?' she said. 'And thanks for all your help today.'

Tessa smiled a shy goodbye to Kathy, whose eyebrows went up in response, and stayed that way as she watched the girl walk away. 'Tell me it's not true,' she said when Tessa was safely out of earshot.

'It's not,' Allyson responded.

'But you want to kill her all the same.'

Allyson laughed. 'No, of course not,' she said, and to avoid any further probing she went off to find out if anyone else wanted to come into the house for a drink.

Bob was a long time taking the kids back and returning the bus. Eventually Allyson had to call taxis to take everyone to the station. She'd tried his mobile a dozen times, but he had it switched off, and she'd reached such a pitch of anxiety by now that there was just no way she could stop herself fearing the worst. Though whether the worst had him smashed up in an accident, or in full flight to a love nest with Tessa, wasn't terribly clear.

She stared down at the bath she'd filled in an attempt to disguise her fears to her guests and make them think she was so unruffled by Bob's disappearance that she was planning, as soon as they left, to take a long, soothing soak before he came home. She'd even lit candles, and scented the water. Then, when everyone had gone, she continued the delusion by returning to the bathroom and taking off her clothes.

This was a horrible feeling, horrible and frightening. Her body was rigid, as though tensing for a terrible blow. And it was so discouraging, the way her mind kept speeding off down the road to disaster, imagining all kinds of pain and betrayal, when in reality there was so little to fuel the fear. Except maybe the horrifying recall of how many of her friends' husbands had abandoned them for younger women, turning their backs on lifelong relationships, shattering shared dreams and memories, destroying lives and totally screwing up their children. She'd never doubted that she'd stand by Bob were he to be beaten about by a midlife crisis, but she'd never considered what she'd do if he didn't want her – if he chose to break free and tie himself to another woman. There was no room for her in that scenario, no need of her, except maybe as someone to blame for all his ills. She knew a lot of men who had done that, who had torn up their wives, both emotionally and physically, then in a vain and cruel effort to assuage the guilt they laid the blame at the wife's door. 'If only she had been different ...' 'If only she had understood ...' 'If only she had listened ...' A thousand ifs, all designed to justify the cold and callous stranger the husband had turned into. Some men recovered, and after months, even years, of utter hell, their wives forgave them and took them back. But was it ever the same again? What happened to the trust? Was it possible to rebuild it?

She felt suddenly helpless and bewildered as she tried to plot her way through this alien land of adultery and deception. But of course she might very well not be in such a place, for she had to remember that it was her own imagination that was concocting this fear, and pushing her headlong into the jaws of disaster, as though it couldn't wait to get there. So maybe the first step was to try to find out what was *really* happening. The thought had no sooner entered her head than she was taking off her dressing-gown and slipping into the water, as though by continuing with things that were normal she could escape the common sense that might take her further into the thorny territory of lies and betrayal.

Was she completely mad? There was nothing normal about lying in the bath when Bob was so late home. She looked at the time on the radio clock. Actually, he wasn't that late. He'd only been gone an hour and a half, and he might have stopped in at the pub on his way back. So perhaps she should ring the pub. There was a phone right next to the bath, she could use that. It would seem quite airy and casual if Ron heard the swish of water, like she was washing up, or watering the plants, or taking a bath. No panic, no need for concern. Just wondered if Bob was there, because he said he might pop back.

He wouldn't be there and she knew it, so why put herself through the misery of asking? She'd give his mobile another try and if it still wasn't switched on she'd . . . She'd decide after what she'd do next.

It rang, and rang, then to her amazement he answered. 'Bob?' she cried. 'Where the hell are you? I've been trying to ring you . . .'

'Listen, if you think I'm shagging your damned assistant in some ditch somewhere, then get off the line,' he growled. 'I'm waiting for the AA to call back. Bloody bus has conked out on me.'

'Then why didn't you call and say so? I've been worried sick. What about the kids? Are they still with you?'

'No. They're back at the Hall. I'm about three miles from Vic's, and guess what, his bloody answerphone's on, so fat lot of use he is.'

His disgruntlement was suddenly making her laugh. 'Do you want me to come and get you?' she offered, feeling quite elated now by his annoying predicament.

At his end Bob looked down at Tessa. Her ruffled head was resting on his shoulder, her smooth plump legs were curled up on the front seat of his car. 'You could,' he said into the phone, 'but I can't just abandon things here. I'll wait for the AA and they can take me and the bus to Vic's where I'll pick up my car. Tape the match for me, will you? It's on at nine twenty.'

'Surely you'll be back by then.'

'I bloody well hope so. But just in case.'

'Did you call your office to let them know you'll be late in the morning?'

'No. I'll just get up at the crack of dawn,' he said, starting to feel irritated that he'd switched the phone back on, but he'd known she'd be worried and it wasn't fair to put her through that.

'You could be pretty tired,' she said softly.

'I'll survive,' he responded brusquely. 'Listen, I'd better ring off in case the AA's trying to get through.'

'Bob,' she said teasingly, 'I don't think you got what I was saying.'

He had, but with Tessa right there beside him . . .

'I was hoping we could pick up where we left off this morning,' she murmured.

He looked at Tessa, and a sudden wild and graphic fantasy of having sex with them both – Allyson on the phone, Tessa here in the car – broke out in his mind. 'We can do that,' he said, his voice seeming tight in his throat as he attempted to push the fantasy away. But he could already feel himself hardening, surging towards a place where the shame of his disloyalty and disgrace of his conscience were becoming obscured by the might of his lust. He could get Allyson to tell him what she wanted, and while she was talking he could do it all to Tessa.

'I'm lying here in the bath, waiting for you,' Allyson whispered.

He could see her, a translucent web of bubbles covering her nudity, desire glowing darkly in the eyes he knew so well. Oh God, if only she would get off the line. It would be all right, if she would just let him hang up. But even as he was thinking it his hand was slipping under Tessa's skirt, caressing her thigh.

'I'm imagining you stroking me,' Allyson said throatily.

'How does it feel?' His hand was moving higher under Tessa's skirt.

'Good,' she responded. 'Mmm, I can feel your fingers touching me, doing all kinds of wonderful things to me. Oh yes!' she murmured warmly. 'I love it when you push them up inside me.'

'Open your legs wide,' he told her.

Tessa looked at him, clearly wondering if he was talking to her. His eyes told her he was. Oh God, this was a dangerous game, and so unbelievably erotic there was just no way he could stop. Then, putting a finger over Tessa's lips, he switched the phone on to speaker.

'Can you still hear me, darling?' he said. 'I need my hands free if you're going to go on like this.'

It was the sound of Allyson's laugh as it came gently into the car that finally jolted him to his senses. He could hardly believe what he was doing, was so appalled that for a moment he seemed paralysed by the shock of it.

Somehow he managed to mumble that he had to go, the AA had arrived, which made Allyson laugh again, and almost, finally, made him laugh too, for he could see why she would think that was funny. Though all he felt was overwhelming relief that she had no way of knowing what he'd almost done, for the shame was already too bitter to bear.

'Why did you do that?' Tessa said, as he tucked the phone back in its wallet. 'Why did you lie to her? You said the AA was here . . .'

He was incredulous. 'You surely weren't expecting me to tell her *you* were here,' he cried.

Her head went down. 'No, of course not,' she answered. Her hands were bunched in her lap, her fingernails were painted with a dark red polish that she started to pick.

He already regretted his outburst, for the way he'd referred to her had been disparaging and unnecessarily hurtful. But it was a peculiar question and he was still racked with the horror of the unspeakable betrayal he'd just come so close to committing. But that wasn't any excuse for taking it out on her. The crime was totally his, and it only shamed him further to belittle her.

In an effort to make amends he reached out and covered her hands, then touching his fingers lightly to her cheek he turned her to face him. Her eyes were rarely easy to read, they were so frequently masked in caution, and it made his heart ache to see that was how she was looking at him now, almost as though she feared him.

'You should bite back,' he told her. 'When I snap like that, you should bite back and put me in my place.'

Her smile was tremulous, then she made a playful snap at his hand, catching his fingers between her teeth. His eyes were still on her face, and as he traced the sultry outline of her lips he could feel himself falling slowly, inexorably, into the depths of her adoration. She so rarely got angry, and was never judgemental. She just allowed him to be himself, and accepted, even embraced, all his flaws and weaknesses as though they were as vital and precious as any other

48

part of him. He wondered what he would do if she wanted to end their affair. Would he try to stop her? Of course, because he couldn't bear even the thought of giving her up. That he should even be thinking this was madness, but knowing her, wanting her, being so utterly consumed by her was more than madness, it was death to everything he knew and held dear. So why was he here? Why didn't he make himself walk away from her now?

His answer was to lean his head forward and bring her mouth to his. He kissed her in small, tender touches, tasting her, embracing her, pulling her so far into his heart he could barely support the weight of his feelings. When at last he looked into her eyes, she said, 'Do you really love me?'

He answered, 'Yes.'

But she seemed troubled, and sensing she wanted to tell him what was on her mind, he tilted her chin so that she could look nowhere but at him and whispered, 'Just say it.'

She nodded. Then bunching her hands around his, she said, 'Allyson said you were starting a family. In the pub earlier . . .'

He sighed and sat back in his seat. 'We've already talked about that,' he reminded her. 'In the bus on the way to get the kids.'

'But you didn't say if it was true.'

He turned to look at her, letting his eyes roam over the pale softness of her skin that was spattered with the shadows of raindrops. 'It would be extremely irresponsible for me to be seriously considering having a baby with Allyson when I feel the way I do about you,' he said tersely.

She was looking at him so intently, seeming to immerse herself in his every word. 'But you do want to have a baby?' she said.

'Allyson does,' he answered. 'And yes, I suppose I do

too, after all, I'm not getting any younger, and what you see in an old codger like me . . .'

Laughing, she squeezed his hand to her cheek. 'I keep asking myself the same question,' she teased.

'And what answer do you come up with?'

Her eyes slanted out to the night as she thought, then her humour started to fade as she sighed, 'There are no answers. Not for us.' She looked at him again. 'Maybe if we could all live together . . . Allyson and I could share you . . .'

His eyes were like saucers. 'Oh, I can see that going down a treat with Allyson,' he scoffed. But of course she didn't mean it.

She laughed, and they sat quietly then, side by side in the darkness, watching the jagged journey of raindrops as they ran down the window. He knew he should leave, that they couldn't go on sitting here like this all night, but it was so hard letting her go, knowing she had to drive all the way to London, alone and in the dark. He pictured them driving together, cutting through the night in a fast-moving car, secure and warm in their togetherness, untouched by a world outside. Excuses for not going home started sliding into his mind, but each one of them disintegrated into nonsense, for there were no excuses – there were only lies and betrayal.

'I'm cold,' she said.

He started the engine and turned on the heater. Then opening his arms he pulled her against him and kissed the top of her head. He adored the smell of her, it was so fresh and natural, like newly cut grass or ripening fruit. Was that what he had fallen for first, the refreshing, invigorating fragrance of her youth? He thought back to the beginning and how this had started, three short months ago, when she'd touched his hand in the privacy of Allyson's office, and seemed for a moment to be engaged only in that, as though he as a man didn't exist beyond that hand. Then she'd raised her eyes to his and smiled as she'd told him how Allyson had confessed to loving his hands, and she, Tessa, could see why. Looking back, there was a chance he'd known then that this girl was going to change his life, though if that were true, he had to ask himself why hadn't he stopped it then? Easier maybe to ask himself why he didn't stop it now, but he had no answer for that either. All he knew was that of all the women he had slept with throughout his marriage, women that obviously Allyson knew nothing about, and who were much more experienced and even more beautiful than Tessa, none had ever been the threat to his marriage that she was now. No-one had even come close. So why her? Why now? And why weren't the horrendous consequences this could have making a difference?

She looked up at him and waited for him to kiss her, which of course he did.

'What are you thinking?' he asked, as she wound her fingers around his and began to play with his wedding ring.

She laughed, then glanced at him shyly. 'I was just thinking . . .' She stopped and took a breath. 'It's going to sound daft, but I was wondering if we, you and me, were meant to be. You know, like some divine power looked down from the sky and said, those two people should be together, so I got sent to my job just so we could meet.'

Though he laughed at the girlish nonsense, his throat became suddenly tight, for maybe it would explain why he, a man who had always been so in control of his life, now seemed anything but. Then, making light of it, he said, 'I wonder where it sent you from? My dreams or my nightmares?'

'Just from Peckham,' she said.

Smiling, he pulled her back into his arms. 'I should go,' he said after a while.

'I know.'

51

'When will I see you?'

'Whenever you like.' She turned to face him. 'Shall we make love again?'

Her pale, translucent skin seemed to shine in the darkness, her breath was warm on his face, but though he desired her, he didn't want to make love to her again in the car. He wanted to lie down with her, in the bed that smelt of her, the bed that contained all their secrets and absorbed their love.

Her mouth trembled as he told her that.

'But I have to go back to Allyson,' he said.

She nodded. 'Of course.' Then she whispered, 'I don't want you to hurt her. I don't want either of us ever to hurt her, but I think we will, won't we? In the end.'

It was on the tip of his tongue to deny it, but he found he couldn't, so all he said was, 'Don't let's think about it now.'

Chapter 3

The *Soirée* offices and studios were in a specially converted warehouse in Fulham. Though the programme was owned by one of the large network companies, independent premises had been found to accommodate the many staff and freelancers it took to service a show with four transmissions a week, and to house the various technical resources required.

The studio, editing suites, dubbing theatres, dressing rooms, make-up department, hospitality quarters and kitchen were all on the ground floor of the warehouse. The open-plan offices, meeting rooms and production gallery occupied the floor above. The windows looked out on to yet more warehouses, and two straight rows of terraced houses at the end of the street. It could hardly be deemed a glamorous location, but its great bonus was the three-level car park underneath the building, and its proximity to Central London, which, though not good, was certainly better than some of their rivals.

Allyson and Shelley had their own offices, next door to each other at the top end of the production level. Allyson also had her own private dressing room that was fitted out like a luxury hotel suite. She was the show's main presenter, therefore she got most of the perks, which included a white Mercedes saloon car, a generous expense account and a say in who replaced her when she was sick or on leave. Her and Shelley's personal assistants had desks right outside the executive offices, part of the open-plan space, but set slightly apart to show the seniority of their positions. It was a happy and successful team that thrived as much on gossip as any other, which meant that this morning it was buzzing furiously with yesterday's story in the *News of the World*.

It was after eleven thirty when Allyson sailed in, causing an immediate hush which she pretended not to notice and they quickly covered. She stopped en route to her office to talk to Jerry Milne, that night's director, and Jocelyn West, one of the production assistants. As they took a brief look through the opening links, she knew everyone was dying to see how she dealt with Tessa, probably not realizing she'd already seen her the day before at the cricket match. Or maybe Tessa had told them, and they were all feeling a bit fed up now at being deprived of the histrionics and fireworks the story should have produced. Of course, there was a chance they'd known for ages about the rumoured affair, which would mean she was now either an object of pity, or a laughing stock because it had taken her so long to find out.

'You know, I think these last couple of sentences don't quite flow,' she said, pointing them out on the script.

'We'll take it back to the subs,' Jerry told her.

'Are you going to be free at some point for some timings?' Jocelyn asked.

'Grab me after the meeting,' Allyson said, moving on through the random arrangement of desks, 'I should be in my dressing room. Hi Alan. Are you doing Wednesday's show? Great. I'd like to talk about it when you've got a minute. Morning Edmund. How was Scotland?'

'Bloody freezing,' the researcher replied. 'Got some good stuff though. I'll bring it up at the meeting. Karen's got Phyllis Reed for tomorrow night. Did she tell you?'

'Phyllis who?'

'Reed. She's conducting the London Philharmonic at some royal extravaganza on Thursday.'

'Which reminds me,' Shelley said, coming out of her office, 'we need to get a crew out to the rehearsals.'

'Already done,' one of the production managers piped up. 'They're shooting this afternoon.'

Shelley's lips smiled her approval, then she embraced Allyson, who, she thought, was looking rather good this morning, considering, and even seemed quite remarkably cheerful. 'Are we making a regular thing out of the humanitarian angle on Wednesdays?' Shelley wanted to know.

Allyson's blue eyes were eager. 'It wasn't an intention I set out with,' she responded, 'but I think it could be good.'

'We'll discuss it in more depth later.' Shelley was already heading off towards the stairs. 'We're recording at four this afternoon, by the way, instead of three thirty, and transmission's been put back fifteen minutes because of an extended news.'

'Jerry told me. Hi Tessa,' she said, knowing that every eye in the room was on her now that she'd reached her own office. 'Did you call my mother about the donation?'

Tessa was her usual efficient self. Only a touch of nervousness, which was normal, and the vaguest hint of a deepening colour in her plump, healthy cheeks, which was also normal. 'I spoke to her an hour ago,' she answered. 'She's sending it over.'

'Good.' Allyson was smiling. She must call her mother and find out if she'd said anything about yesterday's story. She hoped not. Then, leaning in a little, she put a twinkle in her eye and said softly, 'Everyone's watching us now, so we can either make ourselves look foolish, or them. I say we make it them.'

Tessa's eyes reflected the twinkle. 'How do we do that?' she whispered.

'Just laugh, and make it look as though we're the great chums we've always been. Which we are, I hope.'

Tessa laughed as though she'd just been told a hilarious joke. A bit overdone, Allyson thought, but it would do.

Allyson was still close. 'If I was horrible to you at all yesterday, then I'm sorry,' she said.

'You weren't,' Tessa assured her. 'Though you had every right to be, if you believed the paper.'

Allyson's smile froze. Picking up her briefcase, she walked into her office and closed the door behind her.

'If you believed the paper!' Just what was that supposed to mean? Why would she believe the paper? It was all lies! Everyone was agreed on that, so why say something like that? And why say it in that kind of tone! And before she could stop herself she was hurtling off down the road to outrage and fury, throwing aside perspective and getting herself into a right royal state. But just who did the girl think she was, coming out with statements like that? It was offensive, the way she'd said it, and arrogant. At least it had sounded that way. Well, maybe not offensive exactly, and perhaps arrogant was a bit strong too, but she'd given Allyson something of a shock coming out from behind her submissive demeanour like that. Except she wasn't always submissive, agreeable would probably be a better way to describe her, and that, really, was all she had done, agree with Allyson. And now here was Allyson firing off like a lunatic as though the girl had no right to breathe, never mind speak.

'Looks like a fun day ahead,' she trilled lightly to herself, and taking a steadying breath she crossed to her desk and put down her briefcase. Scripts and videotapes were stacked up on the blue leather sofas, and her chair was occupied by a sack of mail.

'Tessa,' she said into the intercom. 'Could you come in, please?'

The door opened and Tessa was there in all her girlish, tousle-haired splendour and black leather boots.

'Could you get rid of that mailbag,' Allyson said, going to hang up her coat. 'We'll go through it later.'

Tessa did as she was told. At the door she said, 'I've just made some fresh coffee, I'll bring a cup in as soon as it's ready.'

'Great.' Allyson was watching her computer screen as it blinked and whirred into life. 'Are there many emails?' she asked.

'Quite a lot. I've already dealt with those I can. The phone messages are on your desk.'

Allyson looked up, then smiling her famously captivating smile she said, 'Give it five minutes, then buzz me through and tell me my husband's on the line.'

Tessa looked confused. 'Uh, does that mean you want me to get him on the line, or just pretend he's on the line?'

Allyson was already regretting such a fatuous request. 'Pretend,' she said, unable to get herself out of it. 'We're supposed to be carrying on as normal, remember? We both know you're not sleeping with Bob, but out there, they don't know what to believe. Unless you've told them something you're not telling me.'

Tessa shook her head. 'Nothing,' she said.

'Good. OK, you can go now.'

Allyson could feel the colour burning in her cheeks. Why had she done that? It was pathetic, stupid and bloody undignified. She was handling this all wrong. She was making a fool of herself and if she'd just calm down she'd remember that she believed Bob when he said he wasn't having an affair. And the way he'd made love to her last night . . . OK, he was tired after the hectic day, so was she, which would account for why neither of them came, but the way he held her, kissing her and teasing her for the way she'd got him going on the phone, and then how quickly he fell asleep – a guilty conscience would never have permitted such an easy release.

More deep breaths, and a cheery affirmation that she'd get past this in a day or two. It would all blow over and no-one would even remember.

She was at her computer, going through the email, when Tessa buzzed through. 'Ally, Bob's on the line,' she said.

Allyson's shame crawled through her. 'OK, thanks,' she said.

'No, I mean he really is,' Tessa said. 'No pretence.'

Allyson turned hot. Had anyone heard her say that? 'Put him through,' she said, and picked up the receiver.

'Darling?' his voice came down the line.

'Hi. Did you get to the office on time?'

'Yep. Sorry if I woke you when I left.'

'It doesn't matter. We're going into the meeting in a minute.'

'Then I won't keep you. I just wanted to tell you that I've been invited to host this year's Sportsman of the Year awards. Isn't that great?'

'Oh darling. It's wonderful. I'm glad you called to tell me. I was just thinking about you and feeling stupidly insecure over that newspaper thing again.'

'Then I'm glad I called too. Do we have any commitments tonight?'

'I don't think so.'

'So why don't we rent a video and have dinner at home, just the two of us? We can send out for something.'

'Sounds perfect.'

'OK, got to go. Just wanted to give you my news.'

'Love you,' but he was gone.

'Coffee,' Tessa said, coming in the door.

Allyson looked up and smiled. 'Thanks. And sorry about asking you to carry out that silly pretence, even though you didn't have to.'

'Oh, that's all right.' Tessa put the coffee down and was just about to leave when she said, 'Isn't that great news about the Sportsman of the Year awards?'

Allyson's smile was gone, so was her heartbeat. 'He told you?' she said.

Tessa flushed deeply and suddenly appeared so flustered and frightened she could hardly speak. 'No, uh . . . No, I . . .'

Allyson watched her, then a horrible suspicion dawned. 'Don't tell me you were listening in to our conversation,' she said.

'Allyson! You ready for the meeting?' Shelley called out.

Allyson was still looking at Tessa. 'Coming,' she called back. And to Tessa, 'We'll continue this later.'

Allyson's powers of concentration were giving her a rough time as the meeting got going. There were about twenty of them in the room, all with their own agendas, and all in need of green lights, no gos, or further discussion. The stories they ran with were usually decided on by her and Shelley, though today Shelley was taking most of the decisions. If anyone noticed they didn't let on, though obviously there would be no hiding it from Shelley.

For a while, though, Allyson managed to wrench herself out of her inner confusion to take part in the discussion on that night's show. Each episode was set up with Cocktails for the first part, a commercial break, then a filmed insert from one of the reporters, followed by a Night Cap to end with. The most important section was Cocktails. Her guests that night, at the cocktail bar, were a leading Labour politician and his wife. The filmed report was from Colin Quinlan, who'd been following the rehearsals of a new West End show.

'Terry Black's taken over the lead,' Colin informed them. 'He's agreed to come in for the Night Cap slot. I'd like to have got him for Cocktails, but he can't get here in time. My sources tell me there's some dirt to be dished on why Stafford Lawrence backed out. I need to do a bit more background, I'll fill you in, Ally, before we record. We're invited to the opening night, by the way. By we, I mean me, Allyson and Shelley. For Allyson, read Allyson and Bob.'

'When is it?' Allyson asked.

Colin's handsome black face showed his surprise. 'Tonight,' he answered.

Shelley arched a humorous eyebrow. Clearly Allyson wasn't paying attention. Allyson looked at her and mirrored the expression.

'Pretty run-of-the-mill stuff tonight,' Shelley declared. 'Nothing too testing. I'm pencilling in Gordon the Gorgeous Gardener for tomorrow's Night Cap. Has anyone checked to make sure he's free? And by free, I mean he doesn't want paying.'

'Still waiting to hear back from his agent,' Camille, one of the researchers, answered. 'He's promoting a new book, so I doubt he's going to charge.'

'If he does, we'll put in one of the standby Caps,' Shelley said. 'Edmund and Debbie, over to you for Scotland.'

Somewhere during Edmund's brief on what was in the works for Scotland Allyson found her mind straining back towards Tessa. She tried desperately to resist it, but she just couldn't stop going over what it might mean if Bob had told her himself about the Sportsman of the Year Awards. Except he wouldn't have. He'd called to tell her, his wife, and Tessa had listened in. But even Tessa's eavesdropping was ominous . . . After all, why would she do that?

'Ally? Are you OK?'

Allyson blinked, then found herself looking at Shelley. 'Sorry,' she said. 'I was miles away. What were we saying?'

'That the meeting's over unless anyone has anything to add,' Shelley replied.

'No, I'm done,' Allyson said, smiling.

By the time Allyson got back to her office Tessa had gone out for lunch, and the rest of the team were either working through, or had disappeared down to the wine bar. Allyson stayed long enough to make a couple of calls that couldn't wait, then went downstairs to her dressing room where Shelley joined her a few minutes later.

'I'm worried about you,' Shelley said bluntly. 'You lost it in there today and that's just not like you.'

'You don't have to tell me,' Allyson responded. 'I don't know where the hell my mind was. No, that's not true, I know exactly where it was.' She looked anxiously into Shelley's face. 'I hate to admit it,' she said, 'but this is really getting to me.'

'I can see that.'

'I honestly don't think it's true,' Allyson continued, 'the trouble is, it's been put there now, and it's stuck, like a great big ugly stain that I can't get rid of.'

Shelley walked over to the bar and poured them both a soft drink. No alcohol before a recording, and, contrary to what the audience were led to believe, no alcohol on the show either. All glasses contained coloured water, or, at the very strongest, a lemonade shandy.

Allyson curled up in a corner of one of the canary yellow sofas. There was a bank of TV monitors on the wall opposite her revealing static images from the studio, or on-air transmissions. The sound was muted. Behind her was a twelve-foot rack of clothes, all for the show. Most were on loan from designers, whose names were to be credited at the end of the programme.

Shelley handed her a drink and went to sit in an armchair. Allyson watched as she crossed her silk-stockinged legs and let one of her black suede Ferragamo shoes dangle. It was probably impossible, she was thinking, for Shelley to look anything other than supremely elegant, which was great for Shelley, but a pain for her, when she could do with some of that perfect poise right now. 'Tell me honestly, Shell,' she said, unconsciously attempting to tidy up her hair, 'do you think it's true? Do you think he's sleeping with her?'

Shelley drank.

Allyson watched her and felt the cold burn of dread enclosing her heart. 'Oh my God, you do, don't you?' she said. The words opened up a giant void inside her.

'I don't know what to tell you,' Shelley said. 'Have you checked whether it's true about Danny living in the same building?'

Allyson shook her head.

'Is there any other evidence?'

'Not really. Bob treats it all as a joke.'

Shelley's lips tightened at that.

'What?' Allyson said. 'What are you thinking?'

'That it doesn't seem much of a joke to me, when it's tearing you up like this.'

'I was thinking,' Allyson said, after a pause. 'The guy who wrote the story, what story there was . . .'

'There wasn't a story,' Shelley reminded her. 'There was just a sequence of lewdly posed rhetoric and sly innuendo.'

'I know. Which is why I'm not convinced it's true. But the guy who wrote it, do you know him?'

Shelley shook her head. 'His name's new to me.'

'But you do know the editor,' Allyson pointed out.

'So do you.'

'Yes, but it would be easier for you to talk to him, find out if this guy has any more.'

'I could, but we're talking the *News of the World* here, so you can rest assured that if he did have more he'd have printed it. Unless it's uncorroborated of course, but I don't think there was much about yesterday's that was corroborated, and that didn't stop him.'

'Oh God,' Allyson groaned, suddenly realizing her head was throbbing. 'It's not true. It's not true. Please God, don't let it be true.'

Shelley watched her lean back and close her eyes. She was going to have to confront the truth sooner or later, but to tell her before a recording wasn't a good idea. She could go to pieces, and when the dust finally settled Shelley knew that Allyson wouldn't thank her for that. Besides, it was Bob's place to tell her, if he could find the guts.

'I think Tessa listens in to my phone calls with Bob,' Allyson said.

'What makes you say that?'

'Something she said earlier.' She returned her eyes to Shelley's. 'Do you think she's strange? No, I don't mean that. What I mean is, do you think there's something I've missed about her? Something that's not all sweetness and light, the way I thought it was.'

Leaning forward, Shelley took one of Allyson's hands between her own. 'Ally, this is just a minor hiccup,' she said. 'You'll be past it in a couple of days. A couple of weeks at the most.'

'I hope you're right,' Allyson said, suppressing a shudder, 'because the truth is, it's frightening the hell out of me. I mean, we all know how blessed my life has been up to now. It's like nothing ever goes really wrong for me. Oh we have our ups and downs with Bob's fondness for the bottle, and his lapses of confidence, and we definitely went through it when his mother died a few years ago, as I'm sure you remember. And Daddy losing his marbles is tough, but he's that age now and well . . . None of it's very catastrophic, is it? I mean, there are people out there who'd trade their kids for problems like mine. The Golden Child, is what Bob sometimes calls me. Wealthy parents, good schools, influential friends, no struggle to get where I am. No bad experiences with boyfriends. No drugs, no illnesses, no real traumas to speak of at all. Maybe it's my turn now.'

'I never realized you were queuing up,' Shelley teased.

Despite herself Allyson laughed. Then after finishing off her juice, she said, 'Let's drop it. I know it's not true, so let's stop going over it or I'll drive myself nuts.'

'It's a deal,' Shelley said. 'And a good change of subject would be to tell you what Stella wanted to see me about yesterday.'

'Oh my God! I totally forgot!' Allyson cried. 'So?'

'It's a biggie,' Shelley warned.

Allyson's heart lurched. She seemed blighted by a sense of impending disaster.

'The old trout's retiring,' Shelley said.

'No!' Allyson responded. 'Retiring? But she can't be more than fifty. I know she looks ninety, but I always thought she'd go on till the Grim Reaper came to get her.'

Shelley's eyebrows rose. 'Apparently he's on his way.'

Allyson looked stunned. 'You mean she's . . .'

Shelley nodded. 'The big C. She wants to spend what time she has left travelling with her husband.'

'God, I don't know what to say,' Allyson mumbled. 'I feel awful now that I never managed to make myself like her.'

'You're not alone,' Shelley reminded her. 'No-one likes her. I don't think she even likes herself very much. But I've got to admit, I felt pretty sad after she told me. Somehow the world's not going to be the same without her.'

They sat quietly for a while, until Allyson said, 'Did she tell you how long she's got?'

'Six months, maybe less.'

'Oh God, this is horrible news,' Allyson groaned. 'And I don't know what's come as the biggest shock, that she's dying, or that I care.'

Shelley laughed. 'I know how you feel,' she said. 'She's leaving at Christmas, but it's all hush-hush for now. She knows I'm telling you, though. She asked me to so's you'd have enough time to practise the dance you're going to do on her grave.'

'No! She didn't say that.'

Shelley grinned.

'She did. It's just like her. Oh hell, I actually think I'm going to miss her.'

'There's more,' Shelley said. 'She told me that the company's been sold. We've known for ages it was in the offing, but now, apparently, it's happened. It won't be announced for a while yet though.'

'Oh God, I just know I'm not going to like what's coming next,' Allyson muttered.

'You might not be so disappointed. So she says, it's been bought by Leisure and Media Inc.'

'The American cable company?'

'Anglo-American,' Shelley corrected. 'It's based in the States, but it's owned by Nick and Mark Reiner, who, I believe, are both British.'

Allyson screwed up her nose. 'I've got a feeling I've met one of them,' she said.

'You interviewed Mark. He's the one who bought Rowcliffe House in Devon and spent something in the region of five million quid restoring it.'

'Good God!' Allyson blurted. 'The one with the alcoholic wife?'

'The very same.'

'I'm trying to work out whether this is good news or bad?' Allyson said, getting up to start sorting through the clothes rail. 'I wonder if Jackie's already picked me out something for today.'

'Personally I think it's good,' Shelley responded.

'I'm trying to remember what he looks like,' Allyson said.

'Not typically handsome, but certainly passable. Taller than me, incredibly powerful of course and . . .' She let the sentence hang.

Allyson turned round, a canny smile growing on her face.

Shelley was smiling too.

'Filthy rich,' Allyson grinned. 'Wow, this could be good news, provided he's managed to dump the dipso wife.' She immediately turned to the window and looked out at the sky. 'Oh God, please forgive what I said about dumping the wife. I didn't mean to tempt fate. Honestly.'

Shelley was laughing as she got to her feet. 'If he is available,' she said, 'he's going to be a mighty big fish to land.'

'That's what they say about you,' Allyson reminded her.

'Ah, but what they don't know about me,' Shelley responded, 'is that I keep getting thrown back.'

The door closed behind her, leaving Allyson with a fading smile and a growing wish that she could do something to change Shelley's luck with men. Not that Shelley was likely to accept any help, indeed this was as far as she would ever go towards admitting she had a problem on that front. Though in Allyson's opinion, the problem wasn't actually Shelley's, it belonged to the men she got involved with. They were all too often intimidated by her, wanting to dominate her or reduce her to a level they considered inferior to their own, and Shelley just wasn't the kind of woman ever to stand for that, which was good for Shelley. But it had to be a lonely existence, having so few relationships and none that had ever worked. However, with any luck Mark Reiner would change all that, provided, of course, he was free. But she didn't want to get into the wife-dumping thing again, so she settled for reminding herself that if it didn't work out for Shelley and Mark, which was another journey her imagination was zooming off down the road with before anyone had fired the pistol – but if it didn't work out, at least Shelley had the programme which was like her baby, her lover, her life and ambition all wrapped up into one.

It meant the same to Allyson too, for they'd started it together, had developed it into what it was now, and it was as much a part of their identities as it was of their lives. God only knew what they'd do without it, or even who they'd be. And right now, with so much uncertainty going on around her, Allyson was realizing the truth of Shelley's belief that the programme was their own personal refuge for when life got really tough or out of control.

Allyson was already in the make-up room by the time Tessa returned from lunch. There was a chance she'd been with Bob, because he hadn't been in his office when Allyson called, though the sub who'd answered the phone had said he was over at the Arsenal ground, which could easily have been true.

The make-up artist was dusting on the finishing layer of powder when Tessa came bounding into the room, flushed and breathless, and endearingly puppy-like, which was how she generally looked when she wanted to share some good news with Allyson, her 'favourite person in the whole wide world!'

'I'm sorry I'm late,' she gasped. 'They said upstairs you were looking for me.'

Allyson eyed her, then realizing the make-up girl was watching, she said, 'I was worried. Are you OK?'

Tessa nodded. 'Oh yes, I'm fine. But I'd really like to talk to you when you've got a minute. I've got something to tell you.'

Allyson's mouth dried. So she did have some news. Whatever it was, Allyson didn't want to hear it. 'Go and check on things upstairs, then meet me in my dressing room,' she said. 'Have any of the guests arrived yet?' she asked Julian, the floor assistant, as he came in behind Tessa.

'Lionel Godfrey's in the green room. His wife's on her way. Still waiting for Terry Black. Here's your mic pack,' he added, handing it over. 'Hey, Tessa, are you coming to see the band tonight?'

'You mean your band?' she said. 'I'd love to. Where are you playing?'

'The Man in the Moon at World's End. Eight o'clock.'

'I'll be·there,' she promised, and skipped off.

Boy, she was in a good mood. Allyson watched the way Julian looked after her. He was a good-looking kid, shoulder-length blond hair, pale lashes fringing his eyes, and a slim wiry physique. He was probably around Tessa's age, and obviously besotted. Was there a man on the planet who wasn't? Still, with any luck, this one would whisk Tessa off into a wild and passionate romance that required far more energy than a man Bob's age could possibly muster.

Ten minutes later Tessa knocked on the dressing-room door and put her head round. She waited for Allyson to finish on the phone, then said, 'Ally, you look fantastic. That dress is so cool. Whose is it?'

'Bruce Oldfield's,' Allyson answered, tilting her head to one side as she looked in the mirror. It was a short black cocktail dress with a sequined bodice, silver chain straps and a chiffon skirt. It did look good, especially with her hair in a French plait.

'God, I wish I was as slim as you,' Tessa sighed. 'Not that I could ever afford anything like that. Anyway, I'm just dying to tell you my news.'

Though Allyson was irritated by the way the girl was brushing that morning's eavesdrop aside, she wasn't about to get into a scene when she was due in studio in fifteen minutes. So doing her best to strongarm some friendliness past the misgivings, she said, 'So, what is it?'

'I was late back to the office,' Tessa said, her lucid dark eyes shining like stars, her cheeks filling up with pleasure, 'because I went to have lunch with my boyfriend and *we got engaged!*' She thrust her left hand forward to show off the jazzy little diamond on her third finger.

Allyson was reeling. Surely to God she wasn't talking about Bob!

'Isn't it pretty?' Tessa insisted, her big fat cheeks as red as tomatoes by now. 'It was a complete surprise. He chose it himself.'

'It's lovely,' Allyson agreed weakly. Then, laughing to cover her awkwardness, she said, 'I'm sorry, it's just, well I didn't even know you had a boyfriend. You've never mentioned him before.'

'I know, but you're so busy and you've already got so many people ringing you up to talk about their love lives and everything, that I didn't want to bore you with mine. Anyway, his name's Phil and he's an interior designer. He's hoping to get enough money together to start his own business. Meantime, he's working for a company over in Battersea.'

Allyson started to laugh, and knew she was a touch hysterical when she almost offered to finance the wonderful Phil's dream herself. 'Well, I can't wait to meet him,' she said. 'He's a lucky chap.'

Tessa's smile was dazzling. 'You'll love him,' she said. 'He's just the most special person. You'll come to the wedding, won't you?'

'Have you already set a date?' Allyson said, surprised.

'No, but when we do. It would mean the world to me if you were there.'

There was a tap on the door and Shelley came in.

'Shell,' Allyson cried. 'You'll never guess. Tessa's just got engaged.'

Shelley turned a chill gaze on Tessa. 'So I heard,' she said. 'Everyone's talking about it upstairs.'

'Isn't it great?' Allyson said, taking a script from the PA who raced in.

69

'Ready to go in ten minutes,' the PA called over her shoulder, as she raced out again.

'I want a quick word with you about the Night Cap,' Shelley said, holding the door open for Tessa to leave.

Taking the hint, Tessa left.

'You didn't congratulate her,' Allyson protested, lifting up her skirt to slot the microphone's battery pack in the back of her tights.

'Here, let me,' Shelley said, putting down a pile of scripts and turning Allyson round. 'We've just heard that Terry Black's wife's been awarded the Nobel Prize for Literature. She's the writer Anna Godling, in case you'd forgotten. *Hunting Black Daisies*, *Shooting Alice Cain*. Ross is doing a quick background on her, he'll be down in a minute to fill you in. He'll also confirm the title that won her the award. I'm pretty sure it was *Hunting Black Daisies*. Tell me you've read it and I'll kiss your feet.'

Allyson lifted a foot onto a nearby chair. 'Off you go,' she said, picking up the phone as it rang.

'Ally? I got a message you were trying to reach me?'

'Oh hi darling. We'll have to postpone our cosy night in, I'm afraid. We've been invited to Terry Black's opening night. That doesn't feel secure,' she said to Shelley who was still trying to fix the mic pack.

'OK. Where and what time?' Bob answered.

'I think it's the National, but I'll check and call you back. Got to go now, I'm due in studio.' She put the phone down. 'I've got it,' she said to Shelley, who was pushing the wire around Allyson's waist and up between her breasts. 'You going tonight?' she said, clipping the tiny radio mic onto her dress.

'Allyson, can we have you in studio now?' a voice boomed down the corridor.

'On my way,' she called back. Quickly picking up the phone, she buzzed through to Tessa. 'Get the details for the play tonight and call Bob with them,' she said.

70

Shelley walked with her to the studio, then after stopping off at the green room to greet the show's guests, she went upstairs to the gallery to watch the recording. On the way she popped into her office and was on the point of leaving again when she noticed Tessa standing over one of the subs, obviously taking in everything he said, then asking the relevant questions to increase her knowledge of reporting and production. Allyson herself had championed this unofficial training and Tessa's remarkable progress had been the source of much pride on Allyson's part, and encouragement on the part of everyone else. Quite amazing really, what charisma and sparkle the girl had on screen, when she was so quiet and unassuming normally. Though she did have her moments, it was true, especially when she laughed, for it was quite infectious, and despite her shy manner there was certainly nothing mousy about the way she looked, with all that shiny, shaggy black hair, and those big Bambi eyes. She was also quite popular, which wasn't so surprising, for she seemed to have very little ego and a kind of easy, interested quality about her that made people like her. That was provided, of course, one set aside the fact that she was having an affair with Allyson Jaymes's husband, but most people didn't know that, at least not for certain, and for everyone, including Shelley, it was hard to believe that anyone would take such a monstrous bite out of the hand that had so lovingly and generously fed her.

Though Shelley almost never indulged in gossip herself, she couldn't help wondering what, if anything, the others might know about the bashful and bumptious little Tessa's life outside *Soirée*. All Shelley knew was where the girl lived, that she had dropped out of university after the first year, and that if she had a family she never discussed them. Much like the fiancé that had suddenly materialized like a rabbit out of a hat. Had anyone heard anything about him before?

Responding to someone yelling her name, Shelley picked up her clipboard and headed off towards the gallery. As she passed Tessa she was aware of the girl looking up, and felt those wide, innocent eyes moving with her all the way to the end of the room. Just before she disappeared Shelley turned back to look at her. As their eyes met Tessa did her usual blush and glanced away, returning her attention to the sub. She was going out later with a crew and one of the reporters to get some more training. How generous she must think Allyson, providing her not only with the background for a new career, but apparently with a fiancé too. Unless, of course, the mysterious Phil actually did exist. And if Shelley believed that she'd be in even bigger denial than Allyson, though without the excuse.

Chapter 4

Later that evening Shelley was with a group of friends in a far corner of the crowded theatre bar when she saw Bob pressing a path towards her.

'Hi, where's Allyson?' he said, raising his voice over the noise.

'Backstage talking to Terry Black's wife,' Shelley answered. She turned to the people she was with. 'I expect you've all met Bob Jaymes.'

Most of them had, either through Allyson, or through their own professional fields, for they were all connected to The Business.

'Can I get anyone a drink?' Bob offered.

'It's champagne, wine, water or juice,' Shelley informed him. 'I'll come and give you a hand.'

As they made their way through the crowd Bob kept very close behind her. 'You're looking sensational, as always,' he murmured in her ear.

Shelley said nothing, just kept working her way through to the bar. Bob Jaymes was a man she knew better than most, so she was very well aware of his many faces, and tragically few of them were as attractive as the one on his shoulders. Were Allyson not married to him then she might have a better view of the overall picture too, but what marriage would last more than a month if a woman didn't blind herself to her husband's idiocies and weaknesses, much less his philandering and betrayal?

'Cashmere?' he said, referring to the figure-revealing, winter-white dress she was wearing. 'No underwear, I can tell.'

'Geoffrey!' she cried, smiling warmly. 'How are you? It's lovely to see you.'

'Shelley Bronson!' the large elderly man responded. 'I was just talking about you the other day. How are you?'

'Terrific. Let's catch up after the show,' she said.

Bob nodded at the man and continued after Shelley. 'Have I done something to upset you?' he said, as they reached the bar.

Shelley passed him a tray and treated him to a look that penetrated even his thick skin.

'Boy, seems like I'm really in trouble,' he joked.

'Did you buy that girl the ring she's wearing?' Shelley demanded.

His disarming grey eyes dilated. 'What ring? What girl?' he said.

Shelley turned away and reached over for two glasses of champagne. There had been many times when she'd understood perfectly why Allyson was so devoted to Bob, for the man had the charm of the devil and a side to his nature that was as genuinely compassionate and loving as any woman could wish for. But there were equally as many times when Shelley wondered how Allyson could stand the sight of him. Now was one of them. 'She's told everyone she's engaged to someone called Phil,' she said, putting the drinks on the tray.

'Who are we talking about?' Bob enquired.

'The jailbait you've been screwing for the past three months,' Shelley replied, smiling sweetly.

Bob laughed. 'Shelley,' he said, 'I'm beginning to think you might be jealous.'

Shelley looked at him pityingly, then turned back for more champagne. 'Just exactly what are you trying to do?' she asked. 'How did that story leak out?'

'I rather thought you'd have the answer to that,' he countered.

Shelley rolled her eyes. 'Why don't you try asking your child bride-to-be,' she said.

Bob was still grinning. 'You know, there's something I've always wanted to ask you, Shelley,' he said. 'Is it true you're a lesbian?'

Her eyes closed as she shook her head in dismay. More response than that was simply beneath her dignity to give.

'You're forty-two years old, you've never been married, and no-one ever sees you with the same man twice,' he informed her, as if he'd only just realized it. Then his hand went up. 'Correction, we never see you with a man, full stop. So tell me, when was the last time you had an affair? Come on, speak the truth. Say the *truth* out loud.'

Her head went to one side as she smiled straight into his eyes. 'And I thought it was a woman hell couldn't match for fury.'

He scowled. 'So says a man-hater,' he responded, though she could tell he hadn't quite worked out what she'd meant.

'It's an old and trusty tactic to go on the attack when you've got no defence,' she said, disdainfully helping him out. 'It just doesn't work with me.' She moved in a little closer and spoke very softly. 'If I were you, Bob, I'd give that girl up,' and sweeping past him she headed back into the crowd.

Tessa was sitting at a small round table in the middle of the packed pub, her hands stuffed into the pockets of her leather jacket, her chubby white knees poking through the frayed holes of her jeans. The band had finished playing, the jukebox was blaring, though it was only just audible through the din of raised and jubilant voices. As Julian carried two halves of lager through the crowd he was frequently stopped and congratulated – the gig had definitely gone down well.

'Everyone's saying you were brilliant,' Tessa told him, as he sat down.

'Yeah, it seems to have got them all going. Cheers.'

'Cheers,' she echoed. She drank, and pretended not to notice him signalling the rest of the band to keep a distance. Then putting down her glass she said, 'I'm really glad I came. It's a really cool band.'

He gave a nonchalant shrug, and as his eyes moved from the radiant loveliness of her face to the ring on her left hand, he said, 'How come your boyfriend didn't show up?'

'He's working. I might see him later though.'

Julian wasn't good at hiding his disappointment. 'So how long have you been going out with him?' he asked.

She shrugged. 'A few months.'

He drank some more lager, then sat staring at the glass as he put it back on the table. 'That thing in the paper yesterday,' he said, 'about you and Bob Jaymes . . .'

'Oh, that was terrible,' she gasped. 'It got me really upset when I saw it. And then I had to go down to Bath to Allyson's place to help with this charity thing. I wanted to die when I saw her. She was *sooo* not happy with me.'

'What did she say?'

'Well not much really, but I could tell she was upset. Then she started trying to push me and Bob together, like she was trying to prove something, though don't ask me what. It was so embarrassing, and it was horrible seeing how hurt she was. I just wish I could have said something to make her feel better, but I knew if I kept on denying it it was only going to end up making it look worse.'

Though Julian managed to retain his look of understanding and sympathy, he was having a hard time keeping the delight off his boyish face. Not that he didn't think yesterday must have been awful for Tessa, but for some reason Bob Jaymes seemed to be a bigger threat than the mysterious fiancé, which was a bit absurd, but he was definitely feeling more hopeful now he knew that he wasn't in competition with someone as sophisticated and out there as Bob Jaymes. 'I'll bet anything the bloke fancies you though,' he said. 'Everyone does. I mean, all the blokes.'

She laughed. 'No they do not,' she said, slapping his wrist.

'Oh yes they do.'

She turned to him and looked frankly into his face, then laughed when he boggled frankly back. 'What about you?' she challenged. 'Have you got a girlfriend?'

Now he was embarrassed, because the truth was he'd never really had much luck with girls, and it was only because Tessa was always so friendly in the office, and seemed so interested in anything he had to say, that he'd found the courage to ask her to come tonight. 'Well, there's this chick I've been seeing,' he said, trying to sound cool, 'but we're not, you know, serious.'

'And what about your career? Are you going to carry on in telly, or really make a go of it with the band?'

'TV pays the bills, but if we could get a good break, you know, sign some kind of deal, I'd be out of that door faster than you could say *Soirée.* I'd miss it though, it's a good programme to work on. Great crew. Great bosses.'

Tessa was nodding her agreement. 'What do you think of Shelley?' she asked.

He pulled a face, as if to say 'you have to ask?'

'I think she's amazing,' Tessa said. 'She kind of scares me though. I don't think she likes me very much.'

'I don't know if Shelley likes anyone, except Shelley – and Allyson. But she's OK to work for. What about you, do you see yourself staying with the programme?'

'Oh God I hope so,' she answered. 'Allyson's been helping me get some experience, you know, letting me go and work with the researchers and reporters when I'm not busy. Shall I tell you my secret ambition? You want to hear what it is? Well, I've got this amazing dream that one day I'll be just like her. You know, famous and successful and,' she laughed self-consciously, 'right up there in the spotlight where everyone loves me and no-one can touch me.'

She turned to look at him, her big eyes seeming to seek his approval, though her lips were still parted in laughter. 'We used to do a kind of news programme every week at college,' she said. 'I did the reporting for that. I suppose that's what gave me the taste for it. I've done a few pieces to camera lately, you know, for *Soirée*. Allyson says Shelley really rates them, which is great, but I don't know how much good it'll do me, not while all this is going on.'

Julian suppressed the offer of help that sprang to his lips. After all, there was zippo someone like him could do, and she'd probably think him a right prat for even imagining there was. Finally, after racking his brains for something else to say, he came up with, 'So, are you from London? You sound like you are.'

'Mmm,' she answered, drinking. 'I was born in Wimbledon. I live in Peckham now though.'

'And your parents?'

'They're both dead.'

'Oh. Sorry.'

She was staring down at her glass, so it was hard for him to tell if he'd just sent her off on a downer.

'What about brothers and sisters?' he asked cautiously.

'No, just me.' She turned to him and smiled. 'What about you?' she asked.

'Me? Two brothers.'

'Lucky you. I always wanted to have a brother.'

'You could always adopt me,' he said, then groaned. 'God, how corny can you get?'

'You're so funny,' she laughed. 'I think it would be great having you as a brother. For one thing, I could get to go to all your gigs.'

'Then don't forget to bring your friends, seeing as you're not available any more.'

Her eyes narrowed with playful laughter. 'It's a deal,' she said. Then glancing at her watch, 'I think I'd better get going. I told Phil I'd be home by eleven.'

He walked her to the battered old Beetle that she seemed to have abandoned rather than parked on the Kings Road, then after an awkward moment of not knowing whether to kiss her or not and deciding he couldn't because of Phil, which helped him out no end because he didn't have the nerve anyway, he stood watching the car as she drove away. He was trying to compare her with all the other girls he knew, the ones his brothers went out with, but as she wasn't like any one of them he kept coming up blank. And there wasn't anyone he could ask about her either, because he didn't know any of her friends. She didn't even seem that close to anyone in the office, except Allyson, of course, but he could hardly go and ask Allyson, and now he came to think about it he wasn't all that keen to discuss her anyway. For one thing it would feel a bit disloyal, and for another, the idea of being the only one who really got to know her was starting to appeal. He'd feel kind of privileged, being in her confidence, as though he had one up on everyone else, for the general gossip about her was that she could be hiding some dark and dastardly secret because she never invited anyone home, and rarely socialized with any of them either. But no-one was ever really vicious about her, she was much too likeable for that. They were just curious, like he was, and where there was curiosity there was always imagination, and he could imagine lots of things about Tessa Dukes, which was why he was really sorry that he hadn't managed to get in before this Phil bloke, because she was just the kind of girl he could be inspired to write songs for.

'Hi, it's me.'

'Hello you. Where are you?'

'I just slipped out. The party's still going on. Where have you been all evening? I was trying to call you.'

'I went to watch a band.'

Bob turned sharply as the fire-escape door he was next to crashed open and a drunken couple lurched out into the alley. He turned away, hiding his face in the shadows before anyone recognized him. 'I miss you,' he said.

'I miss you too. Can you come over?'

'I don't think so. We're going straight home after this.'

Changing the subject she said, 'The Phil thing seems to have worked.'

'You know, I just don't get you,' he responded. 'I thought you wanted me to leave, so we could be together.' Not that he was actually offering, it was just what he'd thought. Or maybe he was offering, for the idea of feasting himself on her completely, knowing how much she adored him, how much he adored her, how full and different their lives could be if they were together all the time, if they didn't have to worry about anyone else, if the lies could end and the betrayal could be over . . . It was crazy and he knew it, but the urgency that was attached to his longing was reaching a level where he could think of nothing but her, of how much he wanted her, how he hated having to leave her, how terrified he was of another man coming into her life . . . Christ, he'd even started to feel jealous of this Phil character, fictitious though he was, but in his way Phil was coming between them, because he was a ruse to throw Allyson off the scent, when really Allyson should be told . . . Christ, he was going out of his mind. He couldn't tell Allyson. But the insane truth was that Tessa only had to mention another man's name to inflame him with a mad urge to rush over there and claim her as his.

'I do want us to be together,' she was saying, 'more than anything, but I can't lose my job. Allyson . . .'

'I know,' he answered, cutting her off. He had no desire to talk about Allyson. He couldn't stand to be reminded of anything that stood in their way, especially something that could fire up his conscience the way Allyson did. And as for the job . . . That problem was surmountable, 'Because,' he explained, 'they can't fire you. You haven't done anything wrong, not from the company's point of view, and even if they tried you could sue for wrongful dismissal.' Boy, was he glad no-one else could hear him right now, not only because of the despicable disloyalty, but because of the way it proved how deeply, and treacherously, he'd thought about this. But all that aside, he was right, they couldn't fire her, and if they were ever to be together he needed to look out for her and make sure no-one ever tried to hurt her.

'You might be right,' she said, 'but I couldn't do that to Allyson.'

Allyson. Allyson. It always came down to Allyson. But that was a resentment he had to get under control. 'No, of course not,' he said. 'I'm just saying, you wouldn't necessarily lose your job if we . . . Well, you know what I'm saying.'

'I think so,' she said softly.

There was a long and emotion-charged moment as they listened to each other breathing and thought about what he'd just implied. He'd implied it lots of times before, but since the story in yesterday's paper it had all started to feel so much more possible, even, maybe, inevitable.

'I wish you could come over now,' she said.

His head went back against the wall as he closed his eyes. 'God, I wish I could,' he groaned, already trying to think of an excuse. 'But there's just no way.'

'Then why don't I come over there?' she said. 'I want to kiss you.'

'I want to kiss you too, baby, but it looks like we'll have to wait till morning. I'll come over early.'

'Very early?' she said, sighing deeply.

'Very,' he promised.

'I love my ring,' she told him. 'It makes me feel special.'

'I love you.'

She sighed again, and he looked sharply down the street at the sound of footsteps. 'I think someone's coming,' he said. 'I'll have to go.'

'Bob! Bob, is that you?' Allyson called into the darkness.

'Yes, it's me. I'll be right there.'

'What are you doing? Why didn't you use the phone inside?'

He smiled and put an arm round her as she joined him. The phone was still at his ear. If he'd rung off in a hurry it would have looked doubly suspicious. 'I couldn't hear,' he said, 'and I needed to call the office to find out if I'm supposed to be doing this OB tomorrow. I'm still holding on.'

'I wish I was there with you,' Tessa murmured in his ear. 'I love you both so much . . .'

'Alistair Glass is inviting us all back to his place,' Allyson said. 'Do you want to go?'

Bob shook his head. 'No,' he answered.

'Tell her you want to go home with her,' Tessa said. 'Be nice to her. Tell her you want to make love to her.'

The words cut through him. Wouldn't she be jealous to think of him making love to his wife? Wouldn't it tear her apart, the way it would tear him apart to think of her with another man? He looked at Allyson, and, afraid of what his eyes might be telling her, he lowered his mouth to hers and kissed her.

'Can you still hear me?' Tessa whispered.

He carried on kissing Allyson, but he was achingly aware of how desperately he wished it was Tessa. So desperately that he began pushing Allyson up against the wall and pressing his erection against her.

'Bob!' Allyson laughed. 'What are you doing? Someone might come.'

'I'm sorry,' he said, strangely disoriented by the voice in his ear and the woman in his arms.

'If you can still hear me,' Tessa said, so softly that he barely could. 'If you can still hear me . . . Oh Bob, I don't know how to tell you this . . .'

Fear suddenly plunged into his chest. She was going to end it. She was about to tell him it was over . . . That was why she wanted him to make love to Allyson. She didn't want to wreck his marriage. He felt as though he was suffocating. Panic was so close behind. But he had to keep control. Allyson was here. That was why she was doing it. Because she didn't want to hurt Allyson . . . Allyson. Allyson. Always Allyson. But what about him? Didn't she realize what she meant to him? Didn't she understand that he couldn't let her go? She meant everything to him now . . . He couldn't let her go. He couldn't even think about it . . . Then suddenly everything in him came to a crashing halt as he heard her say,

'I keep trying to find the right time to tell you . . . Oh Bob, please don't be angry, but . . . I'm . . . I'm going to have a baby.'

Bob was still shaking as he drove through the night towards home. Allyson's car was up ahead, as usual she was driving too fast, or maybe it was him driving too slow. It was him, he knew it, lagging behind as though to delay the terrible moment when he had to tell her that he had made Tessa Dukes pregnant and was going to leave her.

The blare of a car horn made him jump and set his

pulses racing. He had to pay attention, keep his eyes on the road. But his mind was all over the place. A few minutes ago they'd said goodnight to Shelley and the rest of their friends. Shelley had known something was wrong, but she hadn't said anything, she wouldn't in front of Allyson. Curious that, how Shelley could read him in a way Allyson seemed unable to, even after all these years. But Allyson was probably in denial, telling herself if she just ignored it, pretended it wasn't happening, then it would all just go away. That would be typical of Allyson.

Indicating left he followed her car from Hyde Park Corner into Grosvenor Street and from there down to Victoria. His head started to spin. He could barely see straight, so he pulled over to the side of the road and turned off the engine. If he carried on he'd have an accident and where would that leave Tessa? He couldn't believe the way his thoughts were going and pressed his hands to his head as though to stop them. But it was true, Tessa needed him in a way Allyson never had, and probably never would. Of course he was mad, he had to be, because only a madman would have leapt so readily on this excuse to leave his wife, an excuse that might not even be based in truth, and even if it was, nothing had been discussed, or thought through, or even given a chance to sink in. Did he really want to have a baby with Tessa? No. All he really wanted was Tessa.

He had to drive on. If he didn't Allyson would come back to look for him. He wished to God he could just go straight to Tessa. How much easier it would be if the next few hours were already over, if he'd already left. In truth he didn't really know if he had the courage to do it, wasn't even entirely sure he was planning to. After all, thinking about it, and longing for it, wasn't the same as actually doing it. Was nothing like it, in fact, for he'd never felt afraid before, and that was definitely how he was feeling now. He was going to be turning his back on so much, not just Allyson, though God knew that was going to be the most difficult, but on the lives they had created together, the friends they had, the dreams . . . Oh God . . . The dreams . . . How could he tell her that he'd made Tessa pregnant? What was it going to do to her? He couldn't do it. He just wasn't going to be able to tell her.

Suddenly he felt as though he was choking. His breath wouldn't come, his skin was burning, and his mind felt as though it would explode. But it was too late for his conscience to leap to Allyson's defence now. If it was true that Tessa was pregnant – and maybe even if it wasn't – then surely it would be kinder to get out of Allyson's life now before the lies and deceit got any worse.

His eyes closed and as his head fell back he felt himself being swallowed up by emotions he couldn't even begin to name. In the end he took out his phone and dialled Tessa's number. She answered on the second ring.

'It's me,' he said.

Her voice was quiet, meek, almost afraid. 'Are you angry?' she whispered.

His heart twisted at the fear in her question. 'No, of course not,' he said softly. 'Are you OK? You sound as though you've been crying.'

'A bit,' she said. 'I was afraid . . .' She tried again, 'I was afraid of what you might be thinking. Oh, Bob, I'm sorry about the way I told you. I shouldn't have done that. I've just been trying to find the right moment, and then suddenly it just came blurting out and . . .' Her voice was choked with tears. 'I'm sorry,' she whispered.

'It's OK. You had to tell me sometime.'

'Oh God, I wish you were here. No, I don't mean that. I don't ever want to put any pressure on you. I know you love me and I love you too, but I promise you I'll never tell anyone it's yours. If you want, I'll get rid of it.'

'No! That's not what I want,' he said. 'You know what I want. For us to be together.'

'You mean that hasn't changed?' she said. 'You still do?'

'Yes. I still do.'

He stared out at the night, seeing none of the familiar buildings or passing traffic, knowing only the agonizing effort to summon the words that would set in motion the greatest pain and devastation Allyson had ever known. It was hard. So hard. But didn't his happiness count?

As though sensing his dilemma Tessa said, 'It's enough to know you still love me. You don't have to do anything.'

'Yes, I do,' he said, brushing aside her offer of reprieve. Hard it might be, but he didn't want to put it off, he just wanted it done. Then suddenly he was saying, 'I don't know how long it'll take, but I'm going to talk to her tonight. Then, if you still want me . . .' It was a tease that had found its way stiffly, awkwardly, through the numbing gravity of the crisis they were facing.

'You know I do, silly,' she said. 'I'm just worried about Allyson . . .'

'Let me worry about Allyson,' he said. 'You just worry about you and don't wait up, I'll use my key to get in.'

Allyson was already in the bathroom that adjoined their bedroom when she heard Bob letting himself in the front door. Their flat, which took up the entire second floor of one of the beautiful listed buildings of Cheyne Walk, had been a wedding gift from her parents, one of the several properties that had been in her family for at least four generations. It had changed a lot during the years she and Bob had owned it, for they'd put their own stamp on it now, making it very much more stylized and contemporary, though blending perfectly with the traditional. Everything in it they had bought or designed together, even the exotic French and African antiques had been found during long hot summer holidays together, or by going for the thrill of the auction, which

Bob was so good at. The flat was such an integral part of who and what they were that it was probably as much a part of the fabric of their marriage as they were themselves.

She could hear him moving around in the bedroom, easily able to picture everything he was doing as he flicked on the light in the alcove that served as his dressing room, and started to undress. She'd set the heating to come on while they were out so the place was warm, and she'd turned the bedside lights down low, to make it seem even more cosy. She'd been tempted to run a bath for him, to help him relax after being told that he wasn't going to be used for the outside broadcast tomorrow, but it was late and she had to be up early in the morning. But maybe she should have run that bath, for the way his face had drained at the end of the phone call had told her just how upset he was about being passed over again. It seemed to be happening a lot lately, and his confidence, despite outward appearances, was too fragile to take much more rejection.

Still, he had the awards programme to look forward to, and for now, though she was tired and not really in the mood, she dabbed on the expensive perfume he'd given her last birthday, slipped into one of the negligees she knew he particularly liked, and kept the cabinet door firmly closed on her diaphragm. Making love almost always helped him to relax.

When finally she went into the bedroom she was surprised not to find him still getting undressed. He wasn't even in the room, though his jacket was hanging on the door of the large French armoire where he kept his suits, and his tie had been dropped on the satin- and chintz-draped bed.

Presuming he'd gone to pour them a drink, she pulled on a robe and went to see. The carpet was soft and warm under her feet as she padded out into the hall, where, to her surprise, the only lights burning were those over the hunting prints that lined the oak-panelled walls, prints she'd never been too keen on, though Bob thought they were the *dernier cri* in good taste. As she walked past the two guest bedrooms and second bathroom she was aware of the unease she'd been trying to keep suppressed all night starting to stir.

'Bob?' she called. 'Bob, where are you?'

She pushed the sitting-room door open, but there was no-one in the moonlit darkness, only the familiar sofas and chairs, and the tall casement windows that overlooked the Embankment with its Victorian lampposts, autumnal trees and quaint wrought-iron benches. Beyond the Embankment's walls the river Thames flowed in the darkness, moving gently between two of London's famous bridges. She could see one of them lit up in the distance . . .

'What are you doing?'

She spun round.

He was standing behind her, his shirtsleeves rolled up, a glass of whisky in one hand, a brandy for her in the other. She could smell the whisky on his breath, but she couldn't make out his expression in the darkness, though from the way her heart was thudding she probably didn't want to.

'There you are,' she said, taking the drink. 'I wondered where you were.'

He turned back towards the bedroom. She watched him, fearing that he was going into one of his depressions. Or maybe that was what she wanted to think, because the alternative . . . She cut the thought off and after checking that the front door was deadlocked, she followed him down the hall.

'Mummy called earlier,' she said, closing the bedroom door behind her, and attempting to inject some normalcy into what was starting to feel like a horribly surreal situation. 'She's trying to work out the roster for the villa next summer. The one in Sardinia, not France.

She wants to know if we want it, and if we do, when and for how long?' She was pulling back the sheets, climbing into bed.

He was in the bathroom, fiddling about with his shaving gear, but the door was open, so he could hear her – and he still wasn't undressing.

'Bob? Did you hear what I said?' she asked him.

At last he came into the bedroom, but his whole demeanour was making her wish he hadn't. His hands were stuffed in his trouser pockets, his head was bowed and he was still wearing his clothes. Why was she noticing these things? What difference did it make how long he took to undress? And why was her heart lurching about like this when she had nothing to be afraid of?

'You choose,' he said.

Good. That sounded better. 'OK. Well, I was thinking . . .'

'And take Shelley,' he interrupted. 'The two of you'll enjoy spending some time together, out of the office.'

Allyson kept on smiling as her head went curiously to one side, and she forced a laugh past the clogging in her heart. 'What do you mean?' she said. 'Why would I go with Shelley and not with you? She can come, but . . .'

He sat down on the edge of the bed, on her side, but he wasn't looking at her. Her heart seemed to be getting more clogged than ever.

'I won't be coming,' he said softly.

She stared at him, knowing exactly what he was saying, yet refusing to hear it. 'What do you mean?' she said, feeling her smile start to hurt.

He turned to look at her and her heart felt as though it was tearing in two. So her instincts had been right, the story in the paper was true. *But that didn't explain Phil!*

'You're Phil, aren't you?' she whispered.

He nodded.

'Oh my God.' Her hands moved to her mouth. A bolt

of desperate denial cleaved through her heart. 'Oh my God!' She tried to get up from the bed, but his weight on the sheets was trapping her legs.

'I'm sorry,' he said. 'I'd give anything for this not to have happened, but . . .'

Her chest was heaving. She couldn't make herself think. *This wasn't happening!* The concern in his eyes, the painful regret in his words . . . 'Why are you telling me now?' she suddenly cried. 'Why didn't you admit it yesterday, when it was in the paper, when I asked you *if it was true!*'

He grabbed her fists as she started to hit him, and held them to his chest.

But there was only craziness in her head. Fast irrational thoughts erupting from a disabling panic and anger. She wanted to scream and scream. She wanted to hit him, scratch him, kick him . . . She wanted to tear out the horrible, lacerating realization that he'd got himself engaged to a *child* when he was married to her! How could he have done that? What kind of madness was in his head . . . But no! No! She had to put the brakes on this. She was overreacting, getting herself out of control, when she knew what this was. She knew she could fight it, so she was going to keep calm, and try to be rational. Midlife crises didn't respond well to hysterics. So, making a superhuman effort to even out her breathing and press down the panic, she said, in a voice that shook with unsteady courage, 'How long? How long have you been seeing her?'

'Three months,' he answered.

Her heart recoiled from his words, but she made herself nod, as though she was talking to a friend. 'So everyone knew, but me?' she said.

'I don't think so. We've been as discreet . . .'

He stopped as she turned her head away. It was the 'we' that had done it, the 'we' that had joined him to Tessa, and severed him from her. Oh God no! No! No!

No! She was biting her lip, and holding her breath in a furious attempt to stop herself crying, but tears were already streaking down her face, and the brief show of rationale was taking its curtain.

'I don't understand how you could have done this,' she said, her voice breaking with emotion. 'I just don't understand.'

'I'm not sure I do either,' he responded. 'It just . . . Well, I guess it just happened, and it's something that feels, well, right, I suppose. As though it's meant to be.'

She looked at him wildly. 'What are you talking about?' she cried. 'You're forty-five years old! How can it be right? You're old enough to be her father.'

'I know. But what we have . . .'

Rage flung out her next words. 'What do you mean, what you have? You have nothing except some deluded middle-aged fantasy that you're the answer to some little tart's dream!'

'Don't talk about her like that.'

'I'll talk about her how I like. She's sleeping with my husband for God's sake.'

'That doesn't make her a tart.'

'Don't defend her to me! I'm the one who took her in. I'm the one who . . .'

'Allyson, stop!'

'She's a tart!' she screamed. 'She's a fucking whore who's putting it out for every man she meets, and you, you fucking moron, are so damned conceited that you think you're different. Well, you're not, because she's screwing half the men in . . .' The breath suddenly left her body, and not even the sting to her face was as great as the shock that he'd actually hit her. She looked at him, unable to believe he'd done it. So stunned, in fact, that she no longer seemed able to connect with anything at all.

He stared back, shaken too by what he'd done, and apparently as stunned. Then dropping his head he said, 'I wish to God I could take that back.'

91

Allyson looked away. The slap had deadened her. She was numb, and the deafening sound behind the silence was the slow, devastating explosion of her world. She wanted to reach out her arms, pull it back, enfold it against her and hold it safe. But there was nothing there to touch except her husband, who'd betrayed her, who no longer wanted to be touched by her. Oh God, she wanted this to end. She wanted to walk out of this room and pretend none of it had happened. But she couldn't, and that was what was making it so much worse. There was no going back. This really was happening and it was going to go on happening. It wouldn't be over in a day or a week, it wouldn't even be over in a year. For some people it was never over, which was why she had to fight, had to do everything she could to keep them together and get them through this. He still loved her, she was sure of it, so if the only way she could save their marriage was to go along with this craziness for a while, then she'd have to do it. She could ride this storm, and pull them both through. Except he was the one with all the strength and without him she wouldn't have any. But no. She just had to remember that a lot of men went through this, and though it would probably prove the biggest test to their marriage they would ever have to face, they would make it. And though he'd just hit her, she knew he was sorry, and maybe if it were anyone else but Tessa she might be able to forgive him. But the fact that he'd actually struck her, that he would raise a hand to her, his own wife, because he was so besotted and obsessed with a nineteen-year-old girl . . . No! No. She was losing it again. She could feel it slipping away, and she must get a grip, try to be rational and not get all consumed and het up with panic and jealousy . . . She had to try to see this through his eyes . . . But that was awful too, because Tessa was so young and she could see why he would prefer her . . . No! No room for self-pity. Oh God! Why didn't he say something? Why was he just sitting there as though he was waiting for her blessing? What did he expect from her? Why didn't he just go? But no, she didn't want him to go. She wanted him to stay. So maybe she should talk to him. Try to help him understand that he would get over this, that it wasn't something he should wreck their marriage for. She had to help him because he couldn't be thinking straight, and maybe she could show him how to get back on track.

She took a breath to speak, but no words came out. He turned to look at her, and she tried again. 'Tell me,' she said, 'what do you know about her? What's her background? Do you know, because none of us do.'

She could see the question annoyed him, but she was determined not to back down. 'Yes you do,' he said. 'And please don't let's get into the "she's evil" and "he's in midlife crisis" spiel, because we both know it'll be Shelley talking.'

Fury suddenly blasted its way through the calm. 'Are you suggesting I can't speak for myself?' she seethed.

'No, of course not. I'm just saying . . .' He shook his head. 'It doesn't matter.'

A few seconds ticked by, then getting up he walked into the bathroom and took his robe from the back of the door.

'What are you doing?' she said, following him.

He looked down at her and she was suddenly shouting, 'No Bob! Please! Just stop this. You have to pull yourself together and remember how much we mean to each other. Our marriage is good and strong, you can't go smashing it up for a passion that's bound to pass. Darling, it doesn't even stand a chance of surviving, can't you see that? No!' she screamed, as he started to walk past her. 'No, Bob. Please.' She was clutching his arm so tightly her nails were breaking his skin, but she didn't care. She wanted to hurt him, the way he was hurting her.

'Allyson, don't make me say things that are only going to hurt you more,' he said.

Dread of what they might be whipped through her heart. 'You don't have to,' she sobbed. 'All you have to do is tell me you're not going.'

'I have to go,' he said softly. 'I'm sorry, but I have to.'

She was in chaos. She didn't know what to do. All her calm and rationale was in pieces, blown apart by desperation and panic. If only it didn't feel as though he was tearing everything out of her, maybe then she could find some final shreds of dignity to hang onto. Something to reassure her that it would be all right, that this was just something they were having to go through, but it wasn't the end. He might have to go now, but he would be coming back. He had to come back because they were too much a part of each other, too deeply connected, to be torn apart like this. 'If you love me at all,' she said, 'you won't go.'

He looked down at her, and a long time seemed to pass before his decision not to answer made him turn away.

'I don't know you,' she choked. 'Who are you? You're not the man I married.'

'If you knew how much . . .' He stopped and shook his head.

'How much what? You love her?'

'That wasn't what I was going to say, but . . .' He looked at her again. 'Don't make this any worse for yourself,' he said.

Allyson's eyes closed. There was such a terrible wrenching in her chest that it was making it hard to breathe. She felt dizzy, disoriented, as though she was floundering around in a darkness that knew no end. She didn't even know she was crying as she said, 'Don't you care what this is doing to me? Don't I matter to you at all any more?'

His grey eyes looked sadly into hers. 'Of course you do,' he said.

94

The terrible pain of his admission trampled what was left of her hope. 'But she matters more?' she said.

Still he looked at her. Then finally he whispered, 'Yes.'

Her legs suddenly felt so weak she thought they would crumple, but somehow she managed to turn and walk away. She saw her brandy where she had left it, next to the bed, and going to pick it up she carried it through to the sitting-room, not really knowing what she was doing, or where she was going. She stared down at the drink, glinting in the moonlight. She could hear him moving about, putting things into a suitcase. Panic was rising like a storm inside her. A scalding heat burned through her head, a terrible confusion of loss and survival. She didn't know what to do, how to make any of this stop.

He came into the room. She turned to face him and seeing him dressed, ready to leave, she let the glass slip from her fingers. It fell onto the sideboard but didn't break, just turned over and spilled the brandy. She gazed down at the liquid. She couldn't let him go. He was her husband. She loved him and she'd rather die than let him walk out of that door. 'Don't go,' she whispered. 'Please. Don't go.' When he didn't answer she turned to look at him.

'Stop. Don't beg,' he said.

Her fists were suddenly clenched. 'I will. I'll beg. I'll do anything to make you stay. We need to talk. We should discuss this and try to find a way to work through it.'

'There isn't a way.'

'No! Don't say that! I'm your wife. I love you. I can forgive you for this. We can . . .'

'It's over, Allyson. You have to move on. We both do.'

Bitterness made a sudden surge through the misery and pain. 'Oh God, such a hip little phrase,' she spat. 'What comes next? Closure? We have to have closure?' She put a hand to her head and felt another debilitating swing of emotion. 'I don't know what I'm saying,' she sobbed. 'I don't know what's coming out of my mouth. I just know that I can't let you walk out that door. Bob, I don't want you to go. Please!' She looked at him with dark, frightened eyes and willed him with all her might to stay.

'I'm sorry,' he said, and picking up his case he let himself quietly out of the door.

It was as though he was dreaming. Any minute now he would wake up and find that none of this was happening. He wasn't in his car, driving over to Tessa's. He hadn't just walked out on his wife of eighteen years, nor was he adrift from his emotions as though he was no longer in his body, only beside it.

Yet why would he want to wake up from this? He was free now to be with Tessa as often and for as long as he liked. It was what he wanted, and when everything finally settled down he knew he would find he had done the right thing, for everyone. It wasn't that he didn't love Allyson any more, because he did. It just wasn't in the same way she loved him. For over twenty years he'd put her first, always considering her needs, doing things the way she wanted, keeping his affairs secret to make sure she never got hurt. And why would he want to hurt the woman he loved? He didn't. He just wanted to move on to this new phase of his life now, and be with Tessa, who needed him and loved him, who valued him for the man he was, and who mattered so much to him now he'd rather die than be without her.

Allyson was still staring at the door, the one he had closed, though her eyes were only seeing the terrifying, empty space he had left behind. A few minutes ago he had been there, she could still smell him, hear him, feel him, even. It was as though he had turned into a ghost, a presence she could sense, but not see. She wanted to be strong, she wanted to believe that they really would get through this, that he would come back, but right now she was so afraid she could barely make herself think. Except she *was* thinking, and the thoughts that were tearing through her mind, dragging such painful and torturous images with them, were so horrible and disturbing she wished to God she could make them stop. But her imagination had a will of its own, and it seemed determined to show her everything the way it might be, sparing her nothing. The worst was being able to see Bob going to Tessa, walking in the door and pulling her into his arms as he told her they could start their lives together now. She could see his big, strong body naked with Tessa's, holding her close, making her look at him, making her adore him . . . She could hear them groaning, sense their passion, then hear them laughing and doing all kinds of things together that he'd always done with her. His lips would be kissing Tessa's now . . . She pressed a fist to her mouth to stifle a sob. He was hers. He didn't belong to anyone else, so why was this happening? How could Tessa have done this to her? Why hadn't she rejected him when he made a pass at her? Or maybe Tessa had initiated it. Maybe Tessa really was someone she didn't know, someone she should be afraid of, whom she should never have taken into her life. Maybe beneath that shy and anxious exterior there wasn't only the sparklingly confident young girl they sometimes glimpsed, maybe there was some manically deranged she-devil capable of all kinds of damage and disruption . . .

Her breathing was changing again, becoming faster and heavier, labouring in her chest and seeming to ladle more adrenalin and emotion into her heart. Her head was starting to spin and she could feel a hot, uncontrollable rage spiralling through her. That treacherous little bitch! How dare she do this! Just who the hell did she think she was, even to enter into the sacred arena of her boss's marriage? She should be grateful she ever got a job, that someone like Allyson even took an interest in her, because there were plenty of others Allyson had to choose from. And there would be plenty more, because there was just no way she was keeping her job now. She'd rather kill the girl than have to go on seeing her every day, imagining her with Bob and knowing they were getting on with their lives in a way she never could. And maybe that was the most frightening of all, the way she could see herself heading into a total breakdown if he didn't come back. And it could happen. She'd seen enough of her friends go through it, and right now she couldn't even get herself to go into the bedroom, she was so afraid of the emptiness and pain that were waiting. But that was nothing compared to the way the press were going to pounce on this tomorrow . . . Oh God, how was she going to handle that? It was all going to become public. Everyone was going to know and while Tessa had Bob to help her through it, she was going to be alone, trying to be strong without him . . .

'Shelley,' she said into the phone.

'Allyson?' Shelley sounded sleepy. 'What time is it?'

'I don't know. Shel . . .' She tried again. 'Shel, he's . . .'

'It's OK, I'm on my way. Just pour yourself a stiff drink and stay in the kitchen until I get there.'

Allyson had gone through more than half a bottle of wine and another three circuses of emotion by the time Shelley arrived, which happened to be at a point when Allyson definitely had all the balls in the air and was clearly determined to keep them there.

'I feel so embarrassed now,' she said, 'calling you up in a state like that. I'm fine really. But now you're here, would you like a drink?'

'Just coffee,' Shelley said, 'and the same for you. Hangovers are the worst for dealing with something like this. My God! Did you drink all that whisky?' she cried, seeing the near empty bottle over by the fridge.

Allyson turned to look at it. 'No,' she said. 'Bob was drinking before he left.' Those words almost made her drop one of the balls, but then Shelley was saying, 'Well, we don't want you both hitting the bottle, and we know for certain he will. Now you sit there, and I'll put the kettle on.'

'I feel really terrible about this,' Allyson said, sitting down at the table. 'I mean, I know it's going to be all right. He'll come back, but it's just a bit tough, you know, tonight . . . And hearing it wasn't the greatest thrill I've ever had, but in a way I was expecting it. Well, you know that because I've been telling you for ages that I think he's about to start going through the male menopause and I've always sworn I'll stand by him, which I will, but right now I want to *kill him*. But it's OK, because I might go off my top a bit when it happens to me, and I know he'll be there for me. So I'm going to be there for him and before you know it, we'll be looking back on this and laughing. Well, maybe not laughing, but you know what I mean. And I was thinking earlier that maybe we should sack Tessa, but now, on reflection, I don't think we should. I mean I hate the girl, and I want to smash her silly face in, but we could have a . . .'

'Allyson, shut up,' Shelley said gently. 'You're still in shock and nothing you say tonight is going to make any sense to you in the morning. What you are going to need to prepare yourself for, though, is the press. They're going to get hold of this so fast that it wouldn't even surprise me if they already know. So, I think you should take some time off . . .'

'No! I'm not taking time off!' Allyson protested. 'I'd rather die than let either of them think this was getting to me. Oh no. I'm going to be on that screen tomorrow night, and I'm going to be my usual dazzling self, and let him see that I can survive very well without him, thank you very much.'

Shelley's expression was as sceptical as her reply. 'I'm sure you can,' she said, 'but you've never had any practice at losing someone you love, and I'm sorry to tell you that from here, it only gets worse.'

'That may be so,' Allyson replied bravely, 'but I can handle it. I've got you, and I've got my job, and I don't intend to let either of you down. So I'll be there tomorrow, and if she's there too, I'll . . . I'll . . . smash her fucking face in, is what I'll do.'

Shelley burst out laughing. 'That's the spirit,' she said. 'But in my opinion, if anyone's face needs smashing in, it's his.'

Allyson was up for being rash. 'Then I'll smash his in too,' she declared. 'And I'll show him that I actually don't need him. In fact, I might not even take him back when he wants to come. Do you think I should tell him that? I've got Tessa's number, I could call . . .'

'No,' Shelley said. 'I don't think you should call right now. I think you should just drink this coffee and then try to get some sleep.'

At that all the balls plummeted to extinction. 'I can't go to bed without him,' Allyson said, tears starting in her eyes. 'I know it sounds pathetic, but I just can't.'

'It's OK. I brought some things with me,' Shelley said. 'I'll sleep in one of the guest rooms, so if it gets unbearable in the night I won't have so far to come to rescue you.'

Allyson gave a shaky smile. Nothing was feeling very copable with now, but it was good that Shelley was staying. And it would be good if she went to work in the morning too, because there was just no way her pride could handle it if Tessa managed to turn up and she didn't. But how the hell was she ever going to get to sleep knowing that Bob wouldn't be there in the morning – that he would be in someone else's bed?

Chapter 5

The papers were full if it. Every time Allyson turned on the TV or radio it seemed that they too had little else to discuss but the break-up of the Jaymes's marriage. The desertion of a near-forty-year-old woman for a teenage girl was simply too delightfully salacious to pass over, especially when it concerned two such well-known faces. It was as though the entire nation had become obsessed with it. Her phone never stopped ringing. Journalists and photographers she'd always considered friends were constantly crowding her in the street, demanding to know how she was, if she had anything to say, or if she would take Bob back. She never made any comment, but how dearly she sometimes wanted to scream at them for their obtuseness and stupidity.

The windows of her flat had become the focus of telescopic lenses. Shots of her getting into her car, going into a shop, arriving at the office, were all making the front pages. Her mother was photographed too, at the chemist collecting sleeping pills for her father that the headline claimed were for Allyson. Even the people in the village where she and Bob had their country home were being dug out of their cottages and asked to comment on the break-up. She was under siege, not only in her private life, but in her professional life too, as the programme ratings had shot through the roof. Everyone was watching, looking, she supposed, for signs of how she was handling this. Inwardly she wasn't. But outwardly she was doing everything she could to make it look as though she was on top of the situation and perfectly able to cope.

Achieving that front was the most difficult undertaking she'd ever been faced with, especially when all she wanted was to die, or at the very least to hide from the world and pretend that none of this was happening. She was still in shock, she knew that, but it didn't make the pain, or the longing, or the horrible desperation that threw her into all kinds of madness any the less. There were so many times when all she wanted was to scream and scream, as though the noise would drive out the pain, or would maybe even reach him and make him come back to save her, before she went under. She even considered telling him she had cancer, or she was pregnant, or she would kill herself if he didn't come back. Anything to get his attention, to know that he still cared, maybe even still loved her.

But she did none of it. She simply slipped from one moment to the next, and prayed with all the might in her soul that he would come to his senses soon and end this terrible pain she was suffering, for having to go through it at all was bad enough, but having to go through it publicly was nothing short of torture. Yet in its way it was probably the spotlight that was saving her, for knowing that the whole world was watching her, waiting for her to go to pieces, was what forced her out of bed in the morning and somehow, miraculously, held her together through the day. The nights were a whole different story and she was coming to dread them like she had never dreaded anything in her life. Every minute, every second, was spent either tearing herself apart in grief and denial, or waiting for the phone to ring, bringing the call that would tell her he had made a mistake and was coming home. She'd lost count of the number of times she'd called Tessa's, but she only ever got the machine and couldn't bring herself to leave a message. She guessed they were there, but were screening their calls, just as she was, in order to avoid the press. She tried several times to get hold of him at work, but that wasn't getting her anywhere either, because unless his colleagues were lying to her he hadn't spoken to any of them since the day the news had broken. And knowing that he and Tessa were holed up together, and had each other to help them through this, hurt beyond almost anything else.

Two weeks passed and still Tessa didn't come into the office. Nor did she call. They were difficult weeks for everyone, as the whole team was being bombarded by the press, and no-one knew quite how to behave towards Allyson. She was so pale and drawn that whenever they were around her they spoke in hushed tones as though she were ill. And if anyone caught her eye she was treated to looks of such sympathy it made her feel like screaming. She didn't want to be this object of pity. She wanted them to laugh around her and tease her the way they always did, even though she didn't have it in her to respond.

'If firing the girl wasn't going to land us in even deeper hot water, I'd go right to Stella,' Shelley said.

Allyson shook her head. 'You know we can't do that,' she said. 'If we do there's a chance she'll sue, and that kind of publicity I can definitely do without. Besides, it'll just turn me into the villain and right now, I don't think I could handle that either.' Her face was gaunt and strained and the trauma of the last two weeks was etched deeply around her eyes, one of nature's cruelties that had not been missed by the press.

Shelley went to refill their coffee cups. They were in Allyson's dressing room, where they'd spent a lot of time lately, even sleeping there one night when Allyson had been unable to face going home, and they'd both drunk too much to drive.

'We still don't know for certain that she will be coming back,' Shelley said.

'Oh she will,' Allyson responded. 'Don't ask me how I know that, I just do.' She took the coffee Shelley was handing her and turned to look at the TV monitors. 'I should start getting ready for the studio,' she said.

'I wish you'd take some time off. You're asking too much of yourself, trying to carry on like this.'

Whether she was right or not Allyson had no idea. All she knew was that if she didn't come to the office, and was forced to spend every day in the home that was still so full of Bob, then she'd probably end up doing something crazy. As it was no minute of the day was bearable, but those she spent alone were beyond torment and pain, they were unrelenting hell.

'Do you think it's going to get feudal, if . . . she does come back?' she said, unable to utter Tessa's name.

'I think it'll be hard to avoid,' Shelley replied.

Allyson sighed. 'I thought you'd say that. So I want to talk to everyone, after the recording. I want to ask them not to take sides, and turn the place into some kind of war zone. I'm assuming that most of them will side with me, which might be gratifying for a while, but in the end it won't help. It'll probably just encourage me to do what I really want to do, which is kill her.' She put a hand to her head as a horrible lurching pain twisted her heart. 'God, every time I think of them together . . .' She swallowed hard. 'Oh Shelley, sometimes I mean it, you know, I really do want to kill her.'

Shelley smiled. 'Of course you do,' she said. 'You wouldn't be human if you didn't. But I swear to you that relationship of theirs is destined for disaster. Oh, he might think it's going to work out while it's all new and exciting, and still in the heady heights of passion, but we both know Bob, and I'm telling you, once the novelty starts wearing off he'll soon find out that he can't survive without you.'

Allyson sighed and shook her head. 'Right now, it feels the other way round,' she said dismally. 'But I have to believe what you're telling me, because if I don't . . . Well, there wouldn't seem much point in going on, would there?'

'Then believe it,' Shelley said. 'And don't underestimate your strength, because you've got plenty more than you might imagine. However, I don't think you can keep Tessa as your assistant. That would be pushing yourself too far.'

Allyson looked away and stared blindly down at the floor. Shelley was right, of course, she couldn't have Tessa involved in her everyday life any more, or certainly not in the way she once had been. The strange thing was she was going to miss her, but a bolt of hatred soon wrenched that misguided notion from her head, reminding her of how she loathed and detested the girl whose despicable treachery had turned her into a vile snake in the lush green grass of her mentor's marriage. However, Tessa's future with *Soirée* was something Allyson had given a lot of thought to, and despite the overwhelming desire to kit the girl out with horns and a pitchfork and despatch her off down the Styx, or at the very least to shove her back to where she came from, she'd reached a decision that she needed to discuss with Shelley in order to evaluate its merit.

Shelley listened quietly, thoughtfully, showing some surprise, even doubt, and once looked like she might argue. But by the time Allyson had finished Shelley was ready to accept her suggestion, not necessarily because she considered it the best solution, but it was one that would work. And if Allyson was sure she could handle it, then Shelley would talk to Stella when she returned in a couple of weeks, and get her to put it in motion.

Bob was lying on top of the bed in the cramped bedroom of Tessa's South London flat, feeling ludicrously oversized and clumsily masculine in amongst the flowery Laura Ashley decor, dozens of fluffy toys, and silly girlish fripperies Tessa had scattered about the place. But, small though it was, they'd spent a lot more time in this room these past couple of weeks than they had anywhere else in the flat, as they'd indulged themselves in a never-ending orgy of sex that made even his wildest dreams look tame. For days they'd gone without wearing any clothes at all, only putting on dressing-gowns when the food they'd sent out for was delivered, invariably by undercover journos, who'd seized the opportunity along with the pizza to climb the two flights of stairs in the hope of snatching a few shots of the famous couple, or at least getting one of them to comment.

At first it had been funny, romantic even, fighting the siege together, confined to the badly wallpapered rooms of their 'love nest' with nothing but sex, Trivial Pursuit and TV to occupy the time. But two weeks on it wasn't quite so romantic, in fact it was fast deteriorating into a nightmare of frustration and guilt. Frustration because the press just wouldn't let them move, and guilt, obviously because of Allyson, and the cowardice that was stopping him picking up the phone to make sure she was all right.

Of course Tessa was always on hand with comfort and strength, dark eyes flashing with defiance as she refused to accept that either of them had done anything wrong, since neither of them had had any choice in the matter of falling in love. It had just happened, and berating themselves for it now, and feeling guilty about Allyson, wasn't going to change it. Brave words, considering he knew how terrible she really felt, for he was the one who wiped away her tears every time she cried for all the pain they were causing to someone they cared about so deeply.

It was odd, perverse even, the way their concern for Allyson was creating such a bond between them, but that wasn't something he liked to dwell on, for he preferred to think only of Tessa and her tender and generous heart, that was so easily moved by the plight of others that almost any tragedy she read about in the papers reduced her to tears. She just couldn't bear the idea of anyone suffering, and he couldn't help but be shamed by the way she seemed to mind even more about Allyson than he did. Except that wasn't true, of course, because it was tearing him apart. But she kept insisting it was like betraying her own mother, a comparison that he knew would thrill Allyson about as much as it thrilled him when she teasingly called him Daddy. The disparity in their ages wasn't something he enjoyed being reminded of, nor did her childish little voices during sex do much for him either. In fact, quite the reverse, but he didn't even want to get in touch with the horrendous nature of what it could actually make him feel like were he to go along with it. She'd never put those voices on before, but she'd soon stopped when he'd told her he didn't like it, because her only wish was to please him, not to offend him or make him angry. And there was no doubt she pleased him, for he was still hardly able to get enough of her, despite the terrible strain of the guilt – and the imprisonment. But it couldn't be much longer before those bloodhounds outside found some other juicy bones to unearth and savage and maybe then he and Tessa could start going out again, maybe even return to work. After all they couldn't exist on sex and pizza for ever, and her meagre savings weren't going to last long with a baby on the way, especially if he didn't get up the courage to go and raid his and Allyson's joint accounts some time soon.

'Guess what?' Tessa said, coming into the bedroom with the mail. 'I've got a letter here from Stella Cornbright, the big boss. She's asking me to go and see her.' She looked at Bob with wide, apprehensive eyes. 'Do you think they're going to sack me?' she said.

He shook his head. 'If they were they'd tell you in the letter,' he said.

She sat down next to him and read over the neatly typed few lines again. 'Maybe I should just resign,' she said.

Sighing, he reached up to tousle her hair. 'We've been over all that,' he said, 'and I thought you didn't want to.'

'I don't, but . . .' She turned to look at him, then smiled as he started untying her robe.

They'd spent enough time discussing her return to *Soirée*, and though he thought it was a bit odd that she wanted to go back, it was her life, and if Allyson was prepared to accept her back then it was hardly his place to argue.

'There don't seem to be any reporters out there this morning,' she told him, while watching their reflections in the dressing-table mirror as his fingers rotated around her nipples.

'Thank God for that,' he responded.

She grinned. 'Something tells me you're in a better mood than you were last night,' she teased.

'I am,' he said, moving his other hand down to his penis and idly stroking it.

She stood up and shrugged off her robe. 'I thought I might go back to work today,' she said. 'If it's all right with you.'

He laughed. 'You're the one who has to face it,' he reminded her. 'When does Stella Cornbright want to see you?'

'Next week. I thought I might try to get a lie of the land first.'

He shrugged. 'Up to you.' Then, rubbing a hand over her tummy, he said, 'I don't think we should go public about the baby yet though.'

'Oh God no,' she gasped. 'That's something you'll have to tell Allyson about before we even think about telling anyone else.'

He shifted restlessly as though to escape the unease that swept through him. That particular nightmare could wait, though just the thought of it had had a deflating effect on his ardour.

'Oh dear,' Tessa said playfully, looking at it. 'I imagine you'd like me to do something about that before I go.'

Smiling, he reached out and pulled her down on top of him. 'You're something else, do you know that?' he said, his lips almost touching hers, his arms holding her tightly.

She wriggled a bit, pressing her knees into the bed, and wrapping her feet around the back of his legs until he was halfway inside her.

'Mmmm,' he murmured, rocking his hips slowly up and down. Then holding her face between his hands he began kissing her deeply, using his tongue and his lips, and moving gently in and out of her until she sat back to take him fully inside her.

He raised his knees to support her back and held her hands wide as he gazed up into her face. If only he could feel like this all the time, so right about being here, and so definite that she was everything he wanted. But it was clear that his conscience wasn't going to make this an easy trip, though when it really acted up the whisky helped. Thank God Tessa didn't nag him about that, but she wouldn't, because she never nagged him about anything. She didn't even complain when he started thrashing about in a temper, the way he had last night, when he'd felt so trapped and cooped up, and furious with Allyson for being the source of his misery, that he'd drunk far too much Scotch and had ended up virtually passing out. He wasn't going to admit, even to himself, that it was the fact that Allyson seemed to be coping so well that was becoming so hard to deal with. Not that he wanted her to suffer. Far from it. In fact when he'd first realized she hadn't even taken a break from presenting the programme he'd felt only relief that she was managing to get on with her life, especially as it had acted like a very welcome pressure valve for the bottled-up might of his guilt. But, for some reason, when he'd seen her on the screen last night it had irritated the hell out of him, and made him feel resentful for the way her life didn't seem to be on hold the way his was, nor was she barricaded inside her flat like some rat in a trap.

But this morning, hangover aside, he was feeling just dandy as he lay here with Tessa, his gorgeous, insatiable little nymphet, who was carrying his baby, and for whom he must find a bigger, better home. She deserved everything he could give her for the way she made him feel so much better about himself, his decisions, and the whole wonderful life they had ahead of them.

'Oh my God!' Allyson murmured, coming to a halt. 'Tell me that's not Tessa Dukes standing in my office.'

Shelley was beside her. They were at the far end of the production office, just returning from lunch. The rest of the team was busy on the phones or with computers, though everyone had to be acutely aware that this would be the first time Allyson and Tessa had seen each other since the night Bob had left.

'I didn't think she'd come back until after she'd seen Stella,' Shelley remarked. 'I've got to hand it to her, she's got some nerve.'

Allyson was shaking all over. She'd never felt so out of control, so at the whim of emotions that were conflicting like sworn enemies inside her. But she had to go through with this, she had to see the girl, she just wished to God she wasn't having to do it in front of an audience.

'I'll deal with it if you like,' Shelley said.

'No! No, it's OK,' Allyson said, and before she could give herself any chance of backing down she started across the room towards her office, moving swiftly in an effort to strengthen the weakness in her legs. Just thank God she was carrying a huge pile of mail in her arms so no-one could see how badly her hands were shaking.

Tessa was already watching her, that meek, frightened look she knew so well darkening her eyes, those naturally ruddy cheeks spreading their colour down over her neck and chest. At least she'd had the decency to wear something less revealing than normal, but even so Allyson couldn't stop herself imagining the body that was beneath those jeans and baggy V-neck sweater, the body that Bob was daily, maybe hourly, pounding with passion.

'Hello Allyson,' she said softly, as Allyson stalked into the room.

Allyson stared at her coldly. Then, continuing to walk round her desk, she put down a pile of mail and said, 'I didn't invite you in here, so please leave.'

Tessa's eyes dropped, then taking a breath she said, 'Allyson, please, I think we should talk . . .'

'I said, leave,' Allyson repeated.

'I want you to know that if . . .'

Allyson's eyes closed, then suddenly she seethed, '*Get the fucking hell out of my office.*'

Everyone outside stopped what they were doing. Then Shelley was there, grabbing Tessa by the arm and pushing her towards the door.

'Clear out your desk,' she said. 'We'll find you another by the end of the day.'

Closing the door she turned to Allyson, who was chalk white and shaking so badly she had to sit down.

'I'm sorry,' she said. 'I swore to myself that when this happened I wouldn't make a scene, but . . .'

'It's OK,' Shelley interrupted. 'What did she say?'

'Nothing. Except she thought we should talk.' She dragged her hands across her face and pushed them back into her hair. 'I don't know if I can handle this . . .'

'You are handling it,' Shelley told her. 'You're handling it better than anyone I know.'

Allyson shook her head. 'It's all show, and you know it.' Suddenly her face crumpled and only with supreme

111

effort did she manage to stop herself crying. Had she been at home she wouldn't even have tried. 'Oh God, it's all so horrible,' she choked. 'I hate him, I absolutely despise him, but I still can't stop going over and over in my head all the things I wish I'd done, or hadn't done. What I should have said . . .'

'It's still early days,' Shelley reminded her. 'These things take time.'

Allyson blew her nose. 'Platitudes? Not like you, Shell.'

Shelley smiled too. 'Here's another,' she said. 'It's OK to cry.'

'No,' Allyson responded. 'I do enough of that every night. I don't want to start flooding my days too.' She took a deep breath, which shook as it came out. 'I wish to God I could stop imagining them together. I keep telling myself it's enough to know, I don't have to reproduce it in my own private Technicolor. Anyway,' she said, abruptly straightening her shoulders. 'I've got to get through this, and today's bound to be the worst, so I'll just keep projecting my thoughts to somewhere in the future when he gets tired of little orphan Annie out there and wants to come home. My latest fantasy has me telling him to fuck off and him going demented in some bar that I have to go and rescue him from.'

'Sounds more like reality to me,' Shelley said dryly. 'Anyway, as it's not a programme day you can just go home if you find the sight of her starts really getting to you.'

Allyson forced a smile, then after Shelley had left she sat staring at the phone, her heart thudding away like a drum as she tried to pluck up the courage to call him. Tessa was here, so he could be at the flat alone . . .

Ten minutes later she was still sitting there, rehearsing a thousand different versions of what he might say if she said, and what she would say if he said . . . In the end she got angry and grabbed the receiver. This was her

112

husband, for God's sake, she'd never been afraid to talk to him before, so she damned well wasn't going to be now.

Only after she finished dialling did she realize how badly she was shaking again, and when his voice suddenly came down the line her heart gave such a horrible lurch she thought she was going to pass out.

'Bob?' she said, fighting to stop herself imagining his face, or where he was standing, or how he might be feeling about the fact that his telephone number was no longer the same as hers. 'It's me.'

Silence.

Obviously he was shocked. He needed a moment. OK, she'd give it to him.

'What do you want?' he said finally.

Suddenly she was reeling, knocked so off course by his abruptness that she didn't even stop to consider that it might have been caused by nerves or caution or guilt, she only knew anger that very nearly exploded in a stream of vile and incoherent abuse. But mercifully she had the wit to take a deep breath and remember that everyone outside would hear, so all she said was, 'I want you to get the rest of your belongings out of my home by the end of the day!' And she slammed down the phone.

Immediately she regretted it, for the last thing she wanted was him going into the flat while she wasn't there, and she didn't want to be there with him either, not while he was breaking apart their lives. Oh God, what a mess she'd got herself into now, but she could hardly call him back and tell him she'd changed her mind. But why not? She had every right to, in fact she could do anything she liked, even if it did mean making a fool of herself.

This time the answerphone picked up her call, but she knew he'd still be there, so she said, 'On second thoughts, Bob, I'll send it all round in a taxi, so don't bother putting yourself to the trouble of coming back. Ever!' And once again she slammed down the phone.

A few minutes later she was down in her dressing room, stretched out on the sofa, utterly drained. But it was OK. She was getting through it, and at least the hurdle of seeing Tessa for the first time was now behind her. It could be she was going to regret the decision she'd reached about the girl's future on the programme, but for the time being she didn't have the energy even to think about changing it, so she'd just have to let events take their course and pray that it didn't get any worse than this.

Stella Cornbright was snacking on a packet of crisps as she read through the file in front of her. Her fingers and whiskery upper lip were stained with grease, so were the corners of the pages. Dotted around the fleshy folds of her neck were a dozen corn plasters, covering the spaces from which some sizeable warts had recently been evicted. Funny, the things a person did when they knew they were detaching from the mortal coil. She'd lived most of her life with those warts, but she'd be damned if she was going to take them with her when she went.

In the office outside Tessa waited, hands clasped tightly in front of her, eyes as big as the buttons on her short crushed-velvet dress. It didn't seem right to sit down without being invited, but there was no-one around, and Stella Cornbright's door was closed. She wondered if she should just knock, but decided to give it a few more minutes in the hope Melissa, Stella's secretary, might put in an appearance.

Almost a week had gone by since she'd returned to work, and though she still waited and hoped every day that Allyson would speak to her, Allyson didn't, nor on the whole did Shelley. Marvin, Shelley's assistant, seemed to be taking care of Allyson, which, apart from her unofficial training, left Tessa with very little to do. At first she'd been hesitant about asking any of the reporters or researchers if she could go out with them, presuming that they too were going to freeze her out, but after some initial awkwardness, she'd found that most of the team were willing to go on helping her in much the same way as they had before.

'Oh Tessa, sorry,' Melissa cried, bounding breathlessly in from the rain. 'I had to go and pick up Stella's car from the garage. Does she know you're here?'

'No,' Tessa answered, giving Melissa the once-over as she turned away to hang up her coat. 'Cool sweater,' she said. 'Did you get it round here?'

'No, in Knightsbridge,' Melissa answered. 'Cost a fortune. Hang on, I'll tell Stella you're here.'

She was back in a matter of seconds. 'You can go in now,' she said.

Melissa watched the door close behind Tessa and fervently wished that she could be a fly on the wall. She'd only met Tessa a couple of times, as she rarely had reason to visit the *Soirée* studio, but there'd been so much about her in the papers these past few weeks that Melissa, like many others, almost felt she knew her. She couldn't help wondering what the press would make of Stella Cornbright summoning her to Leicester Square. Probably they'd come to the same conclusion as Melissa, that Tessa was about to find herself out of a job.

Stella Cornbright was staring frankly into Tessa's face, framed in its unruly thatch of shiny black hair. She'd seen her plenty of times before, had probably considered her pretty if she'd stopped to think about it, but it wasn't her good looks she was pondering now, it was what she'd done to Allyson and Bob Jaymes's marriage. Stella could only lament the idiocy in a man that made him behave like a prize buffoon. And publicly too! In her opinion Allyson was probably better shot of him. Still, that was Allyson's business, and this, for the moment, was hers.

Tricky. At least it would have been had Shelley Bronson not come up with a solution. And as there wasn't much doubt that Shelley would have discussed the proposal with Allyson before submitting it, it seemed only sensible to go the route Shelley had laid out. Stella wasn't sure she approved, but she was prepared to give it a go if Allyson and Shelley were.

'Were you followed here?' she said. Her voice was loud and sharp, making the question sound more like a reprimand.

'You mean by the press?' Tessa asked. 'I don't know. I don't always spot them.'

'Mm,' Stella grunted. Then, launching straight into why Tessa was there, she said, 'So, what are we going to do about this unholy mess you've created?'

As it seemed like a rhetorical question Tessa didn't answer.

'Well, it's out of the question for you to continue where you are,' Stella said. 'And I'll be frank with you, if Allyson had personally requested it, I'd be firing you right now. So what have you got to say to that?'

Tessa was momentarily thrown, then, clearing her throat, she said, 'I understand your feelings, and I feel terrible about what's happened, but . . .'

'I don't want to hear your excuses,' Stella barked. 'If you had any real sensitivity you'd be leaving of your own accord. But I can't force you, nor will I try. What I'm going to do is act on the reports I've had on your work performance, all of which are good. That means, young lady, that instead of being thrown out on your ear, you're being promoted.'

Tessa's eyes flew open. 'Promoted?' she echoed.

'To the position of researcher and occasional reporter. Your qualifications show you're academically suited, and your potential, I'm told, is considerable.' Her bulging eyes were fixed on Tessa, demanding a response.

'Thank you,' was all Tessa managed.

Stella closed the personnel file. 'OK, you can go,' she said shortly, and after her beady eyes had escorted Tessa to the door she picked up the phone to call Shelley.

'So she got her promotion,' Allyson said, as Shelley finished her call with Stella. 'Tell me, am I insane? Or just a masochist?'

'You were right,' Shelley replied. 'If we'd got rid of her, like you said, it wasn't only a lawsuit we'd have had to contend with, it would have been the press too. And this way you really do look like you're on top of things.'

Allyson sighed. 'Why do we all have such a fascination with other people's misery?' she grumbled. 'I've got to tell you it's really wearing me down.' She rubbed her eyes, then looked blankly at the frozen image of her own face that was on the screen in front of them. They were in one of the viewing rooms looking at a pre-recorded Night Cap to see if it would work for tomorrow night's programme, but Allyson was barely paying attention. 'He called me this morning,' she said.

'Oh?' Shelley said, intrigued. 'To say what?'

'I don't know, I hung up. I expect he wants some more of his things, but I just can't bear for him to come to the flat, and I can't bring myself to pack them up either.' Her eyes closed, as a wave of despair swept through her. It was so hard to accept that he had another address now, slept in another bed and made love to . . . To a child! Her teeth were suddenly clenched tightly together, as hatred and vengeance began to seethe inside her. She must have been insane to have suggested this promotion. How could she possibly have thought that keeping Tessa on the programme was a way of staying connected to Bob? She hadn't been in her right mind. Why hadn't Shelley seen that?

Shelley was looking at her watch. 'I'm sorry,' she said,

'but I've got to go. I'm having lunch with Mark Reiner, remember?'

Allyson pressed her hands to her face. 'Oh God, everything's changing,' she wailed. 'When's the take-over happening, do you know?'

'There's no date set yet. But he's asked to meet me.'

'Just you, or the other programme heads too?'

'Just me, today. We're each getting an individual grilling, it seems.'

Allyson looked her over. 'Well, you'll be sure to knock him off his feet in that,' she predicted.

Shelley smoothed her hands over her cashmere-covered breasts and leather-clad hips. 'I wasn't sure trousers were really appropriate,' she said, 'but what the hell?'

Allyson smiled, but it was clear her thoughts were elsewhere.

Shelley dropped a kiss on her forehead and quietly left the room.

Going back to her desk Shelley took out a mirror to touch up her make-up. She rarely wore much, with such smooth, olive skin and thick dark lashes, she didn't need it. Just a subtle shade of lipstick and the finest black line to emphasize the exotic shape of her eyes.

Satisfied with the way she looked, she was on the point of putting the mirror back in its pouch when she noticed the message stuck to her screen. 'Mark Reiner has to postpone lunch, will call again next week to reschedule.'

Screwing up the note she tossed it into the bin. Though annoyed, a part of her wanted to laugh. Maybe it was to cover her disappointment, or maybe it was simply relief. Spending so much time with Allyson lately had reminded her just how devastating the break-up of a relationship could be, and she'd charted those waters enough times to know she had no desire ever to go there again. Not that there was any reason to suspect that Mark Reiner would take her there, but she was anxious enough about the meeting to make the wait almost welcome.

'Promoted?' Bob echoed.

Tessa nodded. 'I've been dying to tell you. Where were you?'

'On air,' Bob reminded her. 'I don't understand. Why the hell would they promote you with all that's going on?'

'You were probably right, they were afraid I'd sue if they fired me.'

He grunted and went to pour himself a drink.

The kitchen was so small and narrow that they had to squeeze past each other to get from one end to the other. Normally Bob loved to do that, it excited him, pressing up against her and feeling his erection make the space tighter. This evening he was too preoccupied with this astonishing news, and the godawful day he'd just had with Mack, one of the sports editors at LWT. Sure he'd let them down these past few weeks, but what the hell was he supposed to do with the press camped out on his doorstep, and every female hack in the land baying for his blood? Jesus, anyone with any sense would have stayed out of the way with all that going on. And since when was having a couple of jars at lunch time such a major crime? As he recalled, Mack had been in the pub too, and Bob was prepared to bet his next contract that it wasn't shandy the barman was pulling into Mack's glass.

They made him sick, the whole damned lot of them. Subs messing about with his scripts, producers giving his matches to other, less experienced, reporters, his agent calling up to tell him that the new deal they had in the offing with Sky had hit a few problems. God knew what they were, let his bloody agent sort it out, it was what he paid him for, wasn't it?

'She's up to something!' he snapped, suddenly remembering Allyson as he emptied what was left of a bottle of gin into a cheap glass. He'd presumed, at the very least, that Allyson would have Tessa removed from the programme, and sidelined somewhere else in the company. Having her promoted had never even crossed his mind, and because he couldn't figure out what might be behind it it was pissing him off no end. 'Haven't we got any more?' he growled, looking at the empty bottle.

Tessa smiled benignly. 'It's in the cupboard behind you,' she said. Then, lifting her face, 'Don't I get a kiss, Mr Grouch?'

Reaching out, he dragged her roughly towards him and pressed his mouth hard against hers. She snaked her arms round his neck and pushed her groin against his. Since all she was wearing was one of his shirts, he had only to lift her onto the counter, unzip his trousers and enter her.

It was over quickly, and what followed, the tenderness and the giggling, the teasing and the cajoling, went a long way towards working him out of his bad mood. Though she hadn't long gone off to take a shower before he started feeling sour again, so he opened a fresh bottle of gin and drank a bitter, bolshy toast to Allyson, whose smoothness in promoting Tessa was really getting to him now. He'd tried calling her a couple of times in the last few days, but she was refusing to talk to him, and though he needed to go back and pick up more clothes, he didn't quite have the nerve just to show up. Probably because he couldn't face going through another scene like the one they'd had the night he left, so maybe the answer was just to get himself a whole load of new gear and let the past stay where it was.

'Where are you going?' he said, when Tessa walked into the room half an hour later. He was sitting in front of the TV now, an empty plate on the floor beside him, his fourth drink of the evening hanging loosely in his hand.

'Out,' she answered. She was dressed in black shorts and black tights, a white cable-knit sweater and a long grey raincoat.

'What do you mean, out?' he said, not sober enough to get his mind fully wrapped round this surprise. 'Where are you going?'

'To meet Julian, down the pub.'

His face darkened. 'Julian?' he growled. 'Who the hell's Julian?'

'My brother.'

'You don't have a brother. You told me you didn't have any family.'

'I don't. So Julian said I could adopt him.'

'So what the bloody hell am I supposed to do, while you're out playing brothers and sisters? And how come you've never mentioned him before?'

She shrugged. 'There was nothing to say.'

He stared at her, momentarily at a loss. 'I don't want you to go,' he said in the end, certain that would do it.

She laughed and carried on stuffing things in her handbag.

He was so startled that she wasn't doing what he wanted that he couldn't think of anything to say.

Tessa was still smiling as she dragged a brush through her short, spiky hair, then she confounded him even further when she said, 'Do you wish I was Allyson?'

'What?' he said.

'I was just wondering if you wished I was her, so that this baby I'm carrying would be hers. Is that why you've stopped talking about it? Because you wish it was hers?'

This was just too much for him, so he drained his glass, and started to get up for a refill. He'd almost made it when he staggered back into the chair.

'You've had too much,' she told him lightly. Crossing to the window, she pulled back the curtain and peered down at the rain-soaked street below. 'God, I hope there's no press out there. I'm sick to death of them. They're like insects, crawling all over me.'

She turned round and found him standing behind her. Catching her in his arms he held her tightly. 'Don't go,' he pleaded. 'Stay here with me.'

She smiled softly into his eyes. 'Do you mean that?' she said. 'You want me to stay?'

'Yes.'

'But I have to go. I promised Julian.'

'Who the hell *is* this Julian?'

'He works on the programme.'

'How old is he?'

Her eyes twinkled. 'About my age, I guess. Not jealous are you?'

He meant to deny it but other words slurred from his lips. 'Insanely,' he said. 'I want you all to myself. You know that.'

Detaching herself gently from his embrace, she hooked her bag over her shoulder and walked to the door. 'I'll try not to wake you when I get in,' she said, and left.

After pouring himself another drink Bob slumped back down in front of the TV and stared at it blindly. His head was spinning and he felt nauseous, which was something Tessa never seemed to feel, given her condition. He hated even to think it, but lately he'd found himself wondering if she'd made it up about the baby. It was why he didn't want to talk about it, he didn't want to find out she had, because he didn't want to deal with the ugly manipulation of it. Not that it would change anything. He'd still be here, because it was where he wanted to be.

He took a large mouthful of gin. Why the hell did she have to go off and see this bloke Julian? What did she need a brother for when she had him? He'd given up his wife, was getting regularly dumped on by the press, and she gets promoted and goes off to celebrate with *Julian*.

It didn't seem fair. None of it was fair. Those bloody hacks out there hadn't been married to Allyson. They didn't have the first idea what she was really like. For all they knew she could be some psychotic ego freak with an abnormal attachment to her man-hating best friend.

His glass hit the floor and broke. He left it where it was, too drunk and worked up to care. Why the hell should he give a damn about Allyson? He had Tessa now. She was all he wanted, everything he needed. This was all working out just fine. He'd find himself a lawyer tomorrow and start talking divorce.

Allyson stared out at the darkness, oblivious to the rain zigzagging down the windscreen. Tessa was almost out of sight now, meaning he was up there alone. A few minutes ago she'd seen them at the window. She'd sat here, in the chill space of her car, watching her husband with his arms around the girl she'd taken so warmly and trustingly into their lives.

She tensed with the quick burn of pain in her heart.

It wasn't getting any better. It was only getting worse. Sometimes the ache of missing him was so great it felt as though it was swallowing her alive. Everywhere she looked she saw him, everything she felt was about him. She just couldn't make herself accept that he was no longer a part of her life, maybe because without him it didn't feel as though there was a life. There was only this terrible wrenching inside, and a void that only got wider.

She'd lost weight, a fact several columnists had pointed out to the nation, and she often looked tired, almost to the point of being haggard. But she was a professional, she still carried on with the show. She just wished the camera would stop frightening her so much. It never used to, but now, when she sat there at the cocktail bar and the lens was focused upon her, strange things started to happen inside her head. It was as though her face was contorting, stretching up to the camera, dragging her into a science-fiction journey that delivered her to millions of TV screens, where the world, like vultures, could feast on every part of her misery.

She wasn't really going insane. Shelley assured her of that. It was normal to go off the rails a little and be so afraid when your entire life was being smashed apart as though it was worthless. She often wondered how women with children coped. It had to be so much harder for them. Whoever they were she wanted to embrace them and try to comfort them, but children or no children, there was no comfort for this.

She knew now why the press hadn't descended on her when the *News of the World* first broke the story. Shelley had stopped it. She'd been tipped off it was going to happen, and she'd personally called all the editors to ask them to back off. She'd have to pay for that favour somewhere down the line, probably they both would, but they'd deal with it when the time came.

She looked up at the lamplit window. The curtains were still open, the TV seemed to be on. She could go in there now and beg him to come back. The idea of the kind of scene it would create made her sadder than ever. He wouldn't come, nor would she go up there. She'd just sit here a while longer, and try to muster the courage to go home. To walk into the flat that still smelt of him. To open drawers and find things that belonged to him. To look at the sofa and remember him. To lie in their bed and long for him.

She covered her face with her hands. She just didn't know what to do any more. Her ribs were tender from all the crying, and they hurt now as more huge, racking sobs took hold of her body. She didn't understand what was happening. How could someone who had loved her so much, who had shared so much of his life with her, just turn his back on her like this? OK, she understood about male menopause, or midlife crises, but those excuses just weren't enough to blot out the pain, nor were they any guarantee that he would ever come back.

So much despair engulfed her she thought she would drown in it. Her body was too small to contain it. Her fists pummelling the wheel did nothing to ease it. She reached blindly for her bag and fumbled for the phone.

'Shelley?' she gasped. 'Oh God, Shell.'

'It's OK,' Shelley responded. 'You'll be OK. Where are you?'

'Outside their flat.'

'I'll come and get you.'

'No, I'll come to you. It's just . . .' She struggled for breath. 'I can't go home.'

'I know.'

'Here, drink this,' Shelley said.

Allyson took the brandy. She was huddled into a blanket on the sofa facing the sluggishly flickering fire. There were only two lamps on in the room, the delicate bronze and alabaster Carder, and a reading light behind a big, comfy leather chair. Shadows from the fire danced around the walls.

'I don't know why I did it,' she said. Her voice was nasal, still clogged with tears. 'She went out, left him there alone. I could have gone in, but . . .' Her voice trailed off, she didn't really know what she wanted to say. 'Thank God there was no press around.'

Shelley sat down on the sofa too. Her hair was pinned up, she wore no make-up, was dressed simply in a long silk bathrobe and white satin slippers. Evidence of the work she'd been doing was scattered on the floor around the leather chair.

'So humanitarian Wednesdays is a no go,' Allyson said, changing the subject.

Shelley's eyes showed her regret. 'I tried,' she said, 'but Stella wouldn't buy it. She believes that ultimately people just don't care. She's not objecting to the occasional topical interview, you know, if something other than the normal tragedy occurs in Sudan, or a British aid worker gets killed in Bolivia. Just not a regular thing.'

Allyson nodded. 'Doesn't seem like much is going my way lately, does it?'

'That'll change.'

Allyson made a gesture of impatience. 'I don't understand why he wants to live in that dreadful part of town, in a flat that's smaller and grottier than the one we had when we first met.' She sighed and her breath shook. She stared bleakly down at her brandy. 'I suppose it's a measure of how much he loves her, that he'll put up with it.'

'It won't take him long to get fed up,' Shelley said. 'He's too fond of the high life.'

Allyson drank and sat quietly watching the fire. 'I keep asking myself, what it is about her?' she said after a while. 'I know she's young and pretty, but so are thousands of girls. So what is it about Tessa Dukes?'

'You could ask what is it about any of us,' Shelley said. 'No-one's got any idea what attracts us to the people we're attracted to.'

'He's never done anything like this before,' Allyson protested. 'We've always been so close. And it wasn't as if he wasn't getting sex at home. So why did he need to go elsewhere? And why to *her*? Look,' she continued, rummaging in her bag. 'I've been cutting articles out of the paper about her. We were the ones who interviewed her, but no-one, none of us, really knows anything about her. No, I know what you're going to say,' she cut in, as Shelley made to interrupt, 'it was my decision, and I accept that. I could see she'd had problems somewhere along the line and I wanted to give her the chance of a fresh start. Everyone deserves that, but God knows, if I'd thought for a minute she'd make that start with my husband . . .' She took a breath. 'I'm a fool, Shelley. I

126

should have checked up on her more. I mean, she's just come out of nowhere, ruining my marriage, tearing my life to pieces and turning my husband into a man I don't even know. And now I keep asking myself, who is she, for God's sake? How can she do this? I didn't expect any thanks, but I certainly didn't expect anything like this.'

Shelley's eyes went down. Should she tell Allyson that the way she was fixating on Tessa was, in its own perverse way, normal at times like this? To turn a rival into a monster was a way of trying to derive some comfort, or of creating excuses for a rejection that was just too painful and merciless to bear. But that wasn't what Allyson wanted to hear, what she wanted was to have her suspicions confirmed that there was something strange about Tessa, that Tessa and some deep-rooted psychological disturbance was totally responsible for what was happening to her and Bob's lives, and that she, Allyson, must fight to save her husband before he was destroyed by this horrible phenomenon. It was all so dramatic, yet, in its own tragic way, normal. And who could say, Allyson might be right, Tessa could be suffering from some kind of psychosis, but other than becoming the object of Bob's obsession, which had to be his problem rather than Tessa's, as far as Shelley could make out the girl was rather boringly normal. This perhaps did beg the question what did Bob see in her, for God, and Shelley, knew how many affairs the man had had during his marriage, but not even Shelley had brought him close to leaving Allyson, and though she might be a good deal older than Tessa, she was certainly much more Bob's type, considering his bent for social climbing . . .

This led her on to Allyson's belief in his fidelity, which was an aberration that probably should be addressed, for the only astonishing part of that wasn't that Allyson could be so naive, because most wives were, but that the press hadn't trumpeted his serial adultery all over the front pages by now. Though Shelley had to concede they probably didn't know about most of it, since Bob, give him his due, could be pretty discreet when he tried. But this was the British press they were talking about, terriers every one of them, so it was only a matter of time before all the dirty linen was hauled out of the cupboard. God knew, Shelley didn't want to be the one to break it to Allyson, but it was surely going to be better coming from her, here, in the privacy of the flat that was virtually Allyson's second home, than letting her read about it in the papers.

However, even after bracing herself with the reassurance that in the long run it was the kindest thing she could do, it was still with great trepidation that Shelley said softly into the cosy warmth that was embracing them, 'Ally, Tessa isn't the first.'

Allyson was about to drink, but her hand and her heart suddenly stopped. Her drink was in mid-air. But it was OK, it was like a shield, and as long as she didn't move the words couldn't come in, and then she wouldn't have to worry about how to get them out.

Shelley looked at her. 'I'm sorry,' she whispered. 'I wish to God I wasn't the one to tell you, but he's been sleeping with other women, well, for quite some time.'

Allyson remained frozen.

'I'm sorry,' Shelley whispered again.

Allyson leaned forward and put down her glass. Her hand was shaking, her whole life was crumbling again, but she had to let it happen, because there was no way she could stop it. 'How do you know?' she said.

'I just know,' Shelley answered.

Allyson shook her head, telling her that wasn't good enough.

Shelley steeled herself again. 'I was one of the women he tried . . . Well, let's just say, he tried with.'

Allyson took a sharp, quick breath. But it was all right, she didn't have to think about it, because it might not be true. Her nightmares were full of scenes like this, so there was a chance she'd wake up in a minute and none of it would be real.

Her eyes remained focused on the exquisite Night and Day clock by Lalique. After a while it felt strangely soothing, the way the two female figures, engraved so gracefully in the glass, were entwined. One dark, one light. Like her and Shelley. Brunette and blonde. Shelley had so many beautiful things, but of all of them this was the one Allyson loved the most. What she wouldn't give to own a clock like that.

'I always turned him down,' Shelley said.

Allyson's eyes left the clock. It wasn't a dream. 'I suppose it was why he always had such a hard time with you,' she said. 'His ego probably couldn't handle the rejection.' She turned her head and Shelley saw the tears starting to fall from her eyes. 'But men like Bob never can handle women like you. You intimidate them because they're weak and you're strong. Oh God, Shelley, please tell me this is going to end.'

Shelley opened her arms and held her as she cried, smoothing her hair and feeling her tears dampen her shoulder. 'It will,' she promised. 'I just wish I could tell you when.'

'How is it possible to love someone who treats you like this?'

'You'd be amazed how many women do. I've been there myself, but never again.'

'No, never again.' Allyson lifted her head. There was a sudden fierceness in her now. A determination to turn her words into truth. But how could she do that, without knowing how?

Shelley looked into her face and brushed back her hair. 'You're very special,' she whispered.

Allyson gazed into her eyes. She was remembering how Bob had often accused Shelley of preferring women. It made sense now, if Shelley had rejected him.

129

It was what most men fell back on when a woman was able to resist them. She'd never suspected Shelley of it herself. Why would she, when there had never been any signs of it, and when she'd been Shelley's confidante, and shoulder, through so many of the break-ups Shelley had suffered. She'd always put Shelley's failure with men down to them not being man enough to handle a woman like her, but maybe there was more to it than that. Maybe there was something Shelley was denying in herself, and sitting here now, so close that she could feel Shelley's breath on her face ... Her heart turned over. How deeply she loved her, her closest, truest friend. The one person in the world she knew would never let her down.

Shelley smiled and Allyson watched her lips curve. Their mouths were so close, it would be so easy to kiss her. She wanted to kiss her. She wanted Shelley to hold her and keep her safe. She wanted to expand the love they knew so it could embrace them completely.

Very slowly, very tentatively, she closed the space between them.

Shelley's lips were warm and soft. They moved beneath hers, parting and responding.

Allyson's eyes were open, looking at the luxuriant curl of Shelley's lashes.

Somewhere in the distance a siren wailed and the kiss continued. Allyson closed her eyes and increased the pressure of her mouth. Then her hands were on Shelley's shoulders, smoothing the silk, then parting it. Her breasts were large and firm, her nipples were tightly erect. Allyson smoothed her hands over them, loving their feel.

Then the kiss was over.

It was a moment before Allyson realized Shelley had ended it.

They sat there looking into each other's eyes. The glow of the firelight turned Shelley's skin to honey.

'I'm going to put you to bed now,' Shelley said.

Allyson swallowed and felt the strangeness in her head increase.

'No, not my bed,' Shelley said. 'This isn't what you want. It's not what either of us want.'

'But you didn't turn me away.'

'I am now. You needed the warmth and the intimacy, but it wouldn't be right for either of us to go any further.'

'I love you,' Allyson whispered.

Shelley smiled. 'I know. But it's a different kind of love and you're feeling so vulnerable right now you're confusing it.'

Allyson turned away and Shelley covered her breasts. It was the first time she'd ever kissed a woman, but as beautiful and sensuous as she'd found it, she had no desire to do it again. She suspected, in the cold light of day, that Allyson wouldn't want to either.

TESSA

Chapter 6

'Hello Tessa. How are you?'

'I'm OK. Got stuck in traffic, that's why I'm late.' The rosiness of her cheeks told how cold it was outside, but her adorably refreshing smile, when it came, was like sunshine.

'Sit down.' Laura Risby's wiry brown hair was tucked behind her ears, better exposing the calm warmth of a face that was in the twilight of a serene and understated beauty. She got up from her desk as Tessa removed her scarf and coat, going to the coffee pot on a bookshelf nearby. After filling two mugs, she handed one to Tessa and returned to her desk, where a small lamp cast its glow over the open file on her blotter.

Tessa sat in a leather wing-backed chair, her bag tucked in next to her, her face gently illumined by the muted light beside her. The crammed shelves of technical and medical books were lost in the room's shadows, as were the several gilt-framed paintings, and all that was visible through the window behind Laura were the cluttered rooftops of Soho set against the backdrop of a colourless sky.

'I'm glad you came,' Laura said. 'I've been reading about you in the papers.'

Tessa grimaced, and looked at her from under her lashes. 'I guessed you might,' she said sheepishly, 'but I didn't really feel like talking about it.'

135

'Do you now?' Laura asked.

'I'm not sure. It's all been pretty, well, you know.'

No, Laura didn't know, but she could guess, and though, as a psychotherapist, it wasn't her place to approve or disapprove of this affair with Bob Jaymes, she was fond enough of the girl to be more than a little concerned at the way events appeared to be unfolding. 'You're still at the same job,' she said, swivelling in her chair to rest her feet on an open drawer.

'Yes and no,' Tessa answered. 'I'm with the same programme, but I'm a researcher/reporter now. I haven't actually been on the screen yet, though.'

'What about Allyson? Do you come into much contact with her?'

'A bit. But mainly I'm out, you know, on location. I know you've seen the show, so what I'm doing, exactly, is getting together material for the filmed insert that comes after the commercial break. You know, the section where someone reports on weird or unusual things that are happening around the country. It's really cool. I did one of the inserts myself the other day, just for practice. It didn't go out on the air or anything. They're letting me have the tape to give to my new agent.'

Laura's surprise showed. 'Agent?' she echoed.

'Yes. I've got an agent now. Julian, he's this kind of friend, he introduced me.'

'So what's the agent going to do?'

Tessa appeared nonplussed, then, shrugging, she said, 'Well, everyone in front of the camera has an agent. Allyson's got one.'

'I see.' Laura drank some coffee. 'You were always very fond of Allyson,' she said. 'Has that changed?'

'Oh no!' Tessa seemed genuinely distressed by the idea that Laura would even think it. 'She's the kindest, most wonderful person I've ever met, and I can't tell you how terrible I feel about everything that's happened. And sometimes she looks so cut up about it all that I just want to put my arms around her and cry with her. She'd probably go ballistic if I did, but I wouldn't do it, I'm just saying, that's how she makes me feel.'

Laura waited to see if she wanted to expand on that, but she seemed not to so Laura said, 'What about Bob? How do you feel about him?'

'Oh, he's wonderful.' Her eyes were shining as her fingers tightened on the arms of the chair. 'I really love him. I can't believe he left his wife for me. No-one's ever made me feel that special before.'

Given her case history, Laura didn't doubt that. 'Does he love you?' she asked.

Tessa blushed. 'He says he does.' She paused, then nodded happily. 'Yes, I think so,' she said. 'I mean, sometimes he gets in a bad mood, not with me, but with the whole situation, you know. He feels really terrible about Allyson, and he gets angry with himself for not being able to handle it better.'

'How do you think he should handle it?' Laura asked.

Tessa's head went to one side as she thought. 'Well, I think it's better that he's not lying any more,' she began, swerving away from the actual question. 'That was horrible. I really hated it when he was lying to Allyson. I know she probably didn't want to hear the truth, and I didn't want to cause her all that pain, but, you know, when things like this happen, the truth has to come out sometime, doesn't it?'

Laura's professional antennae were suddenly alert. She hadn't expected to get to this point so soon. But it was OK, it was good that they were there, the question was, could she keep them there? 'Like it did before?' she said carefully.

To her dismay Tessa looked sharply away, rejecting the bait, and Laura knew it was going to be hard getting her back. But she was going to try. 'Do you feel at all responsible for what's happened?' she asked.

Tessa reached into her bag, pulled out a bunch of

grapes and began to eat. Laura was familiar with this method of defence, an attempt to appear nonchalant and detached, when in truth she was anything but. 'Want one?' Tessa said, offering the bag to Laura.

Laura shook her head.

A few minutes ticked by, then Laura repeated the question.

'You mean do I feel responsible for Bob leaving Allyson?' Tessa said, chewing. 'Yes, of course I do. It wouldn't have happened if it weren't for me, it might still not have happened if I hadn't told him I was pregnant.'

Laura nodded slowly. That wasn't as big a surprise as it should have been. 'Are you?' she asked.

Tessa inhaled deeply, then helped herself to another grape. 'I wasn't when he left,' she admitted. 'Well, I might have been, but I didn't know it then.'

'But you are now?'

Tessa nodded.

Laura sat quietly for a moment. This manipulation of older people was typical of someone with Tessa's background, so Laura wasn't particularly surprised this was happening, though she could wish that it wasn't proving so costly, tragic even, for those who were involved. But there weren't many circumstances more tragic than those Tessa had come from. 'How is it working out between you and Bob, so far?' she asked.

Tessa took another grape, then her pretty face started to shine with typical teenage rapture. 'He can be such a grouch sometimes,' she said fondly, 'but I can always cheer him up because he really loves it when I do things for him and make him feel pampered and sexy, like he's the best lover in the world. His anger goes away then, and everything's all right.'

'Does he get angry often?'

Tessa nodded. 'More lately,' she answered. 'But he's

having a bit of a bad time getting work, and his money's starting to run out and obviously he's all over the place about Allyson, so I suppose it's more frustration than anger.'

'Does he ever get physical with you, when he's angry?' Laura asked.

Tessa's eyes widened. 'You mean does he hit me? No never.'

The phone started ringing. Laura waited for her receptionist to answer.

Tessa was still eating her grapes.

'Did you manage to get in touch with your mother?' Laura asked abruptly, changing the subject.

Tessa screwed up the top of the paper bag, then suddenly it was open again. 'No,' she answered, pulling out a large handful of fruit. 'I thought it was a dumb idea in the end. I mean, she's dead, and going to a medium was just one of my mad ideas. I only went once.'

'She didn't come through?'

'No.' Then the grapes went back into the bag and she laughed nervously. 'I'm glad really,' she said, 'it would probably have scared the life out of me if she had. Have you ever done anything like that?'

Laura shook her head. 'You mentioned a friend just now, Julian,' she said.

'Oh, yeah, Jules. He's great. He's my brother. Not officially, obviously. I've adopted him.'

Knowing what she did about Tessa, this new piece of information immediately set off all kinds of alarm bells for Laura. 'How old is he?' she asked.

'Same age as me. I think he wants us to be, you know, closer than brother and sister.'

Laura wasn't liking the sound of this at all. 'Is that what you want?' she asked.

Tessa wrinkled her nose as she thought. Laura watched her, knowing that behind her refreshingly frank expression and simplistic manner there was a maelstrom of complexities that had no moral compass to guide them. It wasn't that she didn't know right from wrong, on the contrary she knew it very well, it was simply that she sometimes had difficulty in attaching much importance to either. Though Laura was well aware of the reasons behind this disconnect from her conscience, in the almost two years since she'd been treating Tessa she'd made small progress in its repair. It didn't help that Tessa was such an irregular visitor, but these things couldn't be forced, unless of course Tessa became a danger to herself or society. As yet she wasn't that, and Laura had never believed she would be. However, she had to concede that recent events might call for a re-evaluation of her judgement.

Finally Tessa answered the question. 'No, it's not what I want,' she said. 'I've got Bob. Although Jules is pretty cool. We've kissed a couple of times.' She giggled. 'Bob would go ballistic if he found out. He's *sooo* jealous.'

Laura regarded her innocent-looking face and felt only unease. 'Tell me,' she said, 'does Bob remind you of anyone, someone you know, maybe from your past?'

Tessa screwed up her nose again, then shook her head. 'No,' she said.

'What about Allyson?' Laura asked. 'Does she remind you of anyone?'

Again Tessa shook her head.

'Have you ever told Allyson about your mother?'

'Oh no. I never tell anyone. That's all in the past.'

Laura said, 'Do you think it came as a complete surprise to Allyson when she learned of your affair with her husband?'

'I don't think so,' Tessa answered after a moment's reflection. 'I think she knew all along, but she was turning a blind eye.'

Laura almost groaned. This was so much worse than

she'd expected. 'So you told Bob you were pregnant, which then forced him to make Allyson face the truth?' she said, spelling it out.

Tessa frowned. 'I suppose so,' she answered.

'Are you recognizing any similarities here?' Laura challenged.

Tessa immediately stiffened and suddenly the grapes were out again.

Laura allowed several minutes to tick by, and was on the verge of asking the question again when Tessa said, 'You know, I've been in a bit of a state since everything blew up.'

'In what way?'

'Well, because of Allyson mainly. I wish it hadn't happened to her. Shelley wouldn't have been so bad, but Shelley's not capable of being hurt the way Allyson is.'

Laura wanted to ask, so why did you choose Allyson, but she already knew the answer and it was clear that Tessa wasn't yet ready to face it. So Laura said, 'What makes you say that about Shelley?'

'Well, to begin with Shelley can't stand men, so she wouldn't have been in a position to be hurt anyway. Everyone thinks she's a lesbian, but she's not. At least not according to Bob. He says she came on to him all the time he was with Allyson, practically begging him to sleep with her.'

'Do you believe that?'

'I don't know. He's no saint though. Everyone knows he's been sleeping with other women for years. Allyson was the only one who didn't know. It was kind of an accepted thing, you know, that no-one would tell her. I expect she knew though, and pretended not to.'

Once more Laura inwardly groaned, for there were those fatal words again.

'She's got a lot of friends in the media,' Tessa was saying, 'and everyone likes her. Well, you've probably seen that in the papers these past few weeks. They might be right in her face, not giving her any privacy, or letting up with the stories and stuff, but no-one's ever nasty about her. They're all on her side. Bob's the one who's really getting it in the neck, but then he was the one who walked out, so I suppose that's only to be expected. Anyway, that was why it was such a shock for him when it came out about me and him in the paper. No-one had ever exposed any of his affairs before.'

'Who tipped the paper off?'

'Could have been anyone. People at the office knew, well, I expect some of them did. And I've got neighbours. Someone could have seen him coming and going. Maybe it was one of them who contacted the *News of the World* and this time they decided to run the story instead of hushing it up to protect their precious Allyson.'

Laura registered the note of bitterness. 'So what now?' she said.

'Now,' Tessa responded, 'I think I'll have to get an abortion. I mean, I can't have a baby when I've got a whole new career starting up, can I?'

'What about Bob? Does he want the baby?'

She nodded, and looked away. 'I'll have to tell him I had a miscarriage,' she mumbled, digging back into her bag of grapes.

'Tessa,' Laura said firmly, 'I want you to tell me who you think Bob and Allyson are representing in your life. You know what I'm asking, so please don't pretend not to.'

'It's OK, I won't pretend,' Tessa said, coming back so fast that this time she did surprise Laura. 'You think Bob's the father figure and Allyson's the mother.'

'Don't you think that?'

'I can see why you do.'

Laura said gently, 'Can you see that you're punishing them for something they had nothing to do with?'

Tessa's lips trembled as she tried to laugh. 'I don't

think Bob's being punished, not with all the sex I give him,' she said.

Laura looked at her until Tessa's eyes dropped and spotting her hand in the bag of grapes she began rummaging around.

'It's been almost two years since your breakdown, when you had to drop out of college,' Laura reminded her. 'You've come to understand a lot about yourself and what happened in that time.'

'I know,' Tessa answered. Her hand came out of the bag empty.

Laura's eyes were on hers. 'So why are you denying it now?'

'I'm not. I can even say it now,' Tessa responded.

'I'm listening.'

'But I don't want to,' Tessa said. 'I hate saying it. I hate the word, because the whole thing makes me sick.'

Laura fired the next question. 'Then why did you have to make Julian your brother? Why not just a friend?'

'I don't know. What difference does it make? I suppose because I always wanted a brother who was a friend.'

'Unlike the one you had.'

'Totally unlike the one I had.' Tessa looked at her watch. 'I'm going to have to cut this short,' she said. 'I promised to be home early. Bob's been told he's not hosting the Sportsman of the Year awards now, and he's really upset.'

In dismay Laura watched her go for her coat. 'Would you like to make another appointment?' she said.

'I'll have to give you a call,' Tessa replied. 'I'm so busy these days I might not have the time,' and with a hurried but extremely polite goodbye, she was gone.

Laura sat staring at the door, and shaking her head in frustration. She needed to see this girl so much more often, especially now she'd got herself embroiled in this horrible mess that had such sinister similarities to what had happened in her past. In fact, Laura was very firmly of the opinion that Tessa, with the extraordinary power a bruised and damaged mind often had, had managed to manipulate the entire affair, setting it up to be a sad and potentially disastrous restaging of earlier events that had spiralled so horrifically out of her control. Not that Laura thought for a moment that Tessa's love for Bob and Allyson wasn't genuine, because it almost unquestionably was. Tessa had it in her to love very deeply, it just wasn't always easy for her to apply her emotions in a normal and socially acceptable way.

'This is all that matters,' Bob panted. 'Just me and you. Screw everyone else!'

Tessa giggled. 'I knew this would make you feel better.'

'Oh God!' Bob cried. He was going to come any second.

'Do it harder, harder,' Tessa urged.

His hands were on her hips, he was kneeling over her, the hair on his chest rubbing harshly over her back.

Suddenly the phone rang. Before he could stop her Tessa had picked it up. 'It's for you,' she told him, passing it back.

He was about to protest when he remembered that sometimes they liked to screw while having normal conversations on the phone. It was a great turn-on. 'Hello?' he said.

'Hello? Bob? It's Peggy here. '

His bloody mother-in-law! Who the hell had given her this number? Allyson of course! 'Yes Peggy,' he said. Tessa was still kneeling beneath him. He was still inside her, though no longer filling her completely.

'Bob, dear. I know this is none of my business, but Howard and I, we've been talking, and we want you to know, well, that we understand how sometimes when a man reaches a certain age, that he can, how shall I put it?

Act out of character. It's not so unusual, you know. Most men go through it. It wasn't really talked about in our day, of course, but now . . .'

'Peggy, this isn't a good . . .'

'No, no, I understand. I'm bothering you. But Howard and I, we just wanted you to know that if you need any help, if you feel . . . Well, you know what I'm saying, dear. Howard knows a lot of good doctors. He was one himself once, remember? Not that sort of doctor, of course. Not his area at all, the mind.'

She wasn't kidding. These days, if the old boy saw a heatwave, he'd probably wave back.

Tessa crept out from under him, leaving him on all fours, his ardour gone.

'We're not trying to suggest there's anything wrong with you,' Peggy continued. 'Just if you need a recommendation . . .'

'Thanks Peggy. I'll bear it in mind,' he snapped.

'OK, dear. Enough said.'

As the line went dead, he hurled the phone against the wall and ended up with his hands on the floor, his knees still on the bed.

Tessa burst out laughing, and realizing how ridiculous he must look, he managed a laugh too.

'Who was it?' Tessa asked.

'My mother-in-law,' he responded, picking himself up.

'What did she want?'

'What do you think? To try to get me back with her daughter.' He was on his feet now, trying to get past her. 'Christ! There's no room to swing a cat in this place,' he growled, stubbing his toe on the bed.

She was grinning again, and, seeing it, he suddenly scooped her up and rolled back onto the bed with her.

'We've got to get a bigger place,' she said, as he wrapped her tightly in his arms.

'I know.'

145

She lifted her head up to look into his eyes. 'What about somewhere smart, like Chelsea?' she suggested.

He looked at her for a moment, wondering if she was being deliberately obtuse in suggesting Chelsea, but there was only the usual guileless expression in her lovely eyes. Nevertheless, the allusion to his previous life had reopened the door to his depression, and letting her go he rolled onto his back and stared up at the ceiling.

'What's the matter?' she said.

'Nothing. I need a drink,' and propelling himself off the bed he went to get one.

Tessa lay where she was, idly stroking the pink, fluffy squirrel that was squashed between the pillows.

'Where's the gin?' he shouted from the kitchen.

'I threw it out. You drink too much, and then you get angry.'

He appeared in the doorway, clearly straining to hold onto his temper. 'Have you got any idea what kind of a day I've had!' he demanded. 'First of all I'm told I'm no longer needed for the awards. Then I find out that Duncan Grueber, a snot-nosed kid half my age, is covering the big match for Sky tonight. Then my insufferable mother-in-law and her barmy husband ring up accusing me of having some kind of male meno-pause. And *who*, might I ask, put that thoroughly modern notion into their heads? Their daughter, that's who. And now *you* throw away the gin. So, what's going on here? Are you in some kind of conspiracy, all of you? Are you trying to drive me into the nuthouse?'

Tessa looked up at him and smiled. 'We can always go down the pub,' she suggested. 'Jules might be there.'

'Fuck Jules.'

Mischief sprang to her eyes. 'What, both of you? At the same time? Kinky.'

He came to stand over her and took the hand she held out to him. 'You know, I think you'd like that,' he said, wrapping his fingers round hers, and suddenly feeling absurdly insecure.

'I might,' she confessed. 'If you would.'

He stared down at her, his eyes scanning her face as he tried to work out whether or not she was serious. He guessed the 'if you would' told him she was. But he wasn't, so the question was irrelevant. 'I need a drink,' he said again.

'More than you need this,' she teased, stroking him.

He'd liked to have said no, but it would have been a lie. He needed a drink, and he needed one badly, because on top of everything else that had happened today, he'd been notified by the bank that all the funds in his and Allyson's joint accounts were frozen until their marital difficulties were resolved, one way or the other. Obviously they wouldn't have been able to do that if Allyson hadn't contacted them to make the break-up official, which meant there was a damned good chance that divorce papers were about to starting winging their way.

Inside he was panicking. It was as though everything was slipping away from him, and not even the fact that he'd considered initiating a divorce himself made a difference, because he hadn't done it, and in truth he wasn't convinced he would have. And he definitely wouldn't have contacted the bank. Christ, he needed to get to his money. He was practically broke already and the hundred and fifty quid that was in his own account was going to get him about as far as the middle of next week, if he was lucky. It was all right for Allyson, with her fancy trust funds and inherited wealth to bail her out, but it sure as hell wasn't all right for him. Especially not with Tessa setting her sights on a flat in bloody Chelsea.

'Go down the pub and get some gin,' he said, sinking onto the edge of the bed and burying his face in his hands. 'I'll wait here.'

To his relief she was her usual compliant self, and toddled off without criticism or comment. It wasn't until she'd been gone for over half an hour that he remembered Julian, and her suggestion of a threesome, but by then he was too beside himself craving a drink to care about Julian, or that she'd gone out in only her overcoat and boots. Or maybe it was the fact that Allyson would very probably be tucked up all nice and snug in their Chelsea apartment right now, laughing her head off at the trick she'd pulled with the bank, and almost hysterical over the stunt she'd pulled with her parents that was getting him so worked up. She could be such a bitch when she wanted, and no doubt it was that other bitch, Shelley Bronson, who'd put her up to it all.

Getting sharply to his feet he went into the bathroom and began rummaging around in the the flower basket on the window sill where Tessa kept her nail polish, hairslides, perfume samples and . . . Yes, it was still there – the little white wand with two blue stripes across its centre window that showed that even if Tessa hadn't been truthful when she'd first told him she was pregnant, she was certainly being truthful now. So let Allyson and Shelley laugh, let them laugh all the way to hysteria and back if that was what they wanted, because it was going to be a whole different story when they found out Tessa was expecting a baby.

His eyes closed, and despite the anger that was usually so effective in deadening everything in its path, he was having a hell of a struggle to beat down the fear and misgivings that were erupting all over his mind. For, in truth, the last thing he wanted was to tell Allyson about the baby, because no matter what she did to hurt him, he'd rather die than use this pregnancy to punish her for depriving him of his money. She didn't deserve that. She didn't deserve any of this, but as usual his miserably inept conscience was attempting to put in an appearance long after its chance to make a difference had passed.

He dropped the test back in the basket, and went to find his clothes. He had to have a drink, something to help him escape the hideous mess he was in, and maybe, if he drank enough, he'd manage to link up with the feeling of liberation he'd had when he'd first believed Tessa was pregnant. Oh, what delightfully deluded times they had been, when he'd actually thought that her pregnancy was a God-given sign to the path of his destiny, providing him not only with the permission to walk out on his marriage, but with an absolution from guilt and indecision because he'd had no choice. Well, it certainly didn't feel like a heavenly blessed liberation he was experiencing now, in fact it was so far from anything that even resembled liberation he might just as well consign himself straight to hell and be done with it.

A few miles away, in the centre of London, Allyson and Shelley and a few of their friends were applauding loudly as the final curtain came down on an exceptionally spirited and imaginative production of *La Bohème*. Still clapping, Shelley leaned over to speak in Allyson's ear, and Allyson nodded that yes, she was feeling OK. She'd thrown up during the interval, and in truth she was feeling a bit nauseous again now, though not in any real danger of imminent disgrace. Were she not one hundred per cent certain that she wasn't, she'd probably be surfing around happily in the belief she was pregnant right now, but her body was currently and aggressively engaged in a refute of that, which was why she was looking so pale and drained, and feeling unspeakably tired.

As they got up to start making their way outside Allyson was only too aware of the way people were whispering and muttering to each other, watching her and making her feel so horribly pitied and conspicuous that she could feel cracks appearing in the veneer of airy laughter and interest she was affecting as she and her friends discussed the performance. This wasn't actually her first excursion back into the social scene, but tonight was proving particularly hard, even though she'd managed to enjoy the opera, and had actually stumbled right into some genuine laughter earlier, when Shelley had told her how her mother had called Bob to offer him some help with the menopause. But though she'd found it funny, she secretly wished that Shelley hadn't given Peggy the number, for Allyson was very protective of her parents, and the last thing she wanted was Bob turning on them and hurting them even more than he already had.

Still, it had provided a moment's light relief, and might have provided even more than that were she not feeling so awful about what she'd done today. At the time she had felt so driven and vengeful that she'd derived a deliciously vindictive enjoyment from instructing the bank and her lawyers, she'd even flounced into Shelley's office after and declared herself an empowered and surviving woman. It had taken all of ten minutes for that to wear off, and now she hated what she'd done – not because of how enraged she knew Bob would be when he found out, but because it had been necessary to do it at all.

However, other motives aside, it was all part of her attempt to be practical about the break-up of her marriage, and afterwards, because it wasn't a pro-gramme day, she'd taken herself off for one of her regular visits to a women's refuge in Ealing. She'd been going there for years, getting to know the women, talking to them and listening to stories of the kind of break-ups she doubted she could ever survive. She never discussed her own, though obviously everyone knew about it, but since the size of her pain couldn't even be measured against that of women who had been beaten and abused, abandoned while pregnant, left penniless and battered, and in some cases were lucky to be alive, she felt it wholly inappropriate to mention her own small acquaintance with suffering. However, she did derive some kind of therapy from going, for while reaching out to the women she was able to set her own hurt aside and think only of them. It was also helping her to cope with the wild swings of her emotions, and the burning need for revenge she felt every time she thought of how happy Tessa and Bob might be.

God, how badly she tormented herself with that.

'See you in the morning then,' Shelley said, turning to her as they finished saying goodbye to their other friends outside the Opera House. 'The news of Stella's retirement should've had time to sink in by then.'

'More press on our heels,' Allyson commented. 'At least it'll be for a different reason this time. When's it actually being made official?'

'Sometime next week, as far as I know. Stella's in control. The new takeover should be announced at the same time.'

Allyson nodded thoughtfully, then, after embracing Shelley, she headed off through the late-night glitter and bustle of Covent Garden to where she'd parked her car. She knew Shelley was excited about the takeover, and probably she would be too, were she able to conjure a clearer picture of what it might mean. Not that she imagined the programme to be in any jeopardy – the ratings were good again, and it had a pretty high profile, as well as a dedicated following – but her near-constant state of insecurity was making her suspicious and mistrustful of the world, and terrified of where the next blow might come from and just how devastating it might be. To combat it she tried counting her blessings, like her parents; her friendship with Shelley; her many other friends whom she'd been neglecting lately but who still called to make sure she was all right; the wonderful flat she lived in; her success and the programme – there was so much for her to be thankful for. And though there were times when none of it meant anything without Bob, she tried to cut those thoughts short and move past them.

Tonight, though, it was proving hard, obviously because she'd just put the end of her marriage in motion. Everyone had said it was too soon, that she didn't need to do anything yet, but they were wrong. She had needed to do something, and if that was what it took to get Bob to face the absolute reality of what he had done, then so be it. It was a drastic measure, and one she discovered, when she replayed her messages when she got home, that didn't appear to have paid off in the way she had secretly hoped.

As she listened, she could be in no doubt that he was drunk, for she barely understood half of what he said he was slurring his words so badly, and there was so much background noise from whatever pub he was in. But his fury reached her loud and clear, so did the fact that he had somehow twisted events round in his mind to enable himself to blame her for the break-up of their marriage. He should have left her years ago, he ranted. She'd never needed him, had always considered herself to be better than him, just because her family had money and property and his father was only a dirty old labourer on a building site. Well, she could stick her money and her damned property. He was well out of it, and happier now than he had ever been.

Though the harshness of his words cut right through her, the very fact that he was so drunk told her not only that she'd hurt him very badly, but that his suffering was perhaps greater than she'd imagined. Because it was instinctive she found herself wondering what she could do to help him, the way she always had when he was feeling insecure and beaten down by the world. The sudden recollection of where he was and who he was with ripped that impulse out by the roots, providing even more space for the fiercely bitter urge to cause Bob and Tessa every bit as much pain as they were causing her.

Chapter 7

The news of Stella Cornbright's retirement and impending death had brought the *Soirée* offices to a standstill. It was early in the morning, Shelley had told them all just after the previous day's recording, and now, after a night to think about it, everyone had something to say. With Allyson and Shelley yet to put in an appearance, they were free to air their views and recycle the gossip they'd already managed to glean about Stella, and about Mark and Nicholas Reiner, whose takeover of the entire company was apparently going to be officially announced the following week.

'Someone told me the Reiners are actually British, not American,' Debbie, one of the researchers, said.

'They are,' Jerry Milne confirmed. 'I directed the show that Mark appeared on back whenever it was. He sounds American, but apparently that's because he grew up over there. His roots are here in Blighty.'

'I remember him,' Hayley said. 'He's quite young, isn't he?'

'If you call thirty-six young,' Frankie, the production manager, who rated anyone over the age of thirty as past it, said bitchily. 'Didn't his wife have a problem with drink?'

'All that money, and still the woman has problems,' Jocelyn, the PA, lamented.

'I heard they were divorced,' Debbie chipped in.

Alan was shaking his head. 'I read an article about them in one of those county magazines a couple of months ago. They were still together then.'

'More to the point, what's he going to do with the company?' Edmund demanded.

'I can answer that,' Marvin said, coming in the door.

They were all ears. As Shelley's assistant, Marvin's information was sure to be good.

'Apparently,' Marvin said, enjoying the attention, 'he's moving the transmission to eleven thirty and bringing in another presenter.'

Tessa's eyes rounded.

'Don't listen to him,' Alan chided. 'He doesn't know any more than we do.'

'Straight up,' Marvin insisted. 'My sister's friends with Melissa, Stella's secretary. I got it from her.'

They all looked at each other, still not sure whether to believe him. Even so, they were impressed with his source.

'It'll kill the show if he does that,' Hayley protested.

'It's Allyson's show. He's not going to change the presenter,' Edmund pointed out.

'If he does it'll be over Shelley's dead body,' one of the editors piped up.

'I also heard he wants the programme to go live,' Marvin added.

'At eleven thirty!' Jerry exploded. 'Does the man think we don't have lives?'

'And who the hell watches at that time of night?' Alan said. 'We might as well all pack up and go home now.'

'You might have to,' Edmund responded. 'If he's planning to change the presenter, he could be planning to change all of us too.'

'Oh, listen to him,' Jocelyn grumbled. 'And aren't we all forgetting something? Stella Cornbright's *dying*, for God's sake!'

'Say it a bit louder and you'll save *Variety* the print

space,' Shelley commented as she and Allyson walked in. 'I know the official announcement's not until next week,' she continued, 'but these things have a way of leaking out, so if anyone calls from the press beforehand, trying to get some inside information, play dumb. Stella wants to handle it her way, we should pay her that respect. When I spoke to her last night she was hoping the Reiners' arrival on the scene will overshadow her departure. As for any of the rumours you may have heard, I'll be better placed to put you in the picture after my meeting with Mark Reiner.'

'Which is when?' Alan wanted to know.

'Today.'

Allyson was staring across the room at Tessa, whose shaggy dark head was bowed over a newspaper. Allyson was certain the engrossment was feigned, and felt a dizzying rush of hatred, for it was thanks to that little bitch that she and Bob wouldn't be spending today, their *nineteenth wedding anniversary*, together. And the story the bitch was reading – was it the one about Bob's drunken rampage last night, when he'd got himself thrown out of a pub and threatened to beat up a policeman? How was Tessa Dukes feeling about that, Allyson wanted to know, sitting there in all her plump, oversexed glory looking like butter wouldn't melt? Did she feel any kind of responsibility for the state Bob was in? Did she know what the word meant, even? Maybe Allyson should go and drum it into her head with a blunt object. And what kind of rumours had the girl been listening to, just before Allyson and Shelley arrived? Allyson hadn't heard any yet, but there were never any departures and takeovers without gossip and conjecture, and Allyson was blistering with outrage that Tessa might have heard something before her. Then Tessa looked up, and realizing she was in danger of drawing everyone else's attention to the moment, Allyson turned away, saying, 'Marv, I've got a mountain of mail to get through, can I hijack you for the morning?'

'If it's OK with Shelley,' he answered.

Shelley waved an assenting hand. 'OK, everyone, let's get past the spleen and speculation, we've got a show to get on the air. And today's guests are?' She looked at the board. 'Mm,' she grunted when she saw the names that were chalked up for Cocktails. Then her face brightened. 'Josh Burrows for Night Cap. I'd forgotten he was coming in. New film?'

Edmund nodded. 'I gave Ally the video . . .'

'Which she sat up and watched last night,' Ally finished. 'Totally absorbing, absolutely forgettable.'

'Film insert?' Shelley enquired.

'We're shooting it this morning,' Edmund answered. 'It's one of Tessa's stories.'

Shelley's eyes lost their warmth as they moved to Tessa.

'Uh, it's this writer in North London,' Tessa said, stammering slightly. 'She's got one of the world's biggest collections of dolls. It's seriously spooky. The neighbours swear they hear them screaming in the night.'

'Sounds like something for Hallowe'en,' Shelley remarked.

'Collectors always give me the creeps,' Jocelyn piped up.

'I'll remember that next time you all club together for an art deco piece for me,' Shelley responded drily.

'Obviously we've missed Hallowe'en,' Tessa said. 'Do you want us to shoot it and keep it for next year?'

'Shoot it, yes. Then let's schedule a couple of interviews around it and use it another night. Get a horror-movie star in for Cocktails and something suitably ghoulish for Night Cap. Who's producing today? Alan? Take a look at the inserts on the shelf and see if there's something we can use for tonight.'

'Debbie, did you manage to get a selection of reviews for this film?' Allyson asked.

'Still working on it,' Debbie replied. 'But you'll have them by lunch time.'

'I also want to know how it went down in the States,' Allyson added. 'And whoever's working on the Hobson Brothers for Cocktails, I only want the lunacies of the past couple of months.'

Deciding it might not be a good idea to let the North London author know that her precious dolls were going to feature as part of a horror special, Tessa called her and simply confirmed their filming schedule for later in the day. Then she went to check the crew had the right directions, before going over everything with the reporter to prepare him for the interview.

Allyson stayed in her office all morning. She knew Shelley was on edge about her lunch with Mark Reiner, but they were both too busy to discuss it. However, no amount of work was going to allow Allyson to forget the significance of the day, nor would it stop her remembering that cold sunny afternoon, nineteen years ago, when her father had walked her down the aisle and she had looked into Bob's eyes and known, beyond any doubt, how deeply she was loved. And she'd always felt that way, throughout all the years of their marriage, especially when he'd sprung such anniversary surprises on her as a cruise down the Nile, weekends in Paris or Rome; tickets to a concert in Rio. So many romantic and memorable gestures from a man who had ended up smashing it all to pieces with his lies and deceit, and was probably too hung-over this morning even to read the date on the newspaper, never mind the sordid details of the obscene spectacle he'd made of himself the night before.

Obviously he was in a much worse state than she'd imagined, to be going around getting himself into fights and threatening to assault a policeman, and the anniversary present she'd sent him, a taxi full of his bills and belongings stuffed into bin liners, wasn't going to do much to cheer him up either. She felt bad about doing it now, but what was concerning her more was the article's cutting, though maybe exaggerated, account of his ailing career. No-one, it claimed, wanted to use him any more, because since the break-up of his marriage he had become unreliable and abusive and was all too regularly turning up to the job drunk. One editor had actually been quoted, and the fact that the man had agreed to his name being published was a sure sign of how bad it was. And coming on top of the blow she herself had dealt him yesterday with the bank . . .

She looked out of her office, across to where Tessa was talking on the phone. Her heart twisted. Was she talking to Bob? Was she trying to soothe the humiliating effects of the article? The very thought of such an intimacy, of the girl shoving her fat ugly feet into yet another pair of Allyson's marital shoes, sent all sympathy for Bob fleeing for cover as another storm of hatred broke.

'Allyson Jaymes,' she snapped into the phone.

'Hi. It's me.'

Her heart stopped dead, as the sound of his voice slammed a lid on all the raging frustration and anger. God knew how she had hoped for a call this morning, though in truth she'd never expected it to come. It was why she had bundled up his clothes and his mail, and despatched them in the oldest, smelliest taxi she could find, out of sheer anger that he wouldn't remember. So she'd punished him before he'd even had a chance to commit the crime, and now here he was, remembering. Except she was worse than a fool for even thinking that way, because, of course, he was about to start ranting about the cab full of symbolic resentment, and then he'd get onto the blocked bank accounts, and from there he'd revisit her responsibility for all his ills . . . But maybe she could give him the benefit of the doubt. Wait to see what he said before she started letting rip in defence. So, in her best neutral voice, she said, 'Hello. How are you?'

His laugh was dry-throated and achingly familiar. 'Lousy, actually,' he admitted. 'Did you see the *Express*?'

'Yes.'

There was a long, tense silence as she waited for him to apologize, or at least refer to, the obnoxious and offensive diatribe he'd left on her machine last night, though there was a good chance he had no memory of it, which was partly borne out when he said, 'Can I see you? I want to talk.'

Allyson's chest was suddenly so tight, it was hard to breathe. Eight long and bitterly hard weeks she'd waited to hear those words, and now he'd spoken them she didn't know what to say. It wasn't that she didn't want to see him, she was just afraid of what he might want to talk about. Please God, not divorce. OK, she'd put it in motion, but he wouldn't have had the papers yet, and she'd been planning to call up and stop them. Then a few rays of hope struggled their way through the dread, reminding her that there was a chance he wanted to talk about getting back together. But she shouldn't let herself get too carried away with that, so maybe she should ask him now what he wanted to discuss.

His answer was irritatingly and cryptically short. 'Things,' he said.

Up went her hackles. 'You mean like money, and the fact you can't get to yours any more,' she snapped.

He sighed, which annoyed her even more. 'Why did you do that with the bank accounts?' he said.

'Why did you leave?' she shot back.

She actually heard his hand scrape over his unshaven face. Not the sound of a man who was getting ready to fight. 'Can we talk?' he repeated. 'I'll come over to the flat this evening, if you're free.'

It was on the tip of her tongue to remind him, gently, what day it was, but more self-protective hostility

160

barged its way through. 'If you think you can control yourself,' she said tartly.

'What the hell kind of an answer's that?' he snapped.

'The last time I saw you, you hit me,' she reminded him. 'And you haven't exactly been behaving in a way that suggests I'd be safe around you since,' she added spitefully.

'Well, if you're going to be like that . . .'

'No! You're the one who's being like that. I've always been prepared to talk – even if it is to discuss the terms of a divorce.'

'Are you going to be there, or aren't you?' he growled.

'Come about seven,' she said. 'And leave your temper at the door.'

After putting the phone down she went straight into Shelley's office and closed the door.

'So, what do you think he wants to talk about?' she said breathlessly, when she'd finished recounting the details.

'What do you think?' Shelley countered.

Allyson shuddered. 'Could be anything,' she answered.

'Well, that narrows it down,' Shelley commented dryly. 'What if he wants to come back?'

'Oh God, don't even say it,' Allyson groaned as her stomach churned. 'I don't know. I mean, obviously I want him back, but . . .' She dashed a hand through her hair and started to pace. 'I've got all kinds of things going through my head right now,' she confessed. 'I'm even managing to delude myself into thinking that he's planning to spring another one of his wonderful anniversary surprises, but of course, he won't, because he hasn't even remembered, and if he does he'll make himself forget again, which means he'll probably turn up drunk and we'll have a horrible fight and instead of threatening to beat up a policeman he'll satisfy himself by beating up me.' Her face turned pale. 'Oh my God,' she gasped. 'Are you doing anything this evening?'

Shelley almost laughed. 'Are you serious? It'll send him right off his head if he sees me there.'

'That's for him to deal with,' Allyson replied.

'Allyson, he's not going to beat you up,' Shelley said firmly.

'He'd never hit me before two months ago,' Allyson reminded her, 'and think how you're going to feel if he does beat me up and you weren't there to stop it.'

'Oh God,' Shelley laughed, 'you really know all the buttons to press, don't you?'

'You could hide,' Allyson suggested. 'He won't even have to know you're there.'

Shelley laughed again. 'OK. I'll be there,' she said. 'But I'm not hiding.'

Allyson grinned, and was on the point of leaving when she suddenly turned back. 'In case you thought I'd forgotten, good luck with your lunch.'

Shelley's smile vanished. 'Don't!' she groaned. 'I haven't been this nervous in years.' Then a light of mischief sparked in her eyes as she said, 'But that's nothing to what he's going to be feeling by the time I'm through.'

Allyson laughed, and as she had no doubt about Shelley's powers of seduction – or anything else – she left the office feeling perfectly secure in Shelley's ability to pilot them through the turbulence of the takeover.

It was rare for Shelley to walk into a restaurant without turning heads; it was also rare for her not to run into several people she knew, and this restaurant proved no exception, as she was stopped several times whilst being shown across the clinically styled room of the Pharmacy to a reasonably secluded window table. Though she was five minutes late, there was no sign of Mark Reiner, nor had the hostess offered a message, but he had to come

162

from the City, so was probably caught up in traffic.

Shelley looked businesslike and beautiful. She wore her luxuriant dark hair in a chignon, allowing full view of her exquisite, finely honed features that were, as usual, enhanced by an expression of detached serenity. The silk shirt beneath her soft black suede suit was vaguely transparent, with no lace bra to spoil the smooth plane of the fabric. Her long legs were sheathed in silk hold-up stockings, creating no unsightly evidence of suspenders beneath her skirt, nor was there any unbecoming trace of a panty line. It made her feel more powerful and feminine knowing how she was, or wasn't, dressed beneath her outer garments.

As she glanced casually at the menu she was mulling over the rumours that had started to circulate about the changes Mark Reiner was planning. Though they were probably less than ten per cent accurate, she was fairly certain he'd want some, so she was ready to put forward her own proposals. She'd have liked to be even more sweeping and controversial than was currently reflected in the outlines she'd brought with her, but certain loyalties, and a conscience, had made her hold back. Even so, the documents in her briefcase contained ideas and budgets that were, if nothing else, audacious, though she would only hand them over if things appeared to be going her way. She felt confident they would, for she had already made up her mind to make a friend of Mark Reiner.

A few subtle enquiries had told her that Mrs Reiner had returned to the States and a divorce was in the offing, so Shelley had taken home a videotape of the programme he'd featured in, and watched it several times in order to better acquaint herself with the man who was about to become her new boss. It was why she was experiencing such anticipation and even apprehension about this meeting, for there had been a lot in the programme, which had been recorded during one of her rare absences, to convince her of how remarkably suited they were. And the first glimpse of the tall, extremely striking and well-dressed man, as he walked into the restaurant and was greeted warmly by the hostess, did nothing to alter Shelley's view. If anything it only augmented it, for Mark Reiner in person appeared to be something else altogether from Mark Reiner, two years ago, on TV – and she hadn't imagined it could get any better.

He had to be at least six foot three, which was extremely pleasing as it was rare for Shelley to meet a man she didn't have to look down on. And the fact that he was six years her junior made him even more appealing, which was unusual, for younger men didn't normally do it for Shelley, nor did long hair, but the way his was combed straight back from his face, and curled over the white collar of his shirt, lent him an air of unaffected yet trendy distinction that was wholly alluring. And the fluid movements of what was clearly a well toned and muscular physique, clothed in a black Armani suit, were so entirely male that the sexuality he seemed to exude was, though subtle, totally compelling. In fact, to Shelley's mind, he had the look of a man who would know a woman's body more intimately, and more cherishingly, than she did.

Shelley stood up as he approached the table and smiled as she shook his hand.

'Shelley,' he said, his deep brown eyes looking directly into hers. 'I'm sorry if I kept you.'

The American accent she had expected, even though she knew he was British by birth, but the warmth of his tone unsettled her slightly, though she wasn't entirely sure why, until she realized that it was the discerning intensity in his gaze which seemed to be reading her in a way most men never could. Though it wasn't possible to tell what he was thinking, her instincts were responding with the kind of shivers that suggested he too was making an assessment not entirely confined to the professional.

A light of humour flashed in her eyes as she said, 'I'm glad to meet you.'

His hand was still holding hers, but he let go as he waved her back to her chair. 'Did you order a drink?' he asked, sitting down too.

'Evian for me,' she said to the waiter.

'For me too,' he said. He looked at her again and raised a single eyebrow in a mock- conspiratorial kind of way, which made her smile.

His face was slender and darkened by the few hours of growth since he'd last shaved. His deep-set eyes were narrow and remained quietly assessing within the lambent burn of their humour. Though in his way he was strikingly handsome, his features were irregular and individually ugly, for his nose was large and slightly hooked, and his mouth was too wide and rather thin. Yet the imperfections were obscured by the magnetic potency of his stare and the dynamic charm of a perfect white smile. And as their eyes continued a friendly, yet explicit appraisal Shelley could feel small waves of pleasure eddying through her at all the promise that lay within this one extremely confident and powerful young man.

'Would it be suitable for me to offer congratulations on your acquisition of the company?' she said, her dark eyes showing irony.

'I'll accept them if you're offering,' he replied, matching her expression.

She lowered her gaze to his hands, and allowed her imagination a moment or two with their unquestionable potential, then returned to his face. Barely two minutes had passed and already the chemistry was loading the air. She gave a fleeting thought to a time when they would be naked together, but though it was extremely tempting to let her mind linger, expand on it even, now wasn't the time, so she dismissed it. On a personal level all she wanted from this meeting was to go away knowing he found her attractive, and if she was reading him correctly that goal had already been achieved.

'Shall we decide what we're going to eat first?' he suggested, as he was handed a menu.

His manner had taken a few paces back from the intensity, which allowed an easier, less demanding tenor to the proceedings, so that after Shelley had chosen the veal special, and he had selected the lamb, they fell effortlessly into a conscience discussion on vegetarianism, which somehow led them to various places in the world they'd both visited, which led to a discovery that they had once been in Morocco at the same time. By the time their meals arrived they were talking about music and Shelley was forced to dab away tears of laughter as he told her some outrageous Country and Western song titles someone had recently sent him on the email.

'You're making this up,' she accused, breathlessly.

'I swear,' he protested. 'Apparently they're all genuine. What about this one? "Drop Kick Me Jesus, through the Goalposts of Life."'

Shelley had just taken a mouthful of water, and almost choked. 'Oh my God,' she gasped when finally she could. 'Stop, I can't laugh any more.'

'"Mama Get the Hammer there's a Fly on Papa's Head,"' he quoted.

They were both laughing so hard that it was infecting those on nearby tables.

Shelley picked up her fork and watched him do the same. She was still on the brink of laughter. 'I thought we were here to discuss the future of *Soirée*,' she said finally.

'Indeed we are,' he agreed and took a mouthful of food.

'Do you want to give me your comments, or shall I start with my proposals?'

He seemed amused. 'You're that confident that I intend to keep the programme going?' he said.

Shelley didn't miss a beat. 'Do you?' she said.

He arched an eyebrow. 'Let's hear your proposals. Just give me bottom lines. If need be we can go into detail later.'

She cut a slice of veal and ate it first, giving herself a moment to regroup her thoughts. In many ways they were off to a good start, but that hint about axing the programme had thrown her, and though she couldn't really believe that was his intention, she was still wondering if her defences had been shanghaied by an extremely effective though utterly ruthless *modus operandi*, which entailed disarming a person completely before going in for the kill. If she was right, then he was about to discover that she was not easily felled.

'To begin with I'd like to propose a fifty per cent increase in budget,' she said, expecting an immediate protest, or at the very least a widening of the eyes. However, she received neither, so taking advantage of his controlled composure, she continued. 'The extra funds would enable us to travel around the country and transmit from other cities, maybe even other countries, lending a more international appeal.'

He nodded, and carried on eating.

'Allyson, that's Allyson Jaymes, the presenter,' Shelley said, 'wants to devote one show per week to humanitarian efforts and causes.'

'Do you support that?'

Shelley was briefly halted by the sharpness of his tone, which suggested that perhaps he didn't. 'I'm ambivalent,' she answered, deciding now wasn't the time to take up arms.

He nodded for her to go on.

'That's it,' she said. 'We're a successful programme, so I don't see any reason to make changes just for the sake of it.'

He picked up his glass, finished eating then drank.

He had now become impossible to read, which perversely, considering the threat he might be posing to the programme, was making him more attractive than ever, and almost as a reflex action Shelley took off her jacket and hung it on the back of her chair.

For his part, though he was looking into her face, at that moment he wasn't really seeing her. He was thinking, considering what she'd said, and evaluating the body language that wasn't at all hard to read. He'd heard what a powerfully sexy, and intelligent, woman she was, and he certainly wasn't going to argue, nor was he going to deny that he greatly admired women like her, who made their sexuality work for them. However, it was going to be interesting to see how far she would go with it – or perhaps, more relevantly, how far he would go.

'I've been watching the programme these past few weeks,' he said.

Shelley sat back as a waiter cleared the table. She could feel her nipples brushing against the silk of her blouse.

His eyes drifted upwards to hers again. 'I've also looked at the ratings and read the audience straw polls,' he continued evenly. 'Unless you can convince me otherwise, I think the programme should be reduced to three nights a week, and a new presenter should be brought in. Cocktails is too stuffy and elitist. It should be reinvented as Happy Hour with younger guests and a much younger host.'

Though she didn't show it, Shelley was reeling. 'What brought you to these conclusions?' she asked.

Impressed by the deliberate mildness of her tone, he said, 'The general trend of the ratings is down. Some shows do well, but the figures indicate that the programme, if it's to continue,' *if it's to continue!* 'is in need of a shake-up. I often find where people have been

168

involved in the same project for a number of years, they either become too close to it to see its flaws, or so attached they simply make excuses for its weaknesses. I say this, because I don't want you to feel that I'm criticizing you as a producer. Everything I've heard about you assures me you are excellent at your job, and I think, hope, you will find the challenge of a new shape to your programme extremely stimulating as well as rewarding. To focus on three nights a week will make your team sharper in their choice of material, and to bring in new, and certainly younger, blood is vital for the image of the programme.'

Shelley might have laughed had it not seemed such an inappropriate thing to do, for what he'd just outlined were all the changes she longed to make herself, but loyalty to the team, and particularly to Allyson, had always prevailed. 'I want to get this straight,' she said carefully. 'Are you suggesting we get rid of Allyson Jaymes?'

His eyebrows rose and he couldn't help wondering what she would do if he said yes, that was in his mind. 'Not at all,' he answered. 'What I'm saying is we need someone younger to front the show.'

'So where does Allyson fit in?'

'She could continue with the Night Cap slot.'

Shelley was watching him closely. Though relieved that he wasn't suggesting they cut Allyson altogether, she was still wary. 'And Allyson's suggestion for the humanitarian show?' she said.

'Is completely wrong for the new image we'll be aiming for.' He paused a moment. 'I'm sorry, I know she's a good friend of yours, but we need to move with the times, and Allyson Jaymes is simply too old for the direction we need to take.'

Shelley lowered her eyes. His determination, tinged with ruthlessness, was pushing her loyalty to Allyson into a distant second place. Then her head came up as he

169

said, 'I'm afraid we'll have to postpone the details of my proposals to another time.' He was taking out a credit card and signalling to the waiter. Then looking across the table he let his gaze rest on hers. His eyes were so intense that the pressure felt almost physical and as she looked back she felt a stab of pure lust cut through her.

'I've a feeling we're going to get along well,' he said. 'I'm certainly looking forward to finding out.'

The evening was chill and dark as Allyson tramped through the drizzling rain from her car to the flat. Rumours of Stella Cornbright's early retirement, and Mark Reiner's takeover, had already made the papers, the *Standard* was full of it tonight, along with all the speculation she'd got wind of in the office earlier. So now everyone thought that, on top of everything else she'd been through lately, she was about to be removed from her job. If she didn't have such great faith in Shelley she might have been more worried about that, but Shelley was perfectly capable of mounting a winning campaign when necessary, and if there really was anything to be concerned about, then Shelley would have called her straight after the lunch, before going on to meet Stella. Allyson's heart gave a sickening thump of doubt. Or would Shelley have called? She certainly hadn't let Allyson know that one of Tessa's film inserts, with Tessa appearing, was being aired tonight. It would be Tessa's first time on screen and Allyson wanted to do all kinds of drastic and violent things to the girl – and to herself for the intense stupidity of ever suggesting Tessa should be promoted instead of pulverized. However, there was a certain comfort to be gained from the fact that Bob was going to be with her this evening, instead of out celebrating with *Soirée*'s very own Tellytubby – at least there might have been, were she not being so mercilessly buffeted about by nerves.

Opening the front door, she dumped her shopping

on the floor, and scrabbled for the light switch as her mobile phone started to ring inside her bag. Finally locating both, she prayed hard that it wasn't Bob calling to say he'd changed his mind, and bravely pressed the button.

'Hi it's me,' Shelley said. 'Where are you?'

Relief expelled Allyson's pent-up breath. 'Just got in,' she answered. 'Where're you?'

'In a taxi going round Piccadilly.'

'How's Stella?'

'Pretty up, considering. I've left Art Gulliver from Current Affairs holding her hand.'

Allyson pushed the door closed and began to shrug off her coat. The flat was cold and cheerless. She'd forgotten to set the heating. 'How was lunch?' she asked, her voice sounding deadened by all the layers of dread.

'I've got a lot to tell you,' Shelley answered.

At that Allyson's imagination erupted through the inertia and within milliseconds she was being dumped from her job, divorced from her husband, rejected by the public and utterly destroyed by a killer nervous breakdown.

'What time's Bob supposed to be getting there?' Shelley asked.

'In about an hour. You know, I was thinking, you don't have to come. I'm sure I can handle it.'

'I'll come,' Shelley said. 'If it's a reunion he's after and you find you're interested I'll leave. I don't want to take the chance of him hitting you again, and if he turns up drunk . . .'

'OK,' Allyson said, cutting her off. She didn't want to think about Bob being drunk. 'Was Stella's monitor on while we were recording?' she asked.

Shelley's hesitation was answer enough.

'So who authorized Tessa's report?' Allyson wanted to know.

'Alan. But he checked with me first. It was the right

bridge to get us from the Hobsons to Josh Burrows tonight. I'm sorry, I should have warned you.'

Allyson's voice was devoid of emotion. 'She was good,' she said. Her mouth was dry, her face felt numb.

'She learned from you,' Shelley replied. 'Listen, we're about to go into the underpass, so I'll lose you. I should be there in half an hour. Maybe less.'

Allyson rang off and went to put on the kettle. Then smothering her face with her hands she fought back the sudden urge to weep, most of all in that moment for her father's loss of mind. In the past he'd always been the one to make things better. Now he barely remembered who she was, and her mother was so upset by Bob's desertion and the terrible exposure they'd all suffered in the press, that Allyson was usually the one to comfort her. She felt so isolated, so utterly adrift, for she couldn't even say, thank God she had Shelley, because after today . . . Except she had to remember that it had been *her* decision to keep Tessa on the programme, and Shelley had a lot on her mind right now, with Mark Reiner taking over and Stella leaving . . . From there it was an easy leap to wondering how it would be if things worked out with Shelley and Mark Reiner, the way Shelley wanted them to . . . Allyson was so used to having Shelley all to herself, it would be strange sharing her with a man. But with Shelley's track record there wasn't too much danger of that . . . Horrified by the cruelty of the last thought, she dug her fingers into her face. How could she be so mean as to wish Shelley more bad luck with men than she'd already had, especially now she'd had first-hand experience of how appallingly painful and destructive it could be.

Forgetting about the kettle she went to put on the heating, then still wrapped in her coat she lay down on the bed. The phone rang several times, but she let the machine pick it up, as she sank deeper and deeper into despair. She had no energy, no fight, no will to carry on.

Things weren't going to work out with Bob tonight, she just knew it, and she wished to God now that she hadn't agreed to see him.

However, by the time Shelley arrived she'd managed to force herself into the shower, which had somehow manoeuvred her out of the bleakness towards a few daring rays of hope. It was possible that Bob might be wanting a reconciliation, and Shelley wouldn't really allow her to be thrown off the programme, and demented with grief as she so often felt, she was still a long way from howling at the moon. In fact, she was coping quite well, really, considering, and to prove it she was even able to laugh at Mark Reiner's Country and Western song titles when Shelley repeated them as she poured her a generous glass of Merlot. Shelley had let herself in while Allyson was still in the shower, so was already halfway through her own glass by the time Allyson put in an appearance. Not that Allyson was surprised to see her, feet up on a thickly padded kitchen chair, the latest copy of *Broadcast* spread open on the table. They'd always had keys to each other's flats, in case of emergencies.

'You're not serious!' Allyson said. 'Someone actually wrote a song called "I Flushed You from the Toilets of my Heart"?'

'So he claims,' Shelley laughed.

Allyson laughed again and drank some more wine. Then, sitting down in a chair opposite Shelley she said, 'Sounds like you two hit it off.'

'We did,' Shelley confirmed.

Allyson looked up and felt her heart contract at the glimmering light in Shelley's eyes. 'So do you think . . .?'

Shelley nodded. 'Mmm, it's possible.'

They smiled, knowingly, and Allyson drank some more wine.

After a while Shelley said softly, 'You're upset about Tessa being on the programme.'

'It was a bit of a shock,' Allyson confessed.

'I know. I'm sorry.'

Allyson forced a smile. 'I should have been expecting it,' she said. Then, attempting an objectivity she was far from feeling, she added, 'It was a good piece. Interesting and funny. She looks good on camera. Well, we knew that already.'

Shelley looked at her as she bowed her head and could almost feel the depth of her pain. 'Ally,' she said.

But Allyson spoke over her. 'So tell me more about lunch,' she said.

Shelley's eyes moved to her reflection in the night-blackened window. Allyson was bound to have heard the rumours, or read the paper, by now, so there wasn't much doubt about what she was really asking – and Shelley couldn't have felt worse, for she knew that Allyson would be trusting her to keep the programme format exactly as it was. Were it not for the fact that Mark's vision of a younger, more upbeat style of programme chimed so perfectly with Shelley's own, then Shelley would indeed be fighting, but how could she when it wasn't a fight she wanted to win? However, she reminded herself that nothing had actually been decided yet, so there was no point running with the fear that Mark's plans could prove an end to their friendship as well as to Allyson's position on the programme, they'd just have to cross that bridge when they came to it.

So, prevaricating, she said, 'There's not much to tell. We mostly talked generally. You know, about TV in the States compared to here, that sort of thing.'

'Nothing about the future of *Soirée*?'

Shelley continued to avoid her eyes. 'Only in the abstract.'

Allyson was quiet, and Shelley felt a crippling guilt when she looked up and saw the fear on her face. 'Which of the rumours is true?' Allyson said.

'I don't think . . .'

'No, it's OK. I can tell by the way you're holding back. He wants to replace me.'

Shelley reached for Allyson's hand, but Allyson moved it away. 'It's not as bad as that,' Shelley said. 'He wants you to continue with the Night Cap.'

Allyson felt sick. 'And the Cocktails?' she said.

Shelley was searching desperately for a way to postpone this, but it seemed her hesitation had already answered.

'He wants someone younger, doesn't he?' Allyson said.

Shelley nodded.

Allyson stared at her, ready to crumple beneath the horrible weight of rejection. Then a sudden anger and bitterness swept into her heart, reminding her she was a fighter, not a loser. She wasn't just going to sit here, getting bashed to a pulp by a fate that deserved, at the very least, to be battled, and in a burst of feverish resentment she cried, 'Of course, we're in a youth culture and at forty I'm past it. How could I possibly have thought I could carry on, when I'm crashing through the doors of middle age and embarrassing the life out of those who go gently.' She snatched up the bottle and splashed more wine into her glass. 'You know what's so damned cruel about this?' she demanded, only dimly aware of how badly she was shaking. 'What's so damned cruel is that I feel twenty-five. Don't you? I never think of myself as forty. Forty isn't an age that applies itself to me, in my head. I don't even know what it feels like to be forty. Except used up. Over the hill. A waste of good air space. At least that's how it feels for me. Not for you though. It's different for you, isn't it? You're not getting pushed aside to make room for some airhead with tattoos where I've got cellulite, and stardust where I've got wrinkles. Did you fight for me, Shelley? Did you tell him it's *my* show?'

Thrown by the outburst Shelley said, as calmly as she could, 'We didn't have time to get down to specifics. He just gave me his thoughts and then he was gone.'

Allyson started to speak, but seizing the ground Shelley stopped her, 'Listen, I know it hurts to hear you're too old, but if we can think of a way to make your age work for you, instead of against you ... I believe he's a reasonable man. If we can come up with something, he'll at least give us a hearing. I'm sure of it.'

'*Soirée* is *my* programme!' Allyson cried. 'Why the hell should I be trying to come up with something? Did he look at the ratings? Does he know how much publicity I get?'

Not wanting to get into an argument about whose programme it actually was, Shelley said, 'He's looked at everything, and the ratings, Ally, are starting to drop again.'

'And that's my fault?'

'No. I don't know. We've been using this format for eight years, without a change. Maybe it's getting tired and we didn't notice. Maybe what we need is a new concept.'

The doorbell sounded, announcing Bob's arrival.

'Oh God!' Allyson cried, as a whole other fear sprang up inside her. 'Just what I need.'

'Shall I tell him to go?' Shelley offered. 'You don't have to see him.'

'No. I do.'

'Why?'

'I don't know!' Allyson snapped angrily. 'Maybe to get it all over with at once,' and getting up she went to the entryphone and buzzed him in.

As she opened the front door she could hear his footsteps coming up the stairs, but by the time he came in she was back in the kitchen. From where she was sitting she could see him, and suddenly she wished

Shelley wasn't there. He'd never liked Shelley, and right now she didn't either.

'Hello,' he said. Though he was still in shadow, she could see he looked terrible, but then she probably did too.

She attempted a smile. Her defences were in chaos, not knowing where they were needed, and so terrified they might miss their cue that there was every chance they'd put in a wrong appearance and blow everything to pieces. For the moment, though, they seemed content to wait in the wings, as he closed the door and looked uncertain about taking off his coat. In the end he seemed too uncomfortable to do anything, which was horrible, because it made them seem like strangers, when he was her husband and this was their home. This was where they had shared everything of each other's lives, and now he was too nervous even to look at her. She wanted so badly to walk out into the hall and into those arms that she knew so well, but it might not be what he wanted, so she stayed where she was, listening to the unsteady thump of her heart. 'It's still raining out,' he said awkwardly.

She nodded.

'Is it OK if I take off my coat?'

That made her want to cry, but all she did was nod.

It was bewildering, trying to match this man and his humility with the drunken, abusive voice on the phone, or with the easy confidence and humour she'd known for so long.

'Are you going to say anything?' he demanded.

She jumped at his tone, but realizing his belligerence was caused by nerves she said, 'How are you?'

He came forward. The light moved across his face and her heart twisted. His belovedly familiar features were ravaged with exhaustion. She wanted to sit him down, soothe him and tell him it would be all right, yet somehow she knew already it wasn't going to be.

'It is money, isn't?' she said. 'That's why you're here.'

His eyes went down and she wondered how much pride he had left. She guessed she was about to find out.

'I think the BBC are going to drop me, permanently,' he said.

It was probably the wine that almost made Allyson laugh, for she wouldn't normally find their imminent state of unemployment funny. But she didn't want to tell him about her, so all she said was, 'I'm sorry.'

He waved a dismissive hand, then came on into the kitchen. He was almost at the table before he saw Shelley, and the aggression and anger that leapt into the air the instant he did told Allyson that she had made a disastrous mistake in asking Shelley to be there.

'Well,' he snarled, 'I suppose I should be thankful it's her and not some beaten-up bimbo and her snot-nosed kids.'

Knowing he was referring to the shelter for battered women and children she'd recently been photographed coming out of, Allyson didn't respond. Nor was she offended, for despite the way he was behaving, she knew that the real Bob could summon up a compassion for others that was easily as great as her own.

'Hello Bob,' Shelley said mildly.

He turned to Allyson. His face was twisted with rage. 'You do it to spite me, don't you?' he sneered. 'It's all done just to piss me off or make me look bad. Cosying up with those dykes at the shelter, making out like you're some kind of battered wife yourself. And now here you are with your great dyke friend. Can't make a move without her, can you? You never could.' He pushed his face up to hers. 'I thought we were going to talk?' he hissed.

Allyson wiped the saliva from her face. None of it felt real. Her emotions were distant, her reactions felt like those of somebody else. 'What do you want to talk about?' she asked.

He turned to Shelley. 'Not with her here. Either she goes, or I go.'

'You don't get to make any demands,' Allyson told him. 'She's here because I asked her to be. Because the last time I saw you, you hit me.'

'And now that makes you a battered wife?' he scoffed. 'So you call on your lesbian chum for protection.'

'Stop talking about her like that!' Allyson cried. 'She's done nothing to you, so . . .'

Shelley stood up. 'I'm going to wait in the sitting room,' she said to Bob, 'because I can see that as long as I'm here you're going to carry on behaving like the asshole you are.'

Allyson saw his fist tighten and grabbed it with her hands. As soon as Shelley was gone she let go and picked up her glass. 'What do you want to talk about?' she said, as calmly as she could.

He slumped down in the chair Shelley had vacated, but she could see his temper was still raw. 'Aren't you going to offer me a drink?' he said.

'No.'

He picked up the bottle anyway, and refilled the glass Shelley had left. 'Why did you ask her to be here?' he said. 'It would have been all right if it was just me and you.'

'Would it?' she said. 'Did you read the *Standard* tonight?'

He seemed thrown for a moment, then said, 'No. Why? What are those bastards saying about me now?'

'Actually, it wasn't about you, it was about me. And the programme.'

'So what's new? The darling of the press gets herself a few more pages of free publicity?'

Allyson looked at him and through the muddle of hostility and confusion she tried to find the man she loved. She was sure he'd come in here, had been there at the door, but where was he now?

'What the fuck are you looking at?' he said irritably.

'I don't know,' she answered. 'What's happened to you?'

'Oh, for God's sake, a typical Shelley comment if ever I heard one. Why can't you be your own person for once?'

'Bob, what have I done to make you hate me like this?'

His eyes were refusing to meet hers, but she could see them burning up with frustration, which told her that though he didn't appear drunk, this wine was probably topping up more than a few shots of gin. 'What you did with the bank,' he mumbled. 'You've really fucked me up.'

'Bob, you left me for a girl barely out of a gym slip,' she reminded him sharply, 'a girl who I trusted every bit as much as I trusted you, so do you seriously think I give a damn what you might be suffering now, because of the bank? And look at you! What the hell's happened to you? You're a mess!'

'I don't have any fucking money, that's what's happened to me!' he yelled.

'Not all your work's dried up, you must be earning something ... Or no, don't tell me, what you are managing to get you're spending on booze. Well, we've been down that road before, haven't we? So let's see how good Tessa is at bailing you out, shall we? She gets paid well, so ...'

'Don't come your uppity fucking madam bit with me!' he cried, slamming his fists on the table. 'She doesn't earn enough for us to get the kind of flat we should be in, and well you know it. So, OK, you want to gloat, you go right ahead and gloat, because you're right, we're squashed up in a shithole of a bedsit somewhere at the back end of nowhere, while you're here in *my* home, sitting on *my* money ...'

Fury blazed from her eyes. 'This is *my* home,' she seethed.

'Wrong!' he shouted.

'It was a wedding present from *my* parents!'

'But it's in both our names. And I've checked with a lawyer. This flat is as much mine as it is yours, and I want to sell. I've got an estate agent coming round,' he glanced at his watch, 'in about twenty minutes.'

Allyson was white. Dimly she wondered how much more she could take. First her husband, then her job, now her home. Then suddenly she was on her feet. 'Get out!' she spat. 'Just get the hell out of here and don't contact me again unless it's through a lawyer.'

'I told you, I've got someone coming . . .'

'I don't give a damn who you've got coming. You won't be here, so . . .'

'I'm putting the country house on the market too.'

'No!' she cried. 'You've got no right to do this.'

'You're the one who wants a divorce,' he reminded her.

'Because you left!' she screamed. 'Because you're the one who's sleeping with a kid half your age and you don't care who knows it. And what about all the other women, Bob? What about all the years you deceived me, made a fool out of me? Everyone knew, didn't they? Everyone, but me. So don't come here snivelling to me now that you haven't got any money. Because I couldn't give a fuck. And answer me this, Bob. Where's your precious little baby whore tonight? Why aren't you with her, celebrating? Surely she told you she's on the telly tonight. Hah, you didn't know, did you? Seems like things are working out really well for you, Bob.'

'Bitch!' he snarled. His glass tipped over as he lunged across the table, but he didn't reach her. 'She told me,' he spat.

'Oh yeah, right,' she said.

'*She told me*!' he thundered. This time the table skidded across the floor, and before she could move his hands were round her throat. 'You bitch!' he sobbed as he tried to choke her. 'What are you doing to my life?'

'Let go!' she gasped. 'Bob, let me go.'

'Let her go!' Shelley yelled, coming in the door.

His grip loosened and, struggling for breath, Allyson wrenched herself away and went to stand over the sink.

Bob and Shelley were motionless in the silence, both staring at Allyson, until Shelley turned to Bob and said, 'Just go.'

Visibly shaken, and still breathing hard, he brushed past her and went to get his coat. 'Tell her,' he said, suddenly turning back at the door, 'she's got to sell. Tessa's having a baby, we need a decent home.'

Shelley spun round to look at Allyson, then suddenly she was behind Bob, physically shoving him out of the door.

For a long time after he'd gone neither Allyson nor Shelley spoke. Shelley put an arm round Allyson's shoulders, but though Allyson didn't push her away, she didn't welcome the comfort either. Her eyes were dry, the shock, the utter devastation, was almost palpable on her face. In those few short words Bob had not only annihilated any hope she could ever have that he might come back, he had destroyed the entire fabric of everything they had ever meant to each other. She was still reeling, hardly able to push past the numbing wall of pain and confusion. In a little less than eight months she would be forty, not too late to have children, but at about that time her husband, the man she wanted to have children with, would have one with somebody else. He would be at the bedside of . . . But even her rabid imagination shut down in the face of such unprecedented heartache.

Finally she turned to Shelley and said, 'I'd like to be left alone now, if you don't mind.'

Shelley's arm was still round her. 'Allyson, I . . .'

'I'll be OK,' Allyson said, moving away. 'I've got a lot of things to work out, and I'd like to be alone while I do it.'

Shelley looked deeply reluctant. 'Please tell me you're not planning to do anything . . .'

Allyson shook her head. 'No. I'm . . .' She took a breath, but no more words would come. It didn't matter because she didn't want to say any more. She didn't want to let anything that was inside her go out into the world. She needed to be contained, apart, shut off from all the hurt that was trying to crush her, disconnected from those she had trusted and who were now betraying her.

'Allyson,' Shelley said again.

'Just go,' Allyson snapped, and turning away she walked along the hall to her bedroom, refusing to give Shelley the reassurance she was seeking. Let Shelley stew, and let the rest of the world go to hell, because right now she couldn't think of a single reason to go on with her life, so she was damned if she was going to pretend to Shelley that there was one.

Bob was due back any minute, and Tessa knew that there was a very good chance he was going to be in a bad mood. He wouldn't have enjoyed going to Allyson cap in hand for money, so she wouldn't ask him how he'd got on straight away, especially not with Julian being here, because he probably wouldn't want to discuss private matters in front of someone he'd never met before. And anyway, it could wait, because they were going to celebrate her first time on telly in a very special way, which was why she had invited Julian to come round.

She smiled at Julian, as he sifted through the CDs over on the sideboard and tried not to show how nervous he was. It was easy to make Julian do things, even when he didn't want to. Her real brother hadn't been like that. It had been the other way round with him, which was why she liked Julian so much. It was better being the one in charge. Before, everyone else had been in charge. Now she'd turned it all around.

As the opening bars of a Back Street Boys number began to play on the CD, Julian returned to the armchair he'd been sitting in earlier and attempted to beat time to the music. It wasn't much of a cover, because his fingers were out of rhythm, and he still looked so anxious he might bolt any second. Tessa smiled again to put him at his ease, but it didn't seem to work, and when the door suddenly opened and Bob came in Julian leapt straight to his feet.

Tessa was sitting on the sofa, her back to the door, her legs curled in under her. 'Hi,' she said, reaching a hand over her shoulder to Bob.

'Who's he?' Bob demanded, glaring at Julian.

'That's Jules,' Tessa informed him, giving Julian a wink.

Bob's expression turned even uglier. 'What's he doing here?'

'I can go,' Julian said. 'I just . . .'

'No. Sit down,' Tessa insisted, getting to her feet. 'Bob, you old silly. Just calm down, will you? Let me get you a drink,' and taking his hand she led him into the kitchen. 'I taped the programme so you could see it,' she told him, reaching into the cupboard for a fresh bottle of gin. 'You got my message, didn't you, telling you I was going to be on?'

'What's he doing here?' Bob repeated.

Tessa turned and gazed up into his eyes. 'I invited him,' she said. 'Now, don't I get a kiss?'

He touched his lips to hers, but she caught his face in her hands and used her tongue to ease him gently into a calmer frame of mind.

'Better?' she said when she'd finished.

His eyes were less hostile now, and she could tell he was mildly aroused. 'Where's that drink?' he said gruffly.

'Coming right up.' As she poured she slipped a hand between his thighs, then kept shooting him glances, until, rolling his eyes, he said, 'OK, what are you up to? And what the fuck *is* he doing here?'

Tessa put her head back so he could kiss her again, which he did, groaning softly as her hand increased its pressure. 'Get rid of him,' he murmured. This was just the kind of antidote he needed to help settle him down after the nightmare he'd just been through.

'I can't do that,' she said. 'He's here to, you know.'

No, he didn't know.

'You know, what we talked about,' she said, handing him his drink.

He took a generous mouthful then looked at her again.

'You know, me and you two,' she giggled.

He was about to drink again, but at that he stopped. He didn't speak for a moment, as his mind began playing with the recognition of her words. Then, to be certain he was understanding this correctly, he said, 'Are you saying what I think you're saying?'

She grinned. 'He said he'll do it.'

Bob's eyes were bulging. Jesus Christ, she was serious. But the hell was he getting into anything like that, and slamming down his drink he marched back into the sitting room. 'Time to go,' he said to Julian. 'There's been a mistake . . .'

Tessa was right behind him, clutching his arm. 'Bob! He's my friend,' she cried. 'I invited him here.'

'It's OK,' Julian said, grabbing his coat. 'I've got to go. Really.'

'No!' Tessa protested. 'It's my big night, we're supposed to be celebrating.'

Bob looked at her hot flushed cheeks and bright, feverish eyes. She really did want this.

'You promised,' she said sulkily to Julian.

'Tessa. Can't you see you're embarrassing the boy,' Bob barked.

She crossed swiftly to the door to block Julian's way. 'You promised,' she repeated.

Julian looked helplessly at Bob.

Bob stared at them both, then suddenly he felt so exhausted, so battered by the entire craziness of the past two hours, that, unable to deal with this any more, he turned back into the kitchen. What was the point in fighting her? He had no intention of going along with it, so why was he wasting his energy protesting, when all he really wanted was to drink himself into oblivion in an effort to escape that abominably ugly scene with Allyson that kept playing itself over and over in his mind. Jesus Christ, it had all gone so horribly wrong, had soared so frighteningly out of his control that even now he couldn't be sure how it had happened. Except Shelley being there had started it. He knew that much. If only Allyson hadn't done that, but even the misery of having Shelley witness his humiliation was no excuse for the way he had ranted and raved at Allyson, tried to choke her, and had then thrown . . . His mind recoiled from the unspeakable cruelty of how he had told her about the baby. He was never going to be able to forgive himself for that, never, and he doubted she would either.

Filling a glass with gin he drank it down in one go, then filled the glass again. The shame was still there, crawling around all his excuses and forcing him to see himself for the weak, contemptible specimen he was, not only for the way he'd told her about the baby, but for the appalling self-delusion he'd gone in there with, when he'd actually thought he could enlist her help in extricating him from the terrible mess he'd got himself into. He'd even managed to convince himself that once she realized how bad things were for him she'd offer to give him the flat, for the baby's sake of course, or maybe she'd work it all out so that he could go back to her and she would somehow take care of Tessa. Christ, what kind of idiot was he? And just what kind of fool did he take his wife for, to actually make himself believe that her kindness and compassion for others would extend itself to making a gift of her own home to the two people who had hurt her the most?

His heart was thudding beats of self-hatred, along with a hot, painful denial that he had actually done what he had. He drained another glass of gin in the hope that its burn would nullify the awful truth. The trouble was, Allyson had always understood in the past, had always been there to rescue him from the dark and tangled places he stumbled into without really knowing how. So he'd allowed himself to believe that she'd do it again. And he might have gone on believing it, had Shelley not been there to strip away the delusion and leave him staggering around blindly in the glaring reality of his madness. So really it was Shelley's fault that everything had gone so disastrously wrong. And it was Allyson's too, for letting Shelley be there.

Refilling his glass he walked unsteadily back into the sitting room, and blinked when he saw Julian instead of Tessa. 'Like a drink?' he said, trying to remember the boy's name.

Julian looked undecided, so Bob went back to get him one anyway. He was finding it hard to get his mind round any kind of coherence now, there was so much going on in his head. Allyson, Shelley, Tessa, Julian. Every one of them was a problem, but though his thoughts seemed to start out all right, they kept losing direction and floundering off into areas of total confusion. And Allyson, God damn her, was so together over there it made him want to ... He staggered back from the brink of that one, drank some more gin and lunged off in another direction that allowed him to concede that Allyson was probably hurting as much as he was, might even be missing him, but he only had to look at her to see how well she was handling it. She had everything. The flat. The money. A job. Friends. A wealthy family ... And if she hadn't pulled that stunt with the bank things might have been different for him.

So whichever way he looked at it, whatever sympathy he tried to muster for the way she might be feeling, he always ended up in the same damned place, that the horrendous mess he was in was all thanks to her.

Picking up the drinks he carried them through to where Julian was still sitting stiffly on the edge of the sofa. 'Where's Tessa?' he slurred, handing Julian a glass.

'In the bedroom,' he answered.

Bob looked at the door and tried to focus. Then he suddenly remembered the purpose of Julian being here, and, turning to look at the boy again, he almost laughed. Christ, the whole thing was so bizarre. Here he was, the famous Bob Jaymes, a man of wealth and property, stuck in Peckham with no money, a pregnant teenager and the other half of the teenager's whim.

He slumped down in a chair and continued to stare at Julian, watching him squirm and doubting very much that the kid had the guts to do what Tessa wanted. 'So, have you ever done anything like this before?' Bob asked, nodding towards the bedroom.

Julian shook his head. He tried to drink and it dribbled down his chin. 'I – I'm a virgin,' he said.

Bob blinked as though he hadn't heard right, then suddenly he wanted to laugh again. But the urge was obscured by a confusion he could find no shape to. He drank more gin. Everything was starting to feel strange, kind of distorted and . . . He tried to get to his feet, but the ground was moving . . . He tried again. This time he made it, but as he lurched upright the walls seemed to be closing in on him.

'Are you all right?' he heard Julian ask.

He looked down at the boy, whose pale, anxious face was rotating in a blurry kind of cloud. 'Yeah, I'm fine,' he slurred. 'I just need some air.'

As the door closed behind him Julian heard him stumble on the stairs and swear crudely. Then a few seconds later the front door slammed shut. Julian looked over at the bedroom and wondered what Tessa was doing. He felt uneasy, as though he was a part of something he didn't understand. He got to his feet and went to the window. The street outside was dark and empty. No sign of Bob. He wondered what he should do. He hadn't really wanted to come here, but Tessa had been so insistent, and on such a high after her first transmission, that he just hadn't been able to say no. He turned to look at the bedroom door again. He could hear her moving around, and suddenly her promise of sex, of allowing him to take part in her most treasured fantasy, as she'd called it, seemed to have a dark, unnerving edge to it. It wasn't right. Nothing about this was right, from Bob being so drunk, to his own ludicrous presence here. Then, like Bob, he suddenly needed some air, and before he could get sucked any further into the bewildering depths of whatever was going on, he snatched up his coat and left.

In the bedroom Tessa was carefully folding her clothes. Today had been such a great day, and now tonight was going to be even better. She felt flooded with fondness for Bob, and for Julian – and kind of edgy and excited about what they were all going to do. She was even starting to toy with the fantasy of having Julian move in with them when she and Bob finally went to live in that enormous flat on Cheyne Walk. She wasn't quite sure how Bob had handled that yet. It could be that Allyson would prefer to sell the flat and give Bob his share of the money, rather than move out so that Bob and Tessa could move in. Tessa could hardly blame her for that, though she'd definitely prefer to live there, given the choice.

'OK, I'm ready,' she called out, turning to look at herself in the mirror. She smoothed a hand over the small mound of her belly. She'd always been that shape, so couldn't claim that it was the baby starting to show.

'Hey you two,' she shouted, turning to the door and waiting for it to open.

Still no-one came, so in the end she opened the door herself, and discovered to her amazement that the sitting room was empty.

She wasn't angry, she was simply startled and disappointed, and concerned about Bob, because he might be off getting drunk somewhere again.

She found him, half an hour later, in a dark corner of the pub, staring blindly at a full glass of gin. Loud music was blaring from a jukebox in the corner, and bright, flashing lights strobed around the near-empty room.

Sitting down next to him, she buried her hands deeply in the pockets of her oversized coat. 'Are you OK?' she asked.

He didn't answer, merely continued to stare at the glass.

Tessa picked it up and took a sip. His eyes remained rooted to the same spot.

Putting the glass down again, she reached up to smooth back his hair. 'Is Allyson going to let us have the flat?' she asked softly.

He took a breath, but no words came out.

'It's all right,' she said soothingly. 'I'm not sure we've really got any right to it . . .'

'We've got every right to it,' he slurred. 'So she either lets us have it, or she has to sell.'

'And the country house?'

He didn't answer.

She cupped her hands around his face and turned him to look at her. 'Was it really terribly hard?' she said gently, her black eyes showing her concern.

Still he didn't answer.

She kissed him softly on the mouth. 'It's all right, I understand how you must be feeling,' she said. 'But please, don't be angry with me. We need a good home for our baby, that's all that really matters.'

His eyes weren't focusing on her. They were somewhere else, in a place he didn't know and didn't

190

want to leave. Then dimly he became aware of her pulling faces in an effort to make him laugh, so to satisfy her he attempted a smile.

'What happened to Julian?' she asked, taking another sip of his drink. 'Did you frighten him off?'

His eyes drew focus for a moment, and seemed to drag his mind with them. He thought of Allyson and how he'd wrecked everything just to be with this girl. He didn't seem able to sort out why now, yet somewhere deep inside the bewildering fog in his brain he knew that despite the whole rotten mess, the regrets, the pain, the fear and the shame, he still couldn't say that he wanted to give her up. Maybe what he wanted was to have them both. His wife and the secure, stable, and fulfilling life they'd always had, and Tessa, this girl whom he never seemed able to get enough of.

'Julian?' she prompted with a smile.

Oh yes, Julian. His vision was blurring again, but he could still see her, smiling at him with those beautiful lips that he got so lost in. Had Julian ever got lost in them? 'Would that really turn you on?' he said. 'To be with two men?'

She laughed, and drew his hands into hers. 'You know it would,' she said. 'We talk about it all the time when we share our fantasies.'

'Have you done it before?' he asked.

Her smile widened, telling him she had.

'Who with?'

She looked over at his drink, then fishing out the lemon she began sucking out the juice.

He waited until she put it down again. 'Who with?' he repeated, feeling that for some reason it was important to know.

She was still staring at the lemon, then with a smile she picked up his hand again and drew it inside her coat, onto her bare flesh. 'It doesn't matter. They're dead now,' she said.

Chapter 8

The UK head office of Leisure and Media Inc was on the south side of Russell Square in the centre of London. It was from here that Mark Reiner ran the successful media and catering empire he and his older brother, Nick, had built up over the past twenty years. Though Nick was headquartered in New York, they did their best to meet up at least once a month, which more often than not turned out to be in New York. This month, however, Nick and his wife, Claudia, had flown to London. Claudia wanted to shop and catch up with old friends. Mark's wife, Heather, had not come with them. She'd checked into the Betty Ford Clinic six weeks ago and didn't expect to be out in time to celebrate their divorce. Not that she'd have celebrated with Mark, more likely she'd fly straight to the exclusive multimillion-dollar mansion that she and her new budding movie-star lover had recently acquired. Mark was fully aware that it was the settlement he had made on her that had paid for the Hollywood hideaway, but that didn't rankle anywhere near as much as the loss of the Devonshire home he had spent millions restoring.

Though his marriage had been a resounding failure, the business triumphs of the past twelve years had been spectacular. He and Nick had come a long way from the lowly west country roots that had been transplanted to Idaho, USA, when Nick was twelve and Mark was eleven. After college they'd headed straight for New York. Within a year they'd owned one small restaurant on the Upper West Side, not as fashionable then as it was now. Nick had persuaded a local radio station to promote them heavily, and, to make a long story short, they'd ended up buying into the radio station, opening up more restaurants around the city, gradually going into hotels and then into television. Claudia, Mark's sister-in-law, now ran the TV cable company the two brothers owned in the States, while Nick concentrated on their catering interests, which included a small, extremely upmarket chain of hotels sited in London, New York, Paris, Gstaad, Hong Kong, Sydney – and Ravello, Italy, when the conversion was complete. For his part, Mark had been working for some time now on buying up the British TV station he'd recently acquired. It had provided him with a good reason to base himself in London, and now the takeover was assured he would remain headquartered here, making the restructuring of the station his priority.

And boy, was he making himself unpopular. Already he'd announced plans to axe two lightweight current affairs shows, a struggling drama serial, two spectacularly bad situation comedies, and a local news programme that was so dull a half-hour of fly-fishing would have pulled in more viewers. Along with the programmes would go many of the producers, directors, writers, researchers and presenters whose combined years of service totalled somewhere around a large city's population. At some point he would hire a programme controller to replace Stella Cornbright, someone not only to oversee all the changes he had made, but with the vision to improve on them. He had several candidates in mind, from both sides of the Atlantic, but had yet to begin even preliminary talks.

Oddly, the programme that was giving him the greatest pause for thought was *Soirée*. His first inclination had been to cancel it altogether, but after watching for several nights he'd decided it had a certain style and the ratings, whilst certainly down on the early years, were still respectable. The lunch he'd had with Shelley Bronson a couple of days ago had also gone some way to persuading him that it was worth keeping the show going, at least until the end of its season run in May. If she'd given any sign of resisting his changes he might be taking a different view right now, but as it stood, provided something was done to sharpen up the pace and bring in younger viewers, he was OK with it staying. His guess was that he'd suggested changes Shelley had long wanted, but until now she'd allowed her friendship with Allyson to take precedence over her judgement. So he was going to be the bad guy, which was fine by him, he was in this to make money, not friends.

'Get Shelley Bronson on the line,' he said through the intercom to Corinne, his assistant. 'Then call Max Weatherby and tell him I'll join the video conference with New York at eleven thirty.'

While he waited he turned to his computer to pull up the company's investment portfolio. As he perused it, he rocked gently back and forth in his giant leather chair. Outside trees were being buffeted by fierce winds, which ripped away their leaves and carried them into the traffic that was constantly circling the square. Mark's office was on the first floor of an old Regency building that still retained all the charm and character of its original high ceilings and creaking wooden floors, which had now been covered with luxurious black carpet. Everything in his chief executive's suite was of the highest quality and outstanding workmanship, from the hand-made Italian desk and bookcases to the sumptuous leather sofas and armchairs. There were two original Pollocks hanging either side of the Swedish birchwood TV cabinet, and more garishly colourful and intriguing abstracts on the other walls, all done by the young American artists that he and Nick were sponsoring. The offices of the finance director and company lawyer were housed in the same building, with more original art hanging on their walls, and equally as tasteful furniture in the more modern, Italian style to finish off the exceptionally elegant and de luxe look of the young and extremely rich media company.

He was still scrolling through the latest figures when his assistant buzzed through to announce that Shelley was on the line. Picking up the phone he clicked his assistant off and connected himself to the call. 'Good morning,' he said.

'Hello.'

He smiled and sat back in his chair. Her voice was as sultry as he remembered, and he had no difficulty in picturing the fullness of her lips as she spoke. 'I enjoyed our lunch the other day,' he told her. 'Sorry I had to rush off.'

She said nothing.

Amused by the silence, he said, 'I watched the show the night before last.'

'And you want to talk about Tessa.'

Of course she would know that, it was almost certainly why she had slipped the girl into the programme, to get his attention, and show him that she already had young talent on tap. 'How much experience does she have?' he asked.

'Virtually none. But that needn't be a problem.'

'I'll trust you on that. Would the start of the New Year be too soon to turn things around?'

'No,' she answered.

He looked down at the notes he'd made on their meeting. 'Send me a breakdown on what you'd do with a fifty per cent increase in budget,' he said.

'You'll have it by the end of the day.'

'Then we'll discuss it over dinner,' he said.

'Bibendum. Eight thirty,' and without waiting for an answer he rang off.

Allyson had spent the past two days, and nights, trying to come up with something sensational with which to impress Mark Reiner. It was either that, she'd decided the night Bob had told her Tessa was pregnant, or five bottles of paracetamol and the lower oven of the smart Bosch unit. And if all her efforts to hang onto her job failed, then the paracetamol and gassed-up oven always remained an option. Indeed, there had been plenty of times over the past forty-eight hours when the second option had come very close to promotion, and in truth she was so exhausted now, as she sat at her desk and stared blurry-eyed at her computer, that desperation was hampering her ability to think straight, and tiredness was threatening to make her emotional.

For a moment she seemed not to know what the time was, though she thought it was still morning, and the huge pile of mail beside her probably confirmed it. It might not be a bad idea for her to read some of that mail, she was thinking, for she received so many letters of support and encouragement these days, telling her what an inspiration she was to others, and how deeply moved her viewers were that she continued her work with those in need, despite her own misfortune, that the kindness of those letters frequently sent strength and hope streaming back into her heart. How considerate some people were, that they bothered to take the time to write those letters. And how odd that it should be hundreds of faceless strangers who were now providing the anchor in her life, preventing her from drifting even further into depression, or drowning in the ceaseless waves of despair.

This morning, though, she didn't feel she could read them. She was too close to the edge already, and the kindness contained in the neatly typed or boldly scrawled words rarely failed to move her to tears. And she didn't want to cry, not here in the office, where people would see her. Tears were for the privacy of her bedroom, just like dread of the future was for the privacy of her heart.

So she turned away from the letters, and was about to print out the proposals she'd drawn up to show Mark Reiner, when she found herself looking across the office to where Tessa was sitting. A wild and raging hatred surged into her heart. Then came the panicked terror of the months ahead, when she'd have to watch that girl growing big with Bob's child, and feel herself growing smaller and smaller in the might of the pain. So maybe it would be better if she left the programme altogether, freed herself from having to see the girl every day and went somewhere new, another company, another city, maybe even another country.

Minutes later she was still staring at Tessa. With her shaggy dark hair, rosebud lips and glittering ebony eyes she looked so young and radiant. So happy and in love with the world. Everyone had complimented her on her piece the other night, even Allyson. She'd spoken to her warmly, even affectionately, for she hadn't wanted anyone even to guess what was going on inside her.

Shelley knew, though, which was probably why Shelley had refrained from adding to the praise. But the restraint had done little to ease the tension between them, they'd barely spoken since the night Allyson had asked Shelley to leave.

Finally Allyson turned back to her computer, and after printing out her plan for survival she tried to concentrate on that night's show. The names of the guests were in front of her, but no matter how long she looked at them they weren't sinking in. All she could think about now was her age, and that if she was too old there would be no survival. But maybe there was a chance she could prove Mark Reiner wrong, show him

197

what a loyal following she had, how the ratings dipped when she wasn't there to host.

She went through the rest of the morning in a daze, somehow managing to respond to anyone who spoke to her, and even took part in a discussion on an item in that day's news. Not for a moment did she reveal the fear that she was going to be cast aside, that this hi-tech warehouse that was virtually a second home was no longer going to be a place to which she would come every day. She kept reminding herself that nothing had yet been decided, and even if it ended up going against her Shelley had said the Night Cap slot could still be hers. But wasn't that going to be even more humiliating than being thrown off altogether? And if she stayed she'd have no choice but to watch Tessa getting fatter with child and more famous for her little film slots and happier going home to Bob every night . . . Oh, no, no, no! Please God, no! This couldn't be happening. Somehow she had to find the energy to fight back and make something work for herself.

'Can I come in?' Shelley said, tapping on the door of the dressing room just after lunch.

'Of course,' Allyson said, feigning a lightness she hadn't felt for so long she was amazed she could still mimic it.

'God, it's been crazy today,' Shelley sighed, closing the door. 'My phone's been ringing off the hook.'

Knowing it was because of the official announcement of Mark Reiner's takeover, Allyson made no comment.

Shelley looked at her watch. 'I know you're due in make-up any time,' she said, 'but I've got some news, so maybe you could meet me back here after the recording?'

Allyson didn't show how frightened she was, or angry that Shelley was able to carry on as though nothing had changed. Shelley hadn't even mentioned the baby. But that was OK, Allyson didn't want to discuss it, not even with Shelley. And besides, she was due in front of the camera soon, and now she was fighting for her life she couldn't afford to let her terrible fears and misgivings show.

It wasn't clear how she got through the programme, or how she performed. She simply responded to the countdown, spoke to the camera and interviewed her guests. They recorded as-live so the filmed insert was played in. Today's was a story on an absurd neighbourhood feud somewhere in Oxford. Richard was the reporter. He was twenty-seven, young enough for his job to be safe. At the end she watched the credits roll. Tessa had researched Richard's story. Obviously her job would be safe too.

'Do you know what?' Allyson said when she found Shelley waiting in her dressing room afterwards. 'I think I'll have a drink. I mean a proper one. What about you?'

Shelley looked surprised, then decided it might be a good idea. 'Vodka and tonic. Light on the vodka,' she said.

Wearing a floor-length Ungaro creation with a slit up the front to mid-thigh and a drop back that descended to her waist, Allyson crossed to the drinks tray. She'd spent some time after the show talking to the guests, and seemed slightly clearer now, and calmer than she'd been an hour ago. As she poured, Shelley was chattering on about how well the recording had gone, so maybe she could take some heart from that and remind herself that no definitive action had been decided on, so there was really nothing to worry about yet.

How was it possible to be so wrong?

As Shelley told her the news, about trying Tessa out for the Cocktails, Allyson could feel the blood draining from her face. The pounding of her heart crescendoed until it was so loud it seemed to drown out Shelley's words. But she heard them, every last one of them.

Her drink remained in its glass. Her hands wouldn't

move, her voice was gone. Her entire world was moving to a place far beyond her reach. First her husband, then her home, now her programme. Was there anything left for Tessa Dukes to take?

Her eyes were dry as she turned them to Shelley. 'And you agree with him?' she said. 'You think Tessa should take the first half of the show, leaving me the Night Cap?'

'I didn't put it to the test,' Shelley confessed, 'but it's my belief, if I don't agree, he'll axe the show altogether.'

'He dislikes me that much?'

'It's not personal.'

Leaving her drink Allyson walked over to the clothes rail and started to change.

Shelley watched her, and was shocked to see just how thin she had become.

When she was dressed Allyson picked up her bag and started to leave.

'Don't you want to discuss it?' Shelley said.

Allyson stopped, and turned round. 'What's there to discuss?' she answered. 'You've already made up your mind. Based on a single report by one pretty young girl, you and Mark Reiner have decided to rub my face in . . .'

'Oh Ally!' Shelley groaned. 'Don't see it like that. It's not . . .'

'This programme is the one thing I had left to hang onto,' Allyson cried.

'Ally, it's a cruel world, you know that, especially for women, and even more so for women in your field, where age matters – maybe even more than talent.'

'But Tessa's got talent too? Is that what you're saying?'

'Probably. Possibly.'

Allyson's face was tight with anger. 'You know, I always thought you didn't like her,' she said caustically.

'I don't, much. But I don't want to lose the show. It means as much to me as it does to you.'

'But you get to keep it!'

200

Shelley looked as awkward as Allyson had intended.

'Correction, reinvent it. Without me,' Allyson added, fiercely.

Shelley was shaking her head. 'Look, I know you think I've betrayed you,' she said, 'and if you want me to put up a fight for you to keep the Cocktails, I will. But trust my instincts on this, Ally. If I insist on you keeping the entire show Mark Reiner will just pull the plug.'

Allyson's eyes went down. Emotions were building inside her, pushing her to a point where she might explode with the pain. 'Why her?' she said, her voice shaking. 'There have to be a thousand other girls out there who could bring youth and talent and whatever else you're looking for to the show, so why does it have to be *her*?'

'If you didn't have personal issues with her, you'd be suggesting her yourself,' Shelley said.

Though she hated to hear it, Allyson knew it was true, but that didn't change the fact that Shelley had to know how this was destroying her. 'What about the baby?' she demanded. 'What are you going to do when it starts to show? And how the hell do you think I'm going to feel, sharing a programme with the kid *who's pregnant by my husband*?'

Shelley's eyes remained on hers. She'd already thought of that, and the truth was she didn't know how Allyson would feel, because it would probably be worse than anything Shelley could imagine. 'The baby could be a problem,' she admitted. 'I'll need to discuss it with Mark.'

Allyson stared at her hard. Was Shelley saying what she thought she was saying? Shelley stared back, and though no words passed between them, Allyson felt that she might just have been thrown something akin to a lifeline.

'Have you told her?' Allyson asked. 'Does she know she's about to become a star?'

'No.'

They were quiet then, Allyson standing rigidly at the door, Shelley perched awkwardly on the arm of a sofa. Allyson was still horribly worked up and terrified she was going to cry.

'Ally,' Shelley finally said.

Allyson looked at her, then without another word she turned and walked out of the door. She didn't know where she was going, wasn't even sure if she could drive, but she had to get away from Shelley, from this building, and from the beautiful, blissfully happy girl upstairs whose youth and good fortune were taking over her life.

'So how did she take it?'

'Badly, I think,' Shelley said. 'She left the building and I haven't been able to find her since.'

Mark Reiner's eyes were charting the wine waiter's movements as he opened a bottle of vintage Bordeaux and poured some into a glass for Mark to taste. After approving it, Mark said, 'Are you worried?'

'A bit. She's been having a rough time of it lately. Tessa Dukes is living with her husband.'

'Allyson's husband?' he said, showing surprise.

Shelley nodded. Clearly he didn't read the tabloids, though there was a good chance he'd been out of the country when the story had first broken. His expression was once again inscrutable, but she could see this news had made an impression.

'Is she going to accept the Night Cap slot?' he asked.

'I don't know. She probably needs time to think.'

'Of course. Have you spoken to Tessa yet?'

'No. Not until I've found out what Allyson intends to do.'

He seemed thoughtful for a moment, then raising his glass he touched it gently to hers, and Shelley could sense the subject of Allyson's position on the programme sliding down his list of priorities as he allowed his eyes to roam the smooth, candlelit planes of her face, while his imagination was hopefully taking him a whole lot further. She knew she intrigued him, as he intrigued her, and she wondered how ruthless he could be. How professional? How controlled? All the time she'd been dressing for the evening she'd felt the sharp bite of lust accompanying her decisions about what to wear. Her dress was knee-length, heavily sequined and halter-necked. Knowing the selection she had made to go underneath would drive him wild, were he to see it, was enough. She had no intention of seducing him yet, for toying with him this way, and with herself, both satisfied and intensified the desire. It also began adding an edge to their discussion that meant no matter how professional the subject, the personal was always there, flowing like a slow, sultry river through the *double entendres* of their softly spoken words and deliciously intimate looks.

'I've looked at how you would spend the budget increase were you to get it,' he said.

'And?'

His eyes dropped momentarily to her mouth. 'I'm impressed,' he responded.

Her dark, sensuous gaze remained on his as the compliment folded its promise warmly around her. 'So do I get the increase?' she said.

'Not as much as you've asked for, but I imagine you figured that into your request.'

Shelley's eyebrows flickered upwards.

'If you're going to be basing one programme a month out of a European city,' he said, 'I should put you in touch with the other side of my organization. We have several hotels on the Continent that could offer special deals.'

'I'll inform the programme manager,' she said, still holding his eyes with her own, and feeling the blend of their awareness as her breasts rose and fell with her deepening breath. She took another sip of wine and watched him watching her. Though there was an unquestionable irony in his eyes, his features, she thought, were more austere than she'd first noticed, and the harsh masculinity of his body was inviting her imagination to experience the force, maybe even the violence of his passion. A small sigh of anticipation shuddered through her, and her eyes fluttered briefly closed.

'How did you become a producer?' he asked.

'The usual way. Through researching.'

'You didn't want to present?'

'If I'd chosen presenting, what's happening to Allyson would be happening to me now,' she said.

'But you're not married.'

'I was referring to the programme.'

'Were you ever? Married?'

'No.' Then she added, 'The last significant relationship I had ended eight years ago.'

He was clearly surprised. 'I find it hard to believe that a woman like you has lived all that time without a man.'

Her eyes were burning. 'I haven't,' she said.

He cocked a single eyebrow, telling her he had received the message, then their food arrived and as he watched her eat, the fork gliding smoothly from her lips, the wine moistening them, her fingers circling the stem of the wine glass, she knew the power of her sensuality was affecting him deeply. He probably hadn't expected her to turn him on this much, and though she hadn't started out with the intention of going this far, she was finding very little reason now to continue holding back.

However, she was in no rush, so they continued to talk, about the programme, about life, until their plates were taken and they were offered a menu for dessert.

He declined for them both. She looked at him in surprise then felt her skin start to burn, as he said, 'I think it's time I fucked you.'

Her lips parted as her breath became suddenly heavy. 'Yes, I think it is,' she said.

He drove them to her apartment. Neither of them spoke, except for her to give him directions.

She led him up the single flight of stairs and unlocked the front door. Her heart was pounding. She was on fire for him, and the moment they were inside he grabbed her, bringing her harshly against him. She looked into his eyes and continued to look into them as he crushed her mouth with his and drew the hem of her dress up to her waist. His hands moved over the gossamer-fine rubber straps that were binding her body, and as she sensed the sudden charge to his lust, she began tearing at his shirt, pushing it with his jacket from his shoulders and biting his neck.

He spun her round and rammed her back up against the wall. His cock was so hard it hurt. His trousers were undone, and as she slid down to her knees he pulled the dress over her head and saw more rubber straps.

She sucked him hard and bit him. Her tongue was all over him. He grabbed her shoulders and brought her to her feet. The black straps circled her waist, her breasts, and disappeared between her legs. They covered nothing. She was totally revealed to him in a cage of black rubber. It was blowing his mind.

In her high heels she matched his height. She took him by the hand and led him to the sitting room. Everything was as elegant and benign as she was bewitching and brazen. He took hold of her breasts in their triangular black frames and groaned aloud as she grabbed his cock, scratching her nails along the length of it. The pain was exquisite and intense. He bit the hardened flesh of her nipple. She cried out, but didn't push him away.

Then she was walking across the room. Her buttocks were bare, two tight ribbons of rubber held the cheeks apart. She reached the sofa and glanced over her shoulder. Her dark eyes were smouldering with immeasurable lust.

Parting her legs she bent over the sofa. She was speaking to him now, telling him what she wanted in a language that was inflaming him beyond any point of control. He came up behind her, stooped and bit into her flesh. She moaned and writhed and bent more steeply. He stood up, raised a hand and brought it crashing down on her buttocks. He did it again and again.

The stinging pain was electric, sparking through her genitals, rushing to her clitoris. Wave after wave hit her, pushing her through one orgasm to the next to the next. She was dizzied by lust, breathless with pleasure. He widened her legs more, pushed a hand between them, his fingers right up inside her. His fist was like nothing she'd felt between her legs before. She could hear herself screaming, begging him for more and yet more. She came into his hand, gripping it over and over. Then suddenly he thrust his cock to the core of her and her legs lost power. He held her up and rammed her.

His orgasm was explosive. It pounded into her with unmerciful force. She was bucking beneath him, coming again and shuddering with the might of it. He pulled out of her quickly, spun her round and pushed her to the floor. He lay over her, entered her and began a new journey to the end. Her legs and arms entwined him, her mouth and tongue assailed him. She stayed hot for him all night, matching the vigorous slamming of his hips and harsh demands of his body with her own.

The next morning she woke him with fresh coffee and croissants. As he ate she did things to him, and to herself, that stole his appetite for food and concentrated it solely on her. He could see how harshly he'd used her through the night, but she seemed to want more, only more.

When the time came it was all he could do to drag himself away. He watched her dress and became aroused all over again. She was sensational. She oozed more femininity than an overcrowded harem. She walked him to the door, kissed him, and before he knew it he was inside her again. She was incredible. Indescribable. Insatiable.

It was the middle of the afternoon. Allyson hadn't made an appointment. She simply turned up at Mark Reiner's office and demanded to see him. She'd worked out everything she was going to say, was determined to deliver it as calmly and succinctly as possible and then listen quietly, unhysterically to his response.

Despite this inner coaxing of discipline, she was horribly agitated and not entirely sure she wasn't verging on the dreaded nervous breakdown. Last night had been one of the worst of her life. If it were possible, literally, to cry oceans, she felt she'd shed every one of them, and her entire body felt bruised now from the power of the storm. Around midnight she'd driven to Tessa's flat half-demented with grief, so desperate to see Bob she hadn't cared what kind of scene she might cause. When she'd got there she sat outside, feeling herself filling up with so much hate and despair that all she'd wanted was to go in and kill them both.

All the way home she'd tried to think of a way to get Tessa out of their lives. Murder seemed the only solution. But unless she could come up with a perfect plan she'd never get away with it. And even if she could, she didn't have what it took to go through with it. Maybe she could pay someone else, but she had no idea how to go about that, and it upset her even more to know that these were nothing more than the wild, deluded ramblings of a rejected, middle-aged woman who was thrashing around all over the place in a desperate bid to keep her life together.

She'd spent this morning at home, working frantically on the plan to save her career. Today was Friday, there

207

was no programme, which was why she was able to be here in Mark Reiner's office now.

The last time they'd met was when she'd interviewed him. She remembered almost nothing about it now, so he obviously hadn't made much of an impression. She was glad, because if she hadn't been intimidated then, there was no reason for her to be now. Of course she hadn't been fighting for her life then.

He kept her waiting more than half an hour. She didn't care. He hadn't known she was coming, and there was no point going in there already worked up over something he might have been unable to avoid.

His assistant made no attempt to talk to her. She was glad about that too. She wasn't sure she had it in her to put on her smiley, presenter's face today. There was a pile of newspapers on the coffee table. She wondered if he'd seen them yet, if he'd read the bitterly incisive article on how even women like her, at the top of their professions, could be brought to their knees by a husband's desertion. Allyson's pain was showing, it said. The programme was suffering.

She noticed a box of Christmas trimmings on the floor, but Christmas was something she just couldn't think about.

Suddenly his door opened and the jolt of her heart made her queasy. She turned round to look at him and immediately felt worse, for his towering height, dark good looks and inscrutable manner were reminding her of his power, and she felt appallingly wrong-footed and diminished by it.

'Allyson,' he said, smiling. 'I'm sorry to have kept you. I was on a conference call to New York. Did you get some coffee?'

Allyson shook her head. Oh God, she remembered now, he was younger than her, only by two or three years, but those years were suddenly frightening her, as though they were a tangible threat to her existence. Then struggling past her misgivings she said, in her best affable voice, 'How are you? It's good to see you again. How's the house? It was in Devon, wasn't it?' Too much. Too many questions.

'It still is. It belongs to my wife now. Soon to be ex. Come in.'

She followed him through, and smiled politely as he waved her to a chair. She was OK now, past those initial ravings, and slipping calmly back into the steadying grip of poise and control. For some reason his eyes had made her feel better. They were narrow, unreadable, and disturbingly knowing, so why they'd soothed her she wasn't entirely sure. She thought he seemed a good match for Shelley and she wondered how they'd got on last night. But she didn't really care. All she cared about was saving her job, which in the end was going to mean her sanity.

As he watched her sit down he could see how much this was costing her. There was so much pain etched in her eyes, and fear, that he was reminded of what Shelley had told him, that her husband had left her, for a younger woman, for Tessa Dukes.

Trying not to flinch under his scrutiny, Allyson wondered what he was seeing. But it wasn't important. All that mattered was how she should begin. He didn't seem annoyed that she had barged in on him like this, as she had expected, if anything he seemed curious, interested even, which should have been more encouraging than it was. 'Shelley's told me about your plans for the programme,' she said, her voice sounding oddly harsh and discordant.

He nodded, and waited, politely, for her to continue. She'd said nothing that he could adequately or helpfully respond to – when she did he would reply with the truth, which he knew was going to be brutal for her. He wished she'd spared herself this, but could see the desperation in her eyes. He sensed that there was something about this fight that was going to be make or break for her, and he had a momentary vision of her being escorted out of his office, screaming hysterically, begging to keep her job. He hoped that didn't happen. He was at least going to try to spare her that.

'I think,' she said, 'that you've probably got a point. The show does need a younger image.'

His surprise showed. 'I hope that means you're willing to stay with the Night Cap,' he said.

'Maybe.' She took a breath. 'I would like you to consider using someone else to host the Cocktails,' she said. 'Happy Hour,' she corrected.

'You mean instead of Tessa Dukes?'

She nodded.

He didn't answer straight away, so she continued.

'I'd also like to become one of the new-style programme's producers,' she said.

His eyebrows went up, then, looking at the pen he was holding in both hands, he said, 'Have you discussed any of this with Shelley?'

She shook her head. 'No.'

He nodded. On the face of it he didn't consider this to be a bad idea, though he'd envisaged Shelley surrounding herself with a younger team. 'What would you bring to your producership?' he asked, looking at her again.

'A long-time knowledge of the programme, and the business,' she answered, wishing her heart would stop thudding so loudly. 'Many contacts from just about every walk of life . . .'

'In terms of programme content.'

'In terms of programme content,' she echoed, 'I'd like to produce a weekly round-up of how young people are getting involved in helping others. Whether it's the sick, the elderly, or the homeless.'

He recalled Shelley telling him this was Allyson's particular passion. He also recalled how Shelley hadn't pushed it. She was right not to, it wouldn't work. 'It's not the direction we're going in,' he told her.

Allyson's eyes were suddenly stinging. She felt short of breath, and horribly thrown off course by the understated though definite veto, before she'd even had a chance to present her case.

'In my opinion, people don't want to hear about those who are worse off than themselves, at least not in this kind of programme,' he said. 'There are other programmes that deal extremely effectively with those kinds of subjects.'

'Current affairs and news,' she replied, in a voice that was shaking. 'They don't get the kind of ratings *Soirée* does. And if we're going to aim for a younger audience . . .'

'No,' he said. 'Social issues are not on the agenda for the new *Soirée*. It's a light-entertainment programme . . .'

'It's always had style and sophistication,' she protested. 'What you're aiming to do is bring it downmarket . . .'

'My aim is to up the ratings and attract a broader cross section of the viewing public. Right now, it appeals primarily to your age group and older.'

'And they don't count? People my age and older don't matter in this youth-oriented society? Is that what you're saying?'

'What I'm saying is they don't make up the entire spectrum of the viewing public.'

'OK, I accept that. I mean, obviously they don't, but the entire spectrum does care about those worse off than themselves. I believe that a light-entertainment show, if it handles the subject correctly . . .'

'I don't want to argue about this,' he interrupted.

Suddenly she was on her feet. 'Then what do you want to do?' she shouted. 'Throw me out like I don't matter? Cross out my life because it's upsetting your balance sheets? You're wrong about what people want, do you know that? You're all about money, but the

211

people out there, they're about care and compassion. They're about life and its hardships, something you know nothing about. They want to help, they want to make life better for themselves and for those worse off than they are. They need to know where they can go to get help, or give help. We can show them how to do that, in an informative, entertaining way. But you don't want to, because you don't think young people will watch it. You think all they want is gossip and music, light, inconsequential rubbish to escape into at the end of those long difficult days of being twenty something with the burden of a whole life ahead of them. And you're right, they do want all that, but they need more, they'd be stimulated by more. But you don't believe it'll bring in the advertisers, which is all TV is about to you people from America! Well, I'm a shareholder of this company and I'm telling you this is what I want to do, regardless of how much money it makes. And it *will* make money. I'm telling you now, it *will*.'

Her cheeks were flushed with anger, her small body was vibrating with passion. He was surprised by the extent to which her attempt to make herself heard was affecting him, though it would do nothing to change his decisions. 'Being a shareholder isn't going to help you,' he said, adding a hint of gentleness to his tone.

Her fists were clenched, she was struggling to hang onto her temper. 'Don't patronize me,' she seethed.

'I'm afraid it's true.'

'Why don't you at least give it a try!' she implored. 'Test it out from now until the end of the season. If it doesn't work we can drop it next year.'

He was shaking his head and suddenly she couldn't stand any more. 'Then fuck you!' she yelled. 'Fuck you to hell.'

'Allyson, this isn't personal . . .'

'Who's making it personal? I'm talking about a programme . . .'

'I mean, I didn't come to my decisions with the intention of hurting you.'

'Then give me a chance! Don't throw me on the scrap heap. Let me do this.'

'You've still got the Night Cap slot,' he reminded her.

'That's like offering a mother a part of her child!' she cried. 'And don't you think I've got my pride? Don't you read the things they write about me in the press? Everyone knows what's happened to me, so just how do you think I'm going to feel, sitting at Tessa Dukes's feet four nights a week, down there in the Night Cap slot while she stands tall with the rest of what's always been *my* programme?'

'Three,' he corrected. 'I'm reducing the transmissions to three a week. Which is another reason we can't pursue your proposal. There won't be enough airtime.'

Allyson looked at him. Her taut, tired face was ashen, defeat was crawling through her limbs like lead. She was getting nowhere, she was wasting her time. Turning round, she picked up her bag and started towards the door.

She looked so small and vulnerable, so weighted by loss, that it could only be pride that was holding her erect. He spoke her name without really knowing why. 'Allyson.'

She turned back. She looked so fragile she might break.

Though not sure what he wanted to say, he didn't want her to leave like this.

In the end she was the one to speak. 'The next time you look in the mirror,' she said, 'I want you to ask yourself, are you really always right, or are you just in a position that makes it that way, regardless of truth.'

An hour later Allyson was sitting alone in her dressing room when Shelley knocked on the door. It had been a horrible drive back from Central London and she was still badly shaken from a horrific near-miss she'd had when she'd driven through a red light at the junction of Brompton Road and Sloane Street. She hadn't even seen the other car coming. Nor had she been able to respond when the other driver had yelled at her so abusively that a passer-by told him to clean up his act.

'Can I come in?' Shelley asked.

Allyson nodded.

Closing the door behind her Shelley said, 'I'm not sure if we're friends . . . The last time we spoke . . .'

'Let's forget it,' Allyson said dully. 'We've fallen out before and survived.'

Shelley sat down on one of the armchairs. 'How are you feeling?'

Allyson's eyes dropped, then, sighing, she said, 'OK.' She didn't have the energy to tell her about the disastrous meeting she'd just come from with Mark Reiner. Or maybe he'd already told her and that was why she was here. Either way, what did it matter?

'I was wondering,' Shelley said, 'if you'd given any more thought to staying with the Night Cap slot. I don't mean to pressure you, but Mark wants the new format to start right after Christmas.'

Allyson's insides twisted. So it was all going to happen that soon. She felt as though she was on the nightmare float of a happy family carnival, where only she could see the looming menace of madness. But that was because only she was facing it. She raised her eyes to Shelley's. 'So how did it go between you two last night?' she asked.

Shelley couldn't disguise her pleasure, though her expression was self-mocking, and a touch smug. 'Just about the best,' she said.

'You mean ..?'

Shelley nodded. 'All night. It was incredible.'

Allyson thought about the cold and forbidding man she'd just met with. Or was it only because he didn't want to do things her way that she saw him like that?' 'So do you think it'll develop into something?' she said.

'Between you and me I think it already has,' Shelley answered. There was real warmth in her tone and colour in her cheeks. Then, remembering she was talking about the man who was devastating Allyson's career, she sobered up. For a moment she even considered apologizing, but that would only get them into territory that was just too sensitive to chart right now.

'When are you seeing him again?' Allyson asked.

'We didn't make any plans. I guess one of us will call.'

Allyson looked down at her hands. *Christmas was coming and everyone had someone but her. Bob would be spending it with Tessa. Oh God! How much worse could it get?* 'I don't have an answer yet about the Night Cap,' she said. 'But you'll need to start prepping Tessa, so don't let my indecision hold you up. If I decide not to do it she can just take over the whole thing.'

'I wish you'd do it,' Shelley said.

Allyson looked at her and wondered if that was true. 'Tell me, does my salary drop, now I'm not going to be featuring so large?' she said.

It was a good question, though not one Shelley wanted to answer right now. 'We can discuss fees when you've decided what you want to do,' she said.

Chapter 9

Tessa had never been comfortable around Shelley. Shelley was one of the few people who'd seemed to dislike her from the start, and had so far proved impossible to win over. In fact, it was amazing to Tessa that Shelley hadn't found a way to sack her when Bob had left Allyson, especially considering how close she was to Allyson. Instead, weirdly, she was making all Tessa's wildest dreams come true. First the researcher's job with some occasional reporting, and now this giant leap to hosting the first half of the show starting in January. None of it made much sense, but who cared about sense when she was going to be on TV three nights a week, chatting up rock stars and showbiz celebs, as well as getting the low-down on all the gossip and becoming as famous as Allyson.

'Under the new format one report a week will come from somewhere else in the country,' Shelley was saying, as she looked at Tessa across the elegant satinwood desk that was so Shelley it couldn't belong to anyone else, 'and once a month we'll transmit from a location in Europe. How up are you on the rest of the world?'

'I read the papers every day,' Tessa answered.

'Do you have views?'

'Usually.'

Shelley wasn't interested in what they might be. The

girl was intelligent, she knew that, an extremely fast learner, a quick thinker and an unusual personality. She also had the right measure of naivety to strike a note in her interviewing that Shelley had already observed made a refreshing contrast to those who'd been at it for years. Nevertheless this wasn't the kind of job that could be stepped into overnight without some kind of help. 'You'll need to undergo some intense training between now and January,' she said. 'I'm hiring a number of experts in all fields to get you ready. You'll also get an image enhancer and a personal publicist.'

Tessa was grinning widely. 'Wow,' she said. 'What about my own dressing room?'

'Let's concentrate on the important issues first, shall we?' Shelley responded coldly.

Tessa flushed. 'Sorry,' she mumbled, immediately retreating into the persona of a shy, anxious-to-please beginner.

Shelley fixed her with a harsh, relentless stare that, after a while, made Tessa squirm. 'Is it true you're pregnant?' Shelley suddenly demanded.

Tessa's face drained.

'Don't lie,' Shelley warned. 'I need to know.'

'Yes, it's true. But if it's going to get in the way of this job, I'll have an abortion.'

Just like that. Not even a second thought. Shelley couldn't say she was surprised, but she was disgusted. 'It'll get in the way,' she informed her.

The meeting was suddenly over and Tessa was back at her desk. She looked around for Allyson, but there was no sign of her. Did Allyson know about this? She must. Was that why she wasn't here? She had to be livid. But it was hardly Tessa's fault that she was getting all these breaks, was it? And really Allyson should be proud, since it was Allyson who had set Tessa on this road, and Tessa certainly hadn't lost anything of her desire to please her, despite all that had happened.

217

Anyway, right now, even before she called Bob to tell him her news she must get herself booked into a clinic. She'd always thought it a shame her mother hadn't done that when she was pregnant with her, but the way her life was going now she was glad she hadn't. It was all turning out OK at last.

It was nine o'clock and Bob was still waiting for Tessa to come home. She'd left a message on the machine to say she had some great news but wanted to wait till she saw him to tell him. But she wasn't back yet and when he called they said she'd left the office around six.

He hated being alone, for unless he was drunk he became easy prey to his conscience, and found it almost impossible to blot Allyson from his mind. But he had to do that or he'd go off his head thinking about her, worrying about her, wanting her to understand why he'd done what he had, and why he couldn't come back. She wouldn't speak to him any more, so he couldn't explain the way he was feeling, which was a shame, because he was sure it would help her to know how sorry he was. But if she wouldn't listen, he couldn't tell her, and there was no point getting himself into a state about it, when that wasn't going to help anyone. So he tried only to think about Tessa, and how much she loved him, and cared for him, and did everything she could to help him through this hellish time in his life. She was exceptional really, for she never baulked when she had to give him money, even when she knew it was for booze, nor did she ever deprive him of sex, or the comfort and understanding he craved when things got so bad that he drank himself to the point of throwing up all over her. She was always so patient and tender with him, soothing him gently with her hands and her voice, never judging him, only ever wanting to please him. OK, her moods could be a bit odd from time to time, but show him someone's who weren't? And why shouldn't she assert herself once in a while, she had every right to, and it only surprised him, and sometimes irritated him, because it was so rare that she ever did.

In the end, unable to stay in the flat any longer, he finished the gin in his glass, tucked the rest of the bottle into his pocket, and went out to look for her. But she wasn't in the pub and he didn't know where else to try. As far as he knew she didn't have any friends, except Julian, but Julian was in the pub so she wasn't with him.

'I haven't seen her today,' Julian said. 'There's no programme on Fridays so I don't go in.'

Bob nodded. Now he was here he might as well have a couple of drinks. He ordered himself a large gin and a pint of Guinness for Julian.

By the time Tessa found them at half past ten they were both roaring drunk, and attempting, loudly, to discuss Chelsea's latest performance as though it were the most important issue on the planet, if only they could get the words out right. She watched them from the door, slamming their fists on the table, shaking their fingers, Bob dominating the scene, both physically and vocally. Not that Julian seemed to have a problem with that, in fact they appeared to be doing some serious male bonding over there. A bit like father and son. That might have been funny had she not just come from a session with Laura, but she didn't want to think about that now, it raised too many issues that really ought to be forgotten, and she was already wishing she hadn't gone.

'There you are,' Bob said, when he saw her. 'I was getting worried.'

'Really?' she said, not without irony, after all it had taken him long enough to realize she was there.

He pulled her mouth down to his and kissed her. 'Are you OK?' he asked.

She nodded, and sat down next to him. 'Hi Jules,' she said.

'Hi.'

She was tired, and strangely, considering what a great day she'd had, a bit depressed. 'You seem in a good mood,' she said to Bob.

He shrugged, as if to ask why he shouldn't be. She could think of plenty of reasons, but she wasn't going to remind him. He knew, without her pointing it out, what a dreadful mess his life was in, so she only looked at him and smiled.

'You sure you're OK?' he insisted.

'Sure,' she said, trying not to recoil from the smell of the gin.

'Then could you lend me some cash? It's my round.'

Tessa got out her purse and handed over a ten-pound note. Then, realizing he wasn't in much of a state to stand up, she took the money back and went to get the drinks herself.

'So where've you been?' he said, when she came back.

She looked from his pale, shiny face to Julian's earnest attempt to look sober, then, knowing that neither of them would remember in the morning, she said, 'There's this shrink I see sometimes. I was with her, then I walked around for a bit.'

'Oh.' Bob blinked, then turned to Julian. Julian didn't seem to know what to say either.

'So, do you want to hear my good news?' she said, brightening her smile. 'As of January I'm going to be presenting the Cocktail section of the programme, which they're going to call Happy Hour.'

Julian's eyes grew wide.

Tessa was still grinning. 'Shelley told me today. And my agent's going to ask her for a great big fat fee, which means, Bob, that we might be able to buy Allyson out of the flat and go and live there after all. Wouldn't that be great? Us, in Cheyne Walk, overlooking the river.'

Bob's brain wasn't working as fast as it should.

Tessa moved over to sit on his lap. 'Aren't you proud?'

she said, snuggling into him.

'Yes.' He was looking at his empty glass. He needed another drink, badly.

'You can come to visit,' she told Julian. 'As often as you like.'

'You're not serious about the flat,' Bob said.

'Why not?' she said, sounding surprised. 'You were all for it a few weeks ago.'

He was swaying slightly in his seat, and knew he wasn't capable of really making his point, whatever his point was. 'Her parents . . . Her parents gave us that flat when we got married,' he said weakly.

Tessa smiled. 'Which makes it half yours, silly,' she reminded him. 'So we'll buy the other half and make it all yours. After all, I deserve a nice place to live in, don't I?'

'Yes, but . . . There are thousands of nice places. I don't see why it has to be that one.'

'I thought it was what you wanted. You said you were happy there, and you know how much I want you to be happy. And if you're worried about Allyson . . . Well, just remember that it's because of her that you can't get to your money, and if you're right about her putting a word in with the editors and producers, not to give you any work . . .'

A dark flush spread over Bob's face. Had he said that? He couldn't remember, but it seemed likely.

'Can you believe it?' Tessa said with a fond incredulity to Julian. 'There's his wife doing everything she can to totally screw up his life and now he's too squeamish to go and buy her out of a flat that's already half his. You are a silly, Bob,' she told him.

'Get me another drink,' Bob suddenly slurred. 'And you don't have the money yet, so before you start thinking you can afford even a quarter of a flat on Cheyne Walk . . .' He lost his train of thought, and blinked in the direction of the bar.

Tessa laid her head on his shoulder. 'I'm making you

angry,' she said. 'Please don't be angry. If you don't want us to buy the flat, we won't.'

His head was spinning now, and she was feeling heavy on his lap. 'OK, then we won't,' he mumbled.

Her eyes drifted across to Julian and she winked.

'Hi,' Shelley said. 'How are you?'

'Pretty good,' Mark responded, sliding into the other side of the banquette. 'Did I keep you waiting?'

'I was early,' she told him. Though her smile was warm, waves of unease were threatening to trespass on her cherished serenity. This was the first time she'd seen him since Thursday. It was now Sunday lunch time. They'd spoken a couple of times on the phone, calls she had made, neither of which had elicited a desire on his part to see her again. So she'd invited him to her flat for Sunday lunch, which he'd accepted, but suggested they ate out.

So now, here they were, and though he appeared relaxed enough about being there, she couldn't help wondering where the chemistry had gone.

'Have you been here before?' he asked, looking round.

'A few times.'

'Nice place.'

She nodded. They were so formal when all she wanted to discuss was their night together, and how ready she was for it to happen again. Surely to God he was too. 'I'm getting a team together for Tessa,' she said. 'They start work on Tuesday.'

His eyebrows went up. 'You've already spoken to her?' he said.

'Yes.'

For some reason he didn't seem thrilled.

'Is there a problem?' she asked.

He smiled. 'No,' he answered. 'I presume, if you've spoken to Tessa, that Allyson's decided about the Night Cap.'

'She's letting me know tomorrow.'

They took the menus from a waitress and listened as she recounted the specials. After making a selection they ordered drinks. Shelley chose wine. She felt she needed something stronger than water.

Mark ordered a vodka. He too felt the need for something stronger than water. He'd given a lot of thought to what had happened between him and Shelley on Thursday night, then to the meeting he'd had with Allyson the following day, and he was furious with himself now for having allowed himself to get involved in personal matters, when he'd only just taken over the damned company. Shelley was one of his employees for God's sake, the producer of a programme he might ultimately axe, so how the hell was he going to do that if they were literally in bed together? God knew he'd had a bad enough time dealing with Allyson, feeling like the biggest shit of the century, and he wasn't even involved with her. She'd certainly got to him, though, as he'd hardly been able to stop thinking about her since. But regardless of the decisions he might make there, or maybe because of them, there was no doubt in his mind that this thing with Shelley had to be stopped now before it went any further.

'Did Allyson tell you she came to see me?' he said.

Shelley's surprise showed. 'No. When?'

'Friday. She tried to talk me out of using Tessa for the Happy Hour.'

Shelley took a moment to digest this. 'Is that why you didn't seem overjoyed to hear I'd put your plans in motion? You've had a change of heart.'

'No. The show still needs a younger image, and Tessa's the answer if we want to turn it around fast. If we decided to audition we'd have to delay the change until the start of next season. I don't want to do that.'

'So?'

'So nothing. I was merely wondering what Allyson had decided.'

Shelley got the feeling there was more, but for some reason she didn't want to ask. Instead, she moistened her lips and fixed her eyes on his mouth. 'It's Sunday,' she said, 'why don't we forget about work and talk about . . . Other things.'

Their drinks arrived, then the food, and despite all her attempts to bait him he stubbornly refused to move from the general to the personal.

In the end, embarrassed and angry, she said, 'I'm sorry, but am I supposed to be pretending that Thursday never happened?'

His eyes went down, but she saw his discomfort.

She laughed bitterly. 'Oh, I see . . . You got what you wanted . . .'

'Shelley, listen,' he said. 'What happened on Thursday, well, it was something else. The best. I don't know anything, anyone who can compare.'

'But.' Her heart was pounding.

'I don't think it should happen again.'

She felt her face drain. She didn't want to believe what she'd just heard. At last she'd found a man she could call her equal, a man she already knew she wanted to share her life with, and he was telling her he didn't want her. It didn't make any sense. They'd been more intimate than most couples ever got. How could he not want it to happen again?

'Is there someone else?' she said.

He glanced up as their coffee was delivered. 'Shelley, you're an exceptionally beautiful and desirable woman,' he said. 'I've got great respect and admiration for you, but if we're going to have a relationship that works, it should remain professional.'

'Even though we've already got as personal as it's possible to get?'

Again he looked awkward. 'I'm sorry,' he said.

'Sorry that it happened, or sorry that you're a bastard who led me to believe you felt the same way I did?'

'I don't recall us discussing feelings,' he countered.

'Oh,' she laughed angrily, 'so you think I put out like that for every man I meet?'

'Frankly, I don't know,' he responded. 'All I know is that you blew my mind, and I'm not sorry it happened. You're a unique and beautiful woman, but as for anything else, well I'm afraid that's as far as it goes.'

She was so stunned she was unable to make herself think. She couldn't look at him. She didn't want to see the regret in his eyes. This was the man she had decided to love. The man who could match her intellectually, physically, sexually. How could she let him go? She couldn't. She had to find a way to talk him round, and being hostile wasn't going to do it. So she managed to smile, winsomely, seductively, as she said, 'Why don't we go back to my place and talk this over?'

He smiled. 'If we went back to your place the last thing we'd do is talk.'

She laughed. So he did still want her. 'We could be really good together, can't you see that?' she said.

'We already were,' he responded. 'But it's not all about sex.'

'I wasn't just talking about sex.'

He glanced at his watch. 'I've got to go,' he said and signalled for the bill.

It was like a slap. A slap that reverberated right the way through her.

Their departure was so swift she could barely remember getting into her car. And later, when she got back to her flat, she didn't want to think about how she'd sat there pleading with him, trying to cajole and seduce him, had almost even bared her breasts to remind him ... Thank God she hadn't done that, but the humiliation of the way she'd behaved anyway was still so great it burned her all over.

As Allyson walked down the stairs of the farmhouse,

she was remembering the hot summer's day when she and Bob had first found it, and how thrilled they had been to discover their dream home in such idyllic surroundings, despite its neglected and dilapidated state. Then had come the long and arduous task of restoring it, followed by the weekend-long party they'd thrown when they'd finally been able to move in. There wasn't a single cushion or rug, painting or book they hadn't chosen together, all found in local antique shops, country fairs and community sales. Like their flat in Chelsea, this house was a part of them too, something they had lovingly created together, and taken such pride in whenever their friends came to stay. And the villagers who'd been popping in all weekend with cakes, or wine, or tickets for the Christmas raffle, were almost like family. She had grown so fond of them all, and could hardly bear the thought of never seeing them again.

She'd filled two suitcases with her personal belongings. Bob's were still there. She'd considered packing his too, but in the end had been unable to do it. Maybe he wanted them to stay here. Maybe he was planning to move Tessa in and make this a home for their baby.

Over her dead body.

Her mother was waiting outside by the car. Her father was in the front passenger seat, staring blankly down over the hillside. A few meagre Christmas lights twinkled over the church spire, thin columns of smoke rose from the old brick chimneys. It was a grey and cheerless day. The sky was low and oppressive, the cold was biting. After locking the front door she put her cases in the boot, then got into the driver's seat. She didn't look back as she drove away. Nor did she look down at the village. She simply kept her eyes on the road and tried not to feel what was going on in her heart.

The drive back to London took less than two hours. She went to her parents' house first to drop them off, and ended up going in for a cup of tea. She didn't stay long, though. She needed to be alone, in her own bed and asleep, away from this horrible day.

'Thanks for coming with me,' she said, kissing her mother goodbye at the front door.

'Will you be all right?' her mother asked.

Allyson nodded and smoothed her fingers over the soft, papery skin of her mother's face. Peggy's eyes were red and swollen from crying, the trip to Wiltshire had been almost as difficult for her as it had for Allyson.

'I wish you'd stay,' Peggy said.

Allyson hugged her again and was about to walk away when Peggy started crying again.

'I'm sorry,' she sobbed. 'I just can't bear seeing you hurt like this. I wish Daddy understood. We're a bit lost without him, aren't we?'

Allyson smiled. They'd just left her father in the cellar, taking refuge from a bomb attack. Driving down to Wiltshire had been hard for him too, in his own way. He hadn't known who they were, or where they were taking him.

'Poor Mummy,' she said.

'Call me when you get to the flat?'

'Of course.'

Allyson was almost at the gate when her mother said, 'You're not old, darling. And that girl, she won't be nearly as good as you.'

'No,' Allyson said quietly, 'I don't expect she will. But sadly, that's not the point any more.'

Shelley was the only one who knew why Tessa wasn't in the studio today. The team of hand-picked gurus who were coaching Tessa in camera technique and interviewing subtleties had been given the day off, they thought, because Tessa needed a break. It was a plausible enough excuse, for they'd been hard at it this past week.

At the moment Shelley was in a screening room viewing videotapes of the results of Tessa's training so far. They were even more impressive than she'd expected, for the girl looked so fresh she might burst, and seemed so strikingly unfazed by the celebrity guests Shelley had talked into rehearsing with her, that she could have been at this for years. She even had a certain style of wit, which, though immature, was not wholly unbeguiling, and the way she oozed fascination was allowing even the biggest of bores to come off well. But that wasn't all, for the camera so magically enhanced the radiance of her smile, and the plump fleshiness of her body, that Shelley could be in no doubt that her appeal was going to be huge.

She'd wanted to come straight back to work after the abortion, but Shelley had insisted she take the day off. Obviously getting rid of a human life was no big deal to her, though Shelley couldn't help wondering if she'd told Bob what she was doing today. Not that it was any concern of Shelley's, nor did she much care. However, she did care about Allyson, which was why she was in two minds whether or not to tell her about the abortion.

On the one hand it could help Allyson considerably to find out that Tessa was no longer pregnant. But on the other, if Tessa hadn't told Bob, and Allyson decided she would, well, the last thing Shelley wanted was Bob creating some kind of scene that might get into the press. If it did there was a very good chance the story would be twisted to make it look as though Shelley, and probably Allyson too, had coerced the girl into giving up her baby for the sake of saving their show. Public outrage would be so great that Shelley would be forced to resign and the programme would inevitably be cancelled. A week ago Shelley might have gone for that, just to spite Mark Reiner, but it hadn't taken her long to realize that it made no odds to him what happened to the programme, he'd simply set up another to take its place. Besides, she wasn't so angry with him now. In fact, after taking some time to get things into perspective, she was starting to feel quite warm towards him again.

Obviously she'd been upset when he'd begun to back off, which was why she hadn't understood the problem sooner. But now she was pretty certain she did, and if she was right then she couldn't really blame him for being so concerned about the intensity of their attraction. After all, he'd only just taken over the company, so it was hardly going to create a good impression were it to get out, and being who they were it almost certainly would. So, for the time being at least, it seemed he had decided to concentrate his energies on turning the company around. And she was OK with that. Were they destined to be just a small-time, hole-in-the-wall affair, it might be different, but something this big could easily run out of control. So, considering what was at stake, the only sensible course to take was a slow and cautious one. It was probably hard for him to articulate that, which again she understood, for not many men would find it easy.

Ordinarily she'd have talked this over with Allyson, as they generally discussed everything, but Shelley was very well aware of how that had changed lately, which was really no surprise considering her failure to stand by Allyson during all these changes. But it was a disappointment, and certainly a great loss, for Shelley was missing the closeness she and Allyson had always shared. She was also, behind all the guilt and concern, slightly upset with Allyson, as it wasn't like her not to mention something as significant as going to see Mark last Friday, and though there was obviously a great deal on Allyson's mind these days there had been plenty of time to bring it up since, but Allyson still hadn't.

Someone knocked on the door and Shelley looked up as a shaft of light from the corridor outside cut across the darkened viewing room.

'Have you got a minute?' Allyson said.

Shelley hit the VCR's pause button. 'I was just thinking about you,' she said.

Allyson glanced at the screen.

Realizing the frozen image was of Tessa, Shelley turned the monitor off and switched on the reading lamp behind her. 'Come in,' she said.

Allyson let the door swing closed, but stayed where she was. 'I just wanted you to know that I've decided to continue with the Night Cap,' she said.

Shelley's expression only partially relaxed. 'I'm so pleased,' she said.

Though Allyson's smile was weak Shelley couldn't help noticing that there was more colour in her cheeks than of late, and her hair looked newly cut and styled. She was still painfully underweight though, and she hadn't been big to start with.

'When it came down to it,' Allyson said, 'it was that or nothing. I don't think I could handle nothing, even if it means having to remain in the same vicinity as Tessa Dukes. And I suppose in some sad, sick way being around her keeps me connected to Bob.'

Shelley removed the files on the chair next to her. 'Come and sit down,' she said.

'I can't. I've got to go up to town. Mark Reiner's invited me for lunch.'

Shelley's smile drained, and her body felt suddenly stiff.

'Do you know anything about it?' Allyson asked.

'No.' Shelley's voice was harsh.

Allyson attempted a shrug. 'He called after the recording yesterday and asked me to meet him at one today. I thought you might know what it was about.'

Shelley attempted to sound casual, as she glanced down at the files. 'No idea,' she said, realizing that Allyson was probably scared half to death that she was about to be fired altogether, and was waiting for some reassurance from Shelley. But how could Shelley possibly give it, when she didn't have the first idea why Mark Reiner would want to see Allyson, especially not for lunch.

'Then let's hope it's not to rescind the offer of the Night Cap,' Allyson ventured.

'No, let's hope not,' Shelley responded, still seeming distracted.

Allyson was almost out of the door before she turned back and said, 'Can I ask? How are things working out for you two?'

Frustration and anger dug into Shelley's heart as she playfully rolled her eyes. 'Oh, you know, still early days,' she said.

Allyson smiled and nodded, then closed the door behind her.

It was several minutes before Shelley started up the video again and Tessa's face filled the screen. But her mind was still angrily exploring the many paths of doubt and suspicion that were opening up all over the place. This was the second time Allyson had been to see Mark in a week, and it was after the last time he'd seen Allyson that he'd decided to put the brakes on his relationship with Shelley. So had something happened that day in his office, something neither of them was telling her about? Except that was crazy, for not only had Allyson appeared convincingly anxious about today's invitation, she was, by Shelley's reckoning, still at least five years from being over Bob. And even without Bob, Shelley just couldn't see Allyson being Mark's type. To start with they wouldn't even look right together, he was so much taller, and bigger than Allyson, and there was just no way Allyson exuded the kind of sexuality a man like Mark Reiner would demand in a woman. He had standards that were exceptionally high, and a skill that justified their being met. Allyson's experiences with Bob, the only man she'd ever slept with, simply didn't equip her to deal with someone like Mark – and Shelley would know, for she'd made love often enough with Bob Jaymes to be aware of how limited Allyson's technique probably was. And Shelley couldn't see Allyson going for Mark either, as Allyson always gravitated towards the needy people, like Bob, and Tessa, and all her little charity cases. And whatever else Mark Reiner might be, he certainly wasn't needy.

Realizing she was getting carried away, stirring up fears and insecurities that had nothing to do with reality, and everything to do with a long and carefully suppressed rivalry she felt with Allyson that Allyson wasn't even aware of, Shelley attempted to ground herself in reason. After all, it wasn't often that she felt this rivalry, though she had to confess that there were times when Allyson's good nature and easy popularity did grate on her nerves. And even though Shelley would never have allowed Bob to leave Allyson during their long, bittersweet affair, the fact that he had never even shown any signs of wanting to had confused and angered her, for she simply couldn't imagine why any man would rather be with Allyson than with her.

With Tessa's face staring back at her from the screen Shelley felt a stab of unease sink into her heart. She had known long before Allyson that Bob was sleeping with Tessa, but it had never crossed her mind that he would leave Allyson for the girl, especially not when he hadn't even come close to it with her. But he had, and Shelley despised him for it now, not only because of how it had so totally devastated Allyson, whom she really did care for despite all the conflicting emotions, but because of the unforgivably insulting gesture it had been to her too. However, no matter how bitterly she was smarting over Bob's aberration with Tessa, it was nothing to how she would feel if Mark were to suffer a similar aberration with Allyson. And with Allyson being on the rebound, and in grave need of some male attention . . .

But no, she wasn't going to allow herself to continue with this. Just because Mark had invited Allyson to lunch, rather than to his office, was no reason to start sharpening up the knives of jealousy and suspicion. In fact, it was crazy to be thinking this way, when people in their positions had lunch all the time, with nothing more personal on the agenda than a shared liking for fish.

Laura Risby, Tessa's psychotherapist, led Tessa to where the car was waiting on an expired metre, a few doors down from the clinic, and settled her comfortably in the front passenger seat. The wind was blowing a bitter gale through the parallel terraces of Harley Street, bending the bare winter trees and scattering clouds of dust up into the elegant white façades. She'd heard on the radio while driving here that they were forecasting snow for Christmas.

'OK?' she said, fastening Tessa's seat belt, and tucking her scarf inside her coat collar.

Tessa nodded. She was pale, but that was only to be expected. She might be a little sore for a couple of days too.

She was going to tell Bob she'd suffered a miscarriage, though Laura wondered if he'd guess the truth, with the baby's loss coinciding so neatly with Tessa's new status on the programme. Either way, miscarriage or abortion, Laura was curious to see if he stayed with Tessa once it really sank in that there was no longer a child. Laura had to hope he didn't, for this wasn't good for Tessa, sleeping with a father figure, though Laura doubted Bob had any idea that was the role he'd been cast in. And the substitute brother could prove disastrous too. But it was the punishment Tessa was both consciously and unconsciously inflicting on Allyson that was the most disturbing. Fate had rather played into Tessa's hands by promoting her into Allyson's position on the programme, but the rest of it, like Allyson's husband,

Allyson's flat and even the complex need for Allyson's approval and affection, was forcing Laura to wonder if it would be wise, even permissible, for her to talk to Allyson. However, considering this new turn of events, she felt it was probably better to wait for a while and see if Tessa's and Bob's relationship broke up of its own accord. She really did think it would, and, if she was right, there would be no need to step outside the bounds of professional confidentiality and interfere.

Mark was watching Allyson as she chose which of the three vegetables the waiter should put on her side plate. The man was clearly delighted to be serving someone famous and had made such a performance out of fileting her sole, he might well have been auditioning. Mercifully he'd finished before it got too embarrassing, but now it seemed that every vegetable on his platter had its own personal history, and Allyson was having to be acquainted with every one of them.

She handled it well, Mark noted with amusement, and brought it to such a smooth and satisfying conclusion that not for a minute would the waiter consider he'd been dismissed. Obviously, being who she was, she'd had a lot of practice at this, but still Mark couldn't help being impressed with the way she'd handled not only the waiter, but the many autograph-hunters too, whose nerve to come seeking a brief word and personal inscription was boosted by a large intake of Christmas spirit – it being less than two weeks to go now. However, with the exception of the waiter, no-one had interrupted for the past five minutes, and with any luck the initial delight of spotting a celebrity was over, and they would be left to get on with their lunch. Not that he imagined Allyson was going to eat hers, it was far too big a portion, and if the way she'd pushed the avocado hors d'oeuvre round her plate was anything to go by, she had no appetite anyway.

'So,' she said, picking up her cutlery, 'we've talked about America, we've discussed the earth-shattering prophecies for the new millennium, we've established that neither of us care much for Christmas, I'm agog to know what comes next.'

His eyes narrowed, showing his amusement. This was a different woman from the one who'd yelled at him in his office a week ago. No doubt equally as spirited, but thankfully less hostile, and though she might look like an injured bird, with her tired, watchful eyes and unsteady smile, she was staging a remarkable show of togetherness considering how tough life must be for her right now.

'So, are you building up for something big?' she pressed. 'Or are you waiting for me to turn hysterical again? Most men don't go for that, but you could be strange.'

He laughed. 'To be frank,' he said, 'I'd like to be able to tell you that I'm going to give you the airtime for your social issues. But I'm not.'

Her blue eyes were holding tightly to his. 'Yet you say you'd like to tell me,' she said. 'That must mean you think they're worthwhile.'

'I never said they weren't. I just don't think they've got a natural setting in *Soirée*. But as a presenter, you do. Which is why I want you to continue with the Night Cap – and why I think you should become a producer, as you yourself suggested.'

Allyson's eyes widened with surprise. Elation was a beat behind. 'Have you discussed this with Shelley?' she asked.

'No. I thought I should discuss it with you first, and make sure it was what you really wanted.'

'It is,' she said decisively. 'I've really thought about it, and I know I don't have any credited experience as a producer, but on the whole it's what I'm doing most of the time. You know, making decisions about what does

235

or doesn't go into the programme, what questions to ask, what angle to take – even what the budget should be.' She stopped, embarrassed suddenly that she might be overdoing the zeal.

'Of course,' he said. 'But we're going to have a slightly new-look programme, and I think your experience and high profile would serve us best for the monthly international transmissions.'

Allyson blinked. This was too much. She'd come here expecting . . . Well, she wasn't sure what she'd been expecting, but after the ghastly scene she'd thrown in his office, and with the way her luck had been going lately, she'd been gearing herself up for something more along the lines of 'Thank you, Allyson and good night' than 'Hello, Allyson, here's your rescue package all laid out, ready to make you shine in a whole new way. Oh, and by the way, I hope you're enjoying your lunch, because I certainly seem to be.' She put down her knife and fork and lifted her napkin. Then, realizing she hadn't eaten anything yet, she picked up her fork again. Only when she looked at him did she realize he was laughing, and to her surprise she laughed too. 'You really are going to have to discuss that one with Shelley,' she said.

'I'm discussing it with you,' he responded. 'Is it something that interests you?'

'That's like asking me if I'm interested in living,' she told him. 'Yes, I'm interested. Though a few days ago I might not have been, but we won't get into that.'

He'd seen the newspapers, so he knew she'd moved some belongings out of her country home at the weekend, but he had no intention of trespassing on that hallowed ground. 'Would it be possible for you to produce the monthly slot, and to continue presenting the Night Caps?' he asked.

She was nodding. 'I would think so,' she answered. 'But we really will have to discuss this with Shelley. After all, she's the boss.'

He waited, with ironic eyes, for her to remember whom she was talking to. When she did, she seemed absurdly and touchingly confused for a moment, then, realizing he was teasing her, she shot him a meaningful look and said, 'OK, you're the boss, but you're not going to be involved in the day-to-day running of the programme, and I think Shelley would like to be consulted before she gets me foisted upon her as her brand new producer of international programmes.'

Sidestepping the Shelley issue again he said, 'Maybe you could give some thought to the kind of shape you'd like your programmes to take. Whether you want to keep it in the exact same style as the domestic transmissions, or . . .'

'I think it should stay the same,' she interrupted. 'At least for the first few months. Coming from a different European city each time is going to make it individual enough, if we start changing format it'll just get confusing.'

'And Happy Hour is something that occurs all over the Continent,' he said, looking right into her eyes.

Allyson flushed slightly, and looked down at her plate, for she realized that this was a gentle reminder that, if this did all come off, she'd be travelling with Tessa. Several pleasing scenarios of ditching Tessa in the Danube, or shoving her off the Eiffel Tower, or making her bungee jump off the Bundesbank on a very long rope, rushed in for inspection, but the reality was, Tessa would be the star of the show and Allyson was going to have to find a way of working with her. A second later her head was up again and she was smiling. 'Of course,' she said, referring to Happy Hour being an international event, 'which is why there's no point going off-piste, so to speak, let's just stay safe and in style for the moment. Shelley will probably be happier with that too.'

He nodded.

She wondered why she kept bringing Shelley's name

up, especially in such a sycophantic way. He was going to think she was incapable of taking a decision unless it was validated by Shelley, which wasn't the case at all. She was just reminding him that Shelley was *Soirée*'s editor and senior producer and as such she should be a part of this plan. She was also, she realized, trying to get him to say something about Shelley that might give some clue as to what his feelings might be, which was not only unprofessional of her, it was also disloyal, for Shelley hadn't asked her to do that. And besides, why should she be concerned about Shelley when, right at that moment, Shelley was heavily involved in preparing the source of all Allyson's misery to take over the main part of Allyson's programme. So where was the loyalty in that?

Mark's eyes were watching her closely as she looked at him again. They were steeped in humour and had that knowing sort of look that seemed to suggest he was reading her mind. Allyson smiled, a little self-consciously, for if he was reading her mind she couldn't exactly feel proud of what she was thinking. On the other hand she was rather enjoying the interest he seemed to be taking in her, and picking up her fork she took a delicious mouthful of fish.

He asked her then about the kind of team she'd need to staff the transmissions, and the approximate budget, as well as any early thoughts she might have on publicity. Ideas soon began spilling out of her, almost faster than she could think them, and though she quickly saw that many of them were unusable, bouncing them around with him was turning out to be an extremely exhilarating and often hilarious process. The glass of champagne he ordered to mark the launch of her new, jet-setty career slipped down rather easily too, as did the next glass, which was to celebrate Christmas and the fabulous start of their very special friendship.

Realizing that she'd got a bit gushy and over the top

with that particular toast she blushed, and winced and said, 'If I'm embarrassing you, I promise it's nothing to what I'm doing to myself.'

Laughing, he clinked his glass against hers again, and replied, 'It's better than when you yell at me.'

Allyson closed her eyes and sank into a laugh. 'Seems as though I'm destined to be a problem whichever way we look at this.'

His eyebrows arched. 'Are you trying to trick me into such corny lines as – if only all my problems were like you? Because I can assure you I wouldn't mind if they were, for one thing they'd make good lunch dates, and for another they'd be pretty good at making me laugh. Now, instead of ogling my dessert like that, why don't you just have it?'

'Oh no!' she cried as he started to pass over his banoffi pie. Then, grinning, 'Well, maybe just a taste.'

Not until they were leaving the restaurant, his hand at the small of her back as he steered her through the crowded lobby, did she realize that she'd just eaten an entire meal for the first time since Bob had left. She'd also drunk three glasses of champagne and was feeling wonderfully flushed and light-headed, and considerably warmer towards Mark Reiner than she had a week ago. In fact, as he handed her into the back of a taxi then got in beside her, she was starting to see why Shelley was so attracted to him. She might be too, were it not for the way her heart plummeted at the very idea of anyone other than Bob occupying that place in her life.

The week leading up to Christmas was pandemonium on all fronts. The offices and studio were decked out in glorious seasonal splendour, with huge towering Christmas trees, some in gold, some in silver, and still others all in red. The set was transformed into a wonderful Alpine cabin, with snow on the windows, a fire in the hearth and a ready supply of hot toddies at the bar. The designers had surpassed themselves this year. So too had the caterers, who were taking care of twice the number of guests, as they all began flooding in for the extra recordings to cover the holiday period. Being so rushed off their feet Allyson had yet to tell Shelley about the new producership she had discussed with Mark – a bombshell that she felt might be better coming from her than from him. She just wanted to pick her moment, sit Shelley down and take the time to explain how well this could work. It wasn't something she was looking forward to, for she was only too aware of how jealously Shelley guarded her position, and having decisions like this taken behind her back was going to do nothing to endear the plan to Shelley.

Then out of the blue Mark called to say he was going to talk to Shelley himself. 'I think it should be put to her in a way that the idea seems to come from her,' he said.

Allyson was intrigued. 'How are you going to do that?' she said, mildly aware of the pleasure she'd felt at hearing his voice. It was making quite a difference to her lately, knowing that she had his support and friendship, especially with Christmas increasing her depression about Bob.

'Leave it to me. All I need you to do is act surprised when she offers you the job. Then accept.'

Allyson laughed, but there was so much noise going on in the office outside that she missed what he said next. 'Hang on,' she said, going to close the door. 'That's better. I'm sorry, what did you say?'

'I was wondering how Tessa's doing with her training?' he replied.

The warmth instantly drained from Allyson's smile. No matter how busy she was, or excited about the prospect of her new position, her hatred of Tessa Dukes, who was going to be spending Christmas with *her* husband, then following it up by taking over *her* role on *her* programme, was never going to wane. In fact there

240

were times like right now, as she looked at that glowingly happy face on the monitors in the main office, when her loathing felt as if it was just getting bigger. 'You'll have to ask Shelley,' she said coldly. 'I'm not involved in the training.'

'But you will be recording the pilots tomorrow?'

'I'm doing my inserts separately. We won't be in the studio together.'

'I see.'

She imagined he did. 'Is there anything else?' she asked.

'No. Well, I guess, Merry Christmas if I don't see you before Friday.'

'Thank you. To you too.'

After she rang off she regretted sounding so sharp, but he surely had to realize that there weren't many instances when Tessa's name could be mentioned without turning her into a wannabe killer, and he certainly hadn't found one. Still, she didn't imagine he'd lose any sleep over her tart little responses, so she wouldn't either, and picking up her script for the next recording, she switched her phones through to Marvin and ran down to her dressing room. On the way she passed Tessa coming out of the small studio, laughing delightedly at the director's lavish praise for her latest *tour de force*. Allyson pretended not to see them, and carried on to her dressing room. Once inside, with the door shut firmly behind her, she closed her eyes and fought back the mounting rage. It was hard, so hard, to keep all this anger and hurt bottled up inside, especially when she was having to turn down so many parties and celebrations in the build-up to Christmas, because she was afraid that going without Bob would be even more painful than staying at home on her own.

The phone rang, and by the time the call ended sadness had blunted her fury, for it had been George, Bob's father, accepting her mother's invitation to join them for Christmas. Poor chap, he was all alone there in his high-rise council flat in Lewisham, still waiting for a place on ground level and too proud to take any help from Allyson. And just as Allyson had suspected, he hadn't had an invitation to spend Christmas with Bob, hadn't even heard from him since the marriage had split up. Hearing that, Allyson's heart had flooded with anguish and pain. How utterly besotted Bob must be with Tessa, and the prospect of their new baby, that he didn't even have time for his own father.

Shelley was in a great mood. She had just attended a producers' lunch which Mark had hosted at the Mirabelle, and now, at his invitation, she was leading the way up the stairs to his Russell Square office for a pre-Christmas drink. Thanks to the lengthy conversation they'd just had in the restaurant she was no longer having to feel quite so bad about Allyson, because after tossing around several different ideas, they'd decided to give Allyson a shot at producing the new Continental transmissions as well as presenting the Night Caps. It certainly sorted out the question of Allyson's fee, though whether or not Allyson was interested in producing, or even up to it, remained to be seen. But at least Shelley had some good news to be going back to her with, something that would hopefully help to ease the tension that was still straining away between them.

'So what are your plans for Christmas?' Mark was asking as they walked into the reception area of his office.

As he'd already told her he was spending the time with his brother and sister-in-law who'd just flown in from New York, Shelley didn't mind admitting to spending the time with her family too. 'My mother and stepfather have a place in the New Forest,' she said. 'I'll probably drive down there. My stepsister and her husband usually come too, with their three delightful kids.'

From the way she said it it was evident she found the

242

kids anything but delightful, which didn't surprise him, she didn't strike him as the motherly sort.

He stopped to speak to his assistant, and Shelley used the opportunity to go and powder her nose. When she returned she could see him already in his office pouring them both a drink. The intention now was to watch the two pilot programmes that had been recorded the day before, with Tessa as the Happy Hour host, and Allyson at the foot of the show taking care of the Night Caps. Personalities and all other issues aside, the new-style programmes were even better than Shelley had hoped for. Tessa's magical quality on screen was richly enhanced by the girl's wonderful gift of infectious laughter, and an impishness that got people to say or do things as though the camera wasn't there. And Allyson was perfect in her new role, almost like a parent who had stayed up later than the kids to talk to the ageing relatives and foreign visitors. Shelley had no doubt that Mark was going to be every bit as impressed as she was, when he eventually got to see the shows.

Closing the door behind her, she put down her bag and took off her coat. She was wearing a close-fitting black cashmere dress and a gold silk scarf. He smiled as he handed her a drink, then touched his glass to hers.

'Merry Christmas and Tessa's success,' he said.

As she drank she kept her eyes on his, and was pleased to see that he didn't look away.

'Did you bring the videotapes?' he asked, going to open the TV cabinet.

She watched as he ejected a cassette from the machine, then putting her drink down she pulled her dress over her head and laid it aside with her coat. Wearing only the gold silk scarf, black hold-up stockings and high-heeled shoes she joined him at the TV and handed him the videos.

He took them, then catching her reflection in the screen he turned round.

'Merry Christmas,' she murmured.

He started to speak but her hand was already twisting round his tie, using it to pull his mouth to hers. She lifted one foot onto the corner of the desk and rubbed herself against him. His hands went automatically to her body, he thought to push her away, but as he touched her and felt the intense hardening of his cock he found himself kissing her back.

'Someone might come in,' he said gruffly.

'I locked the door.'

Her tongue moved back into his mouth as she unfastened his trousers, then holding his cock with both hands she sank to her knees and began to moisten him.

He could stop this, and knew he should, but he also knew he wouldn't, for she had the power to arouse him like no other woman, and if this was what she wanted then he sure as hell was going to give it to her. So as she sucked him hard, while removing his trousers, he stripped off the rest of his clothes and pressed her head in so tight to his groin he could hear her choking.

Letting her go he looked down at her face. Her lips were tender and wet, her eyes were blazing with lust. Still gazing up at him, she circled her tongue round the tip of his cock, then licked a trail right down to his balls, drawing first one, then the other deep into her mouth. He was so big and hard he might come right away, but then she was on her feet, taking his hand and leading him to one of the guest chairs in front of his desk.

As she pushed him down she stood over him, her legs making an arch over his lap as she thrust her pubic hair to his face. He pushed his tongue into it, squeezing her buttocks and sucking her violently as she rotated her hips and moaned with the explosive pleasures of his expert mouth. Then she was lowering herself onto him, her fingers guiding him to her. When he was there, her hands moved behind her, gripping the edge of the desk. Her long, slender legs took her down slowly, until she'd swallowed his cock entirely. Then she raised herself up until he was only just in her. She smiled down at him, then watched as she took him into her again.

'Is this good?' she murmured.

His hands circled her waist as he leaned forward to kiss and bite her breasts. Then she pushed him back and told him to watch as she began sliding smoothly up and down his cock, her magnificent legs bending and stretching with the power of an athlete. It was blowing his mind.

He rubbed her clitoris and watched her come many times before he stood up, laid her flat on the desk and entered her again. He held her legs wide and looked down at her face as he began ramming himself towards climax. When finally he came, in long, exquisite spurts, his thumb was between her legs making her come too. He'd heard about multiple orgasms, but she was the first woman he'd known who experienced them. They were as big a turn-on as the woman herself, and within minutes he was spinning her over and pushing into her from behind.

It was already dark outside by the time she finally put her dress back on. His assistant had gone and the message light on his phone was blinking hard. The sound of Christmas carols and heavy traffic drifted up from the wintry street below.

She was smiling that sultry smile as she came towards him, putting on her coat. He was perched on the edge of his desk, still naked.

'I knew you couldn't resist me,' she said, kissing him.

'I wasn't trying,' he countered.

'But when we last met you said it shouldn't happen again.'

Raising his hands he ran them softly over the cashmere that was covering her breasts. 'Merry Christmas,' he said, and using her nipples to pull her forward he kissed her on the mouth.

Chapter 10

It was Christmas morning. The floor of Tessa's flat was strewn with torn wrapping paper and breakfast dishes, while a carol service from St Matthew's was chorusing cheerily out of the TV. The tree Bob had brought home a few nights ago was standing in the corner, its blinking lights reflecting in the shiny surfaces of the red and gold frosted balls. The mistletoe Tessa had bought was poised with romantic intent over the front door, while fake snow encrusted the corners of the windows giving them a cute, Christmas-cardish sort of look. It was all very festive, except for the faint smell of gas that was leaking from the fire in the hearth, though it was currently masked by the Estée Lauder perfume Tessa had found in a gift from Bob. The slim gold necklace that had accompanied it was back in its velvet pouch on the coffee table, waiting for a special occasion that Tessa would probably also have to pay for, but that was OK, she didn't really mind. She'd given him a pair of Ralph Lauren cufflinks and a book on how to stop smoking. It should have been drinking, but she'd obviously picked up the wrong book, which had made them laugh when he'd opened it, quite an achievement for Bob, considering the pounding throb of his hangover.

Now the presents were open Tessa was in the kitchen, flicking through a cookbook to find out what to do with a turkey. Bob was lying on the sofa, still struggling with his hangover and trying to stop shaking. He hadn't showered yet that morning, nor shaved, and the old pyjama bottoms and T-shirt he was wearing were in need of a wash. He'd do something about himself in a minute, but right now his head was hurting too much to move very far. Tessa, a regular little nurse, had brought him coffee and Alka Seltzer, and gently massaged his scalp, but despite her show of concern he knew she was worried that he'd spoil the day.

'I've always hated Christmas,' she'd told him last night. 'But it's going to be different with you. This year I'm going to love it.'

And he wanted her to, especially after the miscarriage she'd just suffered. He'd come home a few nights ago to find her tucked up in bed, eyes red from crying, and a terrible fear in her heart that he was going to be angry. It had upset him immensely to think she was afraid, though it had been a timely and alarming warning of just how violent his drunken tempers must be getting. Wanting only to comfort and reassure her, he'd slipped into bed with her and held her until they were crying together. Not until later, when she had fallen asleep in his arms, had he given any thought to the fact that he was now free to leave her. But at the time he had brushed it aside, not only because he couldn't just up and go while she was still so upset about the baby, but because he had no idea what Allyson's feelings were now. If she hated him as much as he deserved, then no chance of forgiveness could possibly exist, and even if he could bear to swallow his pride and ask, there was really no point even thinking about it while Tessa was still recovering.

Fortunately she had this new job to keep her mind busy now, and though she still seemed a bit shaky at times, she was throwing herself into all the training and rehearsals to such a degree that he really hadn't seen much of her since the baby had gone. It was a busy time for sport too, but though he'd been in touch with all his contacts he had yet to hear back from any of them. He'd received a cheque though, for a commentary he'd done a couple of months ago, another cheque that had to be deposited into Tessa's account, to start paying off the enormous sum he already owed her. With the payment had come a letter informing him that the company concerned wouldn't be taking up their option on his contract next year. That company had been his last hope, so it was in panic that he'd called up the producer, who, for old times' sake, had agreed to see him. The meeting had been so excruciating that after, when he'd returned to his car, he'd actually wept.

'Why don't you come and help,' Tessa grumbled. 'I've never cooked a turkey before. How am I supposed to know what to do?'

'Just leave it,' he said. 'Who wants turkey anyway?' It wasn't what he'd meant to say, but the last thing he wanted right now was to go out there and start playing happy Christmas cooks.

Coming to kneel on the floor in front of him, she rested her elbows on his knees and looked up at him. 'It's Christmas. Our first one together,' she reminded him. 'We should be celebrating and doing all the things everyone else does at Christmas.'

More truculence barged past his good intentions as he said, 'Then get me a drink.'

Sighing with exasperation she said, 'That's all you ever think about. Did you watch the videos of the two pilots I did?'

He nodded.

'Well? What did you think?' She grinned. 'Was I good or was I just great?'

'You were great,' he told her, smoothing the hair back from her face. 'And you looked incredible.'

'That's what everyone said. Now come and help me with this turkey.'

In the end it was too much effort, so they went to the pub and Bob steadied the DTs with a few stiff gins, while Tessa sipped a Coke, and they made each other laugh by poking fun at all the men who turned up wearing their new Christmas sweaters.

'I should have bought you one,' Tessa declared. 'Did Allyson ever buy you one?'

He knocked back another gin. Yes, Allyson had bought him sweaters, in fact he could hardly remember buying anything without Allyson being there, except surprises for her, of course. He hadn't got her anything this year, how could he when he'd have to ask Tessa for the money? The sad and crazy part of it was that Tessa would probably have given it to him, but how could he give Allyson something Tessa had paid for?

'Let's have another drink,' he growled, angry now that Tessa had made him think about Allyson, whose fault it was that he hadn't got her a present, since she was the one who'd got the bank to freeze his money. 'What are you going to have?'

'Another Coke.'

'It's Christmas Day,' he reminded her testily. 'Why don't you have something stronger?'

She shook her head. 'I'm OK with Coke.'

'A sherry, or something?' he suggested. 'Or what about a cocktail?'

'I've told you before, I don't really like alcohol. It makes me unhappy. Just a couple of sips of yours is enough.'

He was feeling belligerent enough to press it, but then she grinned and kissed him on the mouth, and by the time he went off to get a refill he'd forgotten all about her abstinence and was thinking more about when she might be ready to have sex again. But that was soon forgotten too, and Julian's arrival on the scene a couple of hours later was well timed to help Tessa get Bob home and into bed.

249

'Please don't let on that you know he wet himself,' Tessa said, stuffing Bob's clothes into the little counter-top washing machine in the kitchen. 'He'll get really embarrassed.'

'It's OK,' Julian assured her. 'I won't say anything. But you've got to know he's in a pretty bad way, if he's doing things like that.'

Tessa nodded. 'But we'll only end up having terrible rows if I try to make him stop and I hate rows.' She smiled brightly. 'Let's go out somewhere and leave him to sleep it off in peace.'

'OK. Where do you want to go?'

She shrugged. 'For a walk. That's what people do on Christmas Day, isn't it? Go for walks after lunch. Did you have lunch with your parents?'

He nodded. 'What about you? Have you had any lunch?'

She grimaced. 'I had some scampi and chips down the pub. I bought a turkey, but neither of us knew how to cook it. Anyway, come on, let's wrap up warm and go for a walk by the river.'

Half an hour later Julian was edging his ancient BMW into a parking space on a Chelsea side street, and after locking up he and Tessa, who was colourfully dressed in a bright red Santa's hat, Bob's huge black padded jacket and an outrageous pair of Christmas-tree leggings, strolled out along the Embankment opposite Cheyne Walk.

'Do you think she's up there?' Tessa said, gazing up at Allyson's windows.

'No lights,' he answered, turning his back to the river wall and resting his elbows.

'I'm thinking I should ask for her dressing room,' Tessa said. 'I need a dressing room, now I'm about to do most of the show, and I think I should have the big one. What do you reckon?'

'Where would she go?'

'She could have the one I've been using. It's nice. It's got a telly and its own shower.' She looked up at the darkened flat again. 'I should have brought Bob's key, we could have gone in and had a look round.'

Julian turned to look at her. 'You'd actually do that?' he said. 'While she's not there?'

Tessa shrugged. 'I don't know. Maybe. If we're going to live there, we should take measurements and things.'

Julian continued to look at her, his grey-blue eyes searching her profile as his mind tried to link up with what she was thinking. 'So Bob's going to buy her out then?' he said.

Grinning, Tessa stood on tiptoe and hugged him. Then tucking her arm through his she walked him on towards Battersea Bridge. Despite the bitter cold the sun was shining, and there were plenty of people about, either walking off their Christmas indulgences, or watching out for children on new bicycles or skates.

'Shall I tell you something?' she said as they stopped to look over the side of the bridge. The water that flowed beneath was shiny and black, with vast swirling depths and thickly clogged banks of mud. 'Sometimes Allyson reminds me of my mother.'

When Julian said nothing she turned to look at him, her luminous eyes combing his pale, handsome face. 'My mother killed herself, did I ever tell you that?' she said. 'She had this gun, I never knew where she got it, and she just blew out her brains.'

Through his shock she could see him struggling to find the right words. 'Why?' he finally managed.

'I think it was because she couldn't forgive herself,' she answered, then turned to look back at Allyson's flat.

'Had she done something . . .?' he said.

Tessa smiled. She knew how hard this conversation was for other people, no-one ever really knew what to say. 'It was more what she didn't do,' she answered.

Julian looked up at the flat too. Winter trees and white

251

clouds were reflected in the windows. Evergreen shrubs crowded the balconies.

'I wonder what Allyson would do if she knew I was down here?' Tessa said.

'What would you want her to do?'

'Anything, as long as it's not what my mother did.' She turned to look up at him again. Then smiling she said, 'We ought to be getting back. If Bob wakes up he'll wonder where we are.'

With the day's festivities at an end Allyson was walking down the front path of her parents' Chelsea home, helping Bob's father to a taxi. It was slippery out, and George wasn't too steady on his feet.

'I had a lovely day,' he told her, his breath making wispy clouds in the chill night air.

'I'm glad you came,' she said. 'So was Mummy. We'd have missed you if you hadn't.'

'I could have gone to my sister,' he assured her, 'but well, I always come here.'

'Of course you do.' She opened the rear door and helped him in. After giving him a kiss she told the driver his address and leaned in the window. 'I'll call you next week,' she said, 'find out how you are.'

'You'll always be my girl,' he said, squeezing her hand.

Smiling, she stood back and waved as the taxi drove off into the night. Then pulling her cardigan tightly around her, she ran back inside. Her aunt and uncle were still there, snoozing on the sofa, while a repeat of *Only Fools and Horses* played on the TV. Her mother was in the kitchen cleaning the oven. Her father had retired to the study an hour ago to compose a letter to *The Times*.

She'd spent every Christmas she could remember in this house, unwrapping presents in the morning, getting ready for church, then going to dish out meals for the homeless before returning for their own turkey feast.

Though she hadn't wanted to be anywhere else this year, it had been almost unbearable without Bob. Until the break-up her family had all adored him, and she knew that Christmas hadn't been the same for them either, without his teasing and taunting and outrageous games to liven up the day. Everyone kept looking around, as though expecting him to walk in. Then, when they seemed finally to accept that he wouldn't, a pall fell over the gathering as though there had been a bereavement.

'Daddy's had another bombing,' her mother said, as Allyson started to pack away the cake. It was Peggy's way of saying her husband's incontinence pad needed changing.

Allyson stopped and looked at her mother. Then quite suddenly she started to laugh. After a moment her mother started to laugh too. It had been an awful day, so awful Allyson had almost wanted to put a gun to her head as she tormented herself with images of how cosy and romantic Bob and Tessa probably were, over the river in their love nest. And now here she was at the end of it all, standing in the kitchen with her mother crying with laughter at how wretched their lives were, thanks to the men they loved.

Five days later Allyson was back at the office. Normally she and Bob drove down to the country on Boxing Day and stayed until New Year, but even if she hadn't closed up the house she wouldn't have wanted to go alone, it would have been just too depressing. Besides, she was attempting to get used to the idea that everything was different now. Though she hated even to think it, and could feel everything in her straining to resist it, she knew that the only way she was ever going to get over it was to accept that moving on meant looking ahead to the future her new job was offering, instead of casting about in the past for a thousand vivid and happy memories to torment herself with; or letting her imagination loose on the present when it invariably conjured up all kinds of painful scenarios of what Bob and Tessa might be doing now.

She had no more programmes to record before January, they were all in the can, so she'd come to the office to start getting things ready for her first meeting with her new research team. Thanks to Mark's skilful handling of Shelley, Allyson had been able to have a long and productive talk with her on the phone over Christmas, when she'd put forward the names of those she wanted to poach for her team, which Shelley hadn't objected to even though Allyson felt she was stealing the cream of the crop. Shelley was even enthusiastic about the few sketchy ideas Allyson threw in for discussion, coming up with several suggestions of her own that would certainly work. To Allyson's relief they'd also agreed that she should keep her office, her salary and dressing room, all of which was going to save her an enormous amount of face when her new role on the programme was made public sometime in the next few days.

'It's like the dawning of a new era for us,' Shelley had remarked towards the end of the call. 'I'm just glad that we're going into it together.'

Allyson laughed. 'You didn't really think I was going to let you go ahead without me, did you?' she challenged.

'I have to confess, I was starting to get worried,' Shelley replied. 'It's been a horrible few months for you and I honestly wouldn't have blamed you if you'd decided to walk away from it all.'

'My marriage maybe, but not the programme,' Allyson said. 'Anyway, I'll see you at the office on Thursday.'

Shelley came in around lunch time, so they ran through the rain to the wine bar where they ordered shepherd's pie and chips and a bottle of red wine.

London was like a ghost town at this time of year, so they didn't have too many interruptions as they talked, with people coming up to say hello to Allyson or ask for her autograph.

'So, how was your mother?' Allyson asked as they waited for the food.

'As witchy as ever. Probably where I get it from. What about yours? Still cut up over Bob?'

Allyson felt the bottom drop out of her carefully constructed resolve. Quickly she recovered it and rolled her eyes. 'And some,' she said. 'But it's only been a couple of months. You can't expect her to be over it yet.'

Shelley's expression was wry. 'Was it tough?' she said. 'I guess it must have been.'

'I've been married to him for nineteen years,' Allyson said. 'It doesn't just go away.'

'No, of course not,' Shelley responded, while looking curiously at the package Allyson was taking out of her bag. 'So, have you spoken to your research team yet? Any decisions on where you're going to record your first programme?'

'Nothing's settled yet,' Allyson answered, 'but it should be by the end of next week.' She set a beautifully wrapped package on the table in front of her, then looked into Shelley's face. 'Listen, I know things have been a bit strained between us lately,' she said, 'and it's probably mostly my fault. No, please, hear me out,' she said when Shelley started to protest. 'We've been friends for a long time, and I'm not prepared to lose you the way I lost Bob. So I'm sorry for the way I've been, if I've said anything hurtful, or done anything to upset you . . .'

'You haven't,' Shelley said. 'In fact it's probably been more the other way round.'

Allyson smiled. 'We've come through difficult times before and no doubt we will again,' she said, 'but right now, I just want you to know how much this new job means to me. It's exactly what I need, something fresh

255

and challenging to focus on, and plenty of reasons to get up in the morning.' She laughed. 'Anyway, I'm really glad you came up with the idea, and I'm flattered you think I could do it.'

'Just don't prove me wrong,' Shelley warned. 'I really stuck my neck out with Mark Reiner to get you this position.'

Allyson looked down at the package. The lie irritated her intensely, but she let it go unchallenged. 'I got you this,' she said, handing the package over. 'It's not just a Christmas present, it's a thank-you present too.'

Shelley looked delighted, but that was nothing to how she responded when she opened the package and saw what was inside. 'Oh my God, Ally,' she breathed.

'It's a Marcel Bouraine fan dancer,' Allyson said. 'Circa 1920. It's stamped.'

'This must have cost you a fortune,' Shelley protested. She was lifting the heavy, bronze figurine from the box. 'It's exquisite. Oh my God.' She laughed as her eyes filled with tears. 'I don't know what to say.'

'I'm glad you like it,' Allyson said, smiling.

'Like it! I love it.' The slender female body and open bronze fan were almost animated by the glinting winter sunlight coming through the windows, and the thick gold-veined marble of the base weighed heavily in her hand. Allyson reached out to touch it, turning it to get a better look. They were still admiring it when their food arrived.

'OK, so tell me about Mark,' Allyson said as Shelley packed the figurine away. 'Did you see him over Christmas?'

Shelley's eyes started to shine. 'Just before,' she said. 'We had the most amazing session in his office.'

'No!' Allyson cried, covering her true reaction well. Not that she wanted to have a session in his office, it was just that ... Well, Shelley's involvement with him felt like a threat to her friendship with him, which was nonsense of course, so laughing she said, 'What if someone had come in?'

'The door was locked. But to be honest I don't think either of us would have noticed even if someone had. I'm telling you that man is something else.' She sighed ecstatically and picked up her wine. 'You know, I was really beginning to think there was no-one out there for me. Here I am, forty-two years old, and, well, I can tell you Mark Reiner is definitely worth the wait.' She took a sip of wine, then abruptly changed the subject. 'New Year's Eve,' she said. 'Will it be the Roof Garden, or Jemima and Phillip Gunter's? They always give a good bash. Which do you fancy?'

'I hadn't given it much thought,' Allyson answered, trying to steer her mind away from the image of Bob embracing Tessa at midnight.

'Well, you decide. I'll get hold of Mark and ask him if he wants to come too.' Shelley looked quickly at Allyson. 'You don't mind, do you, if he comes?'

'Why should I? No, that's fine.' She was lying, because it wasn't fine, but she didn't want to get into why when she didn't even know.

After lunch they returned to the office, but Shelley didn't stay long, she was off to Bond Street to find something to wear for New Year's Eve. Something to blow Mark's mind. Allyson carried on working till four, so engrossed in the drawing-up of proposals for her first programme that she soon forgot about Shelley and Mark. And with no-one else in the office to distract her she'd managed to achieve a great deal by the time she started packing up her briefcase to go home. She was on the point of walking out the door when her telephone rang.

'Allyson Jaymes,' she said.

'Allyson Jaymes. It's Mark Reiner.'

Her heart skipped a beat. 'Mark!' she cried, unable to keep the pleasure from her voice.

'How are you?' he asked. 'Did you have a good Christmas?'

'Yes, thank you,' she lied happily. 'How was yours?'

'My brother's here with his wife. It's always good to see them.'

'Oh,' was all she could think of to say to that.

'I was wondering,' he said, 'if you're doing anything New Year's Eve. Nick, that's my brother, has got a table at the Grosvenor House ball, and, well, I'm in need of a partner.'

Allyson's mind went straight to Shelley.

'It's for charity,' he said, as though that would persuade her.

'That's good,' she responded.

He laughed. 'I can come by and pick you up. Dinner's at nine. I guess we should get there around then. If you're free, of course.'

Allyson's thoughts were in such a commotion that she truly didn't know what to say. She wanted to go, of course, but if she did what the hell was she going to tell Shelley? Actually there wasn't a single thing she could tell Shelley that Shelley would find in any way acceptable. Especially not when Shelley was right now somewhere in Bond Street in search of some slinky, sizzling little number with which to dazzle him on the very night he was talking about.

'Mark, I . . .' she began.

'. . . would love to come?' he finished.

She laughed. 'Yes, but . . .'

'You've got other plans?'

'No. It's just . . .'

'Then I'll be by around nine,' he said. 'I'll be the one in the tux,' and the line went dead.

She had to call him back. Right now. She had to explain that she simply couldn't do this to Shelley, even if he could. She had no idea what he was playing at, having amazing sessions with Shelley in his office, then calling up to ask her out, but she couldn't help feeling flattered by the possibility that he might just prefer her to Shelley. But that was nonsense, it wasn't about that, she was sure. And though she found him attractive, there was simply no way in the world she was ready to go out with other men. In fact just the thought of it made her feel too peculiar for words. Bob was the only man she'd ever been to bed with, the only man she'd ever loved. It was going to be a long, long time before she was ready to let someone take his place, no matter how attractive she might find them.

Her dilemma seemed only to increase as she wandered down to her dressing room to get her coat. Bob was going to be with Tessa on New Year's Eve, so why the hell shouldn't she go out with someone too? If nothing else it would show her bastard of a husband that she wasn't sitting at home crying over his desertion any more. And how desperately she wanted him to know that someone else wanted her. Maybe she could go without mentioning it to Shelley. She could always say that she didn't feel up to a party, and had decided to spend the night with her parents.

Her heart turned over as she suddenly realized she was sifting through the gorgeous creations on her clothes rail, picking out something that was stunningly suitable for a ball. Did that mean she'd already made a decision? No, it simply meant she'd have a dress to hand in the unlikely event that she did decide to go.

At nine o'clock on New Year's Eve, dressed in a black Gianni Versace tuxedo, a long black cashmere overcoat and white silk scarf, Mark rang the doorbell to Allyson's flat. A few seconds later the buzzer sounded to release the door, so pushing it open he climbed up to the second floor and found her waiting on the landing.

He stopped when he saw her, and felt his words to be gauchely inadequate as he said, 'You look beautiful.'

And she did, with her fine blonde hair scooped up in a diamond-studded net, her face exquisitely made up, and her slender shoulders bare to the tight black bodice of her dress and tops of her over-the-elbow gloves. From the waist to the ground the dress was a magnificent array of stiff taffeta petticoats, all in black, with high, strappy shoes that had across the toes the same design of diamonds that dropped from her ears and circled her neck.

'Thank you,' she smiled. 'Would you like to come in?'

He followed her inside, to where her black fur coat and small velvet purse were lying on a chair in the sitting room. 'It's fake,' she said, meaning the coat.

He smiled. 'But this isn't,' he said, taking a small boxed orchid from his inside pocket.

Allyson's eyes widened with surprise and pleasure. It was such a touchingly old-fashioned thing to do, bring a girl an orchid to pin on her dress.

'Perfect,' he said, standing back to admire her after she'd finished arranging it.

She looked up into his eyes, then felt herself blushing. 'Thank you,' she said again, and hoped he didn't realize how awkward she felt, and how wrong it seemed for him to be in her flat without Bob being there too. In an attempt to cover it she said, 'You look very dashing.'

'Come on,' he laughed, 'the car's right downstairs.'

It was a black Aston Martin with a cream leather interior and every conceivable electronic gadget right at his fingertips. It was also a warm, mellow enclosure on a freezing, windswept night, with an excellent CD system that was playing the newly composed score for a TV movie due to air on Mark's American cable station in a couple of weeks.

As he drove she asked him more about the movie, and laughed when he confessed he hadn't actually seen it yet. Then they talked about other films they had seen, and plays, what had been in the news that day,

260

everything but why he'd invited her tonight, instead of Shelley. She really wanted to ask, but now the opportunity was there she was afraid it might sound as though she was seeking comparisons or compliments, and maybe she was.

It didn't take long to reach the hotel, to her relief, for by then they'd run out of conversation, which didn't seem to bother him, in fact she wasn't even sure he'd noticed. They left the car with a valet, checked their coats, then followed the crowd slowly through to the huge, baroque-style ballroom. The orchestra was playing a Christmas tune, brightly coloured streamers and tinsel cascaded from the ceiling and balcony, while waiters in smart white jackets and tartan bow ties wove between tables with trays of drinks and expertly presented canapés. Nick and Claudia were already there, and to Allyson's surprise she recognized Claudia from school.

'You were in Miss Egger's class,' Allyson laughed. 'The year above me.'

'And I remember you. You were Rachel Wainwright's best friend,' Claudia declared.

'That's right,' Allyson confirmed. She didn't want to spoil the moment by telling them that Rachel had died over ten years ago. Instead she readily accepted the glass of champagne Nick was offering her, and sat down in the chair Mark was holding out.

The two brothers were very similar to look at, she noted, both being dark-haired and dark-eyed, and both had those awkwardly chiselled features that, while not conventionally handsome, were, in her opinion, strikingly attractive. But there the similarity ended, for Nick was much shorter than Mark and carried considerably more weight. Allyson guessed he was older too, though probably not by much. There was no doubt they were close, and as they baited and rallied each other, and went out of their way to make her feel welcome, she started to relax a little and feel glad she had come. And catching up with Claudia was fun too, laughing about all the eccentricities of their teachers and bemoaning the unfairness of well-remembered and detested school rules. There were moments, though, when her mind seemed to slip out of gear and she found herself coasting around in a confusing sort of detachment as she wondered how she had come to be in this room full of strangers, many of whom knew her though she didn't know them. It felt so odd, as though everyone else was part of a dream that she had somehow, mistakenly, stepped into.

They ate smoked salmon and three different types of caviare, followed by roast duck and the most delicious mustard- and honey-flavoured sauce. A tenor from the English National Opera joined the orchestra, then another band took over and soon people started to dance. The time was slipping by, heading fast towards midnight. Allyson barely noticed, she was having such a good time. She'd stopped thinking about Bob some-where between the baked alaska and her fourth glass of champagne, and was feeling so alive she could probably dance until dawn. Then, before she knew it, the count-down to midnight had begun and suddenly she was thinking about Bob in a way that seemed to be stifling her. She wanted so desperately to be with him she could hardly bear it. It had come over her so unexpectedly that despite her efforts to hide it by cheering in the New Year along with everyone else, she could feel herself reeling off into the black depths of despair.

Sensing her distress Mark pressed his lips to her forehead and hugged her gently. 'Happy New Year,' he whispered.

'You too,' she said, embarrassed for him to see the tears in her eyes.

He smiled. 'I'll get your coat.'

*

As Bob pushed his way through a loud, smoky pub in South London he had no clear idea of where he was going, nor even of where he was, he just knew that he didn't want to be there any more, and wasn't even sure why he'd come. Tessa was on the stage with Julian and his band, helping them bring in an extremely rowdy New Year, and though Bob had had far too much to drink, it wasn't enough to stop him feeling ridiculous. With the exception of the landlord, everyone there was at least half his age and though some recognized him, they didn't seem any more impressed by him being there than he was.

He couldn't help wondering which party Allyson had gone to and though he desperately wished he could be with her, he felt sick inside at the way all his old friends were probably laughing now, as they pictured the pathetic farce of his life, and assured Allyson she was better off without him.

As he stumbled out of the door the freezing night air hit him, sobering him a little, but not so much that he couldn't stand it. Spotting a taxi he hailed it and got in the back. All he had in his pocket was half a bottle of gin and a twenty-pound note. It would be enough to get him home, and something to blot out the misery once he got there.

It seemed like a long time later that the driver finally came to a stop. For a moment Bob was confused. Though his surroundings were unquestionably familiar, this wasn't the street of Fifties terraced houses that Tessa lived on, this was the Embankment, between Albert and Battersea Bridges.

He blinked at the driver, who was watching him in the rear-view mirror.

'You OK mate?' the driver asked.

Bob turned to look up at the darkened windows of his and Allyson's flat. It seemed that in his drunken state he had given Allyson's address instead of Tessa's.

'That'll be seventeen fifty,' the driver told him.

Bob mumbled something, and started digging in his pocket for the twenty-pound note.

'Got to get out to pay,' the driver said.

Bob did as he was told, staggering slightly as he hunted again for the money. At last he found it, and was just handing it over when he saw a flash black Aston Martin turn off the Embankment into the slip road that was Cheyne Walk.

'Come on mate, I haven't got all night,' the driver grumbled.

Bob gave him the money. The driver offered him some change, but Bob wasn't looking. So the driver pulled away into the night, leaving Bob swaying on the edge of the pavement as he watched Allyson and another man getting out of the Aston Martin.

'Would you like to come up?' Allyson was saying, as Mark opened the door for her to get out.

'No,' he said, knowing it was the answer she'd hoped for.

She looked up at him. 'I had a lovely time. Thank you.'

Though he didn't smile, his eyes were on hers. 'The photographers upset you as we were leaving,' he said.

She nodded. She'd been thinking about them all the way back. 'We'll probably find ourselves in the papers tomorrow.'

'Probably.'

'So what do I tell Shelley? She's going to wonder why you invited me instead of her.'

'That's an answer I should give Shelley,' he said.

'But it'll be me she asks.'

'Then tell her why you accepted.'

Allyson's eyes were large and confused. 'I'm not sure I know,' she said softly.

Still he didn't smile. 'I'm sure you can work it out,' he said.

He walked her to the front door, hugged her good-night then turned back to the car. She stood watching him drive away, then taking out her key she let herself into the building. Right now it was hard to know why she'd gone, or even how she felt about going. Certainly she'd had a good time, even though she was embarrassed by the way they'd left early. But she had to ask herself, had it really been worth it for all the problems this was going to create with Shelley?

However, if she'd done it to let Bob and Tessa know what a great time she was having, then considering how many press were at the door when they'd left the hotel, she'd probably succeeded. She wasn't even sure how good that made her feel. But then, when she got inside and saw the pale lilac and white orchid pinned to her dress in the mirror, she smiled, and felt her heart fill up with gratitude. For the moment at least, this evening needn't be about anything or anyone but the man who had gone out of his way to make her feel special for those few short, but deeply significant hours as one year blended into the next – which was a whole lot more than Bob had managed, because not one of the messages she replayed before even taking off her coat was from him.

Across the street Bob was trying to focus on the light at the window. He was feeling nauseous and helpless, and angered by the fact that he was standing out here while she was inside.

He wiped a hand across his face, staggered, then looked up at the window again. She had their flat to live in, and a private income that didn't touch their joint accounts. And now she had some rich bloke taking her out on New Year's Eve, while he stood in the street outside, like some tramp with nothing in his trolley. Her life was going on as normal, as if he'd never been a part of it.

After a while he slumped back against the wall and

pulled his coat more tightly around him. It was freezing out here. He could go back to Tessa's, but he didn't have the money to get there. Then he remembered he had the keys to his and Allyson's flat in his pocket.

Thrusting himself away from the wall he started across the pavement, heading towards the blinding lights of the traffic. He rolled back a few paces, then pushed forward again. Someone honked their horn, and he shouted some unintelligible abuse. Then he attempted to cross the road again.

The last thing he remembered was hearing himself grunt as he hit the ground. No pain, no anything, except the grunt and a few circling stars before the blackness.

When he awoke the next morning he was fully dressed, stinking and dry-mouthed on the hard wooden bench of a police cell.

Though New Year's Day was a bank holiday there was a transmission that night, which was to include Tessa's debut as the Happy Hour presenter. This meant that the whole team was in the office early for the morning meeting that filled everyone in on who the guests were, which film insert was being included and the endless other minutiae that went into making up the studio day. Also on the agenda today was a preliminary discussion on the first of the European-based programmes, which was pencilled for transmission at the end of the month. Probably because it was a novelty it engendered some lively debate and excellent input, which Allyson and her two researchers, Justine and Zac, were thrilled about – after all, it was a little like having your new image admired, and even enhanced.

Finally they moved on to the content of Allyson's Night Cap slots, which were scheduled for bulk recordings in order to keep her reasonably free for all the travelling she was now going to be doing. That took some time to go through, and for a meeting that should have been mainly about Tessa, Allyson couldn't help being aware of how much she was dominating. However, Tessa hardly seemed to notice, and Allyson was pleased to see her showing some signs of nervousness at last. Until now it had all been playtime, but today's studio recording would be the real thing. Had it been anyone else she might have offered some encouragement, as it was Tessa she simply willed her to die.

However, an even greater concern right now was Shelley, who was at an early meeting in town and not due into the office until eleven. It was a moment Allyson was dreading, for, as expected, one of the papers had announced Allyson's 'new love' that morning, with a headline that was generous in spirit, if wrong in belief. 'Happy New Year, Ally!' it had shouted, above a triumphantly worded lead-in telling her that she deserved to be loved after the terrible time she had been through. She appreciated the sentiment, but not the inaccuracy, and wondered what Mark was making of his ludicrous new image as 'Prince Charming'. There were more allusions to the fairy tale, obviously because they'd left at midnight, but they were all too corny and trivial to waste time on, or might have been were it not for how Shelley was taking it. Just thank God she hadn't been there first thing, when the others had been ribbing Allyson about her 'dashingly romantic millionaire prince', who just happened to be their dynamic new boss. Tessa, Allyson had noticed with delight, had been somewhat confused, and possibly even put out about it. Of course there was no knowing exactly what Tessa was thinking, but the girl surely had the wit to realize that this new turn of events couldn't fail to have an effect on Bob.

Shelley arrived as the meeting broke up and cut Allyson dead as she called that day's production team into her office for a briefing. She then continued to go out of her way to avoid Allyson, while making a great fuss of Tessa, until just before the recording, when she walked into Allyson's office and slammed the door shut behind her.

'So,' she said, tight-lipped and obviously livid, 'I call your parents at midnight to wish you happy New Year and you're not there. So I call your flat and you're not there either. I, of course, think you're in bed, hiding from the world, but no! Cinderella's flaunting herself at some fancy ball, having a fabulous time in a Jasper Conran gown and the arms of her new love, *who*, as far as I knew, was just getting started on a relationship with me. So do you want to give me some explanation of what's going on? I think you owe me one, don't you?'

'Probably,' Allyson conceded.

'Well, I'm waiting.'

'Don't condescend to me like that,' Allyson snapped. 'I'm not a child you're reprimanding. I'm a grown woman and as far as I knew Mark Reiner *was*, *is*, getting started on a relationship with you.'

'So how come *you're* at a ball with him on New Year's Eve?' The bitterness of her tone was as cutting as the ice in her eyes.

Allyson had had some time to think about this, and was now pretty sure she knew the answer. 'He invited me,' she said, 'in an effort to divert some of today's press attention from the way I'm being pushed down the agenda on my own show, and having to suffer the humiliation of my husband's junior mistress taking over the spotlight.'

Shelley ignored the dig. 'But you still lied. You must have known you were going out with Mark when you told me . . . .'

'OK, I'm sorry about that.'

'So why didn't you tell me? Why keep it a secret and let me find out in the paper?'

'I don't know why I didn't tell you,' Allyson cried. 'I

suppose because I knew you'd be upset.'

'You're damn right I am. You know how I feel about him. I told you everything that was happening between us, then you, who's supposed to be my best friend, go out with him on one of the most romantic nights of the year. So let's have the real truth, shall we? If you're having an affair . . .'

'We're not having an affair!'

'So why didn't you tell me about going to his office? And what's all the secrecy about the lunch you two had? What are you trying to hide?'

'You're making this sound like some kind of conspiracy, which it's not! And I'm not getting into defending myself either. I've done nothing to hurt you, nor would I. OK, I should have told you about last night, but at the time I didn't know what it was about myself. And to be frank, you'd pissed me off earlier in the day, when you said you'd really stuck your neck out to get me the producer's job. For your information the job was my idea, which is what I went to see Mark about on the day you obviously think I went off to start some clandestine affair. It was also what he invited me to lunch to discuss while you were getting ready to shove Tessa into my limelight.'

Shelley's face was white. It was clear she felt duped, and she was right, she had been, royally.

Allyson threw out her hands. 'Look, I'm sorry,' she said. 'Can we try to forget this has happened? It was a one-off. I told you why he asked me, and as for the job, at the time I felt as though I was fighting for my life. I had to do something.'

'So why didn't you come to me?'

'I did, but it wasn't getting me anywhere. Oh God, I wish none of this was happening. Please, try to understand, when you go through something like this, losing your husband, getting pushed aside because you're too old, having your life publicized and analysed in every detail by the press, well, it's hard to keep things in perspective.'

Shelley showed no signs of backing down. Her dark eyes were glinting with rage, her mouth was pinched with frustration. She started to speak, but Allyson cut across her.

'For God's sake, we can't fall out over a man,' she cried. 'A man who means nothing to me . . .'

'But what about him? What do you mean to him?'

'Nothing! He was just being kind.'

'But why?'

'I don't know. For the reasons I told you.'

'But why would he care about the way *you* feel? What's it to him?'

Allyson's eyes flashed. 'Well, thanks for that,' she snapped. 'It's just what I need, right now, to feel as though I'm not worth the effort.'

'Oh, let's make this all about you, shall we?' Shelley cried, throwing up her hands. 'You and your heartbreak. Why deal with your disloyalty and lies, they don't paint such a great picture, do they?'

'Shelley, if you want answers about last night then I suggest you ask Mark.'

'Oh, I'm sure I'm going to do that.'

Allyson was right on the brink of losing her own temper, but knowing that Shelley's anger was much more justified, she simply glared back, giving herself some moments to calm down. 'I'm sorry,' she said, finally. 'What else can I say, except I'm sorry.'

Shelley's breath was still shallow, but she too took a moment to get her temper back in control. 'You should have told me,' she said, 'instead of letting me find out from the paper like that.'

'I know. It was unforgivable, especially when I know how that feels.'

The malice in Shelley's eyes started to fade. 'If it is you,' she said, her voice barely emerging through the tightness in her throat, 'if he's decided he'd rather have you than me . . .'

'He hasn't.'

Shelley stopped and dashed a hand through her hair. Then forcing a smile she said, 'I'd want to kill you if he had. It's been so long for me, and this time it feels so right . . .'

'I know. And do you really think after what's just happened to me I'd walk off with the man you're crazy about? Besides, I'm so far from being ready for anything new it makes me feel sick even to think of it.'

'But that's you, not him.'

'Shelley, I've yet to meet the man who can resist you. And believe you me, he's no exception.'

Shelley despised the weakness in her that so desperately wanted to believe that. Except why shouldn't she? She only had to remember what had happened in Mark's office just before Christmas to realize that there was a good chance Allyson was right. He hadn't been able to resist her then, so why was she doubting herself now? Probably, she thought bitterly, because Allyson's belief in her irresistible charms was nothing like the truth painted by history. And no matter what spin Allyson put on the reasons he'd taken her out last night, he'd still chosen Allyson over her. Did Allyson have any idea how much that hurt? Did she know how much hope Shelley had invested in that man? OK, she was foolish to do it, but in her heart she just couldn't stop herself believing that he was the one who was going to make some sense of all the waiting and rejection, all the confusion and trying that until now had never brought her anything but pain.

In the end all she said was, 'I hope you're right.'

'I am,' Allyson assured her. Getting to her feet, she walked round her desk and put her hands on Shelley's shoulders. 'I don't know if there's a man in the world who's worth all the grief they cause,' she said, 'but I suppose we have to believe there is. And in the meantime, if it makes you feel any better, I've now got the overwhelming joy of watching Tessa Dukes make her glittering debut on what was always my programme, before she no doubt goes off somewhere to celebrate with the man who was, correction, still is, my husband.'

Shelley groaned. 'How could that make me feel better?' she said, glancing at her watch. Everyone would be in the studio by now, she'd be needed.

'OK, not better,' Allyson responded, 'just aware that that side of my life is still very much dominated by Bob Jaymes, which is the main reason I went last night, in the hope of making him jealous.'

Shelley smiled. She wasn't sure it made it any better, but that was at least something she understood.

Allyson hugged her, then watched her go off to check on the last-minute details for recording, her long shapely legs moving swiftly and confidently beneath the gentle cling of a cashmere skirt, her lovely dark hair falling in short waves over the collar of a cerise silk shirt. Whichever angle she was viewed from there was never any mistaking what an exquisitely beautiful woman Shelley was, which could only make Allyson wonder about the extraordinary perversity of a fate that dealt her such bad hands with men. For her part Allyson honestly didn't want to cause her any more pain, nor was it her intention to, but she couldn't help wondering how long it was going to take for her to really forgive Shelley for making Tessa Dukes the star of *Soirée*.

The cameras were moving into position. Upstairs in the gallery the production team was getting ready to record. Tessa's face was on every monitor, rehearsing with the autocue that contained the opening link. She looked cute and sexy, with her fresh open face and a newly designed skin-tight catsuit. She'd already met the guests, a flighty little actress who was playing the bitch in a new teenage soap, and a car-wrecking stuntman who'd just cut his first single. It was going to make a change for her to interview someone now, after all the interviews she'd given these last few days. Her face was going to be on the cover of at least two glossies when they came out, and *Hello!* magazine had been in touch asking to take shots of her at home. Of course they couldn't do that, but she wasn't going to pass up on the publicity so she'd find a way round it. Maybe one of Bob's rich friends could lend them a place to get photographed in.

'OK, recording in one minute,' the floor manager announced.

A sound man came up to fiddle with her mic, then went away again. Tessa peered through the lights and found a couple of researchers smiling their encouragement. No sign of Allyson, or Shelley. They were probably watching upstairs. She hadn't expected to feel this nervous, in fact it was getting closer to panic.

Then Shelley was walking towards her.

'Are you OK?' she asked.

Tessa nodded, but she looked as scared as Shelley had expected.

'The pilots were fantastic,' Shelley told her. 'Mark Reiner called to say he thought so too.'

'Mark Reiner?' Tessa echoed, obviously pleased.

'We both think you've got something special. Just keep the enthusiasm down a notch, it can get overwhelming, but you're a natural when it comes to letting your guest talk. It took Allyson a long time to learn that.'

Tessa knew then that she was going to be brilliant.

Satisfied that the compliment at Allyson's expense had worked, Shelley squeezed the girl's hand and disappeared into the darkness surrounding the set. It was true, Mark had called, and he'd been as impressed as everyone else with the pilots. He'd had nothing to say about his date with Allyson last night, nor about what had happened in his office before Christmas. So Shelley hadn't mentioned anything either, for she was nothing if not a professional, and minutes before a recording wasn't the time to be dealing with matters that were so very personal. She couldn't help wondering if that was why he'd rung when he had. But even if it was, he'd at least remembered to wish her a happy New Year, and, if she'd heard him correctly, she was sure he'd said something about looking forward to seeing her again soon.

'Shelley? Any last-minute notes?' the director said as she entered the gallery.

'No,' she answered.

'OK, studio, stand by.' The director was speaking into the talkback.

'Can someone verify the spelling of this guy's name?' the caption operator called out from his end of the gallery.

A researcher came forward to check.

'Everyone ready to go?' the director asked.

'Standing by,' came several voices.

'OK, roll tape,' the production assistant instructed.

The tape rolled and the countdown began.

'Good luck everyone,' Shelley said, taking her position the other side of the PA. 'Does Tessa have an earpiece?'

'Yes,' Tessa answered, her anxious face filling up the monitors and making her look younger than ever.

'Be brilliant,' Shelley said.

Tessa smiled.

'Ten seconds, nine, eight . . .' the PA announced.

'OK, on you camera two,' the director said as the countdown ended. 'And cue Tessa.'

Despite two false starts when Tessa tripped up in the opening link, her first real recording turned into a triumph. It took her next to no time to get her nerves under control, and she ended up putting on a show that surpassed even Shelley's expectations. She was entertaining, energetic and impressively professional considering her lack of experience. She caused an audible gasp in the gallery when she asked the actress, point-blank, how much her new breasts had cost, and made them all laugh when she got up to jig about to the stuntman's new hit. As a performer she was outlandish, unconventional and definitely refreshing. She was also on an incredible high by the time she came out of the studio, and ready to party all night.

However, Shelley sobered her up by reminding her that the transmission hadn't happened yet, and then she'd be in the hands of the press. Not that Shelley expected anything but praise in the next morning's papers, she just wanted to keep the girl's feet on the ground, and do what she could to avoid rubbing the success in Allyson's face.

The reviews next morning were much as Shelley had expected, though, ironically, Tessa's limelight was somewhat stolen by Bob Jaymes's appearance in court for being drunk and disorderly. As his arrest had happened on New Year's Eve people were more inclined to laugh than condemn.

Allyson was one of the few who didn't find it funny, and might have called him, had she not been flying off to recce the Sporting Club in Monaco as a possible venue for her first foreign programme. That had to take priority now. Bob's increasing problem with drink and the reasons behind it were no longer her concern. Let Tessa deal with his mess, after all she was the one who'd created it.

Chapter 11

Getting Bob out of bed after a heavy night was no easy task, but Tessa had a day off today and was determined they should spend it together. She'd gone to a lot of trouble organizing things, so she had no intention of letting him spoil it, even if it did mean giving him a breakfast of thick black coffee followed by a fortifying gin.

By ten o'clock he was showered, shaved and dressed ready to go. His face was a bit pale, but he looked pretty cool in his black Hugo Boss jeans and a white Armani shirt, though definitely his mood could have been better. But, as he probably had a head like a wrecking ball, she wasn't going to annoy him by telling him to cheer up. Instead, she carried on running up and down stairs filling up the car with their belongings.

By ten thirty they were ready to leave. Tessa had intended to drive, but he insisted he would, so avoiding an argument she slipped into the passenger seat and adjusted the radio. Very soon they were sweeping through New Covent Garden, heading towards Chelsea, and Tessa was chattering on about Allyson and how she'd gone to France on a supposed recce, but, according to everyone in the office, was apparently meeting up with Mark Reiner, the new owner of the company, whom she'd been out with on New Year's Eve.

'Just shut the fuck up about her, will you?' Bob

snapped in the end. 'I'm doing what you want, aren't I? So you don't have to wind me up any more.'

'I was only saying . . .'

'Don't. Just give it a rest.'

'Sorry.' Tessa turned to look out of the window and said no more.

The photographers and a reporter from *Hello!* were already waiting when they drove into Cheyne Walk. Though Bob had some qualms about what they were doing, he was still angry enough with Allyson to go along with it, and since this was his home too, he reminded himself that he had every right to be there.

Once inside, the photographer started setting up in the kitchen, while the make-up artist took Tessa into the bathroom. This was the first time Tessa had ever been inside the flat, so it was all she could do not to give herself away by exclaiming how fantastic everything was. As far as the reporter was concerned this was where she and Bob lived, so to start drooling over the amazing draperies around the bed, or the size of the rooms, or the incredible black and white marble bathroom with its twin basins, massive shower, jacuzzi bath and French bidet, was going to look a bit odd. So she just went about opening cupboards, doors and drawers with the idle panache of someone who was playing down their extreme good taste.

Very soon she was helping herself to Allyson's cosmetics, then rummaging through her underwear drawer looking for clean tights. Next she took a look in the wardrobe to see if there was anything she might be able to squeeze into. Then she tried the shoe cupboard, *shoe cupboard!* to see if anything fitted her there. Nothing did, so she ended up wearing the daring and glittery stuff she'd borrowed from the wardrobe department, which Bob had carried up in a suitcase.

It was like a game as the photographer clicked away, taking shots of her and Bob in the amazing designer kitchen, looking incredibly romantic as he hugged her in front of him, with all of Allyson's saucepans and utensils hanging on racks behind them. From there they moved into the sitting room where Tessa was photographed on one of the creamy yellow sofas, feet curled under her and looking for all the world as though she were the queen of Chelsea living. No-one mentioned the silver-framed photographs of Allyson and her parents, or Allyson and Bob on their wedding day, or any other of the many photographs that were of friends and family, but none of them Tessa.

All the time the photographer worked the reporter was asking questions about how it felt to be famous, what it was like facing so much success at such a tender age, which designers she preferred, all kinds of trivial stuff that Tessa could handle easily, unlike the more in-depth interviews that wanted to delve into her background and know all kinds of details about her parents and family that she wasn't prepared to discuss. So this was a cinch. All she had to do was change outfits from time to time, move from one room to another to pose in front of all the best features of the flat, like the fireplaces, the paintings, the balconies, the weird and wonderful antiques, and talk about things that ultimately meant nothing. There was an awkward moment, though, when the photographer asked her and Bob to pose on the bed and Bob flatly refused. Knowing from his expression that there would be no point in arguing, Tessa took the reporter and photographer to one side and said, 'He's very private about our life together. In fact, I had a hell of a job getting him to agree to this at all, so, if you don't mind, we'd better call it a day.'

The photographer and make-up artist started packing away their gear while the reporter asked Tessa a final few questions. When they were ready to leave Tessa walked out to the front door with them.

'It's a wonderful place you've got here,' the reporter said, as Bob came into the hall. 'Isn't this where you and Allyson used to live?'

'Yes, but we live here now,' Tessa answered, pulling open the door. 'Thanks very much for coming. Let me know which issue it's going to be in, won't you? And you know where to find me if there's anything else I can do.'

Their footsteps could still be heard on the stairs as Tessa closed the door, then turned to look down the hall to where Bob was standing outside the bedroom. Her eyes were glittering brightly, and her breath was quickening with exultance. 'See, I told you,' she laughed, 'we had to get out of that grotty little place or we were going to go mad.' She ran towards him and he caught her as she threw herself into his arms and circled his waist with her legs. 'We've only been here a couple of hours and already everything feels better.'

She looked down into his face and saw how troubled he was.

'Oh Bob,' she groaned. 'You're home. I thought it was where you wanted to be.'

How could he say yes, but not with you? How could he say anything now the reporter and photographer had gone with evidence of their unforgivable intrusion into Allyson's life? But if Allyson was down there in the South of France with another man, a man she might be intending to move in here, who might already have spent the night in *his* bed . . .

'Bob?' Tessa whispered.

He looked into her eyes, which were full of uncertainty and eagerness to please.

'Do we have to go?' she said, her disappointment already starting to show.

'No,' he said. 'I'm just trying to decide whether we should bring our bags in first, or . . .' he was turning into the bedroom.

279

'Or?' she said, starting to laugh.

'Or whether I should make love to you right now.'

'I'd say there's no contest,' she said as he dropped her on the bed.

'I'd say you're right,' he responded, lying down beside her. And, aware of Allyson's photograph on his nightstand, he began to undress first Tessa, then himself.

Allyson was sitting at one of the two dozen or so long tables that fanned out from the empty stage of the Monte Carlo Sporting Club. With her were Justine and Zac, her researchers, and Monsieur Thibault, a representative of the *Société des Bains de Mer*, the organization that controlled everything in Monaco, including the permissions needed to film.

Being one of the Principality's most exclusive venues, the Sporting Club, where the likes of Stevie Wonder, Liza Minnelli, Rod Stewart and Whitney Houston performed after-dinner cabaret for an extremely wealthy and star-studded audience during the summer months, was an ambitious target for Allyson's first transmission. So ambitious, in fact, that it hadn't really surprised her when her first efforts to book it had met with a disdainful no. However, she wasn't so easily put off, for she was viewing this as a critical test of her producer's skills, so had no intention of being felled at the first hurdle. Her next approach, when she'd finally got Thibault back on the line, had hinted at a hefty facility fee without actually stating how much, and a follow-up fax had detailed the incredibly valuable publicity the programme could offer the Principality for free. They'd now been in negotiation for the past two days, and for the moment at least they appeared to be making some headway. Allyson hardly dared to imagine what a coup it would be if she could pull this off, for the large, circular room, with its vast floor-to-ceiling windows that offered a spectacular view of the

Mediterranean, where millionaires' yachts cruised through the surf and magnificent five-star hotels topped the surrounding cliffs, was a location like no other in the world.

'You say you will need the club for three days,' M. Thibault purred in his charming French accent. His clean-shaven, fleshy face was suddenly cut across by a rogue ray of sunlight and he raised a hand to shield it. 'One to set up, one to rehearse and shoot, and one to de-rig.'

'That's right,' Allyson confirmed. 'There'll be about twenty crew in all, including make-up and wardrobe, and fifty specially invited guests to make up an audience. We don't normally have an audience for the programme, but as this is something of a special case we're changing the rules to create a party atmosphere. Obviously, there'll be the programme guests too, which should number around six, I believe?' She was looking at Zac and Justine, seeking confirmation.

Zac, the lanky, tousle-headed Irish lad who was the senior of the two researchers, pushed a sheet of paper across the table. 'I've drawn up a list of those we've approached,' he said. 'They all live here, in Monte Carlo, some British, some American. I'm still waiting to hear back from a couple, so I'll confirm nearer the time who we're actually going to use.'

'And the audience invitation obviously extends to you and whoever you would like to bring,' Justine added with a fetching smile.

Whether it was the invitation or the smile that Thibault appreciated was hard to tell, but either way Justine's additional touch had clearly done no harm. After giving Zac's list a look-over, Thibault turned back to Allyson.

'You understand that we make you a special rate because it is winter,' he said. 'The Club is not used so much in the winter.'

'We're very grateful to you,' Allyson said, knowing she'd have to cut into the location budgets of future programmes to cover this 'special rate'. 'And if all the facilities check out, for camera access, lighting . . .'

'The Club is already set up for such events,' Thibault interrupted. 'But you must inform us if you have any special requirements. Your dates are January 26th, 27th and 28th, *oui?*'

'*Oui*,' Allyson responded with a smile.

Thibault nodded graciously, then returned to his perusal of the documentation in front of him. 'You are returning to London tomorrow?' he said, after a while.

Allyson replied, 'We leave Nice at midday.'

'Then I shall have an answer for you before you leave. Will you be at the Hermitage again this evening?'

She laughed. 'I'm afraid our budget only ran to one night at the Hermitage. So Zac and Justine are staying at a hotel just outside Beaulieu tonight, and I'm staying with friends on Cap Ferrat. I'll give you the number.'

Justine was already writing it down, her long crinkly red hair flowing onto the table as she bent her head over the page.

Half an hour later Allyson was at the wheel of their hire car driving along the spectacular coast road towards Beaulieu. Justine was in the seat beside her, Zac was behind, and all three of them were having trouble containing their excitement.

'I don't know what I'm going to do with you two if this doesn't work out,' Allyson laughed, as she pulled up outside the quaint, typically French auberge they'd found yesterday while touring the region. 'Will you be able to handle the disappointment?'

'We won't have to,' Zac assured her. 'Thibault's going to come through, I just know it.'

Allyson grinned. 'OK, I'll pick you up at nine in the morning so we can go and recce the Old Town. You gave Thibault the mobile number as well, did you, Justie?'

'Of course. But if you hear from him tonight, don't forget to let us know.'

'As if,' Allyson laughed, and putting the car back into gear, she waited for them to close the doors then drove off towards the Cap.

Valerie and Jean-Marc Clausonne, the couple she was staying with, were old friends of hers and Bob's, so she knew their villa well, having spent many long, lazy summer evenings drinking good wine and eating delicious food on their exquisite veranda that overlooked the wonderfully scallop-edged terraces of the garden, unfolding gently down to the sea. Until now she'd been anxious about returning without Bob, knowing it was almost bound to upset her, but with today having gone so well she was hardly thinking about Bob, not even as she watched the sun setting romantically over the sea, she was just looking forward to seeing Valerie and Jean-Marc.

It didn't surprise her one bit to discover that she wasn't their only guest, for they invariably had friends dropping in from all over the world, who were either there on business, just passing through or availing themselves of the wonderful setting and superb facilities for a two- or three-week holiday. With an eight-bedroomed Italian-style villa, a live-in staff of three, and a daily help of eight, including the gardeners, the Clausonnes could always accommodate.

Leaving her car and luggage to the butler, Allyson walked in through the wide sixteenth-century front doors, across the vast marble hallway with its curiously macabre paintings and stained-glass windows, and out through the sitting room full of pastels and Impressionists, to where Valerie was already pouring champagne into a glass for her, and making ready to introduce her to a suave-looking couple from Boston.

'Darling, you look divine and so undamaged,' Valerie declared, with her own inimitable frankness. She was part English, part Italian, and spoke both languages with a pronounced American accent. She had to be at least fifty, though looked closer to sixty thanks to all the hours she spent in the sun. But there was a real beauty to her face that no amount of lines could disguise, and such a playful light in her eyes that it was impossible for anyone to take offence at her outspokenness.

'How are you?' Allyson laughed, embracing her. 'It's so good to see you.'

'I have been so worried, but look at you!' Valerie cried. 'Look at her,' she demanded of her other guests. 'Isn't she gorgeous? Who would ever believe her husband left her for a younger woman? The man he is, pah! a fool. Allyson, you must meet Marla and Wesley Van Owen. They are very good friends of ours all the way from Boston.'

Allyson greeted the Van Owens, then was scooped into a giant bear hug by Jean-Marc as he came out onto the terrace. Like his wife he had been aged by the sun, and also like his wife he favoured flowing, brightly coloured caftans to eliminate any constriction of the blood flow in their large, overfed bodies.

Two glasses of champagne later they were joined by more friends who lived nearby, and the kitchen staff started to load the table up with food. As always chez Clausonne, the conversation was as stimulating as it was varied and with so many people from such different strata of jet-set life, it shouldn't have been such a surprise when Mark Reiner's name came up.

'Did you say Mark Reiner?' Allyson asked Wesley Van Owen. 'Of Leisure and Media?'

'Sure,' Van Owen answered. 'Why, do you know him?'

'He's my boss,' she answered. 'He's just taken over the TV station I work for.'

'Well, how about that?' Van Owen said, looking at his wife.

'Mark Reiner?' Valerie squealed. 'We know Mark. He is a very good friend. As a matter of fact he was here, staying with us, just a few weeks ago. Isn't that right, Jean-Marc?'

'Had a gorgeous lady with him,' Jean-Marc added, his rheumy eyes twinkling. 'What was her name? Do you remember her name, Val?'

'Jennifer? Jane? Something like that. Was she French? I think she was French. No, maybe she was English.'

Though Allyson kept her smile in place, she was aware of the warmth seeping out of it. But Valerie had said it was a few weeks ago, it could very well be over by now. And besides, it might not have been a girlfriend. It could have been just a friend. And even if it was a girlfriend, and it was still going on, Shelley would get to find out sooner or later without it having to come from Allyson, who'd only be guessing, because she could hardly start asking who this Jennifer or Jane actually was when the subject had already moved on, and when it would almost certainly appear that she was the one who wanted to know.

'So tell us more about this programme of yours!' Jean-Marc demanded, as he prised a succulent langoustine from its shell. 'We are all invited to the party, *non?*'

'If it happens you can count on it,' Allyson responded.

'Give me the name of the person you have to convince,' he said. 'I'll speak to him first thing in the morning.'

Allyson laughed. Jean-Marc loved playing Mr Fix-It, and with so many well-placed friends and influential contacts he generally succeeded. However, in this instance, she wanted to go it alone, and know that if they did manage to secure the Sporting Club it would be through their own efforts. So she made Jean-Marc swear he wouldn't do anything unless, for some reason, M. Thibault turned them down. At that point she might consider letting Jean-Marc pull a few strings.

But there was no need, for at ten the following morning M. Thibault called her on the mobile to announce that he was delighted to offer the facilities of the Monte Carlo Sporting Club to her programme under the terms and conditions they had agreed. The second she rang off Allyson gave a scream of joy, then flung her arms round Zac and Justine as they congratulated her and themselves and swore undying love for M. Thibault and all his descendants. Losing her status as a presenter was hard, but if this first real experience as a producer was anything to go by, then Allyson strongly suspected that working behind the scenes, and out here in the field, was going to prove far more rewarding than anything she'd done before. And that in itself felt like a triumph over Tessa Dukes, not to mention a poke in the eye for Bob, who might have been deluding himself into believing that she couldn't survive without him.

By the time the plane touched down at Heathrow Allyson was so exhausted by all the elation and intense hard work of the past couple of days – not to mention the late night she'd had at the Clausonnes' – that instead of going straight to the office she went home first to shower and change.

After the taxi dropped her off she hurried up the stairs with her heavy bag, only to find that though the key went into the lock, for some reason it wouldn't turn. Baffled, and not a little irritated, she was about to get out her mobile to call a locksmith when, to her amazement, Julian came bounding up the stairs behind her. He stopped dead when he saw her.

'Julian?' she said. 'What are you doing here?'

He looked ready to bolt. 'I just, well, uh Tessa left something here. I've come to pick it up.'

Allyson stared at him, not sure she'd heard right. 'Tessa's been here?' she said, her heart starting to thump.

His colour deepened. 'Uh, I've got to go.'

'No, wait. How were you going to get in?'

He looked at her wretchedly.

'You've got a key, haven't you? They've changed the locks.' She held out her hand. It was shaking, and her knees had turned weak with the shock, but her voice was icily determined as she said, 'Give me the key.'

He didn't put up much of a fight.

Allyson turned to open the door. 'Come with me,' she said. She was so angry she felt violent.

The place was a mess, newspapers and unwashed dishes all over the floor, no attempt to make the bed or pick up towels after a shower, and the kitchen was too horrible to face. She stalked straight into the laundry room, grabbed a roll of black plastic sacks and began filling them.

'Help me,' she snapped at Julian.

Obediently he took a bag and began filling it.

When Allyson was satisfied that everything of Tessa's was gone, she made Julian help her carry the sacks down to the bins.

'You can go now,' she said when they'd finished.

Returning to the flat she called an emergency locksmith who came within the hour. When he'd finished she got into her car and drove to the office.

Tessa was just coming out of the studio. Whether Julian had had time to get to her before she'd gone in to record wasn't possible to tell. Allyson didn't care. She grabbed hold of Tessa's arm, marched her down the corridor then flung her up against the wall.

'If you ever set one foot inside my flat again I'll have you arrested,' she hissed. 'Do you hear me?'

'Let go of me,' Tessa cried. 'Just who do you think you are, pushing me around!'

At that Allyson dealt her such a resounding blow to the face that Tessa staggered sideways into a cupboard.

Allyson turned and walked away.

287

'*Bitch!*' Tessa screamed after her.

Allyson kept going, past those who had stopped to stare, and upstairs to the office. 'See if you can find my husband,' she said to Shelley's assistant as she stalked into Shelley's office.

Shelley looked up. 'What's happened?' she said.

'Nothing. I just wanted to let you know that I'm going to tape our first foreign programme in Monte Carlo. Oh, and if . . .'

The door crashed open and Tessa flew at her.

'What the hell?' Shelley cried, leaping to her feet.

Tessa was on Allyson's back, clawing her hair and trying to bang her head against the wall. 'Bitch!' she was screaming. 'She attacked me. *Bitch!*'

'Get her off,' Shelley demanded as Alan and Jerry ran into the office.

Quickly they grabbed Tessa and prised her away. Allyson stumbled against the desk and brushed the hair from her face. 'I'm warning you,' she shouted at Tessa, 'you stay away from me and what's mine or I'll fucking well kill you.'

The others watched in silence as she walked out of the room.

'I've got your husband on the line,' Marvin told her.

Allyson walked right past him. 'Tell him to die,' she seethed.

Shelley caught up with her in the car park.

'She tried to move into my flat,' Allyson gasped. 'I got back to find the locks had been changed and her and Bob's things were all over the place. I wanted to kill her, Shell. I swear, if I had it in me . . .' She took a breath. 'And as for him, I was considering giving him some money, but he can rot in hell now. They both can, because I've had it. They've turned my life upside down, they've mocked me, humiliated me and now they're trying to destroy me.' Fury was making her breath short, tears streamed down her face.

'It's OK,' Shelley said, as she started to sob with anger and frustration.

'I don't understand it,' Allyson raged. 'How does a man you've loved for more than twenty years suddenly turn into this monster?'

'Because like most men he's weak,' Shelley answered. 'He saw something he wanted and took it, without thinking about you or anyone else. And this is what it's got him. No job, no money and a stupid little cow of a girlfriend who he probably can't stand any more.'

'Then why doesn't he leave her?'

'Because he's got nowhere else to go.'

'He's got me.'

Shelley looked at her. 'Are you sure about that?'

Allyson looked back, her eyes dark with confusion. In the end she closed them. 'God, I hate her,' she said. 'I hate her so much it scares me.'

SHELLEY

Chapter 12

'Mark? It's Shelley.'

'How are you?'

'OK. I was wondering if you watched the recording last night.'

'From Monte Carlo? It worked very well. Congratulations.'

'Thank you. But it was Allyson's programme.'

'Your idea to go international,' he reminded her.

Shelley appreciated his remembering, but could think of no suitable response. It had taken her three weeks to pluck up the courage to make this call, rehearsing what she would say, what he might say, how she would respond and how the call would end up. It all worked very well in the planning, right now though she couldn't think how to proceed.

'Is the crew back yet?' he asked.

'Tonight. Uh, I was wondering, would you be free for dinner?'

'Tonight? I'm afraid not.'

The pounding in her heart increased. She looked down at the scribbles on her notepad, heavy lined triangles, thick circles. An empty square. 'Any night?' She could hardly believe she'd said that, and when he didn't answer she wanted to ring off fast and pretend the call had never happened. 'I was hoping,' she said, 'that we could talk.'

'About?'

'Us.'

Another silence. It was as though a hole was opening up inside her. Panic rushed to fill it, sweeping aside her dignity and forcing words from her lips that she knew already she was going to regret. 'I thought it meant something to you, when we made love,' she said. 'You seemed to enjoy it.' Oh God, where was her pride? This was horrible. Too demeaning for words.

'It was sensational,' he said.

'So why don't we do it again?'

'It's complicated.'

'Because of Allyson?' She didn't give him time to answer. 'She's not ready for another relationship. She's still a long way from getting over Bob.'

'I'm sure.'

'So why don't we carry on seeing each other? You've got to admit we have fun together.' Was this begging? Could this go down as *begging*?

Another pause before he said, 'I'm sorry, but I'll have to cut this call short. I have someone with me.'

'Is Allyson with you? Is that why you won't talk to me?' What wretchedness was making her behave like this with a man she wanted only to impress?

'No. I believe you know where she is.'

Of course she did. Allyson was on her way back from France, aglow with the success of her first programme as a producer. Shelley had invited her out tonight to celebrate, but Allyson wasn't free. She'd said she was having dinner with her mother, but now Shelley had just discovered that Mark wasn't free either . . .

'I have to go,' he said.

Shelley put the phone down. Her hand wasn't steady, shame was burning her all over. She looked out at the production office and could only thank God that no-one out there had any idea what she'd just done. And what must he think of her now? How he must despise her. Her eyes closed as her heart filled up with misery and rage. Oh God, why had she made that call? Why couldn't she just accept that he didn't want her? Maybe she could if it didn't seem to be Allyson he wanted instead. Christ, why did it have to be Allyson? Of course she had no actual proof of it, but she'd always trusted her instincts in the past, and this time they were signalling her loud and clear, because it wasn't only the date on New Year's Eve and the secrecy surrounding their meetings, it was also the way the crisis of Allyson's job had been overcome in a matter of no time at all. Mark Reiner had taken care of that, even if it was Allyson's original idea. Mark Reiner had the power to make things happen, and it seemed he was much more interested in making them happen for Allyson than he was for Shelley. Just thinking that sparked all kinds of violent impulses inside her, for she couldn't stand the idea of Allyson and Mark being together. It was too hard to take, too cruel of fate to give the man she wanted to Allyson Jaymes.

After ending his call with Shelley Mark replaced the receiver and looked across his desk at the frankly questioning eyes that were watching him. She'd just returned on an early flight from France and still appeared flushed with the success of her visit.

Tessa smiled. She had no idea who he'd been talking to as he hadn't mentioned a name. She'd noticed that he'd avoided mentioning hers also, so maybe it had been Allyson. Certainly he'd spoken to Allyson while they were in Monaco, because she, Tessa, had answered Allyson's mobile herself. That hadn't pleased Allyson too much, but she'd only done it because Allyson had been over the other side of the Club and no-one else had seemed inclined to pick up the phone.

After the call Allyson had announced that he'd rung to wish them all good luck. And why wouldn't he? He was the boss, after all. But there had to have been more to the call, simply because of how long it had gone on. And the way Allyson had laughed, and seemed to glow, then taken herself off into a corner so she couldn't be overheard, went a long way towards confirming the rumours that there really was something going on between them.

Now, as Tessa looked into his watchful dark eyes, she smiled. He didn't smile back, nor did he look at her legs, which were amply revealed. In fact, he seemed annoyed, which perplexed her for men usually enjoyed being teased.

'Well,' she said, getting to her feet, 'I suppose I'd better be going. I only came to give you my new address and make sure you were happy with the way I'm presenting the programme.'

'Very,' he told her, though there was no warmth to his assurance.

She looked a little lost. 'You seem as though you're cross with me,' she said. 'If I've done something wrong, I'm sorry.'

He seemed to thaw a bit at that. 'No, Tessa, you haven't done anything wrong. It's simply that I have to be somewhere . . .'

'Oh, yes, I'm sorry. You're bound to be busy. Thank you for taking the time to see me. I really appreciate it.' She watched him as he came round his desk to see her out. Then as he passed she reached for his hand and looked up into his startled eyes. 'If there's anything I can do to say thank you, you know, for the chance you've given me . . .'

'There's no need,' he informed her. 'Just continue to do a good job.'

'Of course,' she smiled.

The door was open, he was standing aside for her to go.

'Bye then,' she said.

'Goodbye.'

She walked past him, then at the last moment turned to look over her shoulder. 'Until the next time,' she said playfully, and after a quick glance at his assistant she left.

Bob was holding the note in his hand, staring at it, and hardly believing it. Yet the words were right there, in Tessa's girlishly round writing, plain to see and even plainer to read.

He sat down on the sofa and winced with the pain of the bruises that covered most of his body. Then he closed his eyes and let his breath go. It was a nightmare. His whole life had been taken over by a nightmare and he couldn't make himself wake up. Not three hours ago he had been mugged coming out of the pub. *Mugged*, for God's sake! In broad daylight, for the grand sum of six lousy quid. The landlord had taken him to hospital, where the gash over his right eye had received three stitches, and his left arm had been set in a cast to repair the break. The kicking he'd received to his legs and ribs had broken nothing, but they hurt like hell nevertheless.

And now he had come home to this.

'Dear Bob,' the note said, 'I'm really sorry to leave without talking things over, but we both know how unhappy you've been lately, and nothing I do seems to help. I wish it did, but I think we both have to accept that there's no point pretending any more. I may or may not have mentioned to you how I thought my new boss, Mark Reiner, was interested in me, and I've decided I'd like to give that relationship a chance. I think the only reason he's been holding back is because I'm living with you. So, I've found myself a new place in Knightsbridge, where you'll be welcome to come and visit any time you like. I really love you and care about you. Tessa. PS: I've left twenty-nine pounds on the table, which is yours from my bank account. Big kiss and good luck. T.'

The money was indeed on the table, but everything

else, the magazines, the wooden candleholder and the cheery French wine coasters, had gone. He hadn't looked in the bedroom, but he knew already that she'd have taken everything except the bed, the nightstands and the Formica wardrobe, because everything bar that had been hers. So too had the vibrantly coloured abstract prints whose frames were still outlined on the walls, and the large collection of books that used to fill up the shelves.

He went into the kitchen and saw that she'd left him a glass, a cup, a plate, two knives, two forks and a spoon. She'd also left some bread and cheese, and a full bottle of gin. Next to the gin was the rent book.

He was halfway through the gin when suddenly he couldn't stand any more. He had to get out. He'd always hated this place and now, without Tessa, it felt like a cell. He had no clear idea where he would go, except he knew it couldn't be to Allyson. Since he and Tessa had tried to move into the flat his shame was so great he didn't have the nerve to face her. Nor could he face his father, whom he hadn't seen since he'd walked out on his marriage. There was always Tessa's new place, of course, but she hadn't actually left the address and he certainly didn't fancy running into Mark Reiner. There was something about that that just didn't feel right, but he was too drunk to give it any focus, and too damn sorry for himself to care. All that really concerned him was where he could go to get out of this prison. And then it hit him, there was only one other place he could go, and fortunately he had just enough money to cover the cab fare.

'Oh my God,' Allyson murmured, as she and Zac and Justine wheeled their luggage into the noisy arrivals hall at Heathrow airport. 'I don't believe it.' She was smiling all over her face, and the closer she got to where he was waiting, at the end of the barrier, the deeper she was blushing. 'Hi,' Mark said, handing her the flowers he was holding. 'Congratulations.'

Allyson started to laugh, and glanced self-consciously at her colleagues who were clearly enjoying the moment. 'Thank you,' she said. 'I wasn't expecting . . . I mean, I didn't know you'd be here.'

His eyes were holding onto hers, even though she was trying to avoid them. 'I had a meeting at a hotel nearby,' he said, 'so I checked what time your flight was coming in and . . . Here I am. Can I give you a ride into town?'

Allyson looked at Justine and Zac again, then threw out her hands. 'Why not?' she said. 'Yes, that would be lovely.'

'It certainly would,' Zac agreed, starting to head out.

Justine kicked him. 'We'll get a cab,' she said, smiling through her teeth.

'But . . .' Zac complained.

'Take no notice of him,' Allyson told Mark, 'he's always like that. He's Zac O'Reilly by the way, and this is Justine Webb. My researchers.'

Mark shook their hands. 'I'll be happy to drive you into town too,' he said. 'I've got one of the company cars, so we'll all fit in.'

'Oh no!' Justine cried. 'We wouldn't hear of it.'

'Why wouldn't we?' Zac demanded.

'Because. . .' Justine responded.

'Listen, please come with us,' Allyson said. 'This is too painful to go through any more.'

Zac and Justine were still arguing by the time they reached Mark's car, though by now Zac was insisting they couldn't accept the lift, and Justine was informing him they had to.

'Just shut up, will you?' Allyson said, as they got into the back seat.

Mark was laughing, and after holding the door open for Allyson to get in too, he slipped into the driver's seat and started up the engine.

'Never been in one of these before, have you?' Zac was saying in the back. 'It's a Mercedes.'

'Oh, and there was me thinking it was a Mars bar,' Justine responded.

'You hungry too?' he said, pouncing on it.

Allyson looked at Mark and saw that he was still laughing. 'What can I do but apologize?' she said. Then to Zac, 'If you ask to be taken to dinner you're fired,' she threatened.

He held up his hands, an assurance he wouldn't dream of going any further.

'It was a great programme you shot down there in Monaco,' Mark said, clearing the ticket barrier and indicating to pull into the traffic. 'The congratulations are extended to all of you.'

'Does that mean we get a share in the flowers?' Zac wanted to know.

'Give me a moment and I'll work out a quiet way to kill him,' Justine said. Then both Mark and Allyson burst out laughing as they heard her whisper, 'You're going too far now, so stop it. I mean it, Zac, button up or I'll do something drastic.'

'Oh, what a temptress she is,' Zac intoned, but after that he managed to keep quiet, at least until they got to the M4, by which time Allyson and Mark had realized that they really couldn't have a proper conversation with those two in the back. So Mark gave her a quick wink, then began asking the researchers what they were working on for their next foreign transmission.

Allyson contributed little, for she was happy just to sit and listen, and allow the pleasure she'd felt at him being at the airport, and was still feeling sitting here next to him in this oversized vehicle of luxury, wash over her. This wasn't the only contact they'd had lately, as he'd called her a couple of times in Monte Carlo, once to wish her and everyone else good luck with the recording, when they'd got on to talking about their mutual friends

Valerie and Jean-Marc Clausonne; and another time when he'd wanted to know the name of the person she'd dealt with at the *Société des Bains de Mer*, so that he could pass it on to Claudia, his sister-in-law, whose cable station in the US was currently shooting a holiday show. On neither occasion had Allyson asked him about the woman who'd been mentioned at the Clausonnes', and she certainly wasn't going to embarrass herself by asking now.

What she did wonder, however, was if the meeting at the airport hotel had been a cover to make his gesture less personal, but just before she got out of the car she spotted the hotel's brochure in the pocket between the seats, so knew that it was genuine. Which meant that he hadn't come all this way specially to meet her. But that was OK. It was nice that he'd come at all. Though how the hell she was going to explain it to Shelley, God only knew.

Shelley was staring at the exquisite bronze fan dancer Allyson had given her at Christmas. It was at the centre of a display case, one of her most prized possessions. It had been a gesture of friendship, a thank-you, but now Shelley wondered if it wasn't really a means of trying to buy off her guilt. It wasn't a generous thought, but it could be an accurate one if Allyson was already aware, back then, that something was starting to happen between her and Mark Reiner.

Shelley wondered where they were now, if they really were spending the evening together, as she'd suspected. If they were she'd like to find them and prove them liars, let them know that they hadn't fooled her, for she knew they were seeing each other and trying to hide it from her. But even if she confronted them, what then? It was hardly going to make him want her, knowing she was stalking him about the town. It appalled her even to think she was considering it, though of course she'd never do it.

The way she was tormenting herself, tying herself up in knots of suspicion and resentment, was almost as bad as it being Allyson who'd come between them. Allyson, who'd attempted to assuage her guilt with a gift that must have cost her at least five thousand pounds. It was that exorbitant price tag that was doing so much to convince Shelley she was right in her suspicions. After all, they'd fallen out plenty of times before, but Allyson had never felt compelled to give her something so precious on those other occasions.

Shelley's eyes moved to the elegant Night and Day clock that Allyson loved so much. It was the only thing Shelley had that Allyson wanted, whereas Allyson had virtually everything Shelley wanted. Or that was how it felt right now, and had many times over the years, while Shelley had been sleeping with Bob, who had never even come close to leaving Allyson for her. And now Allyson was winning the man again.

Around nine o'clock someone rang the doorbell downstairs. Shelley was tempted not to answer, but the ringing became so insistent she had to. When she heard Bob's voice on the entryphone she almost laughed. All that surprised her about him being there was that he hadn't come sooner. She'd have liked to tell him to get lost, but suddenly she felt in enough need of some company to make even his acceptable. So pushing the button to release the downstairs door, she opened her own front door then returned to the sitting room.

A few minutes later he walked in, bringing a cloud of chill night air with him. Shelley looked up from where she was sitting, and her eyes flew open at the state of his appearance.

'What on earth happened to you?' she said.

'I got hit by a bus.'

Though she doubted it was the truth, it still wouldn't have been hard to believe, for his face was quite badly bruised and there was a large gash above his right eye that had obviously been stitched. His left arm was in a sling, and when he moved he seemed to be limping. However, he smelt good, a Versace cologne that was one of her favourites.

'So what do you want?' she asked.

He seemed to flinch at the bluntness of her words, then obviously decided to match them with a bluntness of his own. 'Money and somewhere to sleep,' he answered.

She laughed incredulously. 'And you came here for it? You must be desperate. What happened to Tessa?'

'She left. Got herself a new place in Knightsbridge. Seems I'm too small-time for her now. She's set her sights even higher.'

'Not difficult to get higher than you, Bob,' she remarked.

His mouth twisted, and the old fire she was used to made a fleeting return. 'It was good enough for you once,' he reminded her.

'A lot more than once, as I recall,' she said. 'Do you want something to drink?'

He looked tempted, so tempted that she was amazed when he said, 'No. I'm trying to get off it. How's Allyson?'

Shelley turned away. 'Why don't you ask her?' she said, going to the impressive Betty Joel-designed bar. 'Oh, I forgot, you have to do it through a lawyer, don't you, since you tried to pull that ridiculous stunt of moving into her flat.'

'It's mine too,' he said feebly, then unbuttoning his camel-hair coat he slumped down in a chair and let his head fall forward. 'I'm in a bad way, Shelley,' he said.

There was only disdain on her face as she looked down at him. 'Spare me the self-pity,' she said. 'You were the one who started screwing around with a kid, and you've got some nerve coming round here now that it's all fallen apart. What did you expect, a sympathy fuck?'

303

Raising his head he looked at her with cold, hostile eyes. 'It really pissed you off, that, didn't it?' he said. 'Getting tossed out for someone half your age.'

'Look who's suffering,' she responded.

His eyes dimmed and he turned away.

Shelley carried on mixing herself a martini.

It was several minutes before he spoke again. 'You know, since you brought it up, a sympathy fuck, as you call it, wouldn't go amiss.'

Shelley gave a scornful laugh. 'You're deluded.'

'It wasn't so long ago you were begging me for it,' he reminded her. 'Did you ever tell Allyson that? No, I bet you didn't. You got the papers to tell her about Tessa though, didn't you? It was you, wasn't it, who tipped them off?'

'Yes. It was me. She deserved rescuing from you.'

'Oh, is that what you're telling yourself? If you ask me it pissed you off big-time that I wouldn't leave Allyson for you, so you reckoned you'd pay me back by making my affair with Tessa public. Must have come as a real blow to you when I actually left Allyson for Tessa.'

'Bob, there's only one of us in this room looking at a loser, and it isn't you.'

'Fancy doing that to your best friend. You broke her heart.'

'No. You broke her heart. But I don't think she's suffering any more. It doesn't take long to get over you, Bob.'

He didn't seem to have an answer for that, so she stood watching him as he stared at the fire.

'You're pathetic,' she said after a while. 'To think of everything you've lost for the sake of a fat little teenager. And now she's famous where are you? Left with her footprints all over your face.'

His head came up and she saw something of his pain as he looked her straight in the eye. 'Can I stay here tonight?' he said.

'No.'

From his expression it was obviously the answer he'd expected, but he seemed crushed nevertheless. 'What about some money?'

'No.'

'Shelley, I'm destitute. I can't even afford the rent on the little shithole she left me in.'

'Talk to your wife. Oh sorry, the lawyer. Pity I can't do the same, and make you talk to me through a lawyer.'

He grinned nastily. 'That would be one way of getting yourself a man, wouldn't it?' he sneered. 'To hire yourself a lawyer. Shit, even Allyson's managed to find herself someone else already, but look at you, sitting here in this fucking upscale relic of a movie set, too beautiful and too stuck-up to admit you can't get anyone to go the course. Do you know what, I often thought this about you, Shelley, for one of the most beautiful women I know, you've got to be one of the most resistible. Except when you've got your clothes off. Then you're hot.'

Shelley could feel her temper rising, and was right on the brink of hitting back violently, devastatingly, for the way he'd managed to strike at the heart of her fears. But she'd almost rather die than let him know he had hurt her.

'So Allyson's seeing your new boss?' he said, then frowned as he experienced that vague uneasiness he'd felt earlier when he'd thought of Mark Reiner.

Shelley's heart turned over. 'Who told you that?' she said.

'Is she? Is that who I saw her with on New Year's Eve?'

Shelley looked at him in disbelief. 'It was all over the papers the next day,' she said. Then, 'Oh, I forgot, you were sobering up after your night in jail. You must have missed it.'

'You're such a bitch,' he said, getting to his feet. 'I'm wasting my time here. I thought you might take pity on

305

an old friend, but you don't know what pity is, do you? Come to that, you don't know what a friend is, either.'

Shelley picked up the phone as it rang.

'Shell? It's me. Mummy's had to cancel on me. Do you still want dinner?'

Shelley's smile grew as she realized what this meant. 'My treat,' she said to Allyson. 'I'll meet you at San Lorenzo in half an hour.' She hung up and turned back to Bob. 'Are you still here?' she said.

Shoving his hands in his pockets he walked off to the front door.

'Let me guess,' she said, noticing his limp again. 'You got into a fight.'

'Something like that,' he admitted.

As he opened the door she reached for her bag and took out her purse. 'Here,' she said, handing him a fifty-pound note. 'And don't spend it on booze.'

Taking it he said, 'Was that Allyson on the phone?'

She nodded, and he looked so dejected that for a moment she really did feel sorry for him. Then, remembering something he'd said earlier, she said, 'By the way, you didn't tell me who Tessa's sights have risen to.'

He slammed the door in her face and laughing she went to freshen her make-up.

Allyson watched Shelley coming towards her. Though she was anxious about how the evening would go, she was glad she'd come, because the last thing she wanted was Shelley to find out through office gossip that Mark had been at the airport earlier. He'd dropped Allyson at her flat an hour ago, with no mention of going on for dinner, which she'd half-expected, though he had asked her to come to his office at five tomorrow. She had no idea what that was about, and hadn't asked because Zac and Justine were still in the car. Heaven only knew where he dropped them, though she couldn't imagine he'd played taxi service right to their doors. However, that was hardly any cause for concern when she was sitting here trying to work out what to tell Shelley.

'Hi,' she said, getting up to embrace Shelley as she reached the table. 'I'm so glad you were free. I'm on such a high after the last few days that I just couldn't have stayed in this evening.'

'I'm not surprised,' Shelley smiled, as she handed her coat to a hovering waiter. 'It's a pretty impressive debut. Do you need to edit?'

'Only a few joins. Alan's booked in for a couple of hours tomorrow afternoon. Transmission is still scheduled for next Tuesday?'

'Of course. We've been promoting it for weeks. I hope you've ordered champagne.'

'I was just about to. I see the ratings were up again last week, which must mean that even if I can't stand her, the world loves Tessa.' Though she was still smiling even she heard the edge to her voice, which annoyed her slightly for she didn't want to be affected by this tonight. 'She was good in France,' she said. 'That ridiculous Franglais thing she did really worked. I'm just wondering what we're going to do when the baby starts showing. Apart from shoot her – from the neck up?'

Shelley smiled, then looked up at the waiter as he came to take their order. 'Bring us a bottle of Bollinger,' she told him. 'We'll need a few more minutes with the menu.' After he'd gone she turned back to Allyson, who she could see was fast coming down from her high. Tiredness would do that of course, and the reminder of something she'd obviously rather forget. 'About the baby,' she said.

Allyson's eyes flickered off to one side. 'Let's not talk about it,' she said. 'Not tonight.'

'I think we should,' Shelley replied. 'Mainly because there is no baby. Not any more.'

As the words reached her Allyson felt herself go very still. No baby? Bob and Tessa were no longer having a baby? Did that mean . . .? Her eyes came up to Shelley's.

'I think she told Bob it was a miscarriage,' Shelley said. 'Did you know she's left him?'

This was all too much for Allyson to take in. The shock was so great that she didn't seem able to grasp what any of it might mean. 'When?' she finally managed.

'I'm not sure. I only heard myself today. Apparently she's living in Knightsbridge.'

The champagne arrived, and as Allyson watched the waiter open it she had to remind herself what they were celebrating. Suddenly everything felt very different and for the moment she wasn't entirely sure how she was reacting.

'Here's to you,' Shelley said when their glasses were full. 'And to many more programmes like your first one.'

Allyson smiled as they touched glasses. It was a relief to turn her mind away from this earth-shattering news and think only of how great it had felt, running about that club in Monte Carlo, chatting with the guests who'd turned up in all their finery, organizing everyone into position, making key decisions with the director, briefing Tessa on what to say and do with the couple of rock bands and expatriate sportsmen who were making up the Happy Hour, and then recording her own Night Cap slot sitting on the rocks outside with one of Britain's leading authors. It all felt like an entire world away now, another lifetime even.

Bob and Tessa were no longer together!

'Did you see the spread in *Hello!*?' she said.

Shelley nodded.

Allyson stared down at her drink. 'I still can't believe her nerve,' she said. 'She's just not like normal people.'

'She's found someone else, apparently.'

Allyson's surprise showed. 'Oh?'

'No idea.'

Allyson drank some more champagne. 'Let's stop talking about her,' she said. 'I only want to deal with her as some kind of prop on the show, and after that she ceases to exist. Now tell me about you. I feel as though I've hardly seen you lately.'

Shelley was trying not to jump to conclusions about Allyson's failure to discuss Bob. It was probably just that she needed some time to get over the shock, nothing to do with Mark, and no longer knowing how she felt. 'My life has been like yours,' she said with a smile, 'all work and no play.'

Allyson smiled too, then after a moment she said, 'Did you hear from Mark again? Have you seen him?'

Shelley was shaking her head, then looking Allyson frankly in the eye, she said, 'To tell the truth I thought you were seeing him.'

'Me?' Allyson responded. 'What made you think that?' That wasn't very honourable, but it had come out before she could stop it.

Shelley shrugged. 'Just a feeling I had,' she said.

Allyson's eyes dropped to her glass for a moment. 'Did I tell you I stayed with the Clausonnes when I was on the recce?' she said.

Shelley nodded, obviously surprised by the change of subject.

Allyson looked at her. 'Apparently Mark knows them too,' she said. 'Jean-Marc said he was there quite recently, with a woman.'

Though Shelley's throat felt tight, and her heart was thudding, she knew that this was going to be easier to live with than Allyson seeing him. 'Did they say who she was?' she asked.

Allyson shook her head. 'Jean-Marc couldn't remember, and the subject changed before I could ask.'

Shelley pressed her lips together as she thought. 'So you think he's already involved with someone else?' she said.

'It's possible. It could explain why he's holding back with you.'

Shelley nodded. It wasn't perfect, but it helped.

Allyson said, 'I saw him earlier. He gave us a lift in from the airport.'

Shelley's face felt suddenly stiff, and her mouth had turned dry. This had changed direction so fast she hardly knew what she was thinking. 'You mean he came to meet you?' she said.

'No. Not really. He was out at the airport anyway, and knowing we were about to fly in, he came to offer us a lift into London. Zac and Justie were there too.'

Shelley looked away. She truly didn't know what to say, how even to begin to express the feelings inside her. They were dulled, as though ripped away from their centre, hanging jagged and loose in a vacuum of confusion. But it needn't be as bad as it sounded. There could be another woman, and the airport thing could simply be the coincidence Allyson had described.

'He's asked me to go and see him tomorrow,' Allyson said, desperately wishing he hadn't, for she could see that all this was upsetting Shelley even more than she'd expected.

'What about?' Shelley asked.

'He didn't say.'

Several seconds ticked by before Shelley looked up again, and forcing a smile she said, 'So, do you think you'll go back with Bob, now it's over with Tessa?'

Allyson knew what answer Shelley was hoping for, but it wasn't an answer she could give, not yet. So all she said was, 'If I do, it's not going to happen immediately.'

Laura Risby was sitting alone in her office, a small cone of light falling over the file and tape recorder in front of her. Tessa had spent almost two hours with her earlier, spilling over with excitement and exuberance at her new-found   fame   and   amazing   apartment   in

Knightsbridge. Though Laura was relieved to hear that her relationship with Bob was over, she certainly couldn't feel happy about the new course events seemed to be taking. In fact, as she rewound the tape for the second time, she was toying with the idea of calling upon a colleague for a second opinion. Not that she considered Tessa to be a threat to anyone, at least not in the physical sense, but there was no doubt that her particular kind of behaviour could cause some serious problems for those around her.

Stopping the tape, Laura let it play for a few minutes, making notes as she listened.

'It's great what's been happening to me lately,' Tessa was saying. 'It's right up there with the stars.'

Laura carried on writing as Tessa described more of her jubilation, then having heard enough she spooled forward to the place where her own voice was asking to be told more about Mark Reiner.

Tessa wasn't in the least hesitant in her replies. 'I went to see him today,' she said, 'after I moved my stuff out of the other flat.'

'Did he ask you to come to see him?' Laura asked.

'No. But I wanted to say thank you, you know, for everything he's done for me.'

'Had you met him before?'

'Yes, but not, you know, like on a one-to-one. He was really complimentary about the way I do the show. And the ratings are up, so he's really into me right now.'

'And you say he's seeing Allyson.'

'Well some people say he is. It could be they're keeping it quiet because everyone says Shelley's got the hots for him. There was a rumour that he and Shelley, you know, did it, in his office, just before Christmas.'

Laura made some more notes, then spooled the tape on again.

'How's Julian?' Laura was now asking.

'Oh, he's great. He keeps saying brothers and sisters

don't do the kind of things we do, so I remind him, *duh!* he's not really my brother.'

'So you're sleeping together now?'

'Sometimes. If I'm in the mood.'

'Have you ever told him about your real brother?'

'No. Why would he want to know that?'

'Or your father?'

'Or that. Anyway, they're dead now, so who cares?'

'Have you told him about your mother?'

'I told him she killed herself.'

'Did you tell him why?'

'I don't know why, do I? That's why I'm here.'

Laura stopped the tape, then sat quietly going over it all in her mind. She was sure that Tessa did know why her mother had killed herself, but still wasn't ready to accept it. That wasn't so surprising, these things always took time, and in Tessa's case the reluctance would be as much to do with suppressed anger as with the understandable pain. But she would get there, Laura felt sure of it, and should perhaps be allowed the freedom to work it through in her own way, convoluted and sometimes damaging though that could be.

So once again Laura shelved the idea of calling on someone else's opinion, or breaking a professional trust, and turning off the tape, she put the file away and left the office.

Chapter 13

It had been a hectic day recording six Night Caps, catching up with correspondence, sorting her diary, and starting plans for the next transmission from the ski slopes of Austria. It should be a good show, staging an après-ski with the Brits who were happy about making fools of themselves abroad. Tessa would no doubt excel at chatting to them, and it could be a good idea to get her on a pair of skis too. With any luck she might go over a cliff!

Reining in the thought, Allyson gathered up her briefcase and coat and ran out of the office to her car. On the way up to town, still buzzing from her day, she called in at the women's refuge, where she was welcomed with freshly brewed tea, kiddie-baked biscuits and the latest news on funding. She'd had so little time lately that she'd been unable to visit in person, but she'd been in regular contact by phone, getting updates on how they all were, often talking to the newcomers herself and trying to offer some comfort and sympathy. She understood that her being a celebrity made them feel special, which was probably one of the best parts of being famous, knowing that she could use it in such a worthwhile way. One of the worst parts was when she was hounded by the press, as she had been today, since their fascination with her private life was flourishing again, now that Tessa had left Bob.

Allyson wasn't ready to deal with that. It was like a pile of smouldering ashes, still too hot to put her hands in to find out if there was anything left to be salvaged. She'd think about it when it had had a chance to cool down a little, and when she had a clearer idea of what she really wanted to save. In the meantime, she'd continue answering the probing calls from the press, who were all clamouring to know how she felt about Bob and Tessa's break-up, with the maddening non-committal response of no comment.

They were in Tessa's hair too, of course, and Bob's, but Shelley had been quick on the case regarding Tessa, bringing in a publicist to handle the calls, as Tessa had nothing like Allyson's experience in dealing with the press. Allyson had no idea how Bob was coping with it, on any level, but according to that morning's *Mail* he was still living in Peckham, and still out of work. So far he'd made no attempt to contact her, and though she wished that didn't hurt, it did. However, she had no intention of initiating any contact with him, especially not after that fiasco with *Hello!*

Leaving her car at the refuge she hailed a cab and gave the driver the address of Mark's office. She should be there in plenty of time, if the traffic wasn't too bad, and she could do with these few minutes of peace to collect her thoughts. However, they had barely pulled away from the kerb when her cellphone rang, connecting her to a three-way call with Zac and Justine that took up most of the journey. And she'd only just clicked off that call when another came in from Shelley, pointing out the duplication of a celebrity guest who was being talked about for the ski programme, but was already pencilled in to appear on one of the regular shows the previous week.

It was a problem soon settled, for Allyson was willing to find someone else, and Shelley put forward a few suggestions that could easily work. The call then ended on a friendly note, but there was no mistaking the chill of politeness that had crept into their usual warmth. It was how their dinner had ended up last night too, after Allyson had confessed she was going to see Mark today, and Shelley had tried to disguise her resentment, not only at the meeting, but at Allyson's reluctance to respond to Tessa's split with Bob – and of course to the abortion too. But to Allyson it all felt like quicksand, something that would just drag her back into the horrible quagmire of pain and despair she was still struggling so hard to get out of, and now her grip was tightening on the lifeline Mark Reiner had thrown her, she wanted only to go with it.

After paying the driver she slammed the cab door closed and walked the few paces to Mark's office. She couldn't allow herself to second-guess any more about this meeting, because she'd lain awake half the night wondering about it, and about Bob, and where they all were in their lives, and when she had finally allowed a truth to emerge from the confusion, that if it weren't for Shelley she'd be hoping very much that Mark had invited her here for reasons that weren't entirely professional, she had immediately seen the danger and frogmarched her fantasies straight off to the dimmest and darkest cell of her overactive brain. However, they'd somehow contrived an escape, for she was much more nervous than she should have been as she walked up the stairs to his reception, and excited too, it had to be said – though the fall, if it came, would at least have the happy outcome of easing the tension between her and Shelley.

'He's down the corridor with the finance director,' Corinne, his assistant, told her when she walked in. 'I'll let him know you're here.'

As Corinne picked up the phone, Allyson could feel the flutterings in her heartbeat. She really was looking forward to this meeting.

'He's on his way back,' Corinne said a few moments later. 'Can I get you a drink?'

'No thanks.'

Allyson wandered over to the window. Rush hour was already under way, though she was hardly registering it. In fact she had no idea how much time had passed before she became conscious of Corinne's voice again, and realized she was talking to Mark.

Allyson turned round and was instantly aware of the way he seemed to dominate the room – and reach everything inside her with his magnetic dark eyes.

'I've put the tickets on your desk,' Corinne was telling him as he looked at Allyson. 'Your flight's at eleven in the morning, arriving in Paris around noon. Paul McKenzie's joining you at the hotel tomorrow night.'

'Great,' he said. Then to Allyson, 'Hi. Come in.'

He held open the door and as she passed she caught the warm, male scent of him. His tie was loose and his white shirt was crumpled. She was amused by the way she noticed those details, and felt agreeably disturbed by their impact. But sensing where her imagination was heading she brought it quickly to heel, and stopped at one of his guest chairs. 'So you're going to Paris tomorrow?' she said chattily.

'For the second time this week. We're involved in a buy-out of one of the cable stations. Did Corinne offer you a drink?'

'Yes. I've changed my mind, I'll take a vodka martini.'

Noticing the way the corners of his eyes creased as he smiled made her smile too. 'I'll join you,' he said.

As he fixed the drinks Allyson took off her coat and was about to sit down when he said, 'If we're having martinis we don't need to be formal.'

So she went to sit on one of the comfy black leather sofas, and watched him until he brought the drinks over. There was something quite exhilarating about being here, and allowing herself to sink into the attraction, even though she knew very well that she was far too unsure of herself to permit the kind of thoughts she was having to become a reality. Nevertheless, they were enjoyable.

'Thanks for coming,' he said, as he sat down. 'I know how busy you are, and I'm overdue for a visit to the studio. But it's been kind of crazy these past few weeks. Anyway, here's to you and your continued success.'

'Thank you,' Allyson responded.

As they drank she dropped her eyes from his, not wanting him to see how aware she was becoming of his body, but it was hard not to be when his proximity, coupled with those intensely knowing eyes of his, were dragging her shy and battered libido out into the light and giving it all kinds of ideas on how to get going again. In fact, it seemed so ready for the off that the sheer boldness of it was making her feel as light-headed as the vodka.

'Did I remember to tell you, my family enjoyed meeting you on New Year's Eve?' he said.

The intimacy in his voice stole right into her. 'I enjoyed meeting them,' she answered, looking at him again. 'And I'm sorry if I wasn't, well,' she gave a playful raise of her eyebrows, 'quite myself.'

'You're going through a tough time. I heard about the spread in *Hello!*'

Allyson coloured, and felt ashamed for him to know that Bob had treated her so badly.

The phone buzzed on his desk and he reached behind him for the extension.

'Tessa Dukes is on the line,' Corinne told him.

His eyes moved to Allyson. 'Tell her I'll get back to her.'

'She says it's urgent.'

'The answer's still the same,' he said, and hung up.

Allyson wondered who he didn't want to talk to. Obviously it was a woman, and she wondered if it was the one he'd taken to the Clausonnes' in France.

'I need to ask you a favour,' he said, his attention on her again.

Allyson looked intrigued.

'Nick and I have a hotel in Ravello, Italy,' he said. 'The renovation is complete and it should be due to open sometime in March, enough time to get through the worst of its teething problems before the summer season starts. The favour I'm asking is if you'd consider making the hotel's launch the subject of one of your programmes. From my point of view the publicity would be excellent, and from yours the party would be worth going to. The company publicists will draw up a list of who to invite, it should be suitably celebrity-heavy, and the setting on the Amalfi Coast is extremely picturesque.'

Allyson was laughing. 'You're *asking* me?' she said. 'You're the boss. If you want us to go to Ravello then to Ravello we shall go.'

'It's not an order. It's a request. As the producer you tell me if you're happy about making it one of your programmes.'

'I'd be very happy,' she said. 'Obviously I'll need more information and we'd probably want to be involved in drawing up the guest list, but on the face of it it sounds absolutely perfect.'

Though he was still smiling, his eyes appeared suddenly darker as he looked at her in a way that seemed to be moving past the veneer of professionalism and politeness. 'There's something else I'm going to ask,' he told her.

She waited, feeling a shortening of her breath and a wonderful anticipation tightening her insides.

'Nick normally takes care of the hotels and restaurants,' he said, 'but he can't get over in the foreseeable future. That means I'll have to go to Italy to talk to the new manager and take care of the pre-opening business. As you'll need to recce the place I thought we could go together.'

Allyson's breath had stopped. Her eyes were now on her drink, as her heart succumbed to an extremely unsteady beat. This was clearly a romantic proposal and

318

she wanted more than anything to say yes. But how could she when she knew how much it would hurt Shelley? 'If . . . If you're meaning what I think you might be meaning,' she said, looking at him again, 'then I'm afraid I can't.'

He seemed neither surprised nor put out by her response. 'Because of Shelley?' he said. 'Or because of your husband?'

'Because of Shelley,' she said frankly.

He picked up his drink and took a sip. His eyes remained on hers. Then after glancing at his watch he said, 'There's a painting I'm considering buying in a gallery a few streets from here. Are you free to come take a look?'

Surprised by the sudden change of subject, and slightly thrown, she shook her head. 'I'm due at the children's hospital in half an hour,' she answered. 'I go every Thursday.' Then she added, 'Why don't you come with me?'

He gave it a moment's consideration, then getting to his feet he said, 'OK, let's do that.'

Allyson could never have dreamt what a big deal it was for him to make the hospital visit, because, until he told her on the way there, she knew nothing about the daughter Nick and Claudia had lost to leukaemia at the age of three. It was clear from the way Mark spoke of it how deeply the death had affected him too, so Allyson wondered if this visit was going to be too distressing, since his niece had died less than a year ago. But he insisted they should go. He'd gained a lot of experience with sick children after all the time he'd spent with Michaela and the other kids who'd been in the hospital with her, so why not put it to some use?

And indeed, they'd only been in the cancer ward a few minutes before he had his jacket off and was down on his knees playing trains, making tours of dolls' houses, getting shot at and keeling over, or being jumped on and brutally roughed up. Very soon Allyson was laughing along with the visiting parents at the children's eagerness to claim his attention, and delight when they made him groan in pain or shoot back with gunfire.

Leaving him to it, Allyson went to talk to the nurses and various care-givers, most of whom she knew well from her many visits with Bob, and whom she felt to be equally as deserving of attention.

'Because everyone thrives on praise and recognition,' she explained to Mark when finally they left. 'What the nurses and volunteers do for those kids is wonderful. They need to know they're appreciated. We all need that, but what these people do really matters. It's why I wanted to concentrate one programme a week on recognizing those who do things for others.' She turned and smiled up into his face. 'The soapbox goes everywhere with me.'

Laughing, he raised an arm to hail a passing taxi. 'Where're you going now?' he asked, as the taxi pulled up.

She shrugged. 'Home, I guess. Unless you're free for dinner.'

'I'm afraid not,' he answered. 'But I'll take a rain check?'

'OK.' As she climbed into the taxi she was struggling with the disappointment that he'd said no more about Italy. Had he been free for dinner she might have returned to the subject herself, though to what end she couldn't be sure, except maybe to hear him say that Shelley shouldn't be a consideration. But even if he said it, Shelley still would be, so really there was no more to discuss, was there?

It was nine in the morning when Tessa rang Mark Reiner at his home in Eaton Square. 'I waited three hours for you to call back last night,' she told him.

320

'I'm sorry, something came up.'

'I know. It's in the paper this morning, how you and Allyson visited the children's hospital last night.'

He hadn't seen the papers yet, but it didn't surprise him. 'What can I do for you?' he said.

'Your secretary tells me you're going to Paris today.'

He waited.

'When will you be back?'

'Probably at the weekend.'

'Great, because I've been invited to this charity dinner at the Inn on the Park next Thursday and I was hoping you'd come with me.'

'I'm afraid that's not possible. You should ask one of the directors to go with you, or a reporter.'

'I'd prefer it to be you.'

He looked at his watch. 'Tessa, I have to go,' he said, 'I've got a plane to catch.'

He put down the phone and walked along the hall to where he'd left his luggage, just inside the front door. He'd like to think he was wrong about this, and Tessa was being no more than a needy, slightly temperamental novice of an artiste. But if his suspicions were correct, and she had transferred her affections to him, then he was a very long way from being flattered. In fact, he was far closer to being angry and concerned, for it certainly hadn't escaped his attention that her interest in him had neatly coincided with his in Allyson. Exactly what that meant he wasn't yet sure, but he'd no doubt find out soon enough – just as Tessa Dukes would find out that he was no Bob Jaymes who responded to the tiresomely irrational whims of a teenage girl as though they were some kind of magic charm that was impossible to resist.

A week had gone by since Shelley had learned about the proposed programme in Italy, a week in which she had kept her distance from Allyson. She knew she should tell Allyson to go on the recce, that it was the only honourable course to take, but she just couldn't make herself do it. To sidestep any attempts at confrontation, she made a great show of having far more pressing matters to deal with, which she did, for as the show's editor she had eleven more programmes a month to get on the air than Allyson had. She was also still very much involved in Tessa's progress as a presenter, which was why she was with her in her dressing room, late one afternoon, when Tessa took a call from Mark Reiner.

'Oh, hi Mark,' Tessa cried cheerfully. 'How are you? Did you see the programme?'

Shelley couldn't hear the response, but she saw the glow on Tessa's face.

'How was Paris?' Tessa asked.

His reply was brief, because Tessa was talking again. 'So when am I going to see you?' she asked. 'Tomorrow? That's great. What time?'

Shelley continued to look at the script, slightly stunned by what she was hearing, if she was indeed reading it correctly. Surely Tessa Dukes wasn't setting her sights on Mark Reiner? She suddenly turned cold as she remembered that was the precise phrase Bob had used when he'd told her Tessa had found someone else. But Mark Reiner? It didn't sound very plausible, though Tessa was an odd fish and there was never any knowing what went on in her head. She had to be into self-delusion in a big way though if she thought she was going to get anywhere with Mark Reiner, for, Allyson aside, the man was just too sophisticated to be impressed by the likes of Tessa Dukes.

'OK, well don't forget to come and say hi to me,' Tessa said, 'I'll pass you over to Shelley.' She held out the phone. 'Mark Reiner, for you.'

Shelley's heart skipped a beat. This would be the first time they'd spoken since the day she'd all but begged him to see her, and she'd have preferred it not to be in front of Tessa. 'Hello,' she said coolly.

'Shelley. I'd like to see you,' he said. 'I thought I'd come down there after the recording tomorrow. Will I catch you?'

'Of course. Shall we roll out the red carpet? It'll be your first visit.'

'Keep it low-key. It's a personal matter.'

After he'd rung off Shelley could feel an unsteady sensation swirling through her insides, then noticing that Tessa was watching her she picked up the script and said, 'I think we're finished here, don't you?'

'OK,' Tessa answered. 'But just before you go, did Allyson talk to you about the programme in Italy? The one Mark Reiner wants us to set in his hotel?'

'Yes,' Shelley answered. 'What about it?'

Tessa shrugged. 'I just wondered if we were going to be doing it.'

'We've got the one in Austria to get through first. Is that all?'

Tessa nodded, then went to pick up the phone as it rang again.

Shelley returned to her office, slightly perturbed by Tessa, and extremely anxious about the personal matter Mark Reiner was coming here to discuss. She felt sure it was going to be about the programme in Italy, and she'd give almost anything to avoid it. However, she could be wrong, it could be about something else entirely, and knowing there was a danger she was going to drive herself crazy trying to guess what it could be, she tried to put it out of her mind.

However, by the time the next day's recording began she'd been unable to stop herself exploring every conceivable possibility, from him inviting her to recce Ravello now that Allyson had turned him down, to him getting rid of her so he could hand the entire programme over to Allyson. The latter was nonsense of course, and she had no intention of subscribing to that kind of

323

paranoia, though she had to admit that now the thought had entered her head . . .

But no, swinging back and forth between such sublime promise and destructive fear wasn't only exhausting, it was degrading for a woman like her, who normally knew very well how to deal with men. And despite his apparent reluctance, and even attraction to Allyson, whilst on an upswing Shelley simply couldn't be convinced that Mark Reiner's interest in her was no more than the smoke of an extinguished candle.

After the recording she took advantage of Allyson's absence in Austria by using her dressing room to touch up her make-up and change into something less formal than the suit she'd been in all day. It occurred to her, as she pulled on a pair of cream leather trousers and a black silk shirt, how much she would enjoy having sex with him, right here in Allyson's dressing room. It would be a delicious payback, and a fabulously awkward spanner to throw into the works, should Allyson just happen to find out.

She was still enlarging on this particularly thrilling fantasy when Marvin rang to tell her Mark had arrived.

'Could you show him down here?' Shelley said.

Minutes later there was a knock on the door, and, with a calmness she was far from feeling, she called for him to come in.

'Hi,' she said, looking up from the pile of paperwork she'd provided herself with. 'It's usually noisy in the office straight after the recording, so I thought it would be easier for us to talk here. Did Marvin offer you some coffee?'

'I'm OK,' he said.

She waved him to a seat and wished she didn't feel quite so uptight, or so desirous of pressing her body to his in order to attain the reassuring heat of his response. Smiling, she said, 'So, you're impressed with the way things are going?'

'It certainly seems to be working,' he answered. 'The ratings didn't go up any further this week, but the previous increase was good enough to sustain my confidence.'

She was picturing his long dark hair the way it was when it fell over his face during the vigorous throes of his lovemaking. 'So Tessa was a good choice?' she said.

'Her novelty value appears to be paying off. The real test will come once that runs out.'

'I think she's good enough to keep it going. She gets better all the time.'

He didn't argue with that, he simply took the conversation to where he wanted it to be. 'Can I presume that Allyson's spoken to you about the hotel in Ravello?' he said.

As she nodded she could feel her insides tensing with a deeply unpleasant tightness. 'It's a good idea,' she said mildly. 'It should make an excellent programme.'

'I'm glad you think so.' He waited for her eyes to return to his. 'I need to visit the hotel prior to its opening,' he told her, 'and I want to take Allyson with me. I think she'd come were she not afraid of upsetting you.'

Shelley could feel a slow paralysis creeping through her brain. Her smile had gone and the skin under her clothes cringed with the shame of rejection.

As though sensing how badly she'd taken it, his voice seemed much softer as he said, 'This may be unnecessary, but I want you to know that I'm truly sorry if I led you to think there might be something between us. It wasn't my intention, but I understand that you might have read it that way.'

Still she couldn't speak. His chivalry in taking the blame, when she was the one who had done all the running, was making it so much worse.

He waited for a moment, then said, 'I'd like you to tell Allyson that you don't have a problem with her coming to Italy.'

The words were out before Shelley could stop them. 'Has it crossed your mind that maybe she doesn't want to go and she's using me as an excuse?' she snapped waspishly.

His eyes showed his regret that he was hurting her. 'If she needed an excuse she'd have used her husband,' he said.

'From whom she is still very much on the rebound.'

'I know.' He got to his feet. 'I hope when I next speak to Allyson she'll tell me she's coming to Ravello,' he said.

Shelley remained where she was long after he'd gone, hot tears scalding her eyes, horrible emotions burning her heart. Of course she had no choice now but to tell Allyson she didn't mind about Ravello. How clever of him to come here and ask, no, *tell* her in person. She couldn't say no to that, could she? She couldn't say no to anything, because if she did there was every chance she'd end up losing her job. And where would she be then, with no man, no best friend, and no *Soirée*? Oh God, she hated the world. Hated it. Hated it! And it was only by some miracle of supreme self-control that she stopped herself smashing the dressing room mirror in a fit of uncontrollable rage.

The sun was warm on her face, the breeze gentle in her hair as she stood on the balcony looking down over the clustered red rooftops of the villages below. They were surrounded by lushly ripening orange and lemon groves, that stepped down to the glittering sweep of an impossibly blue sea whose only movement seemed to be in the foam that swirled around the foot of the cliffs. Beside her, almost within reaching distance, were the proudly curved feathers of a tall, carefully tended palm; immediately behind her was the arched doorway that led back into her room, which was cool and airy, with white marble floors and elegant Italian antique furniture.

She'd always loved Italy, for its drama and romance, its artistry and its history, and as she stood there in the fresh morning air she was entranced by the feeling that in these next few days she was going to come to love it even more.

Her feet had barely had time to touch the ground from Austria before she'd taken off again to fly here. They'd arrived last night, in the dark, seeing little of the countryside as they'd driven down from Naples, and talked of previous experiences in Italy, but never of whom they'd been with. The general manager, Giovanni, and his wife had been waiting at the door of the magnificent rose-pink palazzo to greet them, making a big fuss of organizing their luggage, which had to be carried from a splendid courtyard along a narrow cobbled lane to the hotel's front door. The smell of freshly applied paint assailed them as they walked in, along with the glossy, airy vision of an exquisite white marble floor, stark white walls, two polished mahogany reception desks and a new delivery of beautiful silk-upholstered sofas, in blues and creams and golds, that were yet to be arranged in the piano bar. This was at the foot of the marble steps that opened out of the lobby towards windows and a terrace that night had shrouded in darkness.

The recently appointed chef from Milan had prepared a light supper of baked sea bass and grilled vegetables, which they ate in the small staff dining room. Giovanni joined them and wasted no time in briefing Mark on the current state of affairs, which was fraught with typical Italian chaos, and some gloriously theatrical accounts of the tantrums being thrown by everyone from the landscaper to the interior designer. After a while Allyson left them to it, and followed Chiara, Giovanni's wife, upstairs to her room. Everywhere there were gorgeous white arches, with rounded or pointed tops, gilt-framed mirrors, huge lustrous green palms and ferns still in their wrappings, ornate marble fountains yet to be filled and expertly restored antiques that ranged from elegant silk-upholstered chaises longues, to Renaissance-style cabinets containing alabaster and bronze sculptures.

Her room was one of the few that was ready, and though small, everything in it, from the all-white tiled bathroom with its gilt and brass fittings, to the pale lemon silk bedspread and dark walnut nightstands, bespoke an elegance of taste that could only have been acquired by hiring the most gifted designers. She was both pleased and disappointed to find she wasn't sharing with Mark, for despite the yearnings of her body she doubted she'd have appreciated it if he had just assumed she would sleep with him.

Now, hearing a knock on the door, she went to open it and found a maid with a large tray of breakfast. In her broken English the maid said, 'Mr Reiner say he will be joining you.'

Allyson stood aside and watched her lay the black wrought-iron table on the balcony and brush down the neutral-coloured chair paddings. The sun was bathing the terracotta tiled floor and rose-coloured walls and balustrades in a soft, crystalline light and the air was heavily scented with jasmine. When the maid left Allyson went quickly into the bathroom, brushed her teeth and slipped one of the thick white towelling robes over her pyjamas.

A sudden guilt smothered her tremors of anticipation. Shelley had sworn she didn't mind, had insisted she come here, but Allyson knew her too well. She was hurting deeply. But when Allyson had tried to say sorry Shelley had backed away, insisting that she'd blown him up in her mind to be something he wasn't, and that she was quite happy to let go. Allyson didn't believe it, but she'd come anyway, and now she was wondering what kind of friend that made her.

The phone rang on the wall beside her.

'Did the maid bring breakfast yet?' he asked.

As her heart tightened her face broke into a smile, and she turned to the mirror as she said, 'Yes.'

'Then I'll be right there.'

She hung up and took a breath to steady her nerves. Then she looked at herself again. She was probably imagining that the wretched lines around her eyes were fading, and the haunted look that had deadened her for months was now lit up with a radiance that made her want to laugh out loud. But who cared if she was imagining it, it was so wonderful to feel this alive again that she wasn't going to deny it. And the added piquancy of desire, moving deliciously into her senses, was inciting the kind of reckless exuberance that made her skin glow and her heart race along with the fantasies of where the next few days would take them.

When he came he was dressed in casual chinos and a black open-necked polo shirt, and raised a droll eyebrow to find her still in pyjamas.

'Good morning,' she said, opening the door wide.

'Good morning. Did you sleep well?'

'Very.' It felt so gloriously wicked and tempting being in the same room as him and a bed that it made her want to laugh. 'Are you ready for coffee?' she asked. 'It's outside.'

'You pour. I need to make a quick call,' he answered.

'How do you take it?' she asked, going out onto the balcony. For some reason she liked not knowing and having to ask.

'Black. No sugar.'

She didn't listen to the call, though guessed it was to his office. It would be absurd to wonder if it was to the mysterious woman who'd been mentioned in France, for he'd hardly be here with her if he was committed to somebody else. So she let that thought drift off towards the hazy horizon, and smiled happily to herself as she closed her eyes and listened to the church clocks all around the valley chiming out the half-hour.

When he joined her at the table he said, 'I've asked the company publicists to fax over the provisional guest list. We can go through it while we're here.'

'Great.' She passed him a coffee. 'I've been having some thoughts on it, and I've left Justie and Zac making tentative enquiries to find out who's free.' Her eyes were drawn back to the spectacular view of mountains and sea. 'I've got such a good feeling about this place,' she said.

He was watching her with dark, humorous eyes, which made her laugh when she looked back at him.

'Let's just hope the paparazzi don't find out we're here,' she said, 'because the last thing we need is them chasing us about the place on those dangerous motorbikes, or climbing trees with their long lenses.'

'We'll only be here a couple of days,' he said, breaking open a crusty roll, 'so we should be safe. What's on your agenda? I've arranged for a car and driver to take you around, by the way. Someone who knows the area and can give you all the information you need.'

'You mean you won't be coming with me?' she protested.

He laughed. 'Not every time. There are things here I have to attend to, designers to see, more staff to hire, papers to be signed, inspections to be completed. We're about on schedule though, and Giovanni seems to have everything well in hand.'

'So I can count on you for Pompeii and Capri?'

'You can count on me,' he grinned, then groaned as his cellphone rang.

It was Corinne, his assistant, with the messages that had come in overnight, then to take down his instructions on how to deal with them. He hadn't finished the call before the phone rang inside the room. It was Chiara letting Allyson know that Domingo, her driver for the day, was ready when she was, and that there was a fax just coming through for Señor Reiner, which she'd send up to Allyson's room.

An hour later, after a quick jacuzzi shower that did nothing to pummel any sobriety into her simmering state of excitement, she was walking along the cobbled lane with Mark to where the car was parked, in a small piazza in front of the church. He was going over the last-minute details on what she should see that morning, and where she should go, before meeting him down in the village's main piazza for lunch – after which, if he could manage it, they'd go to Pompeii together.

'What time shall we meet?' she said, getting into the back of the Mercedes, and taking her straw hat and bag as he passed it in.

'One. Did you remember your camera?'

'It's in my bag. By the way, do you speak Italian?'

'*Un peu*,' he answered, making her laugh. 'How about you?'

She pulled a face.

'Domingo'll take care of you.'

He closed the door, then after a few words with the rotundly cheerful Domingo, he stood aside for them to begin the dangerous reverse back to the main road.

They began with a tour of the surrounding country-side, so that Allyson could search out some vantage points that would offer the best exterior shots of the hotel, and the ancient hilltop village that overlooked so much staggering beauty. She clicked away happily with her camera, hoping that the weather was going to be this gracious when they came to shoot, for though there was no great heat to the sun, its quality was so mistily beautiful as it streamed through the orange and lemon groves and bathed the ancient village walls in a glistening treacle of light that she could almost feel the cameraman's excitement.

They returned to the small church piazza around

eleven, and walked along past the hotel, down through the narrow, steeply sloping streets that led to the main square where tables and chairs were set up outside the cafés, and small tourist shops spilled their wares out onto the street. The magnificent *duomo* with its wide sweeping steps and decorated façade dominated the piazza, and the ancient stone arch and clock tower set at an angle beside it looked so inviting that she couldn't decide whether to go and explore what was beyond straight away, or to wait for Mark to go with her.

In the end she got caught up in browsing through the garishly painted ceramics for sale, and the cleverly shaped lemon liqueur bottles that ranged from stars, to trumpets, to cottagey houses and thin, elegant pyramids. All the time she was scribbling notes, taking more photographs and then finally she drifted in through the arch under the clock tower, which turned out to be the entrance to the magnificent Rufolo gardens with their historic villa and glorious flowers and fountains. After taking her time to look around, she parked herself on a bench overlooking the sea, and, surrounded by vividly blooming flowers and exotic shrubs, she began working out a schedule for the programme. Happy Hour she'd already decided would be in the hotel's piano bar. The filmed insert would be either Pompeii or Capri, she'd know once she'd done the recces. And the Night Cap could be done in the gorgeous little alcove she'd discovered here in the gardens which had a small fountain at the centre, lush green plants all around it and ancient circular stone walls protecting it. Would that give enough exposure to the hotel? She thought so, since the locale was every bit as important when it came to appeal, and stunning though the hotel was, and packed with facilities, no-one came on holiday without wanting to visit the historical sites or beaches nearby.

'Did you know,' she said to Mark later, as a waiter set

two chilled glasses of local wine on the pink tablecloth between them, 'that Wagner got his inspiration to write the music for *Parsifal* here, in Ravello? And there's a Wagner festival every July? Do you like opera?'

'Occasionally,' he answered, taking the menus from the waiter.

'We should use some extracts from *Parsifal* in the programme,' she decided, giving a little wave to an elderly couple as they came into the umbrella-ed shade of the terrace. 'So what have you been doing this morning?'

He grimaced. 'Definitely not having as much fun as you,' he responded. 'We've just fired the chef and I had to wake Nick up in the middle of the night to tell him some of the rooms are too small.'

Her eyes rounded. 'The chef first,' she said.

'What we had last night wasn't up to standard,' he explained.

'But it was only a snack.'

He merely looked at her, allowing his silence to state the standards of excellence.

'OK,' she laughed. 'So why did you have to wake Nick up? Couldn't it have waited until he'd had breakfast?'

'Sure, but waking him up presses home the importance. There's nothing to be done now, but next winter there'll have to be some major renovation, which will leave us with less rooms, but enough space for the average American giant to get in through the bathroom door. And believe me, at the prices we'll be charging, we're going to need to accommodate the Americans.'

Laughing again, she opened the menu and took a sip of wine. 'What are you going to eat?' she asked a few minutes later.

'Spinach ravioli,' he answered. 'You?'

'Parma ham and mozzarella.'

After they'd ordered they carried on discussing the hotel, then moved on to the programme, concentrating mainly on the logistics, as well as the cost, of getting so many names over to Italy.

'The best answer,' he said, as their food arrived, 'is to charter a plane. And before you start reminding me about your budget, I'll get the company publicists to cover travel expenses with theirs. I guess the crew will fly out a day early to get everything set up?'

She nodded, and ordered two more glasses of wine before the waiter went away. 'You'd better organize for the interior designers to be on hand while they're doing that, just to make sure everyone's aware of what is and isn't valuable. I'll check out the storage and recording space while I'm here. Did you find out if Nick and Claudia are going to be able to come?'

'It's not looking likely, but things could change.'

As they ate their conversation meandered away from the programme, moving easily from one subject to another as they made each other laugh with all manner of stories, and, for Allyson, this journey of discovery into his character was so fascinating and exhilarating she could have continued it all day. It had been over twenty years since she'd last got to know a man this way, and there was so much she wanted to know about Mark Reiner that, in the end, he laughingly held up his hands, saying, 'I refuse to believe I'm as interesting as you're making me feel, so stop before it goes to my head.'

Laughing, she finished up her salad and reached for her empty glass.

'More wine?' he offered.

'Oh God, I'd love more wine, but if I do I'll never make it through the rest of the day.'

A teasing light came into his eyes. 'This is Italy, siestas are permissible,' he reminded her.

'Permissible?' she said, tilting her head to one side, and feeling glad that was the only response he could see. 'I thought they were obligatory.'

The way he looked at her then caused her heart to float

in the dizzying flirtation, while all kinds of sensations started igniting elsewhere in her body.

'Nothing's obligatory,' he said.

She smiled and was trying desperately to think of a suitable *double entendre* when his cellphone abruptly rang, and rescued her from the brink of potential disaster.

She watched him as he listened to the voice at the other end. 'That's great,' he said, starting to laugh. 'Do it.' He paused again and looked out across the square, giving Allyson the impression he was avoiding her eyes. 'OK, I'll see you when I get back,' he said. 'Mmm. Me too,' and he rang off.

Resisting the urge to ask who it was, Allyson ordered a cappuccino and picked up her notes. 'You know, I was thinking,' she said, 'this is going to be a pretty special kind of programme, and it seems, well, a bit exclusive and not very generous to keep it to ourselves. So maybe we should invite everyone else on the programme too. Obviously they're not all going to be able to come, and they're not all going to be able to stay at the hotel, but they do work incredibly hard and this could be a way of, well,' she shrugged, 'showing them they're appreciated.'

He was nodding as he mulled it over. Then finishing his wine he said, 'I'll leave that one with you and your budget. Oh God, here come the roses,' he groaned, as a pretty little gypsy girl came waltzing towards them with a basket of blooms.

'I'll take six,' Allyson said, smiling at the girl.

The girl looked confused.

'*Sei*,' Mark translated, digging into his pocket.

'I'll get lunch,' Allyson offered, 'but you'll have to lend me the money, because I didn't find a bank on my morning travels.'

Laughing, he handed the gypsy girl a wad of lire, then signalled the waiter for the bill. When they were ready they walked back up to the hotel, dropped off the roses, then he drove them himself to Pompeii.

By the time they got there Allyson could have wished he'd dropped off his cellphone too, but she wasn't going to let the constant interruptions spoil the experience, for she'd long wanted to visit this historical site and as they left the car and began walking towards the crumbling walls and damaged pillars that edged the tragic town, she could almost hear the silent echoes of terror that seemed to reverberate down through the centuries.

A gentle breeze carried the rank, earthy smell to her senses as they strolled along the worn cobbled roads and walkways, tramping the journey that nineteen centuries ago had been so carelessly and routinely taken by a people that were to meet such a terrible end. They walked through the ruined basilica, the central baths, the Samnite gymnasium and stopped at what had once been the majestic Temple of Apollo, where she allowed her eyes to travel slowly over the devastated majesty. A bronze statue of the god himself, now green with age, stood in front of an amazingly preserved portico and faced a bust of Diana across the weeded and dusty forum that had probably once been covered by marble or limestone. Worn steps rose from a travertine stone altar to aged marble pillars that now supported nothing, and a dais that was currently home to a museum glass case containing the grisly, fossilized remains of a human being whose bared, two-thousand-year-old teeth were in immaculate condition, and showed the agony of fear in his dying moments. It was moving in the extreme, and made her shudder with revulsion and horror at the way the hot ash had so well preserved such a private and perilous hour.

After a while they walked on, down what had once been a busy market street that still bore evidence of the trading and even the graffiti and advertising that were splashed in perspex-covered colour on the decaying walls. From there they wandered into the narrow residential streets where the remnants of two- and three-storey houses, all carefully dug from the smothering debris of the volcano's eruption, stood deserted and shell-like, seeming somehow bewildered by the loss of enlivening crowds.

'Look here,' Mark said, drawing her over to a comparatively vivid wall painting. In the fading colours they managed to make out two children playing, some ancient script, and what seemed to be the feet of a galloping horse. Allyson looked around the dusty, dark room and stairway and tried to picture the family that had once lived there. Had they escaped, she wondered, or had they perished while attempting to flee the savage outpouring of molten lava and flaming rock?

They walked on, along the narrow streets with their raised stone crossings and deeply etched grooves that had once kept wooden carts on track. It was so peaceful and redolent of the burial ground it actually was. Yet it was somehow sinister too, in its reminder of the frailty and impermanence of human life.

'You know, I had a past-life regression once,' Allyson said, as she stopped to get a shot of the fearsome slopes of Vesuvius that towered over the town. Clouds of grey smoke puffed idly from its crater, a deceptively benign show from the madly boiling depths of the interior. 'I did it for the programme.'

'Oh?' Mark said, settling comfortably on a bench and stretching out his long legs. 'Did it work?'

'Oh yes,' she answered, coming to sit next to him. 'It was amazing. It was like I was here, living that life all over again.'

'You were here? In Pompeii?' he said, surprised.

She nodded. 'At the end, I was,' she said. 'It's where I died, or, as they say, left that particular life.'

He glanced at her, waiting for her to go on.

'I was a dancing girl,' she said. 'In Rome. I danced for the Emperor Titus. I was also his mistress.'

He looked at her again, apparently not sure whether he should be believing this or not.

'My family lived in Pompeii,' she went on. 'My brother and two sisters. I was bringing them money and trying to persuade them to leave the town when the mountain exploded. Everyone knew it would explode, it had been rumbling and spewing out lava and rocks for days, but my family were amongst those who wouldn't leave. And then it was too late. We tried to run, but . . .' She paused for a moment, then said, 'After I died, when I left my body, I could see the Emperor Titus in his palace in Rome, and do you know the most remarkable thing?' Her eyes were trained straight ahead, but appeared to be seeing nothing of what was in front of her. 'He looked exactly like you.'

Mark blinked, looked at her incredulously, then, instinctively knowing he was being had, he said, 'So that's what happened to you! I always wondered. You were a great mistress, but boy were you a lousy dancer.'

Allyson burst out laughing at the way he'd managed to get the last word, then picking up her camera and guidebook she walked on towards the Amphitheatre and Palestra Grande.

By the time they started back to the hotel it was already getting dark, and the effects of the Campari they stopped for en route were making her yawn as she said, 'I'm thinking about dressing up Tessa and a couple of actors and recreating a street scene for the film insert. I'll have to look into the cost.'

'What about Titus and his dancing girl?'

She grinned. 'What about them?'

'Well, if you can improve on your act, I don't mind stepping in to become the man I once was.'

A teasing light shot to her eyes. 'Sounds more like a scene for siesta,' she commented.

His eyebrows made a sardonic arch. 'Now you're talking,' he responded.

Laughing, she rested her head against the back of the car seat and turned to look at her reflection in the window while allowing herself the heady delight of imagining where the evening might end. He surely had to know by now how willing she was to make love, that even sitting here like this was turning into an impossible feat of self-control, for her hands were longing to touch him and her lips were actually parting in a breathy anticipation of his pressing against them. Her heart turned over at the thought of his tongue entering her mouth, then his hands were blazing a trail over her breasts, his urgency was matching hers . . . The potency of the fantasy was so intense she actually moaned aloud and had to cover it quickly with a cough. She turned to look at his profile in the shadowy darkness and wondered if she should tell him what she wanted, or if she should wait for him to tell her?

Shelley regarded the outside of the pub and wondered what artless soul had named it the Romeo and Juliet. Garish coloured bulbs burned around the lavender window frames and though it was hard to tell in the darkness she was sure the jazzy brickwork was painted lime green. Not the kind of place she would normally be seen in, but when needs must . . .

Leaving the relative safety of her car, she locked and alarmed it, then blown about by a chafing wind she ran across the deserted South London street, towards the stained-glass doors. Warmth, and the smell of beer, assailed her as she walked in, along with the latest sound from a rock band she'd probably heard of, but wasn't in the least bit interested in identifying. She looked around the dimly lit room which was a large, irregular oval, with triangular-shaped tables and chairs, and very few people. The bar was an island of tawdriness, with mock

Shakespearean props, and posters of Gwyneth Paltrow and Joseph Fiennes plastered to the pumps.

Spotting the very person she was looking for, alone in a dark corner, she skirted a couple of budding Eric Bristows and headed towards him.

'How did you find me?' Bob said, looking up as she reached the table.

Shelley sat down and unfastened her coat. 'It wasn't hard,' she said, lowering her voice as the music stopped. 'I had Tessa's old address, and there aren't too many pubs in the area. I got you on my third attempt. What are you drinking?'

'Coke.'

She looked impressed. 'So you're managing to stay off it.'

'I wasn't an alcoholic. I drank to . . .'

Shelley looked up from her bag. 'It's OK,' she said, 'you're not the first man to hide from himself inside a bottle. What are you doing about a job?'

'I've done a couple of pieces for one of the tabloids. Other than that I can't get arrested.'

'But you did,' she reminded him.

He eyed her nastily. 'What do you want?' he growled.

'Apart from a vodka tonic, I want to talk to you. Don't worry, I'll get it.'

He watched her at the bar, too depressed to notice the way she turned heads. Maybe he should have left Allyson for her, he wouldn't be in the mess he was in now if he had.

'So,' she said, sitting down again, 'you've been on my mind quite a bit since you came to see me, which is why I came to flush you out.'

'Am I supposed to feel honoured?'

'If you like.' She slipped her wallet inside her slim leather bag, then picked up her drink. 'Would I be right in thinking you'd go back to Allyson if you could?' she said, coming straight to the point.

'I'd go back to a lot of things if I could,' he snarled. 'Even you.'

She gave a mild flicker of her eyebrows and waited for him to swallow his venom. Then inwardly she smiled as he said, 'Why do you ask?'

'Because I don't think I played fair with you when you came to see me. Not that I care about you, you understand, but I do care about Allyson. And if I led you to think she wouldn't take you back, then I'm sorry, because the truth is, I think she would. It's going to take some working at, but despite what a stupid, insensitive, moronic bastard you are, I believe in her heart she still loves you.'

He was shaking his head. 'I think there's a much bigger chance she hates my guts,' he said.

'No. She doesn't hate you. She's just angry with you. If she hates anyone, it's Tessa.'

'She's not the only one,' he snarled. 'What I wouldn't like to do to that bitch for the way she's screwed up my life.'

Shelley said nothing. It was typical of the Bobs of this world to absolve themselves of all responsibility, and blame the woman for their own spineless behaviour. 'I think you should try talking to Allyson,' she said after a pause.

He didn't look convinced. 'How can I? I'm still having to communicate through her lawyer.'

'Because she's protecting herself. You hurt her badly, surely you realize that, so you can't blame her for putting up a defence.'

'So what are you suggesting I do?'

'Tell her you still love her, and ask her to forgive you. You might have to do it through the lawyer, but you know Allyson as well as I do. She's got a very forgiving nature and despite outward appearances, I'm telling you she's falling apart without you.'

'What about Mark Reiner? I wouldn't call seeing him falling apart without me.'

Shelley took a sip of her drink. 'It's all a front,' she said, taking a chance he didn't know Allyson was in Italy right now. The press hadn't found out, so she couldn't see how he would either. 'She's doing it to make you jealous.'

She watched him mull that over for a while and was about to speak again when he said, 'Why don't you tell her you've seen me and talk to her for me?'

'Because then I'd have to admit I betrayed her confidence.'

He reached for his glass but didn't pick it up.

'Bob, look at yourself,' she said, keeping her voice low and full of feeling. 'You're a mess and you know it. You've got no money, no job, no real home to go to. So don't you think your pride's a bit out of place? And that's all that's stopping you, isn't it? You couldn't stand it if she rejected you. But she won't. You're her husband. You've been the biggest part of her life for so long that the truth is, she's lost without you. Like you are without her. You belong together, you two, and you know it.'

His upper lip curled in a snarl. 'What's in this for you, Shelley?' he demanded. 'You never do anything without there being something in it for you.'

Her lovely eyes narrowed as she regarded him, seeming to weigh up how much she should tell him. In the end she said, 'All right, to be blunt, I've got three programmes a week to get out, with an increased workload since the international theme started, and I can't go on carrying Allyson. That's one reason. The other is, she genuinely does love you, though you sure as hell don't deserve it. And I think these past few months have shown you just how much you love her too.'

He looked despondently down at his Coke.

'You just lost sight of it for a while,' she said comfortingly. 'It happens to most of us. So think about it. Work out what you're going to say and then contact her lawyer. Perhaps then you can both get on with your lives.'

After finishing his drink he put his glass back on the table and stared at it.

'Come on,' she said in the end. 'Let's get out of here and find a good restaurant. I'll bet you can't remember the last time you had a decent meal.'

'You're right, I can't. And I never thought you'd be providing me with the next one.'

She laughed. 'You see, Bob, you really never know who your friends are. Do you?'

By the time she dropped him back at his crummy little pad, much later that evening, fed and with some money in his pocket, she knew she'd successfully convinced him that he really did stand a chance of winning Allyson back. In fact Shelley was certain he would, because, knowing Allyson as well as she did, there was no doubt in her mind that nineteen years of marriage was going to mean a whole lot more to Allyson than a few heady days in Italy, however romantic they might be. And Shelley couldn't even be persuaded they'd be that romantic, for when it came right down to it, Allyson, who'd never slept with anyone but Bob, just didn't have what it took to satisfy a man like Mark Reiner.

'Stand over there. No, not there. There,' Mark said, trying to get Allyson in the right spot to be photographed outside Capri's beautiful baroque cathedral, which sat at the heart of the entrancing leafy square with all its colourful cafés and bistros.

'Are you trying to get it so that campanile is sticking out of my head?' she accused.

He laughed. 'Just take a step to your left. OK, that's it! Now, smile!'

'Smile!' she scoffed. 'Can't you be more original than that?'

Mark lowered the camera and glared at her.

343

'OK, OK,' she cried. 'I'm smiling.'

He took the picture, then turning the camera towards the vast, glittering expanse of the Mediterranean with Sorrento in the background, he took another.

'Mm,' she murmured, inhaling deeply of the wonderful spring blossom that was wafting from the trees. When she opened her eyes it was to find him watching her with that lazy, gently mocking humour she was coming to know so well. In its way it seemed to suggest he wanted to kiss her, yet he never did. Not even last night, when he'd walked her to her door and stood so close she could almost feel herself moving into him. But he had merely said goodnight, then waited for her to go into her room, before going off to his.

'Do you want to go see Anacapri?' he said, as she watched the funicular, stuffed with tourists, rising up over the cliffs from the harbour to the town.

'Sure,' she answered, and stepped jauntily back into the rear of their fantastic red open-topped taxi, a perfect relic from the Fifties that made her feel like Grace Kelly meandering around the steep winding roads with Clark Gable – or better still with Mark Reiner, whose bare, tanned legs and taut muscles were creating all kinds of havoc in the realms of bodily desire. She truly couldn't remember ever feeling so turned on by a man before, though she realized that it was probably his casual acceptance of nothing physical that was inciting her to such an unprecedented pitch of lust. And as they were chauffeured through the lazy, but dazzling beauty of the island's glossy white villas, towering green palms and spectacular views of the glittering blue sea and enticing coves, she was allowing herself to indulge in a fantasy so unspeakably erotic that it actually made her blush when she looked at him. Worse still, as he handed her out of the car, was the uncanny feeling she had that he was reading her mind. If he was, then she could feel only dismay that he continued to hold back, except of course

344

they were a long way from the hotel and her visions didn't include anything as tawdry as a quick tussle in the bushes; and even if they did she still had to wonder if the power of what was happening to her was driven by a need to get her own back on Bob. She didn't think it was, but in all honesty, while she was so clouded by these glorious feelings of lust that were being met by intolerable frustration, it was impossible to know anything for certain.

They roamed around the small town of Anacapri, inspecting the endless T-shirt and shoe shops and stopping for coffee at a café overlooking the rather ordinary piazza.

'I don't think this island is going to work for the programme,' she said, stirring the chocolate-covered froth of a cappuccino into the milky coffee. 'Most of it's stunningly beautiful, but it'll take too long to get here, and the budget won't stretch.'

Nodding, he said, 'I guessed you might decide that, but it was worth coming, just to make sure.'

'Of course,' she responded. Then smiling she added, 'I'm having a wonderful time. I feel as though we're on holiday, don't you?'

His eyes were dancing, but he only looked past her as their driver approached the table and asked what they would like to do next.

Mark looked at Allyson, and to her horror she felt her cheeks start to burn. Yes, that was what she wanted to do next, but surely she hadn't said it aloud.

'Maybe we go take a look at where Tiberius fling his wife over the cliff,' the driver suggested with a grin.

'No,' Mark said, still looking at Allyson, 'I think you can take us back to the ferry now.'

It was already dark by the time the ferry sailed into the harbour at Amalfi. They were leaning against the deck rail, huddled warmly in the sweaters they'd thought to

345

take with them and gazing out at the glittering lights that shimmered like fireflies at the foot of the hillside. She was so aware of him standing there, right beside her, and so tensed by the desire that seemed to jolt like electricity between them, that she almost gasped when he slipped an arm around her and pulled her in closer.

For a moment she was rigid. Then she turned to look up at him, her hair blowing in the wind, the taste of the sea on her lips. He lowered his eyes to hers and gazed deeply into them. With all her might she willed him to kiss her. But he only brushed the hair from her face and hugged her.

They drove back to the hotel in silence, taking the dark, winding roads at a speed that made her urgency feel like a world-class sprinter in a race against no-one. He seemed in no rush to get there, and she wondered what would happen when they did. Tonight was their last before they returned to London in the morning, and she just couldn't bear the idea of leaving without knowing what it was to make love with him.

When they got back Giovanni gave them their faxes and messages then went off to bed. Allyson's were all from Zac and Justine, and Mark's were from heaven only knew who. As they walked upstairs she resolved to tell him what she wanted. It just wasn't something she could keep hidden any longer, and if she ended up making a fool of herself, then so be it.

When they reached her door he unlocked it for her, and she took a moment to summon her courage, before lifting her head to look into his eyes. 'Mark,' she said.

He raised a hand to her face, brushing his thumb over her lips. 'Are you sure?' he whispered.

'I'll go mad if you don't,' she answered.

As he continued to look at her, she drew his thumb into her mouth. The symbolic meaning of what she was doing inflamed them both, and suddenly his lips were on hers and he was pulling her to him with all the force she had longed for.

He took her into the room, closed the door and pulled her to him again. His mouth was tender and probing, commanding and harsh. He kissed her neck, and she unbuttoned her dress, letting it fall to the floor, then unhooked her bra. He slipped it down over her arms, then smoothed her surprisingly full breasts with his hands, teasing their tight, rosy nipples and watching the desire cloud her eyes. Then he undressed her completely and ran his hands all over her nudity in a way that almost sent her out of her mind with longing. She watched his face and felt the electric force of desire pulsing through her. And when he dropped to his knees and kissed her all the way down to her pubic hair, she felt the breathless might of exquisite, impelling sensations rushing her to a point where she cried out at the insistent mastery of his tongue.

The bed was just behind her and pushing her back he stood over her, looking at her, as he undressed himself. He lay down with her, pulling her to him and feeling her fingers grip the solid stem of his erection. The tenderness he felt curled through his heart, and was belied by the urgency of his need. He sensed the biting power of the need in her too and knew that whatever the truth of her feelings, in this moment she was his.

She lay over him and pushed her tongue between his lips. Her small body was light on his chest, her legs were open. He pushed himself into her, afraid he would be too big for her. Then his eyes closed as she sat up to take him fully. He watched her as she rode him, his eyes moving between her face and where their bodies were joined. He held her hands, entwining her fingers. Then feeling the mounting pressure inside her, he rolled her onto her back and entered her again.

She gripped his shoulders and stared up at his face. Then, as he looked at her too, she seemed to lose all sense

347

of where and who she was as he began moving his hips in a way that touched every part of her, bathing her in sensations that were almost too powerful to bear.

'Oh my God, my God,' she murmured.

He drew her lips between his, then pushed his tongue into her mouth as he moved himself inside her with a rhythm and a force she could hardly bear. She felt so full of him, so overpowered and enrapt by him. He moved with exquisite slowness, then speed, with such expert knowledge of when she was at the brink, only to bring her back and exploit her again in a torrent of unbearable pleasure. Time and time again he took her to the point where she felt her entire body might explode with the ecstasy. She wanted to scream, to rage, to draw him in tighter and make him feel the immaculate pain he was inflicting on her senses, but she was so lost to anything beyond what he was doing, she could only cling to him and beg him for more, and yet more.

Then at last he let her fly, and as the climactic rush soared through him too he pressed his mouth needfully to hers, wanting her cries inside him as he was inside her.

They continued to hold each other long after their heartbeats were calm. Only their faces were apart, so that they could gaze into each other's eyes. Though he said nothing he knew it was love that he felt for this woman, who was still so injured inside that she might be his for only one night.

Chapter 15

The only good thing about leaving Ravello was knowing that now she'd rejigged the schedule and put the Italian programme ahead of the Austrian, they'd be back again in less than two weeks. The closeness Allyson was starting to feel with Mark was something she wasn't ready to put into words; it was enough just to feel it and know that he felt it too. He'd insisted that he wanted to take everything at her speed, even though she had no idea how fast or slow that was, except she was still a very long way from being able to make any kind of commitment again. She was also quite overwhelmed by the fact that any of this was happening at all. Self-effacement definitely wasn't her thing, but even without the horrible battering her confidence had taken over Bob's desertion, she'd never imagined a man wanting her rather than Shelley. Not even Bob had been immune to Shelley's charms, it seemed, though Shelley, being the friend she was, had always spurned his advances. Which was why Allyson felt so bad about what was happening between her and Mark, for she'd done little to spurn him, even though she'd known she was trampling Shelley's dream. But maybe Shelley wasn't as hurt as she feared, after all there had been no actual relationship between her and Mark, and Shelley knew very well that none of them had any control over the vagaries of love.

However, despite feeling that she had her relationship with Mark under careful control, Allyson had to confess that their parting, when they returned to London, was a much greater wrench than she'd expected. And the flat, when she walked in, seemed horribly empty and cold. For a moment she felt herself sliding towards depression, as the confusion of what had happened with Mark, and what it might mean for her and Bob, started to engulf her. But then the phone rang, bringing a call from her mother, which was quickly followed by a call from Zac and Justine wanting to know how it had gone in Italy; then Alan, the director, was on the line with some preliminary thoughts on crewing. Half an hour later she was on the point of heaving her suitcase onto the bed to empty it when the phone shrilled into life again. This time it was Mark.

'I promised myself I wouldn't do this,' he said, 'but as I'm at a loose end for dinner, I was wondering if you were free.'

'I promised myself I'd say no if you asked,' she replied, 'but if you bring the wine I'll cook.'

He arrived an hour later and they made love straight away. She sensed a new urgency to their passion, that must have been incited by the parting, for the lazy, though unsurpassable tenderness of Italy was replaced by an aggressive need to be as close as their bodies would allow.

Only afterwards, as they lay breathlessly in each other's arms, did Allyson think of Bob, and how no other man but him had slept in this bed. But that was going to change now if she could persuade Mark to stay.

It was never discussed, he just did.

The next morning as she drove to the office her mood was coasting buoyantly about in memories of the night before, as she relived every smile and caress, every word and sensation. Though she knew there were still many complications to overcome, she was content to allow herself these few precious moments of believing that the worst of the pain was behind her, and that everything would work out perfectly in the end. Her heart was suddenly seized by the naivety of that, for one of the messages on her answerphone last night had been from her lawyer saying that Bob wanted to see her. She knew instinctively what it would be about, and then she was sunk in guilt as she remembered how passionately she had once vowed that she would stand by him through whatever crisis middle age might bring. But life had moved on a long way since then, and her feelings had changed in ways she could never have predicted. It was true that a part of her longed desperately to turn back the clock to a time before Tessa, and before Mark, so that they could erase the heartache of these past few months and return to being the people they'd always been. But of course it wasn't possible, so they had no choice but to deal with things the way they were now.

Feeling a sudden urge to speak to Mark she reached for her phone. He was flying to New York in a couple of hours so she'd probably get him on his mobile en route to the airport. But before she could dial the number her own phone rang.

'Allyson Jaymes,' she said.

'Are you missing me as much as I'm missing you?' he demanded.

'More,' she answered, with a smile. 'Where are you?'

'On my way to the airport.'

She groaned. 'I wish you didn't have to go. What time's your flight?'

'Eleven.' He paused for a moment, then lowered his voice as he said, 'Last night was very special.'

'For me too,' she whispered. 'Is there time for me to get to the airport to see you before you go?'

He laughed. 'I don't think so. But you could get a later flight and join me in New York.'

'You know I would if I could. When will you be back?'

'In ten days. Sooner if I can.' There was a moment's pause before he said, 'Are you going to see your husband?'

Sighing, she nestled the phone into her shoulder as she negotiated the mini-roundabout at the junction of North End and Fulham Roads. 'I don't think so,' she said. 'At least not yet. I'm not going to have the time with this programme to arrange.'

He said no more on the subject, which didn't surprise her for when they'd discussed it last night he'd agreed that the decisions she made on her marriage were for her to take alone, especially when their relationship was so new.

They spoke for a while longer, then were forced to ring off when Allyson drove into the multi-storey car park beside the office.

Zac and Justine were already at their desks when she walked in, getting the massive organization of the Italy programme under way. There was no sign of Shelley, which wasn't a surprise, for she'd left a message on Allyson's machine to say her mother had had a mild stroke so she was going to be in the New Forest for the next couple of days. Not for a minute did Allyson think Shelley would lie about something like that, even if she did profess to detest her mother, but she couldn't help wondering if Shelley hadn't welcomed an excuse to avoid hearing about the trip to Ravello. For her part Allyson could only feel relieved that she wouldn't have to be constantly aware of Shelley's sensibilities for a while, though she resolved to call her later to find out how her mother was, and put forward her proposal that Shelley and several others from the team join the party in Italy.

After checking her email, she went back out to the main office to sit with Zac and Justine. They would need to be in each other's pockets during the build-up to this show, and there was a good chance they'd have to rope in a couple more researchers to help them out. She made a mental note to bring that up with Shelley, then after getting Marvin to sort out the processing of her films, she laid out the originals of the copious notes she'd made in Italy which she'd faxed back to the office for Zac and Justie to get on with. They were certainly moving along, but there was still an endless number of details and suggestions that needed to be discussed and before long half the office had managed to join in the planning. It quickly deteriorated into a ludicrous free-for-all, providing a convenient platform for the wits among them, and a great opportunity for those who wanted to toss in holiday memoirs or dream adventures. The party in Ravello was going to be an impossible act to follow, was almost everyone's opinion, until Zac came up with a brilliant idea that made everyone roar with laughter. It was at that point that Tessa walked into the office to find Allyson in the midst of a hilarious group, and looking so flushed with pleasure that it was impossible to think that her trip to Italy had been anything other than a resounding success.

Turning, Allyson saw Tessa and said, 'Ah, just the person. We're talking about doing a programme from Transylvania at the end of April. There's a convention of vampires.'

Tessa's face froze. Were they calling her a vampire?

'What happened to the piece you did on those dolls?' Allyson said. 'The ones who belonged to a North London writer? It could be perfect for this programme. Did you ever edit it?'

'No,' Tessa said.

'Well, there's plenty of time. Just make it good and scary.'

Allyson turned back to the others, and Tessa walked over to her desk. She still felt shaken, even though she knew she'd misunderstood. It was reminding her of when she was at school, and all the times she'd thought she was being laughed at then, even when she wasn't. But all that was in the past now, it had nothing to do with what was happening here, today, so there was no reason to get upset, or angry with Allyson, especially not when it sounded like the trip to Italy was going to be a lot of fun, and when she, as the presenter, would naturally be at the centre of it all.

Three manically busy days had passed since their return from Ravello and Allyson was close to screaming. She'd barely had a minute to herself, and every time she snatched one out of the chaos and picked up the phone to call Mark, he was either in a meeting, on another line or en route to some other venue in the city. She'd got him once, on his mobile, but the reception had been so bad they'd had to ring off. He'd said he would call her later, at home, but she hadn't got in until late and there was no message waiting.

Being in almost constant touch with the company publicists who were handling the hotel's opening extravaganza made her wonder if they were talking to Mark, for their guest list was starting to boast some pretty impressive American names that he could very well be adding. On the other hand, it could be Claudia who was drumming up all the celebrities, since she was the one who ran the cable station and had access to everyone who was anyone in the US showbiz community.

As far as the UK went, since promos for the programme had started to air, she'd been inundated with requests, even bribes, for invitations to the party, so the only problem they were facing on that front was making the decisions on who should or shouldn't be selected. It was huge fun shuffling some of the over-blown egos up and down the guest list and sometimes zapping them altogether, at least for Zac and Justine it was, for Allyson it was turning into nothing short of a nightmare. She was going to have to stop answering her

354

own phone, for it seemed everyone she'd ever known wanted to speak to her now, or see her, or take her to dinner, or invite her to a party of their own.

'No! No! No!' she cried, clasping her hands over her ears as Zac and Justine teased her with yet another chorus of unrefusable offers. 'And if you think it's so funny . . .'

'Allyson! There's a call over here for you,' Hayley shouted out. 'Do you want me to take a message?'

'No, give it to Zac,' she answered, and ran into her own office to grab the phone that was ringing there. 'Allyson Jaymes,' she said into the receiver, then spun round to hold up a hand to whoever was calling her name. 'Sorry, who is it?' she said, blocking her other ear.

'It's Bob, your husband,' he answered.

Allyson's eyes closed as the world outside her office seemed suddenly to recede and the guilt flowed in. Of all the calls she didn't want to take right now . . . 'Bob,' she said. 'You know you're supposed to . . .'

'. . . speak through your lawyer. I know, and I'm trying, but you're not being very responsive.'

'Because I'm really busy at the moment. Listen, I'm sorry. I will get back to you . . .'

'Allyson! For Christ's sake! Is your lawyer giving you my messages? Is she telling you what I want to talk to you about?'

'Yes, Bob, she's telling me, but I just don't have time right now.'

'I don't believe this!' he cried. 'What can be more important . . .?'

'Bob! I have to go. I'm sorry, but I can't discuss anything until after this next programme's out of the way.'

'Surely you can spare a few minutes . . .'

'No! It wouldn't do any good.' Then, realizing how much this must be hurting him, she said, 'It's our marriage we're going to be talking about, it deserves more than a few minutes, surely.'

He said nothing, and a few seconds later she heard the line go dead.

'Allyson!' Justine yelled. 'Giovanni from the hotel's on the line, he has to talk to you. Now!'

Allyson went to take the call and almost collided with Shelley, who was about to come into her office.

'Hi!' Allyson cried. 'I thought you weren't back until tomorrow.'

Shelley's smile was ironic. 'I told you that yesterday,' she said. 'Go take the call and if you can spare me . . .'

'Allyson,' Zac said, 'we've got a problem with Burt Barry making the charter flight. Can we put him on a scheduled flight later in the day?'

'Who's Burt Barry?' she said, taking the phone Justine was holding out.

'A member of Test E-Rone, the band for Happy Hour.'

'Who?' Allyson cried.

'I don't know, something to do with male hormones. Anyway, can we put him on a . . .'

'Yes, if he's one of the interviewees. No to the guests. They either make the charter or they don't make the party. Hello,' she said to Giovanni.

She spent the next few minutes jotting down Giovanni's latest list of instructions and complaints, then zoomed off to find the production manager who was supposed to be organizing the crew, but was outside the scene dock sneaking a quick cigarette.

The rest of the day continued at the same frenetic pace until, at seven thirty, Shelley walked into Allyson's office and said, 'I'm going home now. I'll expect you in an hour for martinis, margaritas or whatever takes your fancy. I'm not in the mood to cook so we can send out.'

'Oh God, Shell, I'd love . . .'

'No arguments,' Shelley cut in. 'You're going to burn yourself out if you don't take a break, so I'll see you in an hour,' and she was gone.

Relieved at being bossed into leaving, Allyson spent

the next few minutes reading through the script she'd sketched out for the film insert, then turned off her computer. There were still a couple of researchers at their desks outside, but the place was emptying fast, and the monitors that usually relayed images from the studio, or off-air news, were all silent.

After checking her watch she picked up the phone and dialled Mark's office number in New York. This was starting to get embarrassing, always being told he was in a meeting or on another call or somewhere else in the city on business. It was as though he was avoiding her, and it wasn't simple paranoia that was making her think that, it was a suspicion that he was giving her some space to decide what she wanted to do about Bob. If she was right, then she wished he'd tell her so she'd know for sure what was happening, instead of sitting here having to guess, and trying to stave off the horrible insecurity that was just waiting to put down roots.

The call connected and as the phone at the other end started to ring she began toying with what she would say if she had to leave a message. In fact she rarely did, though the secretary at the other end must surely recognize her voice by now.

'I'm sorry,' the secretary said, 'he left a few minutes ago for a meeting downtown. Can I take a message?'

'Um . . .'

'Is that Carolyn?'

Allyson froze. 'Uh, no,' she said. 'No, it's . . . It doesn't matter. I'll call again,' and she quickly rang off.

Of course it didn't necessarily mean anything. It was only her fragile confidence and hyperactive paranoia making her think the worst, because Carolyn could be anyone. She didn't have to be the mystery woman he'd taken to France, or anyone else he was either attracted to or involved with. She could be a business acquaintance, an accountant, a lawyer, someone from the bank, or the insurance brokers, the dentist, anywhere . . . So she wasn't going to get worked up about this. She was simply going to pack up her things and drive straight over to Shelley's for an extremely large martini and hopefully some respite from the craziness that seemed to have her under siege right now with no sign of a let-up.

For the fourth time that day Bob picked up the phone and dialled the number of his and Allyson's flat. If she answered, he'd try again to speak to her, and if he got the machine he'd key in the code to replay her messages, the way he'd been doing all week.

He got the machine.

As he listened to the several different voices the tape had recorded, he could feel himself tensing with the dread that Mark Reiner's voice would be amongst them again, wondering where Allyson was, and why she wasn't calling him back. He'd tried her at the office a couple of times, he'd said, but each time she'd been busy on another call and he hadn't left a message.

There was nothing Bob could do about the calls Reiner made to the office, but those he was making to the flat Bob could erase, thanks to this digital wizardry, before Allyson got to hear them. He rang in regularly, and so far he'd wiped out seven different messages. The first ones he'd listened to, so he knew now how far the relationship had gone. He didn't need to torment himself by listening to any more, so the very second he heard the man's voice he hit the buttons that would eliminate the message from existence.

Futile though the gestures might finally prove to be, he had to do something to try and stop the relationship going any further, and this was all he could think of while Allyson was refusing to see him.

Shelley's flat was a wonderfully warm refuge from the cold night outside, with a small flickering fire in the hearth, a lazy jazz tune playing on the CD and martinis already in the shaker.

'Help yourself to a drink,' Shelley shouted from the bathroom, when Allyson called out to let her know she'd arrived. 'I'll be right there.'

Slipping Shelley's key back into her purse, Allyson took off her coat and went over to the bar to fill one of the elegant glasses Shelley used for martinis. The first sip produced such convincing signs of freeing the tension in her head that she took another right away and reached for one of the delicious, wrinkled black olives Shelley must have picked up at Luigi's on the way home.

It wasn't until she put her drink on the coffee table and flopped down on the sofa that she noticed the bronze figurine she'd given Shelley at Christmas, exquisitely displayed in a discreet glass case, with a small, hidden light flooding the smoothly sculpted surfaces of the dancer's fans. As she looked at it Allyson felt deeply moved, for it reminded her of how close she and Shelley actually were, that she would buy something like that, and Shelley would display it so. It was a timely reminder, for she'd been in danger lately of forgetting how much their friendship mattered.

Coming into the room and seeing her looking Shelley said, 'It displays well there, don't you think?'

Allyson nodded, then looked up at her in the cosy half light.

Shelley turned away. 'So, tell me all about Ravello,' she said in a tone that Allyson couldn't quite determine. 'And I don't mean the recce.'

Allyson reached for her drink and took another sip. 'Ravello was great,' she said. 'We had a really good time.'

'How lovely,' Shelley remarked. 'So are you in love?'

Allyson bit back the response the sarcasm deserved, and reminded herself that this was a lot harder for

Shelley than it was for her. So all she said was, 'I wouldn't go that far.'

'So how far did you go?' Shelley enquired.

'We slept together, yes,' Allyson responded. Then, attempting to soften the blow she added, 'But he went off to New York the day after we got back and I haven't heard from him since.'

Shelley frowned. 'So he's dumped you too?'

'I'm not sure, he might have.' In fact, it wasn't what Allyson thought at all, at least she hadn't until now. But it had happened to Shelley, so why not to her?

Shelley went to pour herself a martini. 'Did you ever find out who the woman was he took to Valerie and Jean-Marc's?' she asked, her back still turned.

Allyson's heart tripped. 'No. Why?' she said. 'Did you?'

'No, I haven't spoken to them. I was just wondering if that's what you were thinking.'

'You read me too well,' Allyson said, rolling her eyes. 'Yes, I do keep thinking about her, though to be honest . . . Well, I really didn't think she was an issue . . . I still don't, but I called his office in New York earlier and his secretary asked me if I was Carolyn.'

Shelley walked over to the facing sofa and sat down. 'Who's Carolyn?' she said.

'Precisely.'

After a moment Shelley asked, 'Are you sure she said Carolyn, not Corinne?'

Allyson thought. 'I don't know. I suppose it could have been Corinne.' She laughed. 'I'd like to think it was Corinne. Anyway, we don't really want to talk about this. Tell me, have you decided if you're coming to Italy for the party?'

Shelley flicked back her hair and reached for an olive. 'I'm not sure,' she responded. 'I might not have the time.'

'I wish you would,' Allyson said, embarking on the persuasion she knew Shelley wanted.

'I'll think about it,' Shelley promised.

Allyson's eyes took on a mischievous glow. 'Just think about all those gorgeous American movie stars and obscure European royalty. Not to mention the smouldering Italian waiters.'

Shelley's eyebrows flickered, a small, disdainful attempt to join in the spirit of it.

'We're going to need someone from *Tatler* or *Harpers* to help identify the European royalty,' Allyson said. 'I put a call in to Terri Jankler, she should be up for it.' She reached for her drink, took another large sip then steered the conversation out of the danger zone by saying, 'Bob's trying to get in touch. I think he wants to come back.'

Shelley's eyes widened. 'Well, there's a turn-up,' she commented. 'Though I can't say I'm really surprised now that Tessa's no longer on the scene.'

Allyson didn't say anything.

'Is it good news?' Shelley ventured.

'I don't know.'

'If you're asking my advice,' Shelley said, 'I'd say stick with Mark.'

Allyson couldn't hide her surprise. 'You would?'

'Well, how many more times do you want Bob to cheat on you?'

'But Mark could be doing it now.'

Shelley looked irritated. 'You don't really think that,' she retorted, 'so let's stop the charade, shall we?'

Allyson was angry, but not wanting to get into a row, which could easily happen the way things were going, all she said was, 'We were talking about Bob.'

Shelley went to get the shaker and topped up their glasses. 'How do you feel about him now?' she asked in a friendlier voice.

Allyson sighed. 'I don't know. I mean I care about him still, obviously, and God only knows if I'll ever be able to stop thinking of him as my husband . . . I suppose I did

361

in Italy though, but in the end what happened there might just turn out to be a much needed boost for an ego-crushed woman on the rebound.' She looked at Shelley. 'Do you think I should give him another chance? Bob, I mean.'

Shelley helped herself to an olive. 'I don't suppose there's any harm in talking to him,' she said. 'At least you'll find out what he has to say.'

'That's the problem, I already know what he wants to say, but I've resolved not to decide anything until after we've been to Italy – as though Italy's going to come up with the answers I need.'

'You never know,' Shelley responded, 'it might.'

Later, after Allyson had gone, Shelley undressed, put away her clothes and wrapped herself in a white silk robe. Then she sat in front of the mirror, staring at her reflection, and saw the face of a woman who was suppressing so much rage it was a miracle it didn't show. But she couldn't let it show, could she? Not to Allyson, not to anyone. But particularly not to Allyson, because if there was a breakdown in their friendship, or even the slightest fracture, there was every chance that the results would be so disastrous for Shelley that they hardly bore thinking about. Neither could she endure considering the unconscionable spite of fate, or was it God, that had brought Mark Reiner into her life, showing her everything she'd ever wanted, allowing her to believe that the waiting was over, and that dreams were truly worth having, only then to snatch him away and thrust him into the arms of her emotionally bruised and battered best friend. A friend whose injuries seemed to matter so much to God that he was salving them not only with a new love – *a love that should have been Shelley's* – but with the return of the old love too. So now Allyson could choose, and while she was making up her mind it seemed that God was going to fly her higher and higher in her new career, on a programme and in a role that had always been Shelley's. And there was nothing Shelley could do, because all the power and glory were Allyson's, given to her by Mark Reiner and a protective karma that would sever Shelley brutally from the programme were she to allow her feelings to show.

So she must control them, rein them in and then let them loose on God, or Life, or the Universe, or whatever the hell else it wanted to call itself. Oh, certainly it would be nice if she could continue dumping it all on Allyson, the way she had, in her mind, these past few weeks, but that would be playing straight into God's hands, wouldn't it, giving him good reason to rob her of a best friend, a career, everything she had left that meant anything at all, the way he had just robbed her of a lifetime partner. How it must have amused him to shove Mark Reiner in her face. Nice joke that, great entertainment. Let's torment Shelley for a while before we use her dream to put Allyson back together. Shelley could handle it, because Shelley was used to losing out. She could withstand the heartache and pain, the loneliness and humiliation. After all, she'd had years of practice, since the sparkle of love and shining light of happiness had died with her father, when Shelley was twelve and God had first decided to show her the darkness. That, emotionally, was where he had left her, for there had never been anyone who could replace her father, no-one who could light up her world that way, and God had never even seemed to consider there might be a need. Instead he had given her beauty and success, material joys and the kind of freedom that hurt. In fact, everything that was good in her life was like one huge showy bandage attempting to cover the fatal wounds of neglect. But who the hell cared? What impact did her misery have on a God who wasn't even listening? And why should he listen, why should anyone, when Venus had bestowed all her bounteous gifts on the woman who was crying out for help?

But the crying was going to stop now. So was the pain, so was the longing. And all those trusty little lieutenants of his, like hope, belief, faith, trust, they were wasting their time trying to work their magic on her. She was turning her back on all of it now and letting God know that none of it, *none of it*, mattered any more. Allyson could have Mark Reiner, she could have Bob Jaymes too, and let her be happy with the great abundance of choice God had given her, and while she was at it she could be happy for Shelley's friendship too.

Allyson was laughing and shrieking as the ice-cold champagne trickled down over her body into the madly whirling jets of the jacuzzi bath she was standing in. Mark was beside the bath, a half empty bottle in one hand, a full glass in the other, as he lowered his mouth to her breasts and licked off the champagne. Then, seeing how aroused she was becoming, he took a mouthful of champagne and letting it go over her lips he began sucking and kissing them, as he poured more over her breasts and stomach. His tongue was soon to follow and when he finally reached her most sensitive part she opened her legs to allow him in closer and deeper.

Then his mouth was back on hers and he was holding her hard against him, the coarse hair on his chest rubbing her skin, and the hard muscles of his thighs taking her weight as she raised first one leg, then the other, to wrap them around him and take him inside her.

After a while he stopped kissing her and when she opened her eyes to look into his she saw he was laughing. She laughed too, for she knew that there wasn't much they could do with this position, except feel proud they'd achieved it.

'I could give you a tour of the apartment,' he said.

'Like this?'

'Like this. You've only seen the kitchen and bedroom, and if I carried you through the rest of the place I could say I made love to you in all eight rooms in less than an hour. Or . . .'

She laughed. 'Or?'

He stepped into the jacuzzi. 'We could get right back in here and let those jets drive you wild while I'm right up inside you.'

Her breath caught on his words, for hearing him talk that way only increased her desire.

He kissed her again, then setting her back down in the huge, octagonal bath he settled himself onto one of the padded bench seats and drew her down onto his erection. Then opening her legs even wider, he increased the speed of the jets until moaning with ecstasy her head fell back against his shoulder and she turned her face into his neck.

The sensations were so intense, cutting through her with such harsh, insistent power that an orgasm was devouring her almost before he could move.

'Oh God, yes, yes,' she cried, as his fingers replaced the jet, and his mouth sought hers. Then he was lifting her up, carrying her into the bedroom and lying her down on the bed. As he came into her again she could feel the immense hardness of him filling her and filling her, then pulling back gently before sharply filling her again. Then the pace of his thrusting began building and building, until he was ramming himself into her and crying out her name as the explosion of his climax erupted into the renewed torrents of hers.

Minutes later, as they were still breathless and clinging together, he kissed her on the mouth then rolled onto his side so he was no longer crushing her. Morning sunlight streamed through the open curtains, early-morning traffic honked and roared its way along Eaton Terrace.

'I could get used to this kind of homecoming,' he told her.

Laughing she kissed him again, then went into the bathroom to fetch what was left of the champagne. 'Are you going to fall asleep on me?' she asked, when she came back and saw that his eyes were closed.

Lifting an arm he looked at his watch. 'It's four in the morning, New York time,' he reminded her.

'And nine o'clock here, so I have to leave for work pretty soon.'

He watched her as she sat naked and cross-legged on the bed and refilled the glass with champagne. 'Did you see your husband while I was away?' he asked.

She shook her head. 'No. I've decided to do it when we get back from Italy.'

'We leave tomorrow,' he said.

'You think I don't know that?' she laughed. Then, unable to resist touching him, she scratched her fingers gently over his thighs.

'Did you consider that he might have called in to erase the messages I left you?' he said.

Her eyes came up to his face. 'Yes,' she answered, and though she felt glad to have a reason for why she hadn't heard from Mark, she couldn't help feeling sorry for Bob that he had felt compelled to do something like that.

'Have you reached any decisions?' Mark asked.

She looked away, staring at the luggage he had brought in from the airport. He'd called her as soon as he'd landed, demanding to know how, in this day and age, they'd managed to miss each other's calls for almost two weeks. She'd been so thrilled to hear him that it had been her suggestion to meet this morning, and now here she was, sitting on the end of his huge, masculine bed, not wanting to be anywhere else in the world, yet still managing to feel worried about Bob.

'Only that I'm not ready to make any yet,' she answered.

'Then don't,' he said gently. 'And certainly don't make any for me.'

Not entirely sure how to take that, or even how she felt about it, she resumed the stroking of his legs, and wished she had better control over her feelings so that she could have at least some idea of what she should do.

'I've organized for us to have separate rooms when we get to Ravello,' he said.

She nodded, knowing that if he hadn't done it then she would have, for the press were going to be present in droves and neither of them wanted the party to be about them, when it was actually about the programme and hotel.

'How are things with Shelley?' he asked.

'OK.' She shrugged. 'I think she's accepted us, but she really did . . .' She stopped as she realized she was about to tell him something Shelley would never want him to know, which was how deeply Shelley had believed he was the right man for her. She looked down at his face, and understood the depth of Shelley's disappointment, for she knew how she would feel were he to leave her now. Then she allowed her eyes to travel down over the rest of his body to where her fingers were making him hard.

'I hope you're intending to do something about that,' he said darkly.

Allyson smiled, then tipping the contents of her champagne glass all over his erection, she lifted it from his stomach and set about licking it all off again.

Much later, after they'd showered and dressed for the office, he went to check on the messages that had come in since he'd arrived back. The earlier calls he'd picked up on his way in from the airport, but the phone had rung a couple of times in the past two hours and he needed to satisfy himself there were no emergencies.

There weren't, but Allyson was standing right beside him as the machine replayed Tessa's jubilant voice welcoming him back from the States and telling him how much she was looking forward to seeing him in Italy.

Chapter 16

The majority of the sixty specially selected guests began arriving in Ravello at midday. Most came on the chartered plane that flew into Naples from London, while others, like the charismatic Italian tenor and his wife, and the celebrated French comedienne and her gay brother, motored down under their own steam, which in the Italians' case turned out to be a Lamborghini Diablo, and for the French it was a classic 1940s Lagonda complete with dicky seat and air horn. The chosen Americans, who included a Pulitzer Prize-winning author, four internationally renowned movie stars, a teenage rock legend, and several US-dwelling members of the European aristocracy, would be flying straight into Rome later that day, to be met by a small fleet of limousines that would ferry them down to the hotel.

The weather couldn't have been better, as the sun blazed down on the steep, winding roads that led up to the picturesque mountain-top village, and the wild spring flowers that were shooting up all over were as uplifting as the heady promise offered by the terraces of blossoming vines. Allyson couldn't help being thrilled by all the delight and enchantment as she and Shelley welcomed the guests to the magnificent Palazzo. But though Shelley gushed along with them at the very Italian quaintness of their surroundings, she was much lower-key, sometimes almost to the point of rudeness.

Giovanni was with them, in the small church piazza, standing in for Mark who wasn't expected until the following day, so between them he and Allyson managed to upstage Shelley's disdain in a way that was almost making Shelley worse.

Tessa was in the hotel lobby with Zac and Justine, feeling totally blown away by so much style and grandeur – and all the incredibly famous faces that were flowing in through the giant carved-oak doors. Amazing, really, that it should still surprise her how much smaller everyone was in the flesh, and rather ordinary without all the glitter and lights. But they'd have all that tomorrow night, in quantities that would no doubt outdazzle a Renaissance carnival in Venice. Today, though, the guests felt much easier to get to know, and were all charm and gush as the company publicists escorted them from Allyson's and Shelley's initial greeting, along the cobbled lane and into the hotel where Tessa and the two researchers were standing with Alan, the programme's director. From there each guest was assigned their own personal hostess, who offered a welcome glass of champagne, or tea for those who preferred, and a short friendly chat about the hotel and its facilities as they walked their distinguished charges to their rooms.

'My feet are killing me and my jaw's starting to ache,' Alan complained, smiling through his teeth as Shelley and Allyson finally wandered in to join them.

Laughing, Allyson said, 'You can stand down for a while, the next lot aren't due to arrive until six. Are you OK?' she said to Tessa who was starting to yawn.

'Sorry, yes,' Tessa answered.

'What time did you leave the bar last night?' Shelley asked.

'If I'm going to be honest then it was about two thirty,' Tessa confessed. 'But I wasn't the last to go up. Some of the crew were still there, so were . . .'

'But they don't have to appear on camera today,' Allyson reminded her. Then turning to Alan she said, 'What time are you setting off for Pompeii?'

'About four,' he answered. 'We should be back around nine. Ten at the latest.'

'Then make sure Tessa goes straight to bed when you get back, she's got a busy day ahead of her tomorrow.'

Tessa was grinning. 'You sound like my mum,' she said.

Allyson's answering look was so withering that Shelley actually laughed. 'Nothing ever seems to faze her, does it?' Allyson grumbled, as they strolled across the lobby and down the white marble steps into the piano bar.

'Which is something you should feel glad about when you've got her hosting a programme featuring this many VIPs,' Shelley reminded her. 'How many of the sixty do you reckon you actually know?' she asked, as they sat down at the table where they'd left all their producers' paraphernalia.

Allyson thought. 'About half,' she answered.

Shelley nodded. 'That's what I guessed. Dinner should be interesting tonight, when we choose who we're going to sit with. I mean who rates higher, the exiled crown prince of a lesser-known republic, or the reigning queen of the movie screen? Of course, they'll all be wanting to sit with *you* . . .'

'Let's ask Terri Jankler,' Allyson cut in. 'Being one of the more elite and informed diarists she'll be right up with all that. Which reminds me, she should start coaching Tessa on how to address some of these people . . . Oh smile, we're on Candy's camera.'

'Great!' Candy Egan, a freelance showbiz photographer declared, still clicking away. 'Now get back to work, I want some shots of the heads together, like you were in the planning stages of this shindig. God knows who'll want them, but someone might.'

'Did you get all the guests as they arrived?' Allyson wanted to know.

'Every one of 'em. It's going to be quite some show. Where's the man, by the way?'

'If you mean Mark Reiner,' Allyson answered, 'he'll be arriving tomorrow.'

'So is it true you two were here together a couple of weeks ago?' a reporter from the *Express* asked, as he came to join them.

Shelley shifted in her seat and let out a sigh of irritation.

'I was here on a recce,' Allyson said, smiling sweetly, 'and Mark Reiner happened to be here too, sorting out last-minute details before the opening.'

'So the answer's yes,' the reporter declared, 'and straight from the horse's mouth.'

'Charming,' Allyson muttered, sensing the way Shelley's bristling was getting worse. 'Now push off and interview some of the guests who're outside on the terrace, we've got work to do here.'

As Candy and the reporter disappeared out through the French doors, Shelley signalled for a passing waiter to bring them some tea. 'And a couple of those fantastically decadent cakes you served up when we arrived yesterday,' she added. 'I'm starving. How about you? Are you going to have some?'

'Yes, why not?' Allyson replied. 'But only one, or I'll never fit into my dress tomorrow night.'

'Which reminds me,' Shelley said, as the waiter left, 'I want you to help me make up my mind what to wear. I'll bring what I've got to your room later.' Almost before she'd finished her attention seemed to have wandered, for she was staring up at the lobby, absently watching one of the receptionists open a parcel. 'I think we should take a walk around the village later,' she said. 'But only if you can spare the time, of course.'

Allyson returned to her paperwork. She wasn't going

to rise to Shelley's barbs, any more than she was going to hold her breath for Shelley to make any comment on the hotel, for she obviously wasn't going to, other than to say she was pleased to see that the piano bar was big enough to hold the party without causing too much of a problem for the cameras. Since it was impossible to be anything other than enchanted by the Palazzo, Allyson accepted that perhaps it was too much to expect Shelley to voice her impressions when everything here belonged to Mark, and even if Shelley really had let go of that dream, seeing all this had to be a difficult reminder of some of what that dream had entailed.

However, despite the allowances she was making for Shelley's sensibilities there was no getting away from the fact that Shelley's attitude was becoming increasingly annoying. It seemed just about anything was deserving of sarcasm or unfavourable comparison, and she was so snappy with the crew, impatient with the publicists, and stroppy with the hotel staff that Allyson was already dreading the moment when she'd have to step in. So, in an effort to keep Shelley on a more even keel, and make her feel as though she really did have a role to play here, Allyson was currently seeking her advice when she didn't actually need it.

It was an exhausting business pussyfooting around her this way, which was why Allyson was relieved when the publicists came to rescue her from a discussion that was starting to get tense, and whisk her off to talk to the new chef and his team who were on the brink of rioting over a suggestion that an outside company was being called in to help with the party. That was easily dealt with, as the chef was only rattled because it wasn't his brother's company that was being proposed for the back-up, but it was by the time Allyson left the kitchens.

After further conferences with the publicists, and with Giovanni and his staff, Allyson went to see Tessa and the crew off to Pompeii, then before anyone else could waylay her she darted up to her room to get out of the formal suit and tight shoes she'd been in all day, before she called Mark. He'd fully intended to be here for the build-up to the party, but other business was keeping him in London with no guarantee yet of when he might get away. However, he was viewing this hold-up as a chance for Giovanni to establish himself as the hotel's general manager, as well as a welcome excuse to delay the press's intrusion into his private affairs, which was something Allyson handled with much greater skill than he did.

'No, I don't have a problem with people knowing about us,' he responded, when she got him on the line and teased him about it. 'But you've still got some pretty big decisions to be making, and . . .'

'All right, all right,' she cut in, 'point taken. But I really feel like doing some wildly outrageous things to your body right now, and you're not here to indulge me.'

'With an offer like that I could be on the next flight,' he told her.

Laughing, she said, 'Then you'd be just in time to greet Tim Collins and Natasha Koppell who're flying in from LA tonight, on their own private jet no less. Do you know this golden couple, by the way?'

'Sure, I was at college with Tim, and Natasha happens to be an old girlfriend of Nick's from back before he was married.'

'So did they meet through you two?'

'Yep. As a matter of fact they met at my house in Bel Air, when I still had a house in Bel Air.'

'I just don't know who I'm dealing with in you, do I?' she remarked dryly. Then, changing the subject, 'Have you arranged for one of the limos to pick you up tomorrow? I'm presuming you will be here tomorrow . . .'

'It's all in hand,' he told her. 'Now tell me what you've decided to feature for the travelogue piece.'

As she talked him through the latest plan for the coverage of surrounding beauty spots and places of interest, she wandered over to the window to watch the guests who were meandering through the gardens, or relaxing on the terrace that offered such spectacular views of the glittering sea below. It didn't seem quite real, watching so many easily recognizable rockers and aristocrats getting a kick out of meeting each other, and entertaining each other to celebratory cocktails which were currently being served by a Russian princess and her cute little gigolo boyfriend. This particular princess, who had to be at least sixty, if not seventy, was someone Allyson knew well, and liked enormously, for she was always so lively and mischievous, and so hilariously outspoken on the elixir of young lovers that it was impossible not to fall under her spell after a mere five minutes of knowing her. However, she'd managed to upset Shelley earlier, when she'd offered to lend her her main squeeze of the moment if it would help Shelley to relax.

'Why? Does Shelley seem uptight?' Mark laughed when Allyson recounted the story.

'She's trying to cover it,' Allyson answered, 'but I think she's finding it a bit difficult, being here, you know, having to face all that she might have had, if . . . things had . . . turned out differently.' She'd allowed her tongue to run away with her, and already she regretted the crossover into disloyalty. Shelley might be a pain in the neck at the moment, but she deserved better, and Allyson didn't imagine it was making Mark feel particularly good either, having the disappointment he'd inflicted pointed out.

'It really never got that far with me and Shelley,' he reminded her gently.

'No, of course not,' she said, knowing that in Shelley's mind it definitely had. 'I just think she's having a difficult time all round at the moment, but I'm sure it'll pass.'

'I'm sure you're right,' he responded. 'Now tell me, did Tessa do all the history homework you gave her?'

'Don't remind me,' Allyson shuddered. 'I tested her this morning, and got referred to as her favourite teacher, then this afternoon she had the audacity to tell me I sounded like her mother. You know, the way she behaves towards me, you'd never believe she ran off with my husband. There doesn't seem to be any guilt, or regret, or apology, not even any smugness. As far as she's concerned it's like it never happened and we can be all chummy chummy again. Did you return that message she left you, by the way?'

'No. She didn't ask me to, so I just forgot about it.'

Allyson turned round as someone knocked on the door. 'I think I'll have to go,' she said, tightening the belt of her robe as she got up to answer it. 'I'll call you later, OK?'

'I'll call you,' he said. 'I'm going to be on the move, so it'll be easier.'

Ringing off, Allyson pulled open the door to find Shelley standing there in a dark brown trouser suit that had no collar to the jacket and was buttoned right up to her neck. It was smart, but definitely lacked the kind of style Shelley was known for. 'Hi, are you OK?' Allyson asked, stepping aside for her to come in.

Shelley's eyebrows arched. 'Of course,' she said. 'I've come to show you what I'm wearing to the party tomorrow night. What do you think?' She gave a twirl, then laid the cellophane-wrapped dress she was carrying across the back of a chair.

Allyson couldn't hide her astonishment. It was totally wrong for a party, and Shelley knew it, so what was going on?

'Do you think trousers are OK?' Shelley was saying. 'I've brought a dress as well, but I'm not exactly one of the celebrities, and I thought maybe this kind of thing worked better for a producer.'

'Shelley, anything works on you,' Allyson reminded her. 'And forget about being a producer, tomorrow night you'll be a guest, so you can be as glamorous, or outrageous as you like.'

Shelley smiled as she started to unbutton the jacket. 'I'll put the dress on so you can see that too.'

Going to sit on the end of the bed, Allyson couldn't help but admire Shelley's exquisite, olive-skinned body, as she slipped out of the trouser suit and laid it carefully across the back of another chair. The fact that Shelley was now naked, apart from her shoes, didn't surprise Allyson, for Shelley rarely wore underwear, but it did occur to her to wonder if there wasn't some other, underlying reason for showing off her body this way – for example, to remind Allyson just how sensuous she was.

'Fancy a glass of wine?' Allyson offered, getting up to go to the minibar.

'Sure,' Shelley answered. She finished arranging the trouser suit, then turned to unwrap the dress. It was knee-length, beige, with a brown leather belt, a mock turtleneck and long batwing sleeves. 'How about this?' she said, fluffing out her hair after pulling it over her head.

Allyson looked up from where she was uncorking the wine and almost dropped the bottle. Never in all the years she had known Shelley had she seen her in anything that even approached frumpiness, but this dress was so well on the way that Allyson couldn't think of a single thing to say without being rude. 'Shell, I don't understand,' she finally managed. 'Why would you want to wear something like that when you've got such lovely slinky dresses that show off your gorgeous figure and . . .'

'I don't feel like wearing anything like that,' Shelley interrupted. 'Besides, you wouldn't want me upstaging you, would you?' Her smile was so dazzling that it was impossible to tell if she was teasing or not.

'Anyway,' Shelley went on, 'I don't want anyone looking at me and thinking I look sexy or available, because as I'm clearly completely incapable of holding onto a man, I don't even want to tempt anyone to . . .'

'Shelley, stop this!' Allyson snapped. 'You're an exceptionally beautiful woman, and not even these ridiculous clothes can hide that.'

Shelley turned to the mirror. 'You're right,' she said decisively, looking herself up and down. 'But as I have no intention of stealing your thunder tomorrow night, I thought if I wore something like this . . .'

Allyson's head was starting to spin. It was becoming increasingly difficult to avoid the fight, but she was still intent on trying. 'Shelley, listen,' she said. 'I'm really sorry you're feeling . . . well, so upset at the moment . . .'

'Upset?' Shelley laughed. 'What makes you think I'm upset?'

Allyson took a breath. 'Why don't we drop this?' she said. 'You wear what you want to wear and I'll keep my opinions to myself.'

Shelley shrugged, and said no more as Allyson poured two large glasses of crisp, clear Frascati and passed one to her.

'So,' Shelley said, sipping her drink. 'Are you going to let me take a peek at what you'll be wearing? Oh, I forgot, you showed me this morning. The black dress with the panels?'

Allyson nodded, and refused to mind that Shelley had just made her dress sound so unspeakably plain.

'You'll look good,' Shelley assured her. 'Now, if you've got a guest list handy we should sort out who's going to sit with whom for dinner tonight.'

'Good idea,' Allyson responded, going to rummage in her files for a list that didn't already have notes scribbled all over it. 'Oh God, who's that now?' she groaned as someone knocked on the door.

'Hi, can I come in?' Candy, the photographer, said.

'Well, uh,' Allyson said, glancing back over her shoulder at Shelley.

378

'Hi, Candy. Sure, come in,' Shelley called. 'You're not interrupting anything. Except I'm about to take this dress off before I spill something on it. You don't mind do you?' And before Candy could answer she pulled the dress over her head and began arranging it back on the hanger.

Allyson looked at Candy, who looked at Allyson.

'It's OK,' Candy said, shrugging it off. 'Don't mind me. I just came to ask if I could get a shot of the sea view from your balcony. I've got a mountain view myself.'

'Of course,' Allyson said. Then, to Shelley, 'There's a spare robe in the bathroom. I'll get it for you.'

While she was gone the telephone rang, so she picked up the receiver next to the bidet and had a quick conversation with one of the publicists, which took only a couple of minutes, but when she returned to the bedroom she could hardly believe her eyes. Candy was still out on the balcony, but her back was to the view and her camera was trained across the room on Shelley, who was still wearing no clothes.

'For God's sake, Shelley, what are you doing?' Allyson cried, as Candy started to click. 'Candy stop!' she commanded, going to stand between them.

Shelley was laughing. 'Oh God, Ally, it's so easy to get you going,' she said. 'You don't honestly think that was for real, do you?'

Allyson wasn't sure, though it certainly didn't feel like much of a joke to her, so she threw the robe at Shelley and told her to put it on.

'You're angry,' Shelley said, covering herself up.

'I'm not angry,' Allyson responded. 'I'm just . . .' The last thing she wanted was to get into a scene with someone from the press around, so she said, 'I'm probably just a bit uptight about the party tomorrow.'

Shelley gave Candy a look that made Allyson angrier than ever.

'I'll tell you what,' Allyson said tightly, 'I think I'll go and take a bath, and maybe we should let the publicists work out the seating plan for dinner.'

As it turned out, the publicists' careful structuring of the evening soon dissolved into a wonderfully convivial flow that saw the crème de la crème of international society moving with effortless charm and politeness from one table to another, exchanging anecdotes and memories, and drinking champagne cocktails that were travelling freely about the room on shiny silver salvers. Though no-one had bothered with formal attire, and the Americans who had recently arrived were looking a little crumpled and jet-lagged, it was easy for Allyson to get an early view of just how spectacular the party would be in this magnificent airy hall with all its white arches, cherubic fountains, marble floors and exotic greenery. And once all the glitter and dash of fame, high acclaim, noble birth, and sheer magnetism was added, along with the exquisite designer gowns, beautifully tailored tuxedos and lavishly expensive jewels, it could hardly fail to be anything but the party to end all parties.

'I can see our hotel is going to be booked up for months, if not years to come, after your programme,' Giovanni told her, his handsome dark eyes shining with pleasure. 'Everyone will want to come here.'

Allyson smiled as she experienced a pleasing glow of satisfaction, for though she had no idea what the future held for her and Mark, it was good to be playing a part in the birth of the splendid Palazzo. The thought took her mind instantly to Shelley, who was perched on the edge of a fountain, talking to the Italian tenor and his wife. She looked lovely, in a pale blue silk dress that buttoned down the front, and silver Chanel pumps that were as elegant and graceful as Shelley herself. It was an outfit Allyson had seen before and was so classically Shelley that it made the afternoon's display seem an even greater affront. As if she'd really want Shelley to dress down to avoid upstaging her! And the arrogance of assuming she could! However, retaining any anger over that ludicrous scene was a waste of precious energy, so she should just forget it had happened, especially as Shelley was now heading her way.

'Are you OK?' Shelley said as she joined her.

Allyson nodded, then smiled and waved at someone across the room.

'I'm sorry about earlier, with Candy,' Shelley said quietly. 'It was crass and I shouldn't have done it.'

Allyson looked into her eyes. 'Then why did you?' she asked.

'I'm not sure really. I didn't give it much thought at the time, but I can see now why it upset you.'

'Can you?' Allyson said, wanting to understand it too.

Shelley's answering smile was so irritating that Allyson wanted to slap her. 'I think so,' Shelley answered smoothly.

Allyson was boiling. Obviously Shelley was assuming it was her beauty that had upset Allyson, and though it might well have been, Allyson was furious to think that Shelley could feel so superior. But then she had to remind herself that it was all a defence, a means of trying to reassert herself after the humiliation she had suffered when Mark had chosen Allyson over her.

'So is my apology accepted?' Shelley said. 'Are we still friends?'

Somehow Allyson managed a smile. 'Of course,' she said.

'Then let's mingle.'

As Shelley moved back into the room Allyson watched her for a moment and forced herself to remember how very much Shelley meant to her. They'd known each other for so long, had come through such a lot together, that even if this was starting to prove the toughest test yet to their friendship, Allyson felt sure they both wanted it to survive. Though there were times, like right now, when she didn't want it quite so much.

However, focusing her attention on that was doing nothing to help the programme, so putting down her champagne she slipped out to reception to see if the crew was back from Pompeii yet. It was perfect timing for Alan, the director, was just coming in the door.

'How did it go?' she asked, as the camera and sound guys followed him in.

'Great,' he answered, handing her a cassette. 'Got a bit of flack from officialdom, but Justie greased a few palms and they left us alone after that. Tessa did a great commentary, by the way. Did you write it?'

'Yes. Where is she?'

He turned round. 'She was behind me a moment ago . . . Ah, here she is.'

Allyson followed his eyes to the door, then went suddenly still with shock. Mark was walking in behind Tessa. She felt slightly disorientated for a moment, as though she'd missed something vital, then the feeling started to ebb as his eyes found her and the space between them seemed to close even before he moved.

What seemed like seconds later, before anyone else could register his arrival, they were in one of the offices behind reception and she was laughing as he kissed her, and loving the tumultuous urges and compulsions that made these early stages of their relationship feel so risky and exciting.

'I wasn't sure I'd be able to get away,' he told her, holding her face in his hands, 'but when I knew for certain I thought I'd surprise you.'

'Well, you definitely succeeded,' she scolded. 'I thought for a minute, when I saw you, that I was losing my mind. And let me tell you, you're not the first person today to throw me a curve . . .' His lips silenced the rest of her words, and the pressure of his body quickly began igniting responses that needed much more immediate attention than her state of mind.

'Christ, I'm sorry,' he gasped, when he realized how far they were going. 'I guess I was even keener to see you than . . .' He groaned as her hand tightened around him, then his mouth was crushing hers again, and his hands were pushing inside her panties.

'Let me take them off,' she murmured, and in a second she was naked from the waist down and he was pushing his fingers right up inside her.

'I want you,' she gasped. 'Oh God, I want you now.'

His fingers were gone and pushing his cock between her legs he entered her hard. 'Are you OK?' he panted, as he rammed himself into her.

'Yes. Don't stop. Don't stop.'

'I'm not going to. Oh God, Allyson, do you have any idea . . .' then his mouth was hard on hers as the harsh jets of his orgasm burst into the pulsating grasp of hers, flooding her with the exquisite release of wanting her so much he was unable to hold back.

'Hold me,' she implored, when they were able to speak steadily again. 'Hold me and tell me how the hell we're going to walk out of here without everyone knowing what we've been doing.'

Laughing, he kissed her again, then refastened his trousers as she stooped to pick up her panties. 'I didn't mean for that to happen,' he said. 'Or let's say I did, but I didn't exactly have the front office in mind when I was thinking about this on the plane over.'

'You mean you fantasize about me when I'm not there,' she teased.

'All the time,' he answered.

When they emerged, a few minutes later, there was no-one near the reception desk, and they were soon melding into the dinner crowd as naturally as if he'd just come in from the airport, without the ten-minute inter-lude since he'd entered the door. But now and again they caught one another's eye and couldn't stop themselves exchanging glances that easily gave them away to those who were watching, and, with so many reporters present, plenty were. The only one watching Shelley was Candy, and though there was nothing in Shelley's behaviour to suggest that she was even noticing those looks, Candy felt pretty certain she was. And after the strange episode in Allyson's room earlier there was no doubt in Candy's mind that something wasn't right between Shelley and Allyson – and it didn't take a particularly vivid imagination to work out that Mark Reiner was probably at the root of it.

Though Allyson and Mark slept in separate rooms, he delivered her breakfast personally the next morning, at the ungodly hour of six, when everyone else was still sleeping. This gave them a precious hour together before Allyson had to meet the crew at the Rufolo gardens to start recording the Night Cap. Though they made love as passionately, though less speedily than the night before, it was the memory of what they'd talked about afterwards that lingered with her as she sat on the cathedral steps looking over the piazza, while waiting for the crew to set up in the leafy glade.

'I had a call from your husband before I left,' he'd told her, as she poured the coffee.

Allyson had stopped the pouring and turned to look at him, sitting up in bed with a single white sheet covering his nudity. 'What did he say?' she asked.

'Cutting to the bottom line,' he answered, 'he wanted to know how I feel about you.'

Allyson's heart tripped. 'What did you tell him?'

'That considering his reasons for wanting to know, it would probably be more helpful to find out how *you* feel about *me*.'

Allyson looked away. 'I'm sorry he did that,' she said.

'The man obviously loves you and wants you back,'

he said. 'And what I should have told him was to ask *you* how you feel about *him*.'

Allyson let several minutes pass before she turned to look at him again. She said nothing, but the question, the need to know what his feelings were, was there in her eyes.

Reaching for her hand he pulled her down on the bed beside him. 'I could tell you right now how I feel about you,' he said softly, 'but it's not going to help. If anything it'll only complicate things further.'

She hadn't asked him to elaborate on that, there had been no need to, for the tenderness of his kiss and the whole tenor of his actions told her what she needed to know. And now, sitting here, in this beautiful Italian piazza, with the sunlight streaming down through the trees, and the hypnotic scent of nature floating gently on the breeze, she could feel herself coming to the decision she knew she had to make. She smiled, for a part of her wanted to go to Mark right now and tell him, but she wouldn't because she owed it to Bob to tell him first, which she would, as soon as they arrived back in London. It was awful to think of how much it was going to hurt him, but she had to follow her heart and there was no doubt now that she wanted to be with Mark. Whether she was actually in love with him yet was hard to say, but she thought she probably was, and being so certain he felt the same way made her want to give them the chance to find out.

'OK?' Zac said, coming to sit on the steps beside her. 'You've got a bit of daft look on your face, so I thought I'd ask.'

Allyson laughed. 'Has Lenny Blomfeld come down from the hotel yet?' She was referring to the Scottish composer who was to be the Night Cap guest.

'He's on his way. Did Tessa find you earlier? She wanted to set up a time when the two of you can go over the Happy Hour interviews.'

'We can do it this afternoon while they're rigging. I gave Justie a running order, do you know if Tessa's seen it?'

'I think so. Terri Jankler's doing her stuff this morning, by the way. But I have to tell you everyone's finding it hilarious the way Tessa keeps mixing up their titles. Personally I think she's doing it on purpose, and we should let her get on with it, because it's a nice touch.'

'You could be right,' Allyson said, looking up as Alan came out of the gardens and headed towards them. 'Ready?' she asked him.

'Five minutes,' he answered. 'Our guest arrived yet?'

'I'm here,' Blomfeld's voice boomed out behind them. 'And I've brought someone to join us.'

It was America's latest teen pop phenomenon, who was no mere product of the electronic age, but a supremely gifted musician who had won Blomfeld's heart the night before when she'd sung, unaccompanied, an entire aria from *Aida*. An interview with the two of them would provide a perfect finale to the show, particularly if Allyson could persuade them to perform together, Blomfeld on the piano, and the pop wonder singing something else from an Italian opera. The only problem Allyson foresaw with that was the insurmountable one of being able to afford their performance fees. But it was worth a go, and if their managers or agents refused a waiver, she'd have the interview anyway.

Eventually the camera was ready to turn over, and going into the gardens where the make-up artist was waiting to apply the final cosmetic dabs, Allyson waited for her cue from Alan, then began the link into the Night Cap. While the interview took place Zac and Justine were outside in the piazza burning the phones in an attempt to get the go-ahead for a closing performance, but it simply wasn't possible to obtain in such a short time. So it wasn't long before Allyson and her two guests, having completed an extremely entertaining exchange, strolled back out to the square to find Shelley and Mark drinking coffee together outside one of the cafés.

Allyson stopped mid-sentence, for the picture they painted, of a couple who seemed so relaxed and well suited to each other, caused such a jolt in her heart that it was a moment before she could make her thoughts move beyond it. But then she reminded herself of how much easier it would be, for all of them, if Mark and Shelley could be friends, and if this was the start of it then maybe instead of feeling threatened she should be trying to encourage it.

As she approached them she was smiling, though the warmth drained somewhat when she saw the way Shelley's nipples were so evident through the clinging white fabric of her top. There was simply no way Mark could have missed them, and she found herself wishing that Shelley had explored her new image of dowdiness a while longer.

'Darling,' Mark said when he saw her, and getting to his feet he took her hand discreetly in his and looked into her eyes.

Allyson's hostility instantly melted, not only because it was the first time he had called her that, but because he had said it in front of Shelley. And he so obviously wanted to kiss her that, had the crew and some of the guests not been scattered around the square at that moment, she knew he would have.

'Hi,' she whispered, still looking at him.

Shelley picked up her cup. 'I get the feeling I could be extra to requirements,' she said, finishing her coffee.

'No, don't go,' Allyson protested. 'There're still a thousand things we need to go over for later . . .'

Shelley held up her hands. 'This is your show,' she reminded her. 'I'm only along for the ride.'

'Oh no,' Allyson said, sitting down on the chair Mark was holding out. 'No freeloaders from *Soirée*, I'm afraid.

Besides, I'd really like you to take a look at some of the questions I've come up with for Tessa. I've got the guest running order here somewhere,' she said, flipping through the pages on her clipboard.

'Are you going to have a coffee?' Mark asked her as the waiter arrived.

'Mmm,' she nodded.

'*Un cappuccino*,' Mark ordered.

'Make that *tre*,' Zac added as he and Justine joined them. 'We're making some progress for the closing number,' he told Allyson. 'With any luck we'll be able to record something first thing tomorrow before we leave.'

'Great,' she said, handing a guest running order to Shelley. 'Are you leaving us?' she said to Mark, who was on his feet, with a cellphone at his ear.

'I'll catch you later,' he said to Allyson. 'OK, Giovanni, I'm on my way. Sure, it shouldn't be a problem.' Allyson watched him as he headed off to the cobbled steps that led up to the hotel, then Zac was talking, with Justine butting in, and Shelley was starting to remark on the running order and before Allyson knew it they too had returned to the hotel, with the running order still in hot debate, and the crew in close pursuit.

Through all the mayhem of caterers, decorators, cleaners, musicians and electricians Allyson spotted Tessa in one of the lobby's cosy niches with its fabulous view of the sea, being coached by Terri Jankler, the freelance society writer. Great, that was under way, now she needed to find each of the featured guests and run through their questions; then she should have a discussion on position and lighting with the director, after which she might be able to fit in a good hour with Tessa . . .

'Ally, here's the list of what everyone's wearing.' It was one of the wardrobe assistants, handing her the names of the designers who needed to be credited. 'The princess might change her mind at the last minute and wear a Gucci . . .'

'Great. Give it to Justie,' Allyson interrupted. 'Have you seen anyone from make-up, I want them to do something with Tessa's hair. She needs some jewels in it, or a tiara . . . No, not a tiara . . . Just something sparkly. Will you pass the message on?'

'Sure.'

Allyson turned away, straight into the path of a speeding florist. It was a narrow miss, which earned her a stream of Neapolitan invective, and a gentle shove from a rigger who was trying to get past her with cables. Then Tessa was beside her, insisting she come and talk to Terri, who had just popped off to the ladies', so there was a minute for Allyson to take a look at Tessa's costume.

'I've already seen it,' Allyson told her. 'It's perfect. You'll look amazing. I'll come and find you in a minute, I need to talk to the sound guys first,' and she headed off down the bar where the madness was even greater than in the lobby.

However, by five that evening, by some miracle of organization, all the guests were assembled ready for a rehearsal. This was merely for position and timing, though it called for great feats of memory on the part of some, and even greater skills of dexterity on the part of others. But Alan was nothing if not an unflappable director, and mainly thanks to his cunning and patience they were through by six, at which point everyone vanished to their rooms to start dressing for the great occasion.

At eight o'clock the guests started filling the bar, many of them looking every bit the royalty or movie stars they were. The women wore gowns of silk, taffeta, satin and lace, with sequins that glittered, and jewels that sparked off the exquisite crystal and gold chandeliers above. The pop of champagne corks mingled with muted voices and occasional laughter. The band started to play, drowning the gentle rush of the fountains, and the director's assistants began guiding everyone into place.

Allyson stood in the lobby looking down at the scene. Her fine blonde hair was swept up into a cluster of diamonds with loose, curling tendrils tumbling around her neck, and yet more diamonds were circling her throat and falling from her ears. Her eyes glowed in their dark rims of kohl and her lips were moistened by a delicate frosted pink gloss.

She started to move down the stairs and felt as sensuous as she looked, in her figure-hugging black dress that fishtailed around the ankles and revealed her delicately tanned skin through the shimmering transparent panels that snaked around her body in a way that forbade the wearing of anything beneath. She was looking for Mark, and when her eyes finally found him it was as though he sensed she was there, for he looked up from the people he was with and her heart swelled with the emotion that filled his eyes.

He met her at the foot of the stairs and though she was aware of the flashlights going off around them, neither of them seemed to care, as he took her hand and drew her into his arms to kiss her. Then they both started to laugh as Alan chose that moment to yell, 'OK peasants! Opening positions!'

'Right now,' Mark murmured, 'I wish everyone would vanish so that I could just carry on looking at you.'

'Doesn't she look stunning?' Shelley said, joining them.

Allyson turned to her, smiling. 'So do you,' she said, glancing at Shelley's white silk trouser suit whose jacket was slashed open almost to the waist. Very elegant, very sexy and totally Shelley.

'And you look so dashing,' Shelley said to Mark, 'that I absolutely have to insist on the first dance once the recording is over and the party proper gets under way.'

'Consider it yours,' he told her. Excusing himself, he

went off in answer to a signal from Giovanni, who was already heading back to the kitchens.

'Where's Tessa?' Allyson asked, peering into the darkness of what was now the set. Shelley could outmanoeuvre her all she wanted, with first dances and smooth compliments, she was still going to end up on her own tonight – or if she didn't it wouldn't be Mark Reiner she was with.

'Through there,' Shelley said, pointing. 'At the end of the bar.'

Allyson found her, and her eyebrows rose in approval of the way Tessa looked, for though there were no sparkling gems in her hair, as Allyson had suggested, the way it was wet-combed back from her face was exactly the right look for the strapless red sequined dress that showed off her fleshy shoulders to perfection, and curved over her round, girlish hips in a way only she could carry off. But no matter how good she looked, or how objective Allyson found she could be at moments like this, she was never forgetful of just how much she hated this girl.

'I'll have a quick word with her before we start,' Allyson said. 'Where are you going to watch from?'

Shelley looked over at the small inner courtyard, where the production gallery was set up. 'In there, I think,' she answered.

'I'll join you there,' and taking the glass of champagne she was being offered, Allyson squeezed her way through the guests to where Tessa was being miked up ready to record.

'Are you OK?' Allyson asked her.

Tessa nodded. 'I've got the order glued in my head now, so please don't tell me you're about to change it.'

Allyson smiled. 'No,' she said. 'Now remember, just let it flow. Be yourself, and if you screw up someone's title, or even their name, don't worry, they've come to expect it.'

Tessa giggled.

'If you can get anyone to dance, or sing a duet with you,' Allyson went on, 'go for it, we've got you covered on three cameras, and we can sort out copyright after.'

'Is it all right if I ask them who they're sleeping with?' Tessa asked.

'No, it's not all right,' Allyson answered. 'Just be guided by the questions we went through earlier.'

'You look fab, by the way,' Tessa told her. 'I'll bet Mark Reiner thinks so too.'

Allyson didn't reply.

'He said he liked my dress,' Tessa said. 'I expect he was just being polite though, because I don't look anywhere near as glam as you.'

'Just concentrate on the show,' Allyson advised.

'OK, everyone, stand by. We're on the clock!' Alan's assistant shouted.

Allyson started to make her way back to join Shelley, but she was stalled by a couple of journalists wanting some last-minute info and then by Giovanni who wanted to tell her how lovely she looked. So in the end she watched the recording from the lobby, where she was able to look down on the scene and see everything that was happening, from the moment Tessa began moving along the bar while delivering her opening link to camera, to her first overplayed shock at finding a couple of famous film stars relaxing on the sofas she'd reserved for herself, to the introduction of the garish Happy Hour cocktails, which the princess had already had some practice in serving. It was all going so smoothly, and Tessa seemed to weave such an incredible magic with her cheeky good humour and show of total fascination with anything anyone had to say, that Allyson could sense already what a triumph the programme was going to be, not only for her, but for Mark and the hotel too. Of course, she had no way of knowing then that it was a show no-one would ever get to see.

Not even when the cameras were discreetly taken away and the cables were removed to make room for dancing, were there any signs that anything was wrong with the evening. Food was brought, more champagne flowed and soon the dancing began. Allyson watched Shelley in Mark's arms, then turned away, refusing to be jealous. The next time she saw Mark he was smooching with Tessa, who seemed drunk and vaguely out of control, but was making him laugh, so Allyson didn't bother to step in. Later, she danced with him herself, but was soon whisked away by an insistent politician who'd come with his famous wife. Then towards midnight she couldn't find him, but the sight of Shelley, sitting with a German count and his gay lover, quelled the sudden burn of dread in her chest. Shelley spotted her looking and waved, but Allyson didn't go over. She was suddenly so tired she wanted only to sleep. A few more minutes, she thought, and she'd try sliding away, but she should find Mark first.

'If you're looking for who I think you're looking for,' Candy said in her ear, 'he carried your pretty little presenter up to bed. She passed out, I'm afraid . . .'

Allyson turned to look at her.

'Too much champagne,' Candy expanded, her eyes twinkling with humour. 'Ah, here he is.'

Allyson turned round to see Mark coming towards them. 'How is she?' she asked when he reached them.

'She'll survive. Are you OK? You look pretty tired.'

She smiled. 'You offering to carry me up too?' she teased.

Mark looked at Candy, who took the hint and discreetly backed away.

'You don't have to stay to the end,' he said to Allyson.

'Do you think it would be terrible if I didn't?' she said, stifling a yawn.

'No. You've had a long day and now the adrenalin's run out . . .'

'You're right,' she said. 'Will you come and say goodnight before you go to bed?'

'Of course. But I won't wake you if you're sleeping.'

'You'll just bring me breakfast at the crack of dawn?'

Still smiling after they gave each other a friendly kiss on the cheek, he watched her as she stopped to say goodnight to those who were nearest, thanking everyone for coming and wishing a good journey home to those who were leaving early tomorrow. He was still watching her when she reached the top of the stairs and turned back to blow him a kiss, then with a droll look in his eyes he went to rejoin the party.

As the clock ticked towards two in the morning the last of the revellers began finding their way back to their rooms, and the band, too tired to go on, retired in favour of a Frank Sinatra CD on the hotel system. Shelley strolled amongst the remaining few, still sipping champagne, still smiling, talking, laughing, while all the time she was crying inside. She envied Allyson so deeply, and hated her with a passion for inviting her here, when Allyson should have known how painful it would be. Everything was so beautiful, so suggestive of all her dreams, and in keeping with all she'd imagined, it was breaking her heart.

She thought back to the coffee she and Mark had shared earlier in the day, and to the many times they'd danced throughout the evening. It had felt so right being with him, looking at him, touching him, that she just couldn't accept that they weren't destined for each other. And the way he'd responded to her that morning, and held her in his arms this evening . . .

'You look lovely,' he'd told her.

She'd wondered if he was just being polite. But no, she did look lovely, and the expression in his eyes had suggested that he was remembering just how lovely.

'Thank you,' she'd said, and it was a while before either of them looked away.

'I'm glad you came,' he'd told her during their last dance.

'Are you?' she said.

He didn't answer, but when the music slowed he'd pulled her closer and she'd been so intensely aware of his body it had almost been painful. It simply wasn't possible for him not to be aware of her too, so when the dance ended and they were in shadow she'd lifted his hand and placed it inside her jacket, over her breast. His eyes were burning into hers as he said, 'I've never denied how sexy you are.'

Then it was over and he was moving away to dance with someone else.

Shelley looked around for him now, but apart from the staff she seemed to be the only one left. A tall, lonely figure amongst the debris of the night.

She walked slowly up the stairs to her room, then closing the door behind her she moved through the darkness to the window. She stood very still, looking out on the flickering lights of the hillside and the moon's reflection on the sea below. She heard laughter coming from a nearby room, and the clatter of the staff as they worked below. She wasn't the only one who was awake, yet she felt so alone it was as though the world had somehow emptied.

Allyson was in the room next to hers. Shelley had seen her go to bed earlier, so she was probably asleep by now. She wondered if Mark was too.

She moved, hardly knowing it, across the room and out of the door. Night lights burned in the hallways as she walked quietly past them. This feeling she had couldn't only be hers. He must feel it too.

She turned the corner, knowing that his room was at the end of the hall. Maybe he was expecting her, certain she would come, the way she was meant to, for that was how it felt, that this was meant to happen.

As she approached his door she began to feel an untimely dread of rejection. Could she bear it if he sent her away again? She was so close now. Just a few more steps. Did she really dare to do this?

Then she was suddenly disoriented by the sound of his voice. It was close, much closer than the distance to his room would allow. She looked to one side, and saw that the door she was passing was open. There were voices, speaking so softly she couldn't make out what they were saying. But one of them was Mark's, she knew that. And the other sounded curiously like a child. This was Tessa's room. For some reason, Mark was in Tessa's room.

Shelley listened, her heart banging against her ribs. She should leave, turn away, but something was compelling her to stay. She stepped closer to the door. It was open enough for her to see the heavy furniture against one wall, a rosewood desk, a baroque chair, a mirror . . . Her eyes suddenly dilated. Reflected in the mirror she could see Tessa, on her knees, her face in profile as she gazed up at Mark. He was looking down at her, but it was too dark to see his expression. Then Tessa spoke again, in a meek and tearful voice.

'Please,' she said. 'Please don't be angry with me.'

Mark stooped to draw her to her feet.

Shelley remained rooted to the spot, too appalled even to breathe. She heard his next words but hardly registered them as Tessa moved into his arms. Still Shelley listened and watched, then finally, she turned and walked silently back to her room.

The next morning Shelley and Allyson had breakfast together on the terrace. Allyson's face was white, her eyes were blinded by shock. For some reason, all she seemed to be registering now Shelley had stopped talking, was the fact that the sun wasn't shining today, and the sky, so clear and blue the day before, was now ominously grey and thunderous, casting a pall over the hillsides, in much the same way as Shelley's words had cast a pall over her heart.

'I'm sorry,' Shelley said. 'If I hadn't been coming back from Edgar and Janie's room at that time I wouldn't have seen it. But I did and . . .'

Allyson glanced at her, then swallowed and picked up her coffee. She didn't drink, she simply stared down at the cup. She didn't want to believe it, was resisting it hard, but images and memories kept flashing through her mind: Tessa's voice on his machine; Tessa walking into the hotel with him the night he'd arrived; Tessa dancing with him and making him laugh; Tessa being carried up to bed by him . . . And now this . . .

'You say she called him Daddy?' she said, feeling confused and sick and horribly distanced from reality.

'That's what it sounded like,' Shelley said. She too was pale, having hardly slept all night.

'You don't think . . .?' Allyson couldn't finish the question.

'That it was a sex game?' Shelley said. 'I don't know. It could have been.'

Allyson's eyes closed. 'God, it's horrible. It's almost like . . .' But she didn't want to speak the words aloud. Their meaning was too ugly, too depraved. 'Do you think he was making her do it?'

'I didn't see any force.'

Allyson couldn't stop herself picturing the scene, nor could she stop the revulsion. 'What's it about?' she said. 'Why's she doing this? First Bob, then the programme, then my flat, now Mark. What is it with the girl?'

Shelley glanced up and gave a brief shake of her head to someone who was about to join them.

'How the hell do I handle this?' Allyson said.

'Maybe you should talk to him,' Shelley suggested. 'Ask him what it was about?'

'He left early this morning, for Rome. He's on a midday flight to New York.' He'd come to kiss her goodbye, but it had been so early and she was still so tired she'd barely known he was there. She wondered now why he hadn't told her before that he'd be leaving so early. Or maybe he had and she'd been so busy she hadn't heard him. She tried to think what it could mean, that he'd left so soon after the party. Were there any sinister or unworthy motives she could attach to it? If there were, she could find none. 'I can't believe he'd do this,' she said finally. 'It just doesn't seem like him.'

She was looking at Shelley and Shelley could see the suspicion starting to turn her way. 'I know,' she said. 'And maybe it wasn't what it seemed . . .'

Allyson continued to look at her.

'I know you don't want to believe me,' Shelley said, 'but I swear to you, he was there, in her room, and something was going on . . .'

'Oh God,' Allyson groaned, pressing her hands to her head. 'Why did I ever let that girl into my life? Or maybe more to the point, how the hell do I get her out?'

Chapter 16

Two days had gone by since they'd returned to London, and still Allyson didn't seem able to shake herself out of this trance-like state. But life was easier to deal with that way, just going through the motions, hardly thinking, or responding, only editing or dubbing, making plans for the next programme then getting into her car and going home. Sometimes, during odd moments in the day, she felt an anger that was so intense it would burn her up like a fire, but she quickly detached herself from it, because she was afraid of what she might do if she didn't.

Mark was still in New York. He'd rung several times, but if she was in the office she cut him short by saying she'd call back, and if she was at home she listened to his voice on the machine without picking up. She didn't want to talk to him, because she didn't even want to form the thoughts that were needed to ask if anything Shelley had said was true. She just wanted to put it out of her mind, as though none of it, not him, not Tessa, not the break-up of her marriage, nothing, had ever happened. Besides, even when she was ready to talk, she wouldn't do it on the phone. She'd make herself face him, which shouldn't be hard because she hadn't known him long, so it couldn't be as devastating as when Bob had betrayed her. But it felt that way, and the hatred she'd known for Tessa since Bob had left was magnified now to a degree that consumed her. She couldn't look at the girl without thinking monstrous and violent thoughts, couldn't hear her voice without wishing her dead. Yet she still had to work with her, still had to see her every day and know there was nothing she could do to get rid of her. Her popularity was exploding.

Yet Tessa too seemed different, strangely cowed, as though she was afraid of something only she could see. But Allyson wasn't interested to know anything about her, except to understand whatever insanity it was that was making her want everything that was Allyson's.

It was only just after nine in the morning, but Allyson had already been at her desk for over two hours. There were always a thousand things to do, so she was never in any danger of having to face the torture of empty time. Even so, she knew that by ignoring the wound she was leaving it open to fear and paranoia, as well as to hatred and fury. But maybe that was what she wanted, to nurture it and let it grow so out of proportion that the whole savage energy of it could destroy the horror of being betrayed again . . .

The phone snapped off her thoughts, and reaching for it she said, 'Allyson Jaymes.'

'Allyson. I was wondering . . .'

Allyson went very still.

'I was wondering if we could talk.'

Allyson looked out into the office to where Tessa was sitting, a phone to her ear as she stared at Allyson with a pathetic, beseeching look in her eyes, like a dog that had been whipped and was trying to skulk back to its master.

'Is it about the programme?' Allyson asked coldly.

'No. It's . . .'

'Then there's nothing to talk about,' and she slammed down the phone.

Tessa rang off too, and Allyson watched her as she sat there looking lost and forlorn and so miserably self-pitying that it made Allyson despise her all the more.

Another week went by. Mark was due back in a couple of days, but he'd stopped calling now. His last message had told Allyson that he suspected Bob was tampering with her machine again, and as she never had time in the office he'd see her when he got back. He'd sounded curt and confused, and Allyson had wanted to scream at him that even if there hadn't been anything sexual in that disgusting scene with Tessa, then what the hell was he doing in her room at that hour anyway? For one wildly insane moment she'd considered asking Tessa. The girl wanted to talk, so let her! But what good would it do? She couldn't be relied on to tell the truth, and even if she could Allyson didn't want to hear it from her.

Nor did she want to hear from Bob. She just wanted him out of her life, expunged from existence, rather than have to deal with his pathetic pleas to come home. But she couldn't put off seeing him any longer, he had to be faced, though even after she arranged it she picked up the phone a hundred times to cancel. In the end, though, she took the afternoon off work to psych herself up for the ordeal, so that by the time he arrived she might be in a frame of mind that would more easily allow her to cope with him.

It was an early spring evening, awash with a glowing red sunset. Which symbol should she choose, she wondered, as she opened the door to let him in, spring for new beginnings, or sunset for happy endings? But neither were going to be had here, tonight, she knew that already.

It was evident right away that he'd made an effort, for he was wearing the cologne she liked best, a shirt she had bought him and the jeans she'd always said he looked sexy in. He looked haggard though, and was so apprehensive that ordinarily she'd have wanted to hug him. Tonight, she simply stood aside and tried not to wish that he would turn around and go away.

'Would you like a drink?' she offered as he walked into the sitting room ahead of her.

'Maybe some wine,' he said.

She went to get it and came back to find him sitting on the edge of a chair he'd once slouched in. His elbows were resting on his knees, his hands were clamped together. She could see how hard this was for him, so hard it would be easy to pity him.

'Did your lawyer tell you . . .?' His voice was hoarse. He cleared his throat and started again. 'You know why I'm here?'

She nodded, then seeing his eyes fill with tears she put down the wine and went to him.

He clung to her as he wept, bitterly and so full of shame that it was hard to make sense of his words. 'I'll do anything,' he sobbed in the end. 'I'll get counselling, anything, just please say it isn't too late.'

She looked at his tormented face. She knew this man so well. He was so much a part of her life that he almost was her life. Yet she felt so remote from him.

He grabbed her wrists. 'I know how much I hurt you,' he cried. 'I know I don't deserve your forgiveness, but look at me, look at what I am without you.'

'I'm sorry,' she said, her voice seeming to come from a long way inside her.

'Oh God, Allyson,' he implored, pulling her to him. 'Please don't turn me away. I can't go on living without you.'

'Don't say that. I can't be responsible for your life. You chose this, Bob. You made it happen and nothing I do can change it.'

'But we can put it behind us. I'm starting to get some work again now, so we can move forward and be together the way we should.'

'Until when? The next Tessa?'

'No! I don't want any other woman. Leaving you has made me understand that in a way I never did before . . .'

402

'But what about all the other women, Bob? And Shelley, my best friend.'

He looked shocked and hurt. 'Are you saying you'd rather give me up than her?'

'She didn't betray me.'

Disbelief widened his eyes, and as she looked back at him she could feel something horrible rising up inside her, something she'd always known was there but she'd never wanted to face. 'She slept with me all those years, but the betrayal was only mine?' he said incredulously. And there it was. The suspicion she'd never allowed a voice, that Shelley had lied, that Shelley, her best friend, had been sleeping with her husband all along, that Shelley had betrayed her too.

Her head was spinning. 'What years? What are you talking about?' she said, as if she could bury it all again. 'She said you tried . . .' But she couldn't go any further. She had to accept it, and he wouldn't lie to her about that, not now.

Realizing what had happened, he dropped his head in his hands. 'Oh God, oh God, oh God,' he groaned.

Allyson got to her feet. 'You should go now,' she said.

'No. Allyson, please.'

She pushed his hands away and walked to the door. 'There's no-one I can trust,' she said unsteadily. 'No-one.'

He wasn't listening. 'Just tell me there's a chance,' he begged. 'Tell me you'll think it over.'

'Just leave me alone,' she said. 'All of you. Just leave me alone.'

Bob was standing in Shelley's sitting room, facing the unflinching anger in her eyes, as he told her what had happened with Allyson. He felt foolish, unmanned, yet so desperate that even now he was still clinging to the hope that Shelley would know how to repair the damage he'd done.

But when he'd finished Shelley looked as though she might strike him in disgust. 'You fool,' she spat. 'You bloody fool!'

'But I thought she knew,' he cried. 'She made it sound like you'd told her.'

Contempt twisted her face. 'Are you out of your mind? Why the hell would I do that? She's my best friend, for God's sake!' Again she looked as though she might hit him. 'God, you're pathetic!' she seethed. 'Look at you! How the hell do you think you're ever going to get her back now?'

He looked away, misery and hopelessness engulfing him.

'It's as good as over with Mark Reiner!' she raged. 'You actually stood a chance and you blew it. You moron! You stupid, *stupid* moron.'

'All right!' he yelled. 'I should never have left her in the first place. Don't you think I already know that? And I wouldn't have if Tessa hadn't been pregnant. It's all her damned fault. Everything was all right before she came into our lives . . .'

'You low-down, self-pitying piece of scum!' Shelley spat. 'You were always a cheating bastard and you know it. And to try blaming Tessa when we both know you were happy to screw anyone who'd lie down for you . . .'

'Including you, you stuck-up, self-righteous bitch! You lay down often enough, didn't you? That's how fucking good a friend you are. And I'll tell you this, if it was you who'd been pregnant, I still wouldn't have left, because Allyson's worth ten thousand of you Shelley . . .'

'But she couldn't give you a baby, could she?' Shelley spat viciously. 'You couldn't make her pregnant, like you made Tessa. Made you feel like a man, that, did it? I suppose you know she had an abortion? That given the choice between fame and your baby, your baby didn't even get a look-in. So that's who you gave Allyson up for, a silly little tart who didn't give that for you, or your kid . . . What are you doing? Get away from me!' She was backing across the room, but he kept on coming.

'I said get away!' she shouted.

His fist knocked her flying back across the sofa, then picking up a photograph of her and Allyson he flung it violently into the fireplace before snatching up her purse, helping himself to the money and storming out of the door.

Shelley lay breathlessly where she was, her hand covering the throbbing in her face as his footsteps thundered down the stairs. It was all getting out of hand. Nothing was happening the way she had expected and she didn't know how to turn it around. But maybe she didn't need to. Maybe she should wait a while longer, see what happened in the next few days, for though it didn't seem likely that Allyson would take Bob back now, there was nothing to say she'd take Mark back either. So yes, she should wait, let events unfold a little further, until she had a clearer idea of what she should do.

The following morning Shelley was already at her desk when Allyson arrived. The strain in Allyson's face as she walked into her own office was plain to see, and everyone noticed. Shelley watched them as they looked at each other, hoping someone might have the answer, for clearly something had happened, and this time the newspapers weren't telling them what.

Shelley considered going to talk to her, but this definitely wasn't the place to have the kind of showdown they were heading for, nor was it the time. How must she be feeling, Shelley wondered, with Tessa sitting out there, Shelley in here . . . The world must seem a very strange place for Allyson right now, with no-one to trust and no-one to turn to. So maybe Shelley *should* go and talk to her, if only to help her connect to something as superficial, yet stabilizing, as the day's needs.

But as Shelley reached her door Allyson was already calling across the room to Tessa.

'Have you edited the piece about the dolls yet?' Allyson was asking her.

'No, not yet,' Tessa replied. There was such a hunger in the girl's eyes as she looked at Allyson, such an appeal, that Shelley was reminded again of the night Mark had been in the girl's room. Tessa had seemed the same then as she did now, kind of frightened, eager to make amends, and . . . Well, it was hard to put into words . . .

'If you're in a hurry I can do it tonight,' Tessa was saying.

Shelley knew there was no hurry, for Allyson wasn't due to shoot that programme for another three weeks, so it surprised her when Allyson snapped, 'Yes, do it tonight.'

As she turned back into her office her eyes met Shelley's, and Shelley could see how deeply her pain was cutting. Then she disappeared, and after glancing over at Tessa again, Shelley returned to her desk and picked up her keys.

'I've got to take my car in for a service,' she told Marvin, 'then I'll be popping home for a few minutes. I'll be back before lunch.'

It was early in the afternoon when Allyson answered the phone in her dressing room to find Mark at the other end.

'I don't know what's going on,' he said. 'I don't know why you're refusing to speak to me, but I'm outside, and if you're not here in the next five minutes I'll come in and get you.'

Allyson replaced the receiver, stared at it for a moment, then picking up her coat she walked upstairs to Shelley's office.

'Is she back yet?' she asked Marvin.

'Yes, she's in the screening room,' he answered.

Allyson found her alone in the dimly lit room,

speaking to someone on the phone. An image from the Italian programme, which was due for transmission the following day, was paused on the screen.

Allyson said, 'Did you really see Mark and Tessa together in Italy? Or were you lying about that too?'

Shelley finished the call. 'Allyson, listen . . .' she said.

Allyson was already turning away.

'I wasn't lying,' Shelley cried. 'I swear I saw them.'

Allyson's back was still turned. 'Do you have any idea what all this feels like?' she said. 'Knowing there's no-one you can trust?'

'Yes. I know what that feels like,' Shelley answered.

Allyson turned round. 'You could trust me,' she said, anger twisting her mouth.

'Listen, we have to talk,' Shelley said. 'Not now. Later. Will you let me at least try to explain?'

Allyson didn't answer, and suddenly Shelley was afraid. Everything seemed to be slipping away, moving out of focus, beyond her reach, and she wanted desperately to bring it back. Then she had a sudden, horrible premonition that this was going to be her only chance to say this, so she must say it now.

'Think of loneliness, rejection, never feeling as though you matter,' she cried. 'You know now how some of that feels. That's how it's been for me. All my life. I never learned to value people the way you do. I never understood what it was like to be loved so much by a man that he'd never leave me. You had that and I wanted it. I resented you for all you had and at the same time . . . I loved you.' Her voice was choking with emotion. 'I'll book a table in Dolphin Square for eight thirty. Please say you'll come.'

'I'm looking after Daddy until then.'

'Then I'll book it for nine. If you're not there, I'll wait.'

Allyson sat in the passenger seat of Mark's car, almost numb with exhaustion. So many betrayals, so many lies, could there ever be any trust again? She wanted to sleep now, to curl up in a ball and wait for everything to be over.

She'd already asked him about Tessa and he'd explained, but the words didn't seem to have reached her.

He said them again. 'She was very drunk. I don't think anyone realized how drunk until she passed out and I carried her up to bed. When I left her she was still out cold. Then later, when I was in my room, I heard her crying. Not just crying, she sounded hysterical, out of control. So I went in. Maybe she'd taken some drugs, I don't know, because it was like she was hallucinating. She seemed to think I was her father and that I was going to hurt her. She offered to have sex with me if I promised not to beat her. I couldn't get her to understand who I was. Then she started talking in a childish voice and calling me Daddy. I didn't know what was happening, I'm not even sure I do now. Then she was talking about you. At first I didn't realize it was you, because she kept referring to Mummy. Then she called you by name and . . .' He was shaking his head. 'It was like she had you confused with her mother. God, I don't know what was going through her head. What I do know is it wasn't coherent and it wasn't particularly sane. But she seemed worried about hurting you and kept saying she was afraid of what you might do. Then she threw up all over us both, so I called someone from downstairs to come and take care of her, and went back to my room.'

Allyson was staring straight ahead. She was hearing the words now, but hardly knew what they meant.

'Allyson, you've got to know how much you mean to me,' he said. 'I don't want to push you, I know you've been through a lot, but for God's sake, I love you . . .'

She turned to look at him. So Shelley hadn't lied. He had been in Tessa's room.

Tessa. Tessa. It always came back to Tessa. Just this

408

morning she'd opened a magazine and there was Tessa looming large on the page. And there was she, a small inset at the bottom, a footnote, a last word before the end.

She was still looking at him, searching his eyes and wanting desperately to believe him. Her thoughts were so jumbled she seemed unable to make any sense of them.

'I have to go now,' she said, and before he could stop her she opened the door and got out of the car.

The day's recording was over, the lights in the offices were mainly extinguished, just a few scattered lamps burned that people had forgotten to turn off. There was nobody in the building now except Tessa and Will, who were editing the film about dolls, and Shelley, who was almost ready to leave.

It had been the strangest day, with no sense of reality attached even to the normal routine. It was as though something pivotal was happening in a bizarre, other-worldly kind of way, something that was going to move with a silent and mighty force to change their lives completely.

Shelley knew Allyson had seen Mark earlier, but had no idea yet of the outcome, whether Allyson had accepted his story, or even if there had been a story that could be accepted. She kept wondering what she would do if Allyson told her later that everything was all right, that she and Mark were staying together and that they didn't want her in their lives any more. It could happen, because Mark would know Shelley had twisted what she'd seen in an effort to try and break them up; he knew too, that using Tessa would be the most effective, as well as the cruellest way to hurt Allyson. And what about how Shelley had tried to seduce him at the party? He wouldn't want that to happen again.

She felt suddenly breathless, and there was such

unease in her heart that each thud felt like a blunted blow. Maybe it was tiredness and emotional exhaustion that was lending the macabre sense of detachment to what she was doing, or maybe it was fear of the slow, silent explosion that seemed to be erupting all around them.

She should leave now, go home and change. She'd just check on Will and Tessa first, find out what time they'd be finished.

The edit room door was closed, but Shelley could hear the squealing whir of the videotape rewinding. Then she heard Tessa laugh. All day the girl had looked like an injured bird, but now she was laughing.

The door suddenly opened and Will almost walked into her.

'Oh, Shelley!' he said, his small, squashed face showing surprise. 'I didn't know you were there.'

'Just coming to check how you're getting on,' she said, looking past him to where Tessa was sitting at the control desk.

'It's great,' Tessa told her. 'Really scary.'

Shelley smiled. 'I'll leave you to it then,' she said.

Allyson was standing next to her mother's car in the garage, waiting for Peggy to start the engine.

'Are you sure you're all right?' Peggy asked, peering up at her anxiously. 'You seem ... I don't know... Distracted?'

Allyson forced a smile. 'I've got a lot on my mind. But I'm OK. You have a good time with Aunt Mary. It'll do you good to get out.'

'I won't be long,' Peggy assured her. 'We'll just get a quick bite. I should be back by eight thirty.'

Allyson looked at her mother's ageing, kindly face and felt a lump rise in her throat. The one person in the world she would never doubt, would always be able to trust.

As she watched her drive away she was thinking of

Shelley and what Shelley had said in the office today, about loneliness and rejection, and mattering to someone so much they would never leave. All the pain she was suffering now Shelley had been suffering for years, which made her want to hold Shelley in her arms to comfort her – *then cut her out of her life to punish her*. If Shelley knew what it was like, how could she have inflicted it on someone she cared for?

Dear God, there were so many complex and conflicting emotions that made up a woman like Shelley – or any woman, come to that. Except maybe Tessa. Tessa was different, and Allyson knew she wasn't even close to understanding the complexities and conflicts that made up someone like her.

Going back into the house, she went to check on her father and found him sleeping on a sofa in his den. She stared down at his peaceful, jowly face and found herself wondering what happened to the lucidity when the confusion took over. Was it still there somewhere, operating on another level like a sound that existed but couldn't be heard? Or was it tangled so deep in the subconscious that it could never be found? Who ever knew what really went on in someone else's mind? Whether they were sane or mad, evil or righteous, tormented or even dead. Did the mind carry on working after death? No-one knew, because there wasn't a way for anyone to know. But if it did then she hoped, for her father's sake, that mental tangles came straight again so that he wouldn't have to be afraid any more.

Kissing him on the forehead, she closed the door quietly behind her, then returned to the kitchen. The clock said six thirty. That should give her plenty of time to do everything she had to do – she'd just sit down for a few minutes first though and try not to think any more.

The lights in the edit suite were off. All eight monitors glowed in the darkness, each projecting an identical image. Tessa was alone for the moment. Will, the editor, had received a call from the parking attendant, reminding him that the barrier went down at eight so he should move his car out to the street.

Tessa was seated at the console, watching, enthralled by the house that was filling up the screens in front of her. It was tall, gothic, with stained-glass windows and a forbidding air. The effect on the sound track whistled the same eerie cry as the wind that was sweeping through the streets of Fulham outside. Naked tree limbs swayed across the face of the moon, fallen leaves gusted over the brittle, frosted lawn. The camera tracked in, angling from side to side as it approached the front door. Footsteps crunched on the dark, gravelled path.

The front door was opening, the dubbed effect of a creak stretched with the ominously slow swing. The hall beyond was in pitch darkness, just two narrow strips of blue light shining through the cracks in a far off door. The camera inched tentatively towards the light, a thin, high-pitched strain of music began to move with it.

This sequence was a cheat. It wasn't the author's North London home, it was footage imported from Hammer. But the next mix, as a hand pushed open the door and the screen filled with blue light, took them into a huge, brightly lit room full of every imaginable type of doll. This was the writer's home.

Later would come the interviews; with the writer, and with her neighbours who swore the dolls screamed and flew in the night. But first the camera was going to show the sublime horror of the collection.

They lived on every shelf, every chair, every surface of the high-ceilinged room. A thousand staring eyes, unseeing, unspeaking, yet all-knowing. Bisque-headed, shiny-faced and smiling infinitely winsome smiles. Dressed in delicate, hand-sewn clothes; small, malignant spirits locked in wax, china and porcelain forms. Girls, boys, babies; haughty women, evil old men. Mouths were open; eyes were slanted. Teeth were bared, fury was a solid, unmoving mass. The music dipped and swayed. Cute little dancers and regal skaters poised to come alive. Heavy chords blasted the entry of malformed puppets, and trumpeted angrily at scowling sailors. The camera panned sharply, then settled in benign observation of inscrutable Orientals and halted songsters. A sudden screech emanated from the frame of a spiteful Turk. Insolence and supremacy blazed from the frame.

Tessa didn't move. Her concentration was total as the thrill of fear stole through her senses.

Behind her the door opened, then quietly closed.

'This is brilliant,' she murmured to Will, eyes still riveted to the screen.

A piano was playing, surging through the discord of frantic violins.

Faces flashed across the screen. Ugly, old, tormented, sad. Human emotions trapped in tiny torsos of plastic and clay. She felt Will standing behind her. Her heart was thudding.

A drumbeat exploded. The first blow knocked her unconscious.

The grating, staccato squeals from *Psycho* knifed through the room. A frenzied cutting of crazed, laughing mouths, and fiendish eyes. A shadow bulged on the wall, a nefarious enactment of the final four blows that took her life.

Allyson was running. The wind rushed in her ears, winter's trees were reflected in the moonlit puddles her feet splashed through. When she reached her car she took out her phone. She dialled quickly as she got in and started the engine.

'Shelley?'

'Ally? Where are you? You sound upset.'

'No. I fell asleep and Mummy was late back. I didn't want you to think I wasn't coming.'

'It's OK.' Shelley's voice sounded strained too. 'I'm stuck in traffic. I should be there just after nine.'

Allyson rang off, fastened her seat belt and pulled away from the kerb.

Will, the editor, returned from the car park to find the editing room in silence and darkness. He'd thought Tessa would wait, but it seemed she hadn't. Disappointed, he switched on the light and looked at a schedule on the wall. Later, when he talked to police, he couldn't remember which came first, noticing the droplets of blood on the chart, or the terrible, gut-wrenching smell. All he knew was that when he turned round the sight of Tessa's mutilated skull, the pooling blood and crudely spattered brains loosened his bladder and caused him to sink trembling to his knees. A moment later he was vomiting as he staggered like a drunk to the door.

'Shelley!' he attempted to shout. 'Shelley!'

Allyson was already at the restaurant by the time Shelley arrived. Both women looked pale – the strain of this meeting was harsh.

'There's a bomb scare somewhere in Chelsea,' Shelley said. 'They've closed off half the roads.'

'I heard it on the news,' Allyson said. She felt strangely groggy, as though she'd been asleep for days.

Shelley ordered a drink while Allyson toyed with her own.

'About Bob,' Shelley said.

Allyson closed her eyes. She didn't want to hear it.

'I'm not stupid enough to think you can forgive me,' Shelley said, emotion acting like a burr on her voice. 'I just want you to know that your friendship has been more precious to me than anything else in my life. I wish I'd known how to value it. I wish I wasn't realizing all this when it's already too late.'

414

Allyson's eyes were shining with tears, but none fell.

'Jealousy is a powerful monster,' Shelley said, 'and I've always been jealous of you. But I've loved you too.' As she spoke she was reaching inside the large carrier bag on the floor beside her.

Allyson watched her take out a box, then returned her eyes to Shelley's face as she said, 'This is for you. A token of our friendship.'

As she pushed it across the table Allyson suddenly laughed. She stifled it quickly, but suddenly laughed again.

Shelley looked at her curiously.

'I'm sorry,' she said. 'It's just been . . . Oh God, I don't know how much more of today I can take. Thank you. What is it?' But as she started to unwrap it Shelley covered her hands.

'Maybe you'd better wait until you get home,' she said. 'It might make us both cry.'

Allyson looked into her lovely face and felt her heart filling up with emotion. It was all going to change, everything that had been so familiar and cherished, so central and necessary to them and who they were, was moving on to another plane and there was nothing they could do to stop it. 'I don't want to lose you,' she whispered.

Shelley swallowed the lump in her throat, then looked up as her drink arrived. She was about to make a toast when her phone started to ring. It was ringing for a long time as she tried to locate it in her bag.

'Shelley Bronson,' she said.

Allyson watched her face as its expression turned from surprise, to confusion, to horror and shock. 'What is it?' Allyson said, feeling her blood run cold. 'What's happened?'

Shelley was ending the call. 'Of course,' she was saying. 'I'll come right away.' She clicked off the phone and stared at Allyson, her face bloodless and stricken. 'It was the police,' she said. 'Apparently Tessa's been murdered.'

Allyson's head started to spin. She thought she might faint.

'They want me to go back to the office,' Shelley said. Her eyes drew focus on Allyson. 'Maybe you should come too.'

Allyson couldn't move. Her limbs were weighted with fear. 'Yes,' she managed to say.

Shelley stood up and started to put on her coat. Allyson watched her, then forced herself to her feet and reached for her coat too.

'I had to park miles away,' Shelley said. 'Where are you?'

'Just down the road.'

'Then let's take your car. Don't forget your parcel,' she added, then turned to lead the way out.

By the time they got to the office the place had been cordoned off and the press was starting to gather. Flashbulbs popped through the rotating police lights as Allyson and Shelley got out of Allyson's car. A couple of policemen spotted them and ushered them through. Neither of them answered the shouted questions and demands to know what had happened.

Inside there seemed to be policemen everywhere, some in uniform, some in plain clothes and others in overalls. They saw Will sitting at a desk with a detective. He looked deathly white and as though he'd been crying. A short man with cropped red hair and a stern face approached them.

'Mrs Jaymes,' he said, recognizing Allyson. 'Detective Inspector Hollander.'

Allyson shook his hand. 'This is Shelley Bronson,' she said.

Hollander shook hands with Shelley.

'Where did it happen?' Shelley asked.

'Through there,' he answered, pointing towards the editing room.

Suddenly Allyson started to cry and stuffed a hand into her mouth to try to make herself stop. 'I'm sorry,' she said.

Shelley slipped an arm round her. 'Is she . . . still there?' she asked.

Hollander nodded, then looked round as they were joined by another man and a woman.

'Detective Constable Maine,' Hollander said, introducing the man. Then, indicating the woman, 'Detective Constable Lister.'

Both officers looked grave. Neither Allyson nor Shelley knew what to say.

'We're going to need you to answer some questions,' Hollander told them. 'Mrs Jaymes, perhaps you can take Detective Lister somewhere quiet. Miss Bronson, Detective Maine will take a statement from you.'

Allyson took Detective Lister to her office. It all seemed so unreal. It was like an invasion, the forensic scientists, the ambulancemen, so many police swarming all over the place. And the phones were ringing off the hook. For God's sake someone make the phones stop ringing!

She answered the detective's questions as succinctly and helpfully as she could, knowing that by now everyone must be thinking she did it. She had the biggest motive, all she needed was opportunity. But it was all right, there was no need to panic. They would find out who did it, then everyone would forget they'd suspected her. But her alibi for the past three hours was so weak that it drove white-hot fear into her chest, and blinded her to where she was and why she was there. This was no longer a place she recognized, it wasn't her office, and the person who was with her had mistaken her for somebody else.

But at the end of it, after hours and hours of questions

and black coffee and watching her colleagues come in and out, they told her to go home.

She looked round for Shelley, but someone said Shelley had already gone, so she walked outside into the cold, garishly lit night and followed a policeman as he struggled to open a path through to her car. As she got in she heard a TV reporter telling the world that she'd just come out of the building and as far as they knew no arrests had been made yet.

Allyson drove in a trance back to the flat. She was afraid of being alone, but didn't know who to call. She'd have to speak to her mother and make sure she was OK. She thought of Mark and felt a sudden longing cut through the numbness. But then she thought of Bob, and the numbness returned. After that all she could see in her mind's eye was the image of them carrying Tessa's body away in a bag. It was an image she would never forget.

When she got home the message light was blinking wildly on her machine. Ignoring it she went to pour herself a drink. Her hands were shaking badly. She had to do something to calm herself down.

She sat in a chair, her coat still on. Everyone thought she had done it. They all believed she had finally flipped and smashed Tessa's brains in. She started to cry, so afraid she didn't know what to do. The phone rang. The machine picked up the call and she listened to a reporter's voice telling her which paper he was from and asking her to call back.

After a while she went into the hall and stood over the bags she'd carried in from the car. Two of them were from Waitrose. The other contained Shelley's gift. She stared at it for a long time, bizarre and frightening thoughts whirling round in her head. Her skull felt so tight it might be crushing her brain. Finally she knelt down on the floor and knocked over the other two bags as she took the gift out.

Minutes later the wrapping on Shelley's gift was open, the lid of the box was cast aside. Allyson's hands moved slowly, clumsily over the contents of all three bags. Her mind was barely registering her movements. Finally she was holding a wad of rolled up fabric. She looked at the ugly brown marks. Then carefully she unwrapped it, not wanting to drop the heavy object inside.

When it came free she looked at it, expressionlessly, breathlessly. It was the fan-dancer Allyson had given Shelley at Christmas, beautiful and bronze, and sculpted with such sublime expertise that the light seemed to bring it to life. It was the figurine Allyson had given Shelley at Christmas. It was the elegant Marcel Bouraine Allyson had given Shelley at Christmas . . . It was the figurine . . . The fan-dancer . . . Her chest was heaving, her hands were shaking . . .

Then suddenly the monstrous reality of what had happened erupted like a bomb in her head and as the figurine fell to the floor, she slumped back against the wall, quivering with terror and starting to gasp uncontrollably.

Chapter 17

The first signs of spring had been swallowed into a dark and chilling late afternoon. The sky outside was grey, the suddenly still air was like invisible ice. Detective Constables Lister and Maine had been up all night, so had many of their colleagues. This was a high-profile case and the boss wanted an arrest by the end of the day. It was looking increasingly likely that would happen.

DC Lister stifled a yawn. She'd taken a quick shower in the WPCs' locker room earlier, but it hadn't done much to revive her. DC Maine didn't look any better.

Inspector Hollander was scanning the early statements they'd taken, and lists of already documented evidence. Though he didn't look up, he was listening closely as the two detectives briefed him.

'The time of death has been established as being between seven fifty and eight o'clock,' Maine said. 'Cause of death was pretty obvious, list of suspects tentatively increased to three after Shelley Bronson called late last night to report a bronze figure missing from her flat. She says she first noticed it had disappeared after a visit from Bob Jaymes, Allyson Jaymes's husband. She's not saying she's sure he took it, because apparently Allyson Jaymes has got a key to the flat and could have let herself in any time without Shelley Bronson knowing.'

'And this figure was some sort of gift from Allyson

Jaymes?' Hollander said, looking at the scribbled notes that had been added to Shelley's statement.

'Yes. It's also now been confirmed as the murder weapon since Allyson Jaymes brought it in this morning.'

It was DC Lister's turn. She was a tall, large-boned woman with greying hair and deep-set eyes. She had taken Allyson's statement the night before, she was also who Allyson had asked to see when she and her mother, a proud but frightened-looking old lady, had come to the station earlier with what Allyson was claiming was a gift from Shelley. 'She says she gave the figurine to Shelley Bronson at Christmas, but Shelley gave it back to her last night, wrapped up in a bloodstained make-up gown.'

DI Hollander's face showed his dislike of the way things were going. 'So has someone talked to Shelley Bronson since we got the figurine?' he said.

'I did,' Maine answered. 'I went over to her flat earlier. She got pretty upset when I told her we had the figurine and what Allyson had said about it. She says the gift she gave Allyson last night was a Lalique clock, an item from her own collection that Allyson had always admired.'

'So where's the clock now?'

Maine looked at Lister, who shook her head. 'No-one seems to know,' he answered.

Hollander tugged at his lower lip. 'Things aren't looking very good for Mrs Jaymes, are they?' he commented. 'We've got at least a dozen witnesses who claim to have heard her threaten to harm the girl, and in some instances even kill her. We all know her husband left her for the girl and now, according to Shelley Bronson, she believed her new boyfriend, Mark Reiner, was also having an affair with the girl. Has anyone talked to Reiner?'

'I did,' Lister answered. 'He says he wasn't having an affair with Tessa Dukes, but that Shelley Bronson had intimated to Allyson that he was.'

'Oh, the tangled webs,' Hollander remarked, sighing. 'And Bob Jaymes? Do we have a statement from him yet?'

'Yes, it's there, sir,' Maine answered. 'He says he was at the Arsenal match last night and reckons the first he heard of anything was when he got home and turned on the news. We're still checking his alibi.'

'And the cars?' Hollander asked.

'So far we've checked out Allyson's, Shelley's and Bob Jaymes's,' Lister answered. 'Oh, and the Butler-Blythes', Allyson's parents. All have come back with clean bills of health.'

'Which can mean everything and nothing,' Hollander responded. He looked up. 'So what we're really saying here is that our chief suspect, our only suspect, is Allyson Jaymes, whose only alibi for between six and nine last night is a father who doesn't know what day of the week it is.'

'That's right,' Lister confirmed. 'She says she was looking after him while her mother went for a bite to eat with her sister-in-law. Apparently her mother was slightly late getting back, which was why Allyson didn't get to the restaurant until around nine fifteen.'

'Mmm,' Hollander grunted, still looking at Allyson's statement.

'Meanwhile, Shelley's stuck in traffic caused by the bomb scare in Chelsea last night,' Maine added.

'She was on her way from the office?'

'Yes. She says she left around eight with the intention of going home to change. But when she saw the traffic she realized she wasn't going to have time. So she went straight to the restaurant and arrived just after Allyson.'

'Did she see Tessa before she left?'

'She says only briefly. She went to check on her in the editing room and that was the last time she saw her.'

'And there was no-one else working late?'

'Apparently not. Except the editor, of course.'

Hollander was reading again. Then sighing he looked at Lister. 'What a bloody circus this is going to be,' he grumbled. 'Where's Allyson Jaymes now?'

'Still downstairs with her mother. They've been here all day. I think they're too afraid to go home.'

Maine rubbed a hand over his face. 'I say everything points to her. Let's wrap this up and go get some sleep.'

'Hey!' Lister protested. 'I know we're all tired, but don't let's make any hasty decisions. After all, Shelley Bronson we *know* was at the scene of the crime.'

'And three hours is plenty of time for Allyson Jaymes to get in her car, go to Shelley's flat and get the figurine, take it to Fulham, bash the victim's head in, get back in her car and drive back to Chelsea. And from what you're telling me about the old boy he wouldn't even know she was gone.'

'But we've checked her car. And her parents' car too,' Lister reminded him. 'They're clean. Forensics have been over her flat, but we already know the murder weapon was there.'

'What about Shelley Bronson's flat? Are they checking that too?'

'Nothing,' Maine informed him.

'Yet,' Lister added.

Maine threw her a look. 'I for one am totally satisfied with Shelley Bronson's story,' he said. 'It was bedlam out there last night, just like she said. The bomb scare brought everything to a standstill.'

'But how do we know she was in it?' Lister asked. 'Did anyone see her?'

'Where's her motive?' Hollander asked.

'Allyson claims Shelley was having an affair with her husband, prior to his affair with Tessa. She also claims that Shelley was jealous of her relationship with Mark Reiner.'

'Leading us to?'

'A frame-up, according to Allyson. In other words, if

Allyson's sent down on a murder charge then Mark Reiner might rediscover his interest in Shelley.'

'Rediscover?'

'They had some kind of fling, apparently, prior to Reiner getting involved with Allyson. Both he and Allyson say that he dumped Shelley in favour of Allyson.'

'Ah, the hell hath no fury motive,' Hollander declared. 'Always a good one.'

'But what we all seem to be forgetting here,' Maine pointed out, 'is that there's not a single shred of evidence pointing to her. Unlike Allyson Jaymes, who not only has motive and opportunity, but actually turns up with the murder weapon in her hand. What more are we looking for?'

Hollander turned to Lister.

'The restaurant owner's confirmed that he saw Shelley handing Allyson a box last night that was large enough to have contained the figurine,' Lister said, looking up as a uniformed officer put his head round the door.

'There's a woman downstairs claiming to be some kind of therapist to the deceased,' he told them. 'Name's Laura Risby.'

All eyebrows rose with interest. 'I'll talk to her,' Lister said. 'Just don't get carried away with any arrests until I'm back.'

The longer DC Lister listened to Laura Risby the more she was being forced to admit that things were looking grim for Allyson Jaymes. It seemed that Tessa Dukes had had some kind of fixation on Allyson, which in itself didn't amount to much, but when weighted with everything else could easily add another motive for the killing.

'It was all rather tragic,' Laura Risby was saying about Tessa. 'She grew up in a household where both her father and older brother regularly abused her, sexually,

424

and her mother either turned a blind eye, or simply didn't know. We'll never know which, but it's my guess that she didn't want to know, and when Tessa forced her to acknowledge it her answer was to laugh. It was undoubtedly nervous hysteria that provoked that reaction, but Tessa didn't understand that. They had a terrible fight, during which Tessa tried to strangle her mother. The father broke it up and the next day the mother shot and killed both her husband and her son and then herself. Tessa was sixteen when it happened. When she was eighteen, just after she started university, she had a breakdown, which was when I first met her. We've been seeing each other ever since, though not as regularly as I'd have liked, and I don't think Tessa's ever got any closer to understanding why her mother killed herself. She truly loved her mother, even though she blames her for what happened with her father and brother. They never had a chance to work anything through, and on the surface at least, I'd say Tessa seems to have been more traumatized by her mother's suicide than she was by the abuse. I think what she's been doing since is trying to recreate her family. Bob the father, Julian the brother and . . .'

'Julian?'

'A young man who works for the programme too. But he was with me last night, talking about Tessa and trying to understand why she's the way she is.'

Lister wrote Julian's name down, then nodded for Laura to continue.

'He told me he'd been worried about her lately, since she'd got back from Italy. She'd seemed depressed and withdrawn, and more preoccupied with Allyson than ever. You see, she'd cast Allyson in the role of her mother, someone she loved deeply, but wanted to punish too. She blamed herself for her mother's suicide, and with Allyson, in that cruelly perverse way the mind sometimes has, she was trying to see if she could do it

425

again. I don't believe she wanted to succeed, quite the reverse in fact. She wanted Allyson to be stronger than her mother, that way her own faults might not be so much to blame for the suicide, if they weren't capable of provoking it again.'

Lister inhaled. 'Sounds like the girl had a lot of problems.'

Laura nodded. 'In recent weeks Tessa and Bob broke up,' she went on. 'It appears that Allyson's interest in him had faded, so Tessa's did too. Also, despite what we've read about Bob Jaymes in the press, the drinking, the loss of his professional standing, etcetera, I don't think he proved as malleable as Tessa's father who she could get to do anything in exchange for her favours.'

'You mean she was encouraging her father in the abuse?'

'Sometimes, yes. And her brother. Other times they beat her and forced themselves on her. She says she never discussed it with her mother until the end, but I think she was always trying to tell her mother in other ways. She was an exceptionally intelligent girl, but terribly damaged and very confused when it came to communication. She expected people to understand a lot more than they possibly could. Allyson was one of those people. She wanted Allyson to love her, but at the same time she was doing everything she could to make Allyson hate her, because deep down inside she doesn't feel worthy of love. So going after Bob was an attempt to become a part of the love Allyson shared with him, to feel as though she belonged to them both, as she had to her parents. It was also a way of hurting Allyson, in the same way she'd hurt her mother by trying to make her father love her more. Then, when it became known that Allyson was involved with Mark Reiner, Tessa tried to get involved with him too. As far as I'm aware Mr Reiner never allowed their relationship to go beyond the professional, but Tessa can be very persuasive and I hadn't seen her in a while. Maybe something did happen between them, and maybe that's why Allyson . . . ' She stopped, suddenly uneasy, but Lister knew what she'd been about to say. *Maybe that's why Allyson finally lost control and killed her.*

'So there you have it,' Lister said, finishing up Laura Risby's story for Hollander and Maine. 'One severely damaged teenager with a mother fixation on Allyson Jaymes, whose life she was systematically taking apart.'

'I remember that case,' Hollander said. 'When the mother shot herself after killing her husband and her son. Everyone wondered what would happen to the girl . . . Well, I guess now we know.'

They were silenced for a moment by the horrible tragedy of it all.

'So do we arrest her?' Maine said.

Slowly Hollander nodded. Then rubbing his eyes he said, 'It's not every day we get a suspect who brings in the murder weapon themselves then sits downstairs waiting to be cuffed.'

'Which is what bothers me, sir,' Lister said.

'I know. It bothers me too. But you've heard the evidence, Sheila, now you give me one good reason why we shouldn't arrest her.'

Lister's eyes remained on his, until finally, feeling heavy with fatigue and defeat, she got up from her chair and walked to the door.

Allyson and her mother were in the station canteen, at a table that had been cleared many times of its empty milk packets and plastic coffee cups. They'd been there ever since speaking to DC Lister that morning, when they'd decided between them that the only sensible thing to do was take the figurine, together with the make-up gown it had been wrapped in, to the police.

Allyson looked exhausted. They both did. Neither of

427

them had slept, after Allyson had driven over to her mother's last night to tell her what had happened. It had taken a while to calm Peggy down, for her shock and fear were as great as Allyson's. Then, feeling they should have a man to help them, Peggy had wanted to call Bob, but Allyson wouldn't. She'd wanted only to try and make her father remember that she had been there the entire time between six and nine last night. But of course he didn't. He didn't remember her at all.

'You should go home and see to Daddy,' Allyson said now. 'We could be here for hours yet.'

'Aunt Faye is looking after him. He'll be fine.'

'But you're tired and . . .'

'I'm not leaving you here,' Peggy said.

DC Lister came into the canteen and walked over to them. 'Hello,' she said.

Allyson's heart was in her mouth. Something had happened, she could tell by the policewoman's demeanour.

'I'd like you to come with me,' Lister said, looking at Allyson.

Allyson glanced at her mother, then stood up. 'What's happening?' she said. 'Where are we going?'

Lister looked down at Peggy, then back to Allyson.

Panic swelled in Allyson. 'You're going to arrest me, aren't you?'

Lister nodded.

'No!' Allyson cried. 'I didn't do it. I swear I didn't do it.' She started to turn away, as though to run from the room. Several officers rose from surrounding tables, but Lister caught her and held her tight.

'No,' Allyson sobbed. 'No, no, no.'

'She didn't do it,' Peggy sobbed too. 'I know my daughter. She'd never kill anyone. Please. You've got to believe her.'

Lister looked into Peggy's terrified face and wished

428

there was something she could say, but all she managed was, 'I'm sorry. I'm truly sorry.'

After Allyson's personal effects were taken she was led to a cell and locked in. Her mother sat on a bench in the corridor outside and refused to leave. She had to be near her daughter, couldn't leave her to deal with this alone.

DC Lister made the call to the Butler-Blythes' family lawyer on Peggy's behalf. He was going to sort out the best man for the job, then come with him to the station. He spoke to Peggy, but couldn't persuade her to go home. Lister was concerned about her. She wasn't a young woman, and this trauma was taking its toll. But she understood the fierce and protective love of a parent, she had parents and children of her own.

Were it not for Peggy's vigil Lister might have gone home after the arrest, but not wanting to leave the woman without a friend she lingered awhile, returning to her desk and going over the statements again, trying to find something that would satisfy that niggling doubt in her mind that some crucial factor was being overlooked. But though she searched and searched she just kept coming back to the facts that were right there on the page.

So maybe it was simply that she didn't want it to be true. She liked Allyson, the whole world liked Allyson, and no-one wanted the shining image of a woman who was known for her compassion and kindness to turn out to be the glittering and angelic front for a monster. The problem was, there was nothing in the evidence to support any doubt. What was more, Allyson didn't only have one, she had several motives, as well as a publicly declared intent, the opportunity, and, as Maine had pointed out, ultimately the murder weapon itself. And Lister had to admit, if she had some cocky young kid trying to screw up her life and make her pay for sins that weren't even hers, she'd want to be rid of her too –

though of course she wouldn't resort to murder. But that was her, and no-one was investigating her, so the real question was, would Allyson Jaymes resort to murder?

Lister turned her thoughts to Shelley Bronson, the wronged and rejected woman. The only one who really stood to gain with both Tessa and Allyson out of the way. The gain being the extremely eligible and apparently fantastically rich Mark Reiner, who was repeatedly calling to ask if he could either see or speak to Allyson. Lister noted that the husband hadn't called at all, or certainly not that she knew of, but maybe someone else had answered the phone.

She read Shelley Bronson's statement again, then on a hunch she picked up the phone and called the uniformed officer who had driven Shelley home after her initial interrogation at the *Soirée* offices. The lad wasn't happy about being dragged out of bed, but by the time their call was over Lister's adrenalin was starting to pump. The young officer had merely confirmed everything that was in his report: how he'd driven Shelley back to the restaurant she'd been at earlier with Allyson, watched her get into her car and drive off, then he'd returned to the scene of the crime. The only thing he'd omitted from his report was the make of Shelley's car.

Armed with this new information Lister made a few more calls, upset a few more people by getting them out of bed, then went to consult the large map of south-west London that was pinned to the office wall. The clock on her desk was ticking into the early hours as she traced all the possible routes from the *Soirée* offices to the restaurant, then from the *Soirée* offices to the restaurant via Shelley's flat in Kensington. Had they not all been so tired they'd probably have worked this out a lot sooner, but going without sleep rarely sharpened the mind.

It was just before two in the morning that Lister got a call back from the owner of a car-hire company confirming that one of his staff had rented a black Volkswagen Audi to Shelley Bronson on the morning of the murder. She'd returned it early the next day, already washed and vacuumed, and had paid in cash. The car the young uniformed officer had returned Shelley to, which had been parked a few streets from the restaurant, was a black Volkswagen Audi. Shelley's own car, the one that forensics had gone over, was a silver Lexus.

Lister got on the phone to her colleague, Geoff Maine. 'Shelley Bronson hired a car on the day of the murder,' she said. 'She returned it the next day, already cleaned and paid for it in cash. The roads between the office and her flat weren't affected by the bomb scare, meaning she had time to get home, change and drive to the restaurant by nine fifteen.'

'Jesus Christ, Sheila,' he grumbled. 'What time is it?'

'The reason we couldn't find anything in her car was because she was driving a rental!' Lister almost shouted.

Maine was still coming to. 'So we talk to her in the morning, right?'

'No, we go now.'

'Now!'

'Trust me on this, Geoff. We need to go now.'

Even with no make-up and her hair tousled from sleep Shelley Bronson still managed to look gorgeous. Lister noted the expensive nightwear, the perfume, and the exceptional collection of furniture, all from the art deco period. Lister could even name a few of the designers. For example, she knew who had made the exquisite fan dancer that had been put to such heinous use, she also knew that Shelley had put in a request to have the dancer returned when everything was over.

As Lister had expected, this dead of night visit had unnerved Shelley, though that in itself proved nothing, as a visit from the police at that time would unnerve anyone. And despite her unease, Shelley wasn't hostile, in fact she was perfectly polite as she invited them to sit down and asked if she could get them a drink.

They sat, but refused the drink. Shelley sat too, drawing her fine satin robe more tightly around herself. Lister guessed she was naked underneath, and noticed that Maine was probably coming to the same conclusion.

'So, what can I do for you at this hour?' Shelley asked.

Lister smiled. 'We just need you to clear something up for us.'

Shelley glanced at Maine, showing she would be more comfortable if he were in charge.

Lister continued. 'You said in your statement that you left the office around seven fifty, possibly a little after, and were stuck in traffic more or less until you got to the restaurant.'

Shelley nodded. 'I was going to go home, but when I saw how bad it was I decided I probably wouldn't . . . have enough time.'

Lister noted the slight tremble in her voice. 'Can you remember where you were when Allyson called you on your mobile to say she was going to be late?'

'I think I was by the cinema. The one on the corner of Beaufort Street. I can't say for certain though.'

'And that was about what time?'

'Just before nine, I think.'

'You knew Allyson was babysitting her father that evening?'

'Yes. She told me earlier in the day.'

Lister smiled. 'Good, so that all checks out.' She glanced over at Maine, though not before she'd seen the relief in Shelley's eyes.

Shelley was about to get up when Lister started talking again.

'Why didn't you mention you were driving a hire car on the day of the murder?' she asked.

Panic stripped away the relief. Shelley's lovely face was now deathly pale. If she was wise, Lister thought, she'd refuse to say anything now without a lawyer.

Her voice was husky, cracked. 'My car was in the garage. I always hire another when mine's in the garage. You can check. It's something I always do.'

'And do you always clean it before you take it back?'

Shelley's eyes darted to Maine. 'Sometimes,' she said.

Lister could almost smell her fear. 'We'd like to take a look at the clothes you were wearing on the day of the murder,' she said.

Shelley's eyes were almost wild. 'They're at the cleaners.'

Of course.

'I think I should call a lawyer,' Shelley said.

'Yes, Miss Bronson,' Lister responded. 'I think you should.'

Shelley could feel the cold seeping far into her bones. DC Lister was still with her. Maine had looked as though he wanted to stay, but after some quiet consultation with Lister he'd left. Her lawyer, who was in Wales, couldn't be there until morning.

She didn't speak to the policewoman, she had nothing to say. Her words were all wrapped up inside her, entangled in images of the past two days. She was more afraid than she'd ever been, yet she felt disconnected, apart from the reality of the nightmare, as though it were happening to somebody else and she was just a horrified observer. Her mind was assailed by flashes of all that had happened, and what might have happened. She could see the abstract figure that had walked into the edit suite and stood over the girl. She could see its shadow, looming on the wall, its eyes looking down at Tessa's small, still head, studying the little whorls and tufts of shiny dark hair, hearing the sounds of the film, seeing the unmanicured hands on the console. Then she was hearing the wild and crazy thoughts, seeing the venom, feeling the hate . . .

She stifled a cry at the image of the statue rising, then swinging down brutally on the fragile skull. How many times? Someone had said five.

And now Tessa was dead.

But she couldn't be. It was inconceivable; beyond comprehension that Allyson's plump and pretty nemesis was lying cold and stiff under a sheet somewhere, no longer able to inflict herself on other people's lives. Shelley had never liked the girl and she had no pity for her now. All she had was anger – and a hot, paralysing fear that was blurring her senses and crushing her mind.

By the time she was ready to leave the sun was filtering through the clouds, cresting the rooftops in a sluggish pink glow as a new day began. She felt frighteningly calm. Calm and exhausted. Lister must have thought she might kill herself, because ever since reading her her rights the woman hadn't left her side. Not even while she showered and dressed for what could be the last time in her beloved home, had Lister left her.

She walked into the sitting room and looked around. Her courage was now no more than a plucky flame in a dying fire. How could she bear to leave? What could she do to stop this nightmare going any further? She imagined them all talking about her in the office. It was difficult to envisage the place without her in it. They'd been her family for the past eight years, but they'd all scorn her now. Would Allyson, she wondered.

Quite suddenly she started to scream. The noise tore from her in harsh, petrified cries, breaking her out of the hypnotizing horror of what she was facing. Suddenly it was real. All so horribly, terrifyingly real that she might go insane.

Lister caught her by the shoulders and held her tight.

'I didn't do it,' she sobbed. 'I swear, I didn't do it.' Her face was ravaged, almost demented, her body was shaking so hard she could barely stand.

'It's OK,' Lister soothed. 'It'll be OK.'

'*Noooo!* You don't understand. I didn't do it! I didn't kill her.'

'Sssh,' Lister whispered. 'Of course not.' It was what they all said when finally they realized it was the only thing left to say.

A few miles away, in the chill early morning, a young PC escorted Allyson and her mother through the drizzling rain to their car. Allyson's face was chalk-white, her eyes were bloodshot and shadowed. She was weak with relief, yet heavy with fear. She knew they'd gone to arrest Shelley, but what she didn't know was what Shelley would say, or where any of it would end.

The PC slammed her car door and waited for her to start the engine. As she drove away there was no-one from the press to record her release, no-one to witness her return to freedom – or to tell her how long she might keep it. After all, they'd believed in her guilt enough to arrest her once, what might Shelley tell them to make it happen again?

Chapter 18

Mark Reiner got out of his car and looked across the cemetery to where a small, huddled group stood in the rain. Further away, at a distance that was almost respectable, was a much larger group, most of them clutching cameras and notebooks. It was a horrible, bleak day in every way, for no-one could help feeling the terrible sadness that came with the senseless and untimely death of a young girl who had suffered so much in her short life. The papers had been full of her story since the details had come out, the nightly news never failed to mention it.

Earlier in the day Mark had gone to talk to the staff of *Soirée*. Their sense of shock and grief was evident the moment he'd walked into the office, reminding him of passengers stranded aboard a boat that had lost its engine. He'd sympathized with them, for none of them, including him, had ever known anyone who was murdered, nor anyone who had committed a murder. It was hard to deal with, harder still to understand, and not even the kind of headlines that were being splashed across the papers, like Producer Murders Presenter or A Soirée with Death, seemed to be bringing home the reality. Shelley was still in custody and according to the papers no-one who had tried to see her had so far succeeded.

For his part Mark avoided the press, channelling the

statements that needed to be made through a company spokesman. Nothing had yet been made public about *Soirée*'s future, out of respect to the programme's makers he'd wanted to speak to them first – and in person, though they'd almost certainly guessed that the suspension of transmission was going to lead to the programme being cancelled. That morning he had confirmed that it would be, though he'd also told them that Clive Dansing, who was about to take over from Stella Cornbright, would welcome any ideas they might have for a completely new show. He could see it was the kind of therapy they needed, to help draw them out of the shock, but when they began trying to include him in their discussions he'd informed them that from this point on Dansing was in charge, and would report to Mark only when necessary.

'Are you OK?'

Mark looked at his sister-in-law, Claudia. She'd insisted on coming to the funeral with him, and now they were here he was glad that she had.

Holding an umbrella over them both, he steered her towards the mourners who were starting to file into the chapel. They consisted almost entirely of the *Soirée* team, with the exception of an uncle who had been tracked down by the police, the two detectives who were involved in the case, and Allyson's husband and mother. Of Allyson herself there was no sign, but he guessed she was already inside.

The chapel was cold and dark, but the flowers helped to cheer it, and the candles cast a warm glow over the altar. Mark and Claudia slipped into a pew near the back, and knelt to pray. With his eyes closed Mark thought of Tessa and felt weighted by the unthinkable reality that they were here to cremate her. Knowing what he did now he could only feel the profoundest regret that he had done nothing to help her, for that night in Italy had surely been enough to show him how disturbed and desperate she was. A long talk with Laura Risby had explained more, and though he had no idea if anyone could have truly ended her torment, certainly someone could have tried. And that someone could so easily have been him – and Allyson. It was something they could have done together. But being so tied up in their own affairs, and so focused on what Tessa was doing to Allyson instead of why she was doing it, they hadn't recognized the need for help. And now it was too late. Accepting that was almost as hard as accepting everything else that went with it, but how much worse it must be for Allyson considering the complex role she had played in Tessa's life – and ultimately in her death.

Seeing her at the front, dressed in black and seated between her mother and husband, he tried to imagine the aching futility of what they had been through, unwitting and now badly damaged pawns in a game they hadn't even been aware of until it was over. The trauma of her arrest must have been hard for Allyson, but her release had come so soon after that the worst of this now, apart from the tragedy of Tessa's death, must be knowing what Shelley had tried to do to her. Friends for so long and now this. How badly it must hurt, and he couldn't help wondering if Allyson blamed him in some way too, holding him accountable for the pain he had caused Shelley which in the end had driven her to do what she had. It was impossible to know, for they hadn't spoken since the day of the murder, and it was perhaps still too early for any of them to attach any kind of meaning or understanding to what had happened.

The organ droned on, merging finally into the opening strains of a well-known hymn as the minister entered, the coffin and pall-bearers behind him. As everyone rose Mark felt Claudia's hand on his arm. The small procession passed. He looked at the coffin, and thought of Tessa's ruined body lying peacefully inside. He looked away and tried to sing, though he barely heard the words leaving his lips. He was thinking now of Shelley, and how she might be feeling today, for she surely must know what was happening. Though he'd spoken to her lawyers, he hadn't attempted to see her, and knew that it was unlikely he would until the trial.

Everyone sat, and in their still fragile stupor listened to the minister as he read from the Bible. A while later he asked everyone to pray, then Julian, a young boy from the programme, went forward to read a piece he'd written himself. Like everyone else Mark was profoundly moved, not only by the words the boy had written himself, but by the relief of knowing that someone had cared, and apparently very much.

Then the worst moment was upon them, as the coffin moved slowly, gracefully away from them, taking with it the young girl no-one had ever really known, and now never would. It was the hardest, cruellest test of all, watching the curtains close and knowing that for Tessa it was all over now and nothing anyone did was ever going to make it right. She hadn't deserved such a life, nor had she deserved such a death, and though the capriciousness and challenges of fate were beyond anyone's control, it was inevitable that each in their own way would feel they had failed her.

Outside in the cold again, Mark and Claudia offered their condolences to an uncle who hadn't seen his niece since she was five. But there was no-one else to accept them, and they needed to be given. The man was courteous, though obviously embarrassed. But no-one hung around for long. Eager to be out of the rain and away from the grim rituals of farewell they were soon finding their way back to their cars. No wake had been planned, which somehow made the occasion sadder than ever.

'I feel I should go and say something to Allyson,' Claudia said, as Mark held the door open for her to get into the car. 'Do you mind?'

'Of course not,' he answered.

She was looking up at him. 'You won't come with me?'

'No.'

From where he was standing he watched as Claudia ran over to where Allyson and her mother were talking to a few of the *Soirée* team. For the moment he couldn't see Bob, then he noticed him talking to the detectives. No doubt the press would be drawing their own conclusions from what they were seeing today, and it was partly because of them that Mark didn't want to go over there now, for he – doubtless Allyson, also – didn't want the event of Tessa's funeral to be upstaged by speculation on where Allyson's relationships with her husband and Mark Reiner might now be going. Of course the fact that Bob was with her and Mark wasn't, would provide an easy assessment for now, but Mark knew that there was nothing easy about this, nothing easy at all. And as his eyes met Allyson's for a long and torturous few moments he knew that no matter how hard this was for him, for her it was nothing short of hell.

The days were seeming to merge into one, with no real shape or meaning, as the shock of Tessa's death, her own arrest, then Shelley's, took its time to subside. It was hard to believe that three weeks had gone by since the funeral, though in some ways it felt like three years. Or maybe it was another lifetime, for there was something strangely disconcerting about standing here with Bob, in the front porch of their country home, facing a battery of press who had come to witness the Jaymes's reconciliation being made official.

Bob's arm was wrapped protectively around her as she blinked at the flashbulbs and he dealt with the barrage of questions, confirming that they were now back together and intended to stay that way. Yes, he had made mistakes, he admitted, they both had, but life was full of them and though naturally they deeply regretted Tessa's death, they were legally unable to make any more comment than that.

'Bob! Is it true you're about to sign a deal with Sky?' someone shouted.

Bob laughed. 'It's being talked about,' he answered.

'Did you catch the Liverpool match last night?' someone else wanted to know.

'A great game,' he answered.

'Allyson! Now that *Soirée*'s been cancelled can you tell us what you're going to do?'

Bob's arm tightened around her. 'She won't be doing anything until after the trial,' he told them. 'She needs to rest now, and be looked after.'

Irritated that he'd answered for her, Allyson continued to smile and decided to let him carry on. His euphoria at their reunion was, for many, infectious, and as they were all having such a good time she didn't see any point in ruining it. Not that her answers would have done so, it was simply that she didn't want to pretend a lightness of spirit she was so very far from feeling. A young girl was dead, and her best friend was in prison. There was nothing to celebrate in that, and it felt horrible, callous even, to be standing here pretending everything was all right when it was so very far from being all right that there were times she felt she might be going out of her mind.

Her biggest enemy was fear, for she was so afraid now of what the future might hold, for her and for Shelley, that she could think about nothing else. She tormented herself night and day with the horror of being arrested again, of being locked in the prison where Shelley was now, of ultimately not being able to prove her innocence. Yet no-one thought she'd done it, there was no finger of blame pointing at her, so why couldn't she stop this self-torture and take charge of what was happening around her? It was a rational question that was constantly swept aside in a tide of erratic and destructive emotion, for the very thought of making plans for the future was simply too much, and maybe too tempting for fate. It was easier just to let everyone else make the decisions, organize her life for her so that all she had to do was go along with it, until the trial was over and she knew for certain whether or not she was going to hold onto her freedom.

She was startled back into the moment by someone asking her a question. 'Allyson! Are you in touch with Shelley at all?' they wanted to know.

She started to answer, but Bob said, 'Come on, you guys, you know we can't discuss anything to do with the case. How about you ask us where we're planning to go for our second honeymoon?'

Allyson stopped listening again. She was thinking now about the letter she'd received from Shelley, two weeks ago, asking her to come. It was the first communication they'd had since the murder, and that was all it had said: 'Dear Allyson, I am enclosing a visiting order. Please come. Shelley.'

Allyson had meant to go. She'd even got as far as the prison itself, but at the last she'd turned away. She just hadn't been up to dealing with it then. She'd been too afraid, too disoriented still to grasp the steadying hands of reason. She'd tried to remind herself that she had no need to fear Shelley. Shelley couldn't harm her where she was, and even if Shelley persisted with her claims of innocence, there was still nothing to say Allyson had done it, nothing even to put her at the scene of the crime. But at the time the thought of seeing Shelley, of looking into her eyes and knowing . . .

But she felt ready to see Shelley now. She'd go any time Shelley wanted, but having already been let down once it seemed Shelley wasn't prepared to take the chance again. So Allyson had appealed to Shelley's lawyers, who had come back with the curt and frightening response that Shelley would see Allyson in court, where justice would be done.

When she'd first received that message Allyson had been so angry and afraid that she'd found herself considering all kinds of panicked and irrational acts, like going to the newspapers and giving them a full and graphic account of what Shelley was really like, and what had really happened that night. But of course she didn't know, so how could she do that? How could she do anything but live in daily dread of the trial, and lie awake night after night imagining all kinds of horrific scenarios that would restore Shelley's freedom and reclaim hers. After all, she wouldn't be the first to suffer a miscarriage of justice, nor would Shelley be the first killer to walk free.

Killer. Oh God, how had that word ever come into their lives this way? How could she ever really think of Shelley as a killer when she knew her so well, had loved her like a sister, and even now, despite all the fear and misgivings, she still cared for her deeply. Which was why she had called Pearl, Shelley's mother, in the hope that Pearl could somehow intervene and persuade Shelley to let Allyson visit. Pearl's response had chilled Allyson to the bone. 'Shelley must pay for what she did,' the woman had said. 'I want no more to do with her.'

That Shelley's own mother was so ready to believe in Shelley's guilt had torn at Allyson's heart in a way that nothing else in this whole horrible mess had. Shelley had to have someone to stand by her, it was only right, only fair, but who else was there, except Allyson? And how could she support her when Shelley was so determined to hang her innocence on the proof of Allyson's guilt?

Suddenly aware of what Bob was saying, Allyson felt herself cringing, and wanted desperately to go inside. This ludicrous charade, she knew, had been staged as much for Mark's benefit as for anyone else's, to let him know that Bob and Allyson were still very much in love, despite everything, and were looking forward to picking up the pieces of their lives. She prayed to God that Mark wasn't watching, and if he was she willed him to know it was a lie. She was only here because she couldn't bear what the press would make of it if she was with him so soon after Tessa's death.

Would he understand that? Would he know how desperately she wanted to be with him, to be able to draw from his strength and find some moments of peace in his understanding? But she couldn't do that to him, not while there was still a chance she'd be blamed for Tessa's murder, and when she didn't even know for certain if he was as convinced of her innocence as everyone else seemed to be. Those moments at Tessa's funeral, when their eyes had met and the rest of the world had ceased to exist for a while, were all she had to persuade her that he still cared. But now, after three weeks of such destructive anxiety and self-doubt, the power of that look had diluted and she no longer knew what to believe, especially when he'd made no attempt to call her.

At last the questions began to peter out, and Bob announced they were going inside. Shielding her eyes from the bright evening sun, Allyson looked out at the ragged group with their cameras and notebooks. How loyally they had all rallied behind her, hardly questioning her innocence, and seeming so eager to believe that she, the model of compassion and stability, was wholly intact. Even those who had attempted to put her in the frame of guilt had been unable to prove she was anywhere but at her parents' house during those crucial three hours. So she was the woman who had been gravely wronged, and still was for the doubts and aspersions being cast upon her by Shelley's lawyers and the few remaining sceptics in the press. Maybe one of those sceptics was the pretty young reporter who'd been making eyes at Bob throughout the proceedings. Or no, she wouldn't be a sceptic, she'd only be another pathetic young female who'd fall willingly into Bob's arms were he to give her a sign. Suddenly Allyson wanted to laugh. The girl's timing couldn't be more off, for Bob was still too shaken by how close he had come to ruin to put his future in jeopardy now. But give him a while, Allyson thought, and, crushing the hope that the while wouldn't be long, she turned back inside.

Her mother was standing in the hall, waiting. Allyson hugged her warmly then led her through to the kitchen. This was all proving such a terrible strain on Peggy, who looked so much older now than she had just a few weeks ago. And there was still the trial to be got through.

'Well, I think that went well, don't you?' Bob said, following them in. 'So what do you say we open some champagne to celebrate?'

Allyson looked at her mother, who was about to plug in the kettle. Peggy had wanted this reunion, but only because it was what she was used to. She was too old to welcome change, and things were better kept in the family. It was another reason Allyson had allowed herself to go along with the reconciliation – after the way her mother had stood by her she felt she owed her something in return.

'I'll go and get it,' Peggy said. 'I expect it's in the cellar, isn't it?'

As she left the kitchen Bob walked over to Allyson and put his arms around her. 'So what do you think of the second honeymoon?' he said, starting to kiss her neck. 'Bali OK for you?'

She wondered how he was going to pay for it when his work was still so thin on the ground. But of course they wouldn't be going, so all she said was, 'We can't go anywhere until the trial's over.'

'I know,' he murmured, still kissing her. 'God, I've missed you.'

She knew exactly what that meant, for though he'd been with her virtually every day since the murder, they'd been staying with her parents, and until now she'd insisted on sleeping alone.

'Bob, don't,' she said. 'Mum'll be back any second . . .'

He laughed. 'We're not doing anything she hasn't seen us doing before,' he reminded her. 'In fact, it'd probably cheer her up no end to come back and find us in flagrante.'

'I hope you're not serious,' she said, knowing he wasn't.

He tried to kiss her again, but this time she managed to shrug him off and to give herself something to do, she plugged in the kettle.

She allowed several seconds to pass, staring down at nothing, and feeling his eyes as though they were caging her in. Then she made herself turn round and to her surprise her heart contracted when she saw how hurt and concerned he was, despite his efforts to conceal it.

'I'm prepared to wait,' he told her. 'It doesn't matter how long.'

She reached for his hand. 'Bob, I know this is hard for you,' she said softly, 'and I know it isn't what you want to hear, but I've already told you I don't know if this can work. I'm not even sure if I love you any more.'

His eyes fell away and she thought how much younger he looked when stripped of his panache and charisma. He was left awkward and somehow raw, like a child who'd been abandoned in a place it didn't know. Then a sudden, unbidden thought of Shelley darkened her mind, and the dread that came with it made her turn away from his confusion as though it was an intruder. All she could see now, in the haunting drama of her mind's eye, was the horrifying image of Tessa's final moments, and the feral madness of the woman who had beaten her to death.

Shelley's manner was aloof, imperious, a calculated and convincing performance to disguise the fear that she was

446

too proud to show. She walked into the visitors' room where two suited men were waiting. She was in her daily uniform of jeans, trainers, and a grey striped T-shirt. Her hair was tied back, her olive-skinned face was beautiful and pale.

She surveyed her lawyers with cautious yet uncompromising eyes, knowing that they were going to try once again to persuade her to enter a plea of diminished responsibility, in the hope of reducing the murder charge to manslaughter.

The door behind her closed. She moved towards the one empty chair and sat down carefully. Seeing her wince one of the lawyers moved forward to help her, but she shrugged him away. The pain of rape with hard objects, the humiliation of all she was being forced to suffer in this sealed-up hell of a women's prison, was nothing to the terror of a sentence that would keep her here for years, maybe even the rest of her life. So no, there would be no deals with the prosecution. They had no real evidence with which to convict her, so she was going to take her chances with a jury and plead not guilty. If they found in her favour she'd be a free woman.

'We've got a date for the trial,' Roscoe, the barrister, told her. He was a thin, attractive man of great poise and predictable arrogance. 'It's been set for July 4th.'

Shelley's insides turned over. Eight more weeks then please *please* God . . .

Her solicitor was a kindly man, with a smooth complexion and tender eyes. 'Shelley,' he said, 'I'm going to ask you again to consider . . .'

'The answer's no,' she said, cutting him off.

'But we don't have anything new! We'd hoped to by now . . .'

'What are you looking for? An alibi?' she snapped. 'I don't have one, Ed, and well you know it. But what I do have is a motive, the opportunity and the big fat mistake of not telling anyone about the hire car.'

'So why didn't you?'

'I told you, I don't know.' Her eyes moved from Ed's anxious face to the barrister's, and, suddenly too exhausted to maintain the hostility, she sighed heavily and allowed some of her angst and vulnerability to show. 'I suppose because I thought it would just complicate matters further,' she said. 'That if they knew I'd hired a car they'd think ... Well, what they think now.'

'The garage owner is going to testify that he found nothing wrong with your Lexus,' the barrister reminded her.

'The ABS light kept coming on. I just wanted him to check it out, make sure there was nothing wrong with the brakes. So, he's going to testify that there wasn't.'

'I don't think it's going to sit well with a jury.'

Shelley's eyes closed. Somewhere inside her chest was a wall of resentment and anger and unbridgeable fear. But it would be all right. She would get out of here. She just had to keep remembering that she didn't do it, that she'd already left the building, that she'd been stuck in traffic, that the gift she'd given Allyson was the Lalique clock ...

'Have you found the clock?' she asked, looking at the barrister.

His face showed his discomfort as he shook his head.

They didn't believe her. They thought she was lying about the clock ...

'We've spoken to the police,' Ed said. 'They've searched everywhere, but so far no clock.'

'Did they ask Allyson? I take it they asked Allyson.'

Ed nodded. 'Yes, they asked Allyson. She still says the gift you gave her that night was the fan dancer.'

Shelley covered her face with her hands. Oh God, no, no, no. Everything was going to work out all right for Allyson, because everything always worked out all right for Allyson. But no! Not this time. This time it was going to work out for Shelley . . .

The restaurant was crowded and noisy; pots of steaming pasta and pans of simmering sauces cluttered up the open-plan kitchens, along with deliciously pungent herbs and chefs with high hats.

Bob and Allyson and a group of their friends were at a large round corner table that was laden with wine and water, fresh garlic bread and succulent bruschetta. Though she wasn't facing into the room Allyson could feel a thousand eyes boring into her back, all watching and wondering, dying to ask and longing to know. Was she really as innocent as everyone was saying? Or was she the one who had smashed that poor girl's head in? Such grim and appalled fascination followed her everywhere now.

Todd was talking, holding forth on the wayward shenanigans of the market that day. Janet, his wife, plunged in with some irony while helping herself to more bread. Christian was a novelist whose book was teetering on the edge of success; his wife, Helena, was a fashion designer who modelled her own line. They'd known each other for more years than any of them cared to count, this kind of get-together was regular, and so excruciatingly normal it made Allyson want to scream.

But she didn't. She merely joined in with the wit and repartee, drinking more wine than she should and eating no food at all, until Bob cut her a corner of bruschetta and fed her himself. She even licked his fingers afterwards, allowing it to be the sexual come-on he'd hope for, and evoking the kind of laughter they all enjoyed. It was as though his affair with Tessa, their break-up, her affair with Mark and Tessa's murder had never happened. Which was OK. It was good to pretend it hadn't, because in less than two weeks her entire life would be consumed by the trial, so these evenings with friends were a welcome and needed respite from the angst. They were also a convenient excuse not to be alone with Bob.

'Hey, Ally, did you call Clive Dansing today?' Janet asked her. 'Didn't you say you were going to?'

'Who?' Christian wanted to know.

'Clive Dansing, he's my new boss,' Allyson answered, feeling her insides close up. 'He took over from Stella.'

'You didn't tell me you were going to call him,' Bob accused.

'It was just a thought,' she answered, forcing a smile. 'I didn't do it. But I'll have to sooner or later, if I intend to go back to work.'

'But you won't be going back yet,' he reminded her.

'No,' and in an effort to keep her patience she turned to Todd and said, 'I was thinking of cashing in a few investments. Can I call you tomorrow?'

'Sure,' he answered. 'You know the number.'

The pasta arrived, and the subject of Allyson's return to work was soon forgotten. Except by Bob, but he didn't bring it up again until the ludicrous charade of normality was over and they were back in their own home, getting ready for bed.

'There's no programme any more,' he reminded her bluntly, 'so what do you think you're going back to?'

'I don't know,' she answered. 'But I'm still under contract and maybe . . .'

When she didn't finish he stopped hanging up his clothes and looked at her with accusing eyes. 'Maybe what?' he said sharply. 'You'll see Mark Reiner?'

She was in the bathroom with the door open, but she was cleaning her teeth so she had only to lean over the basin to hide the sudden rush of nerves that had sprung into life. *Yes, of course it was because she might see Mark, was he such a fool that he had to ask?* But she smothered the anger, spat out the toothpaste and drying her mouth she said, 'I keep trying to tell you how afraid I am of this trial, how terrified I am that there won't be a life for me after, but you don't listen, do you? You don't understand what this is like for me, so you don't understand why I need to speak to Clive Dansing, to find out what his plans might be for the rest of my contract, if he even has any. It's my way of trying to see beyond the next few weeks, of projecting my hopes to a place that has nothing to do with the trial. You can't even imagine what a huge thing it is for me to dare to be hopeful, because all you can think about is your jealousy of Mark, and what any of this might do to you.'

He was coming towards hers. 'Oh God, Ally,' he groaned, 'I'm sorry, I'm sorry. You're right, I am being selfish about this, but only because I'm so afraid of losing you. It haunts me all the time, what my life was like when we weren't together, how it would be if I had to live without you again . . .'

'But you only think about me leaving you for Mark!' she shouted. 'You don't think about me going to prison, which is the most likely reason I'd leave you right now. But you don't care about that, do you? Me being locked away for something I didn't do is more acceptable than me leaving you for another man . . .'

'No! No, you've got it wrong,' he cried. 'I know I'm not saying the right things, but you've got to know how much you mean to me, and I do understand what you're going through, I swear I do. But Shelley's going to be found guilty, you know that, so . . .'

'No! I don't know that and nor do you. But let's drop this now, shall we, because I just can't keep going through it.'

Later, as they were lying side by side in the darkness, he said, 'I love you.'

She braced herself and prayed with all her might that this wouldn't turn out to be the lead up to sex she feared it was, because right now she couldn't even bear the thought of him touching her. But it seemed God wasn't

451

listening to her prayers that night, because it did turn out that way, and not, she thought, because Bob was particularly in the mood, but because it enabled him to pretend that they really were pulling through all this.

But they weren't, in fact they were so far from pulling through it that she could only wonder what had happened to the resolution she'd once made that she would be there for him no matter what – and the belief that he would be there for her too. OK, he was here, but she knew it wasn't really for her, it was for him. Their life together suited him, cushioned him from most of the blows and rescued him from the destructive side of his nature. With her he had attained a freedom he'd never have attained alone, a comfort that had much less to do with material goods than with the belief she had given him in himself. She realized now that he wasn't capable of giving that back. He was at the very centre of his world, with no room for anyone else, and she was as much to blame for that as anyone, for she had helped to put him there. But she couldn't consider him and his feelings now, it was time to put herself first, and no matter how unacceptable he found that she was going to begin tomorrow.

'Hello. Mark Reiner's office.'

Allyson's heart was thudding so hard that she almost put the phone down. 'Hello Corinne,' she heard herself say. 'It's Allyson Jaymes. Is Mark there?'

'I'm afraid not,' Corinne answered. 'He's in Los Angeles until the end of next week.'

Disappointment seared through her. Her eyes darted about the room, seeing nothing. Would it be acceptable for her to ask where she could contact him in LA? No, she didn't think so.

'Can Clive Dansing help?' Corinne suggested. 'He's over in the other building, but I can put you through. I'll tell him you're on the line.'

Of course she should speak to Clive, and as Corinne was about to announce her, she could hardly avoid it. But it was Mark she so desperately wanted to speak to. The trial was only two weeks away now, and . . .

Clive Dansing's voice came brusquely down the line. 'Allyson. How are you? I've been waiting for your call.'

Startled, Allyson said, 'Clive, uh . . . I'm fine. How are you?' She'd met him before, a couple of years ago, at the MIP TV Festival in Cannes. He'd been the head of a rival TV station then, and had invited her and Shelley to a party on his company's yacht. 'My leave of absence expires in a couple of weeks,' she said.

'Which is why I've been waiting for your call,' he said. 'I think we should meet to discuss what you're going to do. Have you had any ideas?'

'Some.' How desperately she needed this, to talk about a future that didn't include the trial.

'Good. So have I. I'm sure we'll find some middle ground.'

Allyson's insides tightened. Apparently he was expecting their ideas to conflict.

'How's your diary looking for next week?' he said. 'I can make Wednesday at four or Thursday at ten thirty.'

She opted for Thursday, because it was the last thing he said and Bob was walking in the door so she wanted to get off the line.

'Who was that?' he said, coming into the kitchen.

'No-one. Wrong number.'

He looked at her with reproachful eyes. She almost wished he'd call her a liar, but all he said was, 'I've got the job with Sky.'

'That's great,' she said, knowing it was inadequate, but it was all she could muster.

Going over to the coffee pot he emptied it into a cup and turned back to face her. 'You were talking to him, weren't you?' he said.

God, this was so hard, caring and not caring, living in

the same house as someone who already belonged to the past. 'No,' she answered.

He seemed to take no comfort from that, probably because he knew that it was only a matter of time before she would be in touch with Mark.

For a long time they only stared into each other's eyes. Finally he was the first to speak. 'Tell me the truth, Allyson,' he said, 'do you know where that clock is?'

The question was so unexpected that for a moment she was sure she hadn't heard right. Then suddenly she began to shake with fury.

'I'm sorry,' he said. 'I had to ask. And if you do, then I want you to know . . .'

'Stop!' she seethed. 'Stop before another word comes out of your mouth.'

'Allyson, I'm just trying to say . . .'

'I know what you're saying,' she yelled. 'You're saying that you think I might have done it. *Oh my God! Oh my God!*' Her hands were on her face, then tearing through her hair. 'Have you got any idea what it's doing to me to hear that now, and from you, my own husband? *Oh Christ!* Tell me this isn't happening. Tell me you . . .'

'I'm sorry,' he cried. 'I just wanted you to know that I'd stand by you, no matter what . . .'

'No matter what!' she raged. 'Are you out of your mind? You're accusing me of murder . . . No! No! No! I can't deal with this now. I've got to get out of here. I can't look at you . . .'

'Allyson! Wait!' he implored. 'I didn't mean it to come out that way. It just . . .'

'Get your hands off me!' she yelled as he grabbed her. 'Just don't touch me. How could you do that? How could you . . .' She backed away from him, and grabbed for her coat. 'No, I'm not having this discussion, because you of all people should know that I don't have the first idea where that clock is, and yet *you*, my own husband, are the only one who's doubting me.'

'I'm not doubting you!'

'Then why the hell did you ask!'

'I'm sorry! I'm really sorry,' he cried, trying to put his hands on her to calm her down. 'I was just trying to show you how much I love you, and I chose a really stupid way of doing it. I'm sorry. Oh God, I wish the words had never passed my lips, and I wish to God I'd never set eyes on Tessa Dukes, then none of this would be happening and I wouldn't be feeling you moving further and further away from me ... Allyson, you've got to forgive me, please ...'

The telephone cut him off, and snatching up her keys she wrenched open the front door and slammed it behind her. The clock! The bloody clock. He might wish he'd never set eyes on Tessa Dukes, but dear God she wished she'd never set eyes on that bloody clock.

Shelley was looking at her lawyers, listening to every word they uttered, digesting every nuance and memorizing every twist and turn that was ultimately going to provide her path to freedom. There was less than a week to go now, and she was more afraid, more capable of falling apart and agreeing to the plea bargain than she had ever been. The madness of the not-guilty gamble was eating away at her, sabotaging her resolve and crushing her belief in herself. Perversely her lawyers seemed more confident now than they had at the outset, were willing to believe they really did have a case they could win. After all, no trace of Tessa's DNA had been found in Shelley's apartment, unlike in Allyson's, and the clothes Shelley had worn to the office that day had been retrieved from the cleaners and whisked off to the lab where they'd failed to produce any damning evidence. Allyson's clothes hadn't yielded up any incriminating results either, it appeared, so everything still hinged on what had been in the package Shelley had given Allyson that night at the restaurant.

'Such a shame you didn't let her open it right then,' Ed remarked. 'Someone would have been sure to spot it. Still, you didn't,' he said, noticing the barrister's reproachful look. 'It would just be very helpful if that clock could materialize before the trial began.'

'I think we can feel confident it won't,' the barrister responded. 'So let's go over the witness statements again and make sure all inconsistencies are noted.'

It was a long and laborious process, but a vital one, and painful too as she read what people had said about her. Worst of all was going over Mark Reiner's version of their brief affair, and discovering how little she had meant to him. Of course he didn't phrase it that way, in fact he had assumed total responsibility for her belief that there would be much more to their relationship than the two sexual encounters it had consisted of, and had blamed himself fully for handling the situation so badly. It was a long and eloquent statement, with a consistent tone of regret, some signs of bewilderment and occasional anger, like the point at which he related the way she had put his hand on her breast during the party in Italy. His words then made her burn with shame, though she knew that hadn't been his intention, he'd merely been making the point of how unwelcome and untimely her advances had become. But he expressed nothing with malice, and was never accusatory, seemed in fact always to be careful to allow her the dignity she had failed to allow herself. His chivalry made her feel humiliated and foolish. It also served as a brutal reminder of what she had lost in him. How very alone she felt now with no-one to support her through this, and no-one to care whether she was found guilty or not.

So maybe, she thought, swallowing hard on her misery, it would be better for her to stay here, condemned to a world where there were no men, at least then she wouldn't have to suffer any more of this

456

pain. But just a single thought of Allyson brought her indomitable spirit back to its fighting best, for no matter what the outcome, nothing in the world was going to induce her to let Allyson walk away from this without, at the very least, being made to face the hell of the trial.

'Oh! Allyson!' Melissa cried, suddenly jumping up. 'Have you been there long?'

'Just walked in.' Allyson smiled at the girl who used to be Stella Cornbright's assistant and was now Clive Dansing's. 'How are you?' she asked.

'Frenzied. Clive is . . .'

'Right here.'

Allyson turned round. Clive Dansing was limping towards her. She'd forgotten about the limp. 'Hello Allyson,' he said, holding out his hand. 'It's good to see you again.'

His smile was friendly enough, his handshake was firm, almost warm.

'Would you like to go in?' he said, indicating his office. 'I've just got a couple of things to sort out here.'

Allyson went in and sat down on one of the guest chairs. The room had been redecorated since Stella's day, it seemed brighter now and somehow bigger. She tried to concentrate on the smaller details of change, like the desk, the paintings on the walls, the books on the shelves, but none of it seemed to be reaching her. She'd just come from an interview with Detectives Lister and Maine, so it wasn't really surprising that she was feeling drained and slightly askew from the world. But it was OK, everything seemed to be in order, they'd said. The trial was set to start next Monday at ten, so all Allyson had to do now was decide what she was going to wear. The problem wasn't as facetious as it sounded, for she knew very well that her appearance was going to count for a lot. But she had that more or less worked out, so it wasn't her wardrobe that was causing her the concern right now, it was how her sudden split from Bob was going to be perceived, virtually on the eve of the trial.

Obviously all manner of suspicions and assumptions were going to be drawn from it once it became public, but as Bob himself didn't know yet, it was unlikely to reach the press, at least for another day or two. She'd probably taken the coward's way out, packing her bags and moving to her parents while he was in Yorkshire on a job for Sky, but after the past few months of emotional upheaval and trauma she just hadn't been able to face any more scenes or pleas for forgiveness. Nor, she'd finally realized, did she want to go with him every day to the court and pretend they were a united and loving couple as all the sordidness of his affairs came out. Were she intending to stay with him afterwards, then naturally she'd be prepared to go through it, but that wasn't her intention, and as she wanted their break-up to be something that was apart from the outcome of the trial she had decided to leave before it began.

But she had to put that out of her mind now and run through a final rehearsal of everything she was going to say to Clive. Thank God she'd brought copies of printed proposals, for they could act as a guide during those awkward moments when her mind went blank.

'I'm sorry,' Clive said, coming in but not closing the door. He was looking at his watch. 'Mark should have been here by now,' he said. 'Must have got caught up in traffic.'

Allyson couldn't move. Maybe she hadn't heard right, yet she knew she had. Her heart was thumping wildly, everything in her was starting to tense. Oh God, she wasn't ready for this. She'd had no idea . . .

'Perhaps we could get started,' Clive was saying. 'I know there are certain things Mark wants to . . . Ah! Here he is.'

Allyson turned round, knowing that all her apprehension was there to be seen. She could hardly breathe as she looked at him. He seemed so much taller, so powerful, so . . . She was trying to read his eyes . . . Oh God, if only she'd known. She could have prepared herself . . .

'Hello,' he said. His eyes were on hers. His face was so familiar, his presence so engulfing.

'Hello.' Her voice was throaty and faint.

'I wanted to be here when you came back,' he said.

'You could have warned me,' she responded, then attempted a smile.

His eyes darkened with the irony she loved, then he turned to Clive. 'I think the future programming can wait,' he said.

'Of course,' Clive responded. Then to Allyson, 'If you'll excuse me.'

The door closed behind him.

'So how are you?' Mark said.

'OK. I think.' She laughed. 'You've really thrown me. I don't know what to say.'

'Am I allowed to ask how things are working out with Bob?'

Shaking her head she said, 'They're not.' She longed to tell him why, but wasn't sure she dared. 'I'm staying with my parents.'

He nodded.

She looked into his face. His eyes were still on hers, and she could feel their intensity reaching so far into her that it could be all that was holding her together. Her breath was quickening. She wanted to touch him so badly . . .

As though reading her mind he took a step towards her, and then she was there, in his arms, holding him tightly as he kissed her with such tenderness and passion that she could feel the power of their love searing right through her.

'We'll just get this trial out of the way,' he said, when finally they were able to speak steadily again, 'then we'll go back to Italy and take some time for ourselves.'

'Yes, Italy,' she said. 'Let's go back to Italy.'

Chapter 19

It hadn't taken long to get there. Much less time than she'd expected. She'd been unable to chart the journey, it wasn't possible to see from the back of a prison van. No glimpses of ongoing life, or London streets, no brutal reminders of a world of which she was no longer a part.

She sensed when the van swung off the road and down the ramp to the underground entrance of the court. The press was there, she could hear them, and she was swamped by shame that she, Shelley Bronson, wasn't permitted to walk free, and enter the court with everyone else.

Had Allyson arrived yet, she wondered.

She was so afraid it seemed hard to move. A horrible, churning nausea gripped her insides, utter dread pounded in her heart. She was trying to cut off from herself, to find a place where she wouldn't have to feel all the terrible foreboding that was binding her to the reality of this nightmare, and for moments at a time she succeeded, but only for moments.

Her lawyers were waiting inside. Ed had brought the clothes she'd asked for. A navy silk suit and a pale green silk shirt. Feeling the softness of the fabric next to her skin made her want to cry. It was like the embrace of a long-absent lover.

Just before ten thirty the guards took her upstairs to the court. Her lawyers were already there. As she was led in a terrible silence fell over the room. She kept her eyes straight ahead and walked steadily, rigidly to the dock. It was horrible. So horrible she couldn't stand it. She wanted to scream, or run.

She inhaled deeply.

The room wasn't so bad. It was one of the newer courts. No walls of austere oak panelling, and reminders of dark, sinister crimes with vengeful judges. Just shiny teak benches and lots more light than she'd imagined. It was crowded with people, so many it was as though she was suffocating in their macabre fascination. She knew they were watching her, but she didn't look back. Unless something monumental happened elsewhere in the world, this trial was going to dominate the headlines for at least a week. All the details of her life, her loves, ambitions, rejections were going to be feasted on, picked over, analysed, documented and deplored for the rapacious masses of tabloid readers. They would all have an opinion. The belief in her guilt had already crystallized into certainty. How to break apart that certainty when the world loved Allyson?

Was Allyson outside somewhere?

As a chief witness she wouldn't be allowed in yet. None of them would. Not Bob, not Mark, not anyone from *Soirée*. She was alone in a room full of strangers. And those twelve empty places over there were going to be filled by more strangers, who would decide whether she should regain her freedom or return to living hell.

Every heartbeat hurt.

'All rise.'

The judge entered. His red flowing robes told the world he was of the High Court. His wig sat comfortably over his thinning grey hair.

Shelley looked at him, but he didn't look back.

The indictment was read. As the voice spoke into the pregnant hush it made her feel sick

'Are you Shelley Bronson?'

'Yes.'

'You are charged upon an indictment containing one count, that of murder. In that, you, on the fourteenth day of March . . .' Someone nearby coughed. Shelley didn't move. The clerk was still reading. '. . . did murder Tessa Jane Dukes. How say you? Guilty or not guilty?'

Tessa Jane Dukes. She hadn't known the girl's middle name was Jane. But what did it matter now? When had it ever mattered?

'Not guilty.' Her voice was an echo in her ears. She was shaking hard, her legs were barely able to support her.

The jury was sworn in. The prosecution counsel outlined the case, then the first witnesses were called. They were police officers whose testimony took up most of the day. Shelley had always known that DC Lister had no doubts who had done it. The way she gave evidence showed she had not changed her position. Shelley hadn't been expecting her to, but hearing it told Lister's way was scaring her to death. Until now she really had dared to believe that this nightmare would end, that she would see her beloved home again and be given a chance to pick up her life. By the end of the day she hardly believed it at all – and all she wanted was to die.

Before they took her back to the prison she was allowed to speak to her lawyers. To her amazement they seemed in good spirits.

'All that testimony,' one of them explained, 'and they've still failed to come up with any kind of evidence, or DNA that connects you to the crime.'

Shelley looked at her solicitor, Ed, whom she liked and trusted. He nodded and smiled.

'But all that about me leaving the office and going home to shower and get rid of the bloodstained clothes, when all the time I was stuck in traffic,' she said, fear putting anger into her voice.

'Hypothetical. They've got no proof. Everyone knows

463

there was a monumental jam that night, thanks to a bomb scare, and it's not up to you to prove you were in it, it's up to them to prove you weren't. So far they haven't managed to do that.'

'And the car? God, that all sounded so much worse than I'd expected. I wish to God I'd told them straight away.'

'Don't go losing any sleep over that,' the leading counsel told her. 'The owner of the car-hire company is going to testify that you generally rent from him when your car is in for service. And that when you do you generally give the rental back already cleaned.'

Shelley still looked agitated and afraid. 'What about my neighbour who's going to say that she saw a dark-haired woman leaving my flat around nine? That would leave just enough time for me to get to the restaurant by nine fifteen, after cleaning up the unholy mess I must have been in.' Bitterness was adding another edge to her fear.

'She's not willing to swear it was you,' Ed reminded her. 'She's not even certain the woman she saw was actually coming out of your flat. She was just on the stairs coming down from that direction.'

Shelley covered her face with her hands. What she wouldn't give to be able to go home to her own bed. It had been so long it made everything in her ache. 'Was Allyson there today?' she asked.

Ed nodded.

'You're going to ask her about the clock, aren't you?' she said, turning to counsel. 'When the time comes, you have to ask her what she did with the clock.'

'What do you think she did with the clock?' he asked.

Shelley's eyes were burning. 'I don't know. But it has to be somewhere,' she said.

'Unless she destroyed it.'

Shelley looked at him with such contempt that he actually blushed. 'Why would she take it just to destroy it?' she snapped.

They'd been through this a hundred times before, so the lawyer didn't ask why Allyson would have taken it at all, for they were perfectly aware that it made no sense when Allyson would never be able to admit to owning it. So all he said was, 'Of course we'll ask her where it is.' Then it was time to go.

Allyson wasn't called until the afternoon of the third day. By then both Bob and Mark had been in the witness box, and the tabloid press was going crazy. Getting in and out of court was proving so difficult now that all three of them had to have police assistance. That she and Mark were arriving and leaving together had been noticed, so the second breakdown of her marriage was being crudely splashed over the inside pages, while the trial retained its hold on the headlines. Pictures of Shelley graced every news-stand; mounting belief in her guilt loaded every story.

Despite everything, Allyson's heart went out to her. She could hardly imagine what it must be like to be in Shelley's shoes, though she hoped to God she would never find out.

Mark understood her fear, and talked her through it as often as she needed. She knew that virtually nothing she said made any sense, but nothing about any of this made any sense. There was something so strange, so disconnected from reality, about going into that court every day; sitting there waiting to be called while inside the events surrounding Tessa's death were meticulously and damningly pieced together. In the end they were going to come up with two slightly flawed pictures, one drawn by the prosecution, the other by Shelley's counsel. And either one of them could be the right one.

When her name was called it was as though everything inside her drained away. Her mouth turned dry. Her legs became weak. There was only a solid ball in her chest. Mark was beside her. His hand was on hers as they got to their feet. He couldn't come in with her, but she could feel him trying to fill her with his strength. Thanks to his own testimony the world now saw him as the great seducer of his employees. She wondered how he felt about that. He claimed not to care, that all that mattered to him was her, and that she got through this so that they could get on with their lives.

Bob was nearby. As she walked towards the court-room door she could feel him watching her. They'd spoken only once since she'd left, and it hadn't been pleasant. He'd pleaded, cried, ranted and finally threatened that if she didn't come back he'd testify that he'd called at her parents' house on the night of the murder and there had been no reply. He hadn't done it, and she could only feel sorry now for the pain and bewilderment that had made him want to hurt her in such a terrible way.

An usher was holding the door open for her to walk through. Mark let go of her arm and she entered. It took only seconds for her eyes to find Shelley, and when she did her chest became so tight it was hard to breathe. Maybe it was the way Shelley's head was bowed that made her seem smaller, somehow diminished as she sat there alone in the dock, or maybe it was shock playing tricks with her eyes. This was the first time Allyson had seen her since the night of the murder and it all felt so stupefyingly awry that Shelley should be there, and she should be here, when they should be standing and fighting together, the way they always had in the past. She seemed unable to make herself remember the terrible wrong Shelley had done her, for it was as though they had somehow blundered into the events of another existence and all she wanted was to rescue Shelley from the terrifying injustice that was being thrust upon her. Then Shelley's eyes came up and Allyson felt the room start to spin. It was as though Shelley's hatred was streaming into her like a paralysing venom, and her instinct for survival took a stultifying blow as she realized how determined Shelley was to see her pay for this crime. But she wasn't going to let Shelley win, it wasn't even possible for Shelley to win, because they both knew the truth of that night, so they both knew who had killed an innocent nineteen-year-old girl.

She was led to the witness box and the Bible was placed in her hand. After taking the oath she watched a bewigged and bespectacled lawyer get to his feet. She knew Shelley was watching her, could feel those dark, malevolent eyes blazing right into her soul.

She answered the questions quietly, firmly and always succinctly. Yes, she had been looking after her father that night. No, she hadn't left the house. No, her father was in no mental state to understand whether she was there or not. No, she hadn't gone to the accused's apartment. No, she hadn't taken a bronze figurine from the apartment. Yes, she did know that the figurine had been identified as the murder weapon. No, she did not return to the office after she'd left around five thirty that evening. Yes, she did know that the deceased would be working late, because she had instructed her to.

They wanted to know if she owned a dark wig, but she didn't. Was it easy to get a taxi around where her parents lived? Generally it was. She knew what they were driving at: neither her car, nor her parents' car had yielded up any evidence, so perhaps she had taken a taxi back to the office that night. If she had, they had been unable to find a driver to confirm it, nor anything to suggest she might have disguised herself for the journey. The question of how she might have returned, apparently covered in blood and presumably in a state of great agitation, wasn't addressed.

They moved on.

Yes, she had met the accused for dinner around nine fifteen, when the accused had given her a gift. She hadn't opened it until later, because the accused had asked her

467

not to. No, the gift was not a clock. Yes, it was the murder weapon, wrapped up in one of her own make-up gowns. Certainly she knew which clock was being referred to. No, she had no idea where that clock was now.

And was it her belief that the accused had tried to frame her for the murder of Tessa Dukes?

Objection!

So many objections. Some accepted, plenty denied. They journeyed through the first break-up of her marriage. Her husband's betrayal with her assistant, Tessa Dukes, and with her best friend, Shelley Bronson. They made much of the loss of her senior position on the programme, the downsizing of her public profile. Yes, she had felt humiliated. Yes, she had hated Tessa. Yes, she had threatened to kill her.

Yes to everything.

She had known about Mark Reiner's affair with Shelley. She'd also known that Tessa Dukes had been in Mr Reiner's hotel room while they were all in Italy. No, she didn't believe they'd had sex. No, she didn't know that for certain because she hadn't been there. Was she afraid of losing Mr Reiner to Tessa, the way she had lost her husband? Had she hatched a plan to kill Tessa Dukes and make it look as though Shelley had done it? Had she used her father's impoverished mental state as a cover for getting rid of both rivals? Had she been jealous of Mr Reiner's affair with Ms Bronson? Wasn't Mr Reiner in a perfect position to resurrect her ailing career and alter the course of her foundering public image? It was plain to see how much she stood to gain from a relationship with Mr Reiner. And how much she had to lose should Mr Reiner choose Shelley, or Tessa, over her. So why not make sure that never happened? Why not take whatever steps necessary to prevent history from repeating itself and leaving her abandoned again? With Tessa dead and Shelley in prison, history wouldn't stand a chance.

Allyson was breathless. The faces in the courtroom were swirling around her. Her clothes were tight. Her skin was on fire.

In the end it all amounted to motive, means and opportunity. She had them all.

She had to be guilty.

It was time for Shelley to enter the witness box. She'd known it would come today, her lawyers had told her last night. She'd hardly slept. Not even the convincing ring of Allyson's guilt, nor the murmurs of doubt that were finally being voiced in the press, had been enough to stop the trample of panic inside her head. She wouldn't get a second chance at this. She had to do everything she could now to persuade the jury that though she might have had the means and opportunity, she simply had no reason to kill Tessa Dukes. On the contrary, Tessa Dukes was turning the programme's ratings around; she'd also got Bob Jaymes off Shelley's back after years of harassment. What did it matter that Bob had testified to her plaguing him to leave his wife? It was his word against hers, and he was already known to be a liar and a cheat, whereas she was a beautiful woman. What need would she have to try to steal her best friend's husband? But even if she had, and even if she'd become enraged when Tessa Dukes had succeeded where she had failed, it still didn't prove she had killed Tessa.

There seemed to be even more people in court today. The press and public galleries were jammed full, so too were the benches for witnesses and counsel. Shelley was wearing the navy suit again, this time with a rose-pink shirt. Her demeanour was composed, her dignity was quiet and modest. She knew that many were still disturbed by the shock that they might have judged her wrongly. Some were probably still resisting. But many had to be asking themselves if she really was the scapegoat here; if their beloved Allyson, who was so gentle, so caring and attentive to those in need, who had been a part of their lives for so long, really was the monster who had killed an innocent girl. Unthinkable maybe, but not impossible.

There was no other sound in the room as she took the oath. Inside her was an emptiness that kept flooding with fear and foreboding. She looked at the faces of the lawyers as they swam in and out of focus. She heard her own voice, quiet and tremulous, then strong and entreating. Allyson was there, listening, wondering, waiting. How afraid she must be. How afraid they both were.

'What time did you leave the office on the night in question?'

'A few minutes before eight.'

'Was anyone else there?'

'As far as I knew only Tessa and Will, the editor. Everyone else had gone home.'

'So no-one saw you leave?'

'Not that I'm aware of.'

'Did you see anyone else as you left the building?'

'No.'

So many detailed questions. About what she was wearing. The weather. The car she was driving. At what point she hit the traffic jam. How long she was held up. Where she was when Allyson called to say she'd be late. Did she have a gift for Allyson? Yes. Why? Because relations had been strained between them lately, and she wanted to do something to repair them.

'Why were relations strained?'

'Because of my affair with Allyson's husband. And then hers with Mark Reiner.'

'So you were jealous of her affair with Mr Reiner?'

'Yes.'

'What was the gift you were hoping would restore the friendship between you and Mrs Jaymes?'

470

'A Lalique clock. Allyson had always loved it.'

The lawyer turned away for a moment to speak to junior counsel. Shelley's eyes moved across the courtroom. Faces passed in a blur until finally she was looking at Allyson. Her face was pale, but her eyes didn't falter from Shelley's. Suddenly Shelley felt a hot, uncontrollable rage well up inside her and before she could stop herself she was shouting, 'Ask her where the clock is now. *Ask her!* She knows where it is!'

The judge was calling for order. His reprimand was short and harsh. Her lawyer's eyes showed his dismay.

Her head was spinning. She was shaking. She needed to get away.

The pressure never eased up. The questions kept on coming.

Had she really been in that traffic jam? Wasn't the truth that after she had brutally killed Tessa Dukes, while wearing Allyson Jaymes's make-up gown, she had driven back to her home in Kensington? The record showed that the roads between Fulham and Kensington were unaffected by the traffic jam, so she could have made the journey in under twenty minutes. That allowed her plenty of time to clean herself up, and the car, dispose of the clothes she was wearing, make a parcel out of the murder weapon and make-up gown, and drive over to the restaurant to meet Mrs Jaymes.

'Was it your suggestion that Mrs Jaymes should wait until later to open the gift?'

'Yes, I think so.'

'Why?'

'It had been an emotional day. She looked exhausted and she seemed agitated about something, so I thought it might be better to wait.'

'When the call came to tell you Tessa had been murdered, why did you suggest you return to the office in Mrs Jaymes's car?'

'Because she was parked the closest.'

'Not because you didn't want her to see that you had a hire car?'

'I thought we should get there as quickly as possible, and I'd had to park several streets away.'

'Going back to the gift. You say it was a Lalique clock.'

'Yes.'

'How much would such a clock be worth? Roughly.'

'That particular clock, somewhere between twenty and thirty thousand pounds.'

There was an audible gasp, followed by murmurs that were silenced by the judge.

'A very generous gift.'

'Our friendship meant a great deal to me.'

'So, Ms Bronson, where is the clock now?'

Shelley's eyes returned to Allyson. Allyson was watching her. The tension between them cut through the room like blades of light. 'I don't know,' Shelley answered.

It wasn't over yet. Her innocence, like Allyson's, was far from established. Nothing had yet been said either to prove or disprove any of her claims. The means and opportunity were still as easily hers as Allyson's. But what about the motive? Didn't that start with her self-confessed affair with Bob Jaymes? Wasn't it the truth that she had been trying to break up his marriage for years?

'How did you feel when you discovered that Mr Jaymes was sleeping with his wife's nineteen-year-old assistant?'

'Upset for Allyson.'

'Were you still engaged in a relationship with him yourself at that time?'

'No.'

'Who broke off your affair? You or Mr Jaymes?'

'I did.'

'Mr Jaymes has testified that he did.'

She said nothing.

472

'Who contacted the press to expose Mr Jaymes's affair with Tessa Dukes?'

'I did.'

'Why?'

'Because I thought Allyson should find out what kind of man she was married to.'

'Couldn't you simply have told her that?'

'I could have.'

'Was it because you wanted to punish Mr Jaymes that you did it through the press?'

'Possibly.'

'And you wanted to punish him because he'd rejected you?'

'No.'

The lawyer allowed his scepticism to hang in the air, before moving on to her relationship with Mark Reiner. She'd already heard Mark testify to the power and immediacy of their attraction, and she said nothing to contradict it. Nor did she deny that she was jealous when she found out that Mark had transferred his affections to Allyson. It was all true, but none of it made her a killer.

'How did you feel when you realized that Tessa Dukes was in Mr Reiner's hotel room?'

'Upset, for Allyson.'

'Like you were when you found out about her husband's affair with Tessa? When you alerted the press?'

Her face turned hot. 'I suppose so.'

'So what did you do this time?'

'I told Allyson myself.'

'And how did she react?'

'She was extremely upset.'

'What exactly did she say?'

'That she wished to God the girl had never come into her life.'

'Did you ever hear Mrs Jaymes threaten to kill Tessa

Dukes?'

'Yes.'

The lunch recess was over. Shelley was back on the stand. She was feeling light-headed, as though she had been there for days, maybe weeks. In some ways it was as though nothing had ever happened before this nightmare, and maybe nothing would ever happen after.

'Did you harbour a hope that Mr Reiner might, at some point, rediscover his attraction to you?'

'No. I knew he wouldn't.'

'How did you know?'

'He was in love with Allyson.'

'Did he tell you that?'

'He didn't have to. It was obvious.'

'So you didn't think you could change his mind?'

'No.'

'But if Allyson was no longer in the picture?'

'Objection!'

'Did you make an improper advance to Mr Reiner on the night of the party in Italy?'

'No.'

'You didn't put his hand on your breast?'

'He put his hand on my breast and I didn't stop him.' What did it matter that it was a lie? Who would ever know? And she'd had enough humiliation.

'Do you believe that if Mr Reiner hadn't developed a preference for Mrs Jaymes, he might have continued a relationship with you?'

'It's possible.'

'So this was the second time you'd been passed over for Mrs Jaymes? First was when Mr Jaymes refused to leave her for you. Then, when Mr Reiner dropped you for her?'

Shelley didn't answer.

'Let's go to the clothes you were wearing in the office on the day of the murder. Are they the same clothes as those collected from the cleaners two days later, by the police?'

'Yes.'

'How many black trouser suits do you own, Ms Bronson?'

The air was suddenly trapped in her lungs. 'Three,' she said hoarsely.

'So you could have substituted the suit that became stained . . .'

'Objection!'

The point had been made. Counsel was looking at his notes, giving the jury time to absorb. Then he returned to Shelley.

'Mrs Jaymes has testified that she told you she was looking after her father on the night of the 14th. Is that true?'

'Yes.'

'And presumably you are aware of her father's poor mental health?'

'Yes.'

'So it could be said that you knew Mrs Jaymes wouldn't have an alibi that night, were one ever needed?'

'I never saw it like that.'

'But it could be said.'

'Objection!'

He paused for a moment, spoke to his colleague then turned back. 'Was it your impression that Mr Reiner was engaged in a sexual encounter with Tessa Dukes on the night you happened upon them in Italy?'

'Yes, it was.'

'And why, exactly, were you there at the door?'

She knew it was pointless to lie, for the friends she'd told Allyson she had visited in their room had already testified that it wasn't true. So her lips trembled as she said, 'I was hoping to talk to Mr Reiner.'

'About what?'

'The programme.' It didn't even sound true!

'At two in the morning?'

'Yes.'

'I suggest to you, Ms Bronson, that you were there in the hope of rekindling your affair with Mr Reiner. And that when you found Mr Reiner in Tessa Dukes's room, giving comfort to a girl who was in an inebriated and distressed state, you decided to twist what you'd seen and use it to try to break up Mr Reiner and Mrs Jaymes. But even if you'd succeeded in that there was still Tessa to contend with, wasn't there? Because if that was a sexual encounter you had happened upon, it could be that Mr Reiner would abandon Mrs Jaymes in favour of Tessa instead of you. And you couldn't let that happen, could you? Not again.'

It was as though the ground was shifting beneath her. Questions. Distortions. Allusions. A stampede of fear. A pit of despair. She was no longer reaching the jury. A gulf had opened up between them. Now they only saw her as a rejected, bitter woman. The woman who'd twice tried to steal her best friend's man. Who twice had failed because of a teenage girl. Was it true that she had never been able to sustain a relationship? Didn't she have a history of failures with men? What about her jealousy of Allyson? Just how long had she resented Allyson – for the love of her family, of her public, her husband, and finally of Mark Reiner? How many years had that resentment been building? And what about Tessa? Was it Tessa's youth and freshness that had poisoned Shelley against her? How hard was it for her, a forty-two-year-old woman, to watch Bob Jaymes, whom she'd pursued for years, becoming besotted with a nineteen-year-old girl? Had she felt used up? Discarded? She'd certainly felt bitter. Why else would she have gone to the press? Did she care about her friend Allyson then? No, all she cared about then was punishing Bob Jaymes. What had she cared

476

about on the night of the murder? Certainly not Tessa Dukes. Nor Allyson Jaymes. All she'd cared about then was talking Allyson out of opening a gift in the restaurant, and then making sure they used Allyson's car to return to the office once it was known Tessa had been murdered. And what was the last thing Shelley said to Allyson as they'd left the restaurant that night? 'Don't forget your gift.' Certainly she'd be concerned if it contained such a valuable clock. But wouldn't she have been equally as concerned if it contained the evidence that was going to remove Allyson from Mr Reiner's life, as effectively as she, herself, had already removed Tessa? There was only Shelley's word that there was a clock in that box. And no-one seemed to know where that clock was now.

'Or maybe, Ms Bronson, you do know where it is.'

'No, I . . .' She stopped as panic welled in her chest and her lawyer shot her a silencing look.

'Yes, Ms Bronson?'

Her eyes fell away and she shook her head. 'I don't know where it is,' she said, but her voice didn't have the ring of conviction it needed to persuade anyone she was telling the truth.

Nor, when all her lies were summarized, trivial as many of them were, was there a single benign face remaining amongst the twelve who were watching her so closely.

In the rooms beneath the court Shelley broke down and cried. Hope had gone now, all that was left was despair. It ballooned around her, swallowing her up and suffocating her with fear. She would never leave that prison. She would never return to her precious home. She would grow old and ugly with women who despised and abused her, in a place that was dark and cold, and smelled of raw vegetables and unwashed skin.

Ed tried to comfort her by reminding her that the

picture of Allyson's guilt was every bit as strong, if not stronger. And even if they couldn't swing the blame totally in Allyson's direction, there was still no actual evidence to prove that she, Shelley, had committed the crime.

But his words didn't help her to sleep that night, nor did her knowledge of the truth.

The jury was out all the next day.

Mark took Allyson round to her mother's. The table was set for lunch, but only her father ate. They were all too painfully aware of the way time seemed to have stopped as they waited to see where the sword of Damocles fell. Their words tried to convey optimism and hope, but always they were weighted with dread. For the first time Allyson mentioned an appeal. If she was arrested, and found guilty, she would appeal. It seemed the best she could hope for. The light she needed to get her through the months ahead, should the worst happen.

Mark covered her hand with his. 'Even if Shelley isn't found guilty, it doesn't mean they're going to arrest you,' he reminded her.

'But if they do. I have to think about . . .'

'Darling, there's no more evidence pointing to you than there is to Shelley. Much less, in fact.'

Allyson looked into his eyes. The love she felt for him was growing all the time. He was all that mattered now – him, and her freedom. 'Would you go back to her, if they locked me away?' she asked.

'Stop!' her mother cried. 'They're not going to lock you away.'

Mark smiled and turned back to Allyson. 'We're leaving for Italy as soon as this is over. And no, I wouldn't go back to her.'

Allyson's throat tightened. He was such a special man. Not for a moment did he believe she might be guilty. Please God the jury would think the same way.

Total silence accompanied the jurors' return to the court. After two days of deliberation a verdict had now been reached.

Shelley was unable to look at them. She kept her eyes lowered and her prayers intense.

Allyson was rigid. She was praying too. Her hand was in Mark's, her eyes were on Shelley.

A clerk of the court was speaking, asking the jury if they had reached a verdict.

The foreman of the jury stood. A small, thin woman in her early fifties. 'We have.'

Shelley stopped breathing.

'Members of the jury, on the count of murder, do you find the defendant guilty or not guilty?'

'Guilty.'

Shelley's eyes opened. She was starting to shake. Convulsions were rushing through her. She was out of control. She could hear herself screaming, feel them struggling to hold her down. Panic and denial drove through her. *No! No! No!*

The judge was calling for order.

Mitigation began. But what difference did it make now? They'd found her guilty. They'd taken away her freedom. She would never see her home again, never know what it was to walk in the street, to lie on a beach, to feel a man's desire . . . She would be in control of nothing now. Not the time she rose, the time she slept, when she ate, or showered, worked or played. There was nothing to live for. No sun, no rain, no friends, no laughter. She was a number now. A face amongst hundreds. Her femininity would be coarsened; her beauty would be drained. Shelley Bronson, the producer, was now Shelley Bronson, a convicted killer.

She had to get out! She had to run! Someone, please, help

her! Oh God, don't let this be true!

Someone was holding her. The judge was ready to pass sentence.

Shelley looked at him. His expression was stern, but his eyes seemed kind. He was speaking, but she seemed not to be hearing. Some words broke through. '. . . I sentence you to life imprisonment . . . Recommendation to serve a minimum of fifteen years . . .'

Life! Oh my God! Oh my God!

There was a commotion near the back. Allyson had collapsed. Everyone watched as she was carried from the court.

Shelley watched too. The reporters were rushing to get out, elbowing and jostling each other, desperate to be first with the news. No-one bothered to stay and watch as she was taken from the court. No-one even thought about the van she was put into, or the darkness that now imprisoned her life.

And only she remembered the clock.

Chapter 20

Allyson tilted back her head and felt the sun burn hotly on her face. The air, the sea, the sky were so dazzlingly bright it was as though it was all brand new. She could see for miles. Orange and lemon groves cascaded down the hillsides, silent waves broke over the shore below. Clusters of red-tiled rooftops, tall, rustic houses. She inhaled deeply, as though she could take the beauty inside her and hold it there. It might act as a balm on all the ugliness and fear that had blighted the past few months, and somehow soften the sharp edges of horror that cut so very deep every time she thought of Shelley. But she'd promised herself and Mark that she wouldn't think about her while they were here, for there was nothing she could do to help Shelley now, so she must use this time to heal and forgive and finally move on.

She looked down at the courtyard below where a fountain of lions' heads spurted water into the glistening trough, and smart cane furniture was spread out between towering ferns and palms. The hotel was still in its first season, but already word had spread. It was *the* place to stay. Exclusive, expensive and catering to all refined tastes. The apartment on the top floor was reserved for Mark and his brother Nick, kept available for whenever they wanted to come.

Allyson and Mark had arrived two days ago. Stepping off the plane into the welcoming warmth of the Italian sunshine had felt like stepping into another world. It was what she had needed, to leave England behind for a while, to lose herself in the romance and splendour of a place that she loved. The nightmare of the trial was over, but the wounds, the fear, had left scars that were going to take a long time to heal . . .

She was thinking about it again, but it was impossible not to, for despite their disconnected worlds she still felt tied to Shelley, as though a part of her was in that prison too. She'd stopped swimming in the pool now, for every time she entered the water she felt she might drown under the weight of all the emotion and trauma that had destroyed their friendship. And sometimes the thought of never seeing Shelley again felt like never having any air again.

But mercifully there were moments when she was able to forget.

Now was one of those moments, for she was smiling as she watched the car winding its way up the hill. Mark had been to Naples for a meeting, he'd said, though she hadn't believed him, because today was her fortieth birthday and she knew he was planning a surprise. But she'd gone along with the charade that this was the last meeting he needed to have until this break was over. She wasn't sure how long they would stay, he had put no limits on the time she might need. When she was ready he was willing to talk about her future, whether she would continue in TV, or change her life completely. It was hard to imagine a life without cameras, without Shelley . . . She stopped herself again. She must make herself accept that everything had changed, that a whole new life was opening up to her now, and her heart gave a flutter of excitement as she envisaged it with Mark, and maybe with the children she'd never managed to have with Bob.

The car disappeared as it headed round to the church piazza. Eager to see him, she left the apartment and ran down the stairs. When she reached the reception he was just coming in through the door. There were others around, talking quietly, taking afternoon tea in the shady arched alcoves, browsing through guidebooks out in the courtyard. Allyson didn't care who saw her embrace him and it seemed he didn't care either.

'Hi,' he murmured, holding her close and smiling down into her eyes. 'I get the feeling you missed me.'

She laughed. 'How did it go?'

'OK. The deal's all but done.'

'So you're now an even bigger TV mogul?'

He laughed. 'Are you free? There's somewhere I want to take you.'

It turned out not to be far, just along the lane, under the arch, and back into the church piazza. The sun was beating down, the ancient cobbles were scorched and dusty, and the shutters of the overlooking windows were closed.

The church door was open. Inside was cool and shady, with a damp, earthy smell. Rays of sunlight streaked through the windows, over the empty pews and across the magnificent Byzantine pulpit. Holding her hand he led her up the centre aisle, towards the life-size crucifix which was suspended on chains above the altar. When they stopped she looked up at the face of Christ.

'Don't you think it's beautiful here?' he said, his eyes travelling the faded stone walls that yielded all drama to the sparkling mosaics on the pulpit, then descending with the sunlight to where she was standing.

She was still looking at Christ. 'Yes,' she said, smiling.

'I'd like to marry you here,' he said.

Her heart suddenly swelled, and her eyes were disbelieving as she turned them to him.

'When you're ready. When it's possible,' he added.

'I love you,' she whispered. 'And if there's a question in there, the answer's yes.'

His eyes were full of irony, as, pulling a small box

483

from his pocket, he took out a large, oval-shaped diamond and lifted her left hand.

She watched as he slid the ring onto her third finger, and felt an unbearable happiness filling her heart. Then she raised her eyes back to his as he said, 'Happy birthday.'

A while later they walked slowly back down the aisle. She held his arm and rested her head against it. At the door he stepped out into the sunlight, and she turned back for a moment to look again at the striking image of Christ. Thank you, she said softly.

When they got back to the hotel the concierge called them over. 'Señor Reiner,' he said. 'I forget this parcel arrive for you. It come a long time ago. It say to wait for your arrival.'

Mark picked it up curiously and looked it over. Then, grinning, he turned to Allyson. 'What is it?' he said.

She frowned.

'It says here that you sent it.'

She looked at the sender's name.

At that moment a receptionist told her there was a call for her.

She went to take it, but as she put the receiver to her ear she could feel her heart thudding and barely heard her mother's voice at the other end as she said, 'Hello darling, just wanted to wish you happy birthday . . .'

The parcel, her name! She watched Mark as he walked through to one of the offices.

'. . . and Aunt Faye has said she'll stay with Daddy for a week,' her mother was saying. 'So if it's still all right, I can come over at the weekend.'

Allyson was staring at the door Mark had disappeared through.

'Ally? Are you there, darling? If it's a problem . . .'

'No. It would be lovely,' she said. 'We'll get the limousine to meet you at the airport. You're going to love it here, Mummy. It's so beautiful.'

'I'll call you tomorrow with my flight details, shall I?' her mother said.

'Yes. Love to Daddy.'

She put down the phone and went to find Mark.

He was standing with his back to the door. She looked at the desk in front of him, the torn paper of the parcel, the protective padding and tissue, and though she couldn't yet see it she already knew what it was. The walls were closing in, her heart had stopped beating.

Her name on the parcel. She was the sender.

He turned to face her, deathly pale and uncomprehending. In his hands was the exquisite Night and Day clock by Lalique.

Allyson's eyes were huge as she looked at him. An endless amount of time seemed to have passed. The drumming in her ears was starting to fade, the nausea in her stomach was receding. She could sense his resistance to what this must mean, and wanted desperately to go to him. 'I didn't send it,' she said. She needed air. She needed desperately to be able to think. 'Look at the date. When was it sent?'

He looked at the date. 'March 16th.'

Two days after Tessa was killed. Shelley was in custody by then.

His eyes were on her again. Not yet accusing, only bewildered and questioning.

'If she posted the clock late on the 15th,' Allyson said, 'it would have been postmarked the 16th.'

He was still staring at her.

'Darling, listen,' she said, struggling to remain calm. 'Just ask yourself, what sense does it make for me to send it to you? Why would I do that? Why would I even keep it, if what you're thinking was true?'

She could see he wanted to believe her. It made sense to believe her.

'Darling, don't you understand what she's doing? She

485

sent the clock to you knowing you would react this way. Oh God, Mark! Don't let her do this. Please, don't let her do it.'

The clock was still in his hands. He looked down at it for a long, long time. She was drowning again, spiralling away to a place where she was imprisoned with Shelley, shut away from the world, snatched brutally from the new life they were planning. She didn't move, she could only watch him, and wait, and pray that once the shock was over . . .

After an interminable, unbearable time he finally put the clock on the desk. Then turning to her he pulled her into his arms and held her tight. 'It's all right,' he said, feeling how violently she was shaking. 'It's all right.'

She clung to him and felt the air returning to her lungs. He believed her. Oh thank God, thank God. She was looking at the clock. Thank God.

'What shall we do with it?' she said.

'I guess we have to tell the police it's turned up.'

She nodded and reached out to touch it.

'I'll get it put in the safe for now.'

She looked up at him again, uncertainty still darkening her eyes. 'You really scared me,' she told him. 'I thought . . . I thought maybe she was going to win.'

He smiled. 'It scared me too,' he confessed. Then, turning her to the door, he said, 'Come on, let's go get a drink. I think we both need one.'

'Do you think it's all over now?' she said, after the concierge had locked the clock away.

'I certainly hope so,' he answered, standing aside for her to walk ahead of him down to the bar.

A smartly dressed woman who'd arrived the day before was coming up the steps towards them, and broke into a beaming smile as she saw Allyson. 'Oh, my dear,' she gushed, 'I hope you don't mind me calling you that, but well, I feel as if I know you, and I just wanted to tell you how much I used to love your programme, and how sorry I am for all that you've been through. I never believed, even for a minute, that you could have done such a terrible thing, none of us did, but it must have been a very difficult time for you.' She glanced approvingly at Mark. 'I'm so glad it's working out for you now.'

Allyson smiled. 'Thank you,' she said.

The woman moved on, flushed with the pleasure of having spoken to Allyson Jaymes.

Mark's eyes were teasing as he left her to go to the bar.

Laughing, Allyson wandered out to the terrace to watch the spectacular blaze of the sunset and listen to the idle chatter of the guests. It was incredible, she was thinking, the power of fame. Would she ever have had such support without it? Would anyone have been so ready to believe her? They all felt as though they knew her, as though she was somehow a part of their lives, and she couldn't help wondering if the jury had felt that way too. They watched TV, so just like everyone else it would have been easy for them to see her as belonging to them, like a sister, a daughter, a mother, who had known pain and betrayal, who needed to be shown the same compassion she'd always shown to others. They knew everything about her. Her life had been laid open, she'd had no secrets by the time the trial was over. Yet she was still Allyson Jaymes, the TV personality they all knew and loved and implicitly trusted. It wasn't possible for her to be a killer, not only because there had been no evidence to say she was, but because it just wasn't possible for them to believe it of someone they knew to have such a good and kind heart.

Yes, it really was incredible, the power of fame, because despite the investigation, despite the trial and the verdict, the fact still remained: she could have done it . . .

Out of the Shadows

Susan Lewis

Since Susannah Cates' husband was sent to prison three years ago, life has been a constant struggle to provide for herself and their teenage daughter. Nothing ever seems to go right and the most she hopes for now is that nothing more will go wrong.

Worried by her mother's unhappiness, thirteen-year-old Neve decides to take matters into her own hands. And when Susannah's closest friend Patsy discovers what Neve is up to, she immediately lends her support. As their plans start to unfold they have no way of knowing what kind of fates they are stirring, all they can see is Susannah's excitement, because at last a way seems to be opening up for her to escape her bad luck.

However, the spectre of horror is all the time pacing behind the scenes and never, in all Susannah's worst nightmares, could she have imagined her happiness causing so much pain to someone she loves . . .

'Spellbinding!' *Daily Mail*

'Sad, happy, sensual and intriguing' *Woman's Own*

arrow books